THE LITHUANIAN SHORT STORY
FIFTY YEARS

THE PUBLICATION OF THIS BOOK WAS MADE POSSIBLE, IN PART, BY A GRANT FROM THE LITHUANIAN FOUNDATION

The Lithuanian Short Story Fifty Years

Selected and edited
by
STEPAS ZOBARSKAS

MANYLAND BOOKS, INC. NEW YORK

The Lithuanian Short Story: 50 Years

Copyright ©1977, by STEPAS ZOBARSKAS

All rights reserved. No part of this book may be used or reproduced in any manner whatsoever without written permission, except as embodied in critical articles and reviews. For information address Manyland Books, Inc., 84-39 90th Street, Woodhaven, N.Y. 11421.

ISBN: 0-87141-050-8

Library of Congress Catalogue Card No.: 76-51607

MANUFACTURED IN THE UNITED STATES OF AMERICA

ACKNOWLEDGEMENTS

As I put this book into the reader's hands, I wish to express my deep appreciation to my closest collatorators, Nola M. Zobarskas and Algirdas Landsbergis for their tireless help and advice.

I would like also to express my gratitude to the authors and to the heirs of those authors who are deceased for granting me permission to include their works in this anthology, and to the translators for their laborious but successful efforts. (One should never forget how difficult it is to translate from the Lithuanian, which is one of the world's oldest languages.)

Dr. Rev. Leonardas Andriekus, Dr. Charles Angoff, founder and editor of *The Literary Review,* Kazys Bradunas, and Clark Mills, all of them authors and literary critics in their own right, also deserve our thanks for their suggestions and support.

We are especially grateful to the many friends and supporters who have helped us to disseminate various Lithuanian literary publications among the English-reading public, either recently or in the past. These include Dr. Kazys Ambrozaitis, Joseph J. Andriusis, Dr. Marija Arstikaityte-Uleckas, Dr. Jonas Balys, Vytautas Beleckas, Algis Brazenas, Dr. Nijole Brazenas-Paronetto, Dr. Regina Ciurlys, Dr. Zibute Daugelaite, Right Rev. Dr. Antanas Deksnys, Dr. Joseph Dicpinigaitis, Dr. Jonas Grinius, J. Jakaitis, Marija Jasenas, Dr. Ferdinandas V. Kaunas, Dr. Juozas Kazickas, Kazys Kazlauskas, Justinas Liaukus, Rev. Jonas Pakalniskis, Dr. Jone Peciulionyte, Dr. Zenonas Prusas, Austra Puzinas, Stasys Rudys, Algis Ruzgas, Dr. Alvina Sabanas, Prof. Raphael Sealey, Gytis Serńas, Dr. Rimvydas Sidrys, Dr. Antanas Starkus, Antanas Tveras, Dr. Julio C. Tula, Stanley Vashkys, Vytautas Vebeliunas, Victoria Zayat, Vladas Zemaitis, Jonas Zdanys, Dr. Algis J. Zukas, and numerous other friends, here and abroad. Thanks to everyone.

S. Z.

CONTENTS

A HALF CENTURY OF THE LITHUANIAN SHORT STORY / Algirdas Landsbergis.................9
THE MISFITS / Vaizgantas.................29
THE HERDSMAN AND THE LINDEN TREE / Vincas Kreve....53
VERONIKA / Antanas Vienuolis.................87
THE ORDEAL OF ASSAD PASHA / Ignas Seinius.................120
THE RED SHOES / Jurgis Savickis.................147
BLUE TROUSERS / Petras Tarulis.................161
THE THREE KNOTS / Antanas Tulys.................168
THE HEAVY HAND / Juozas Grusas.................182
THE CROWN PRINCE NEEDS BLOOD / Vytautas Alantas.....196
CAPTAIN BORUTA / Vincas Ramonas.................210
PETRAS / Liudas Dovydenas.................220
A COUNTERBALANCE / Jurgis Gliauda.................230
THE CHINA BOWL / Jurgis Jankus.................244
NOON AT A COUNTRY INN / Antanas Vaiciulaitis.................252
HE WASN'T ALLOWED TO SEE / Pulgis Andriusis.................261
THE QUEEN MOTHER / Kazys Barenas.................269
THE THORN / Nele Mazalaite.................295
SEVEN SWORDS / Juozas Kralikauskas.................304
IN THE HOSPITAL / Antanas Skema.................311
ELENA / Stepas Zobarskas.................327
MIDSUMMER / Marius Katiliskis.................344
THE BRINK OF MADNESS / Aloyzas Baronas.................354
THE ORGAN OF KURKLISKES / Julius Kaupas.................373
HEAVENS ARE FULL AGAIN / Algirdas Landsbergis.................387

TWO STORIES / Vytaute Zilinskaite.. 416
THE STRIPED TROLLEY BUS / Romualdas Lankauskas..... 424
THE OLD WOMAN WITH A GREEN PAIL / Icchokas Meras. 407
THE YELLOW BUICK / Kazys Almenas................................. 431
WILD BOARS AGAINST THE HORIZON / Juozas Aputis..... 457

A Half-Century of the Lithuanian Story

By ALGIRDAS LANDSBERGIS

"IF THE PEOPLE have no heart for a tree like this linden, they won't have pity for anybody," says the protagonist of "The Herdsman and the Linden Tree" by Vincas Kreve (1882-1954), the story introducing this anthology. "It is better to die than to live in times like these."

The herdsman's outcry, both resigned and affirmative at the same time, echoes throughout the volume as one of its leitmotifs as, for instance, in the last sentence of "Wild Boars Against the Horizon" by the youngest contributor, Juozas Aputis (1936-   ):

> With his single eye, Petras Gvildys gazed through white gauze at a frightened white cuckoo perched on a birch tree that grew at the edge of the little island.

Haunted by the tractors—the "wild boars" of the title, the tanks of technology's blitzkrieg transforming the familiar landscape undistinguishable from the scenery of his soul—and almost blinded by his wife in an irrational outburst, Gvildys vainly gropes for answers, flees, and is finally discovered in what seems to be a sanctuary of nature. In this concluding sentence of the story, Lithuania's distant past and present are telescoped into a single image. The earth as the mother, the sacred trees, the cuckoo as the prophet of human destiny—all these are attributes of the ancient Lithuanian world feeling. But has the protagonist really come home to mother earth in the traditional sense, has he become one with nature again; or is this homecoming illusory and he will, after all, remain half-blinded, his marriage ruined and the invincible tractors will go on rooting up the land until one day they reach the sanctuary with the birch and the cuckoo? What may have appeared a simple image turns out to be a complex scene of painful ambiguity as well as a telling summation of one of the persistent themes in Lithuanian Literature: man-in-nature divorcing himself, or being divorced, from his roots and cast out into a puzzling solitude.

Between the noise of Aputis' tractors and the archaic world of feeling still trembling in his protagonist's mind stretches Lithuania's history. A brief digression to review some of the highlights of that history is in order, not only because most readers are unfamiliar with Lithuania's past but also because history sheds considerable light on the stories between these covers.

Contrary to one of the assorted misconceptions, Lithuanians, just as Latvians and Estonians are not Slavs. They belong to the Baltic (or Aistian) people who, according to recent archeological findings, lived in the center of the present European Russia and on the southeast shores of the Baltic Sea already around 2000 B.C. Since then, the Baltic habitat has been considerably narrowed.

For a people who are said to shun extremes, Lithuanians have been saddled with a wildly oscillating history. Soon after the unification of Lithuanian lands into a kingdom in the 13th century, Lithuania rose to the rank of a great Medieval power and held vast Byelorussian, Russian, and Ukrainian territories stretching from the Baltic to the Black Sea. The twin pressures of the Teutonic Knights and of resurgent Moscow pushed Lithuania into an alliance with Poland and by the 16th century the alliance had hardened into a union. The Lithuanian-Polish commonwealth collapsed at the end of the 18th century, when the Russians, Prussians and the Austrians partitioned it among themselves in a remote exercise drill for the Hitler-Stalin Pact of 1939. Most of Lithuania was swallowed by the Russian Empire, an entity that Lenin would aptly describe as a "prison of nations."

The jagged rhythms of Lithuania's history were not conducive for the ripening of a culture. The Lithuanian aristocracy was gradually seduced by the more sophisticated cultural charms of Poland. And so the nurturing of Lithuanian culture was left to the peasantry, as in the Czech lands after the defeat of the White Mountain. The afterglow of a rich mythology, once also cultivated by the ruling class, and a treasure of folklore were preserved in "simple hearts" under thatched roofs—as a vital wellspring for the future Lithuanian literature and a source of admiration for Goethe, Hugo, and Herder.

The 19th and 20th century *risorgimento* in Lithuania was to a great extent a cultural phenomenon. Re-creation of culture and re-discovery of the past preceded the rise of a political consciousness and action. As elsewhere in East Europe and during the Irish Revival, literature suddenly became invested with vatic, existential and political functions. To write a poem or story in the Lithuanian language meant more than to express oneself or provide aesthetic pleasure for the reader; it meant nothing less than adding another proof that the nation was still alive. It was through literature that the "better" past was to be evoked and relinked with the present. The functionaries of Russification were quite aware of all those things and paid the supreme compliment to the power of the word when they prohibited the use of the Latin alphabet in Lithuania (1864-1904). Writing in Lithuanian was therefore equivalent to the defiance of authority, a revolutionary act.

The approximately fifty year span of this anthology covers the period of Lithuania's restored independence (1918-1940), the first Soviet Russian Occupation (1940-1941), the brief Nazi rule (1941-1944). Enough wars, revolts, aggressions, displacements, and murders are crammed into that half of a century to supply much larger countries with a steady diet of calamity for a much longer time.

The short story, both as a genre and an art form, is as young as the Lithuanian story. But theirs is a different youth. In other countries, the short story was a stage in an uninterrupted literary development. A much more difficult task confronted the Lithuanian story writer in the 19th and early 20th centuries. There was hardly any heritage of prose on which to build; the oral narrative tradition (folktales included) was remote; the literary tradition, exemplified by the folksong, was predominantly lyrical. At the time therefore when the short story was asserting itself in Europe and in the United States, the Lithuanian writer had to construct the entire house of prose fiction from its very foundations. And if the enormity of that task were not enough in itself, he had to do it under the most trying conditions: hunted by tsarist censors and the police, constrained by the low educational level of his readers, and haunted by insecurity. His success in creating a Lithuanian story is an exhilarating story in itself; perhaps, the most beautiful one in this anthology.

A national literature, just as nature, does not make leaps. In a few decades Lithuanian prose had to absorb the phases of literary evolution, to digest in frantic haste the schools and trends through which other, more fortunate, literatures have gone at a more leisurely pace. That hurried pace, that yearning to catch up, coupled with a feeling of inadequacy, have endowed the Lithuanian prose with its special dynamics. It has only been since the early 1920s that the writer could begin to consider himself an artist, first and foremost, and not primarily a patriot or teacher, to indulge himself in the luxuries of modernist experimentation, to take trips into the subconscious, or to revel in playful irony. This change of attitudes was preceded by a shift toward West European literature in the second decade of our century, after a long predominance of Polish and Russian influences.

The Herdsman and the Linden Tree is an appropriate story to begin an anthology of a literature in transition. In the herdsman Lapinas, Kreve has created an enduring portrait of traditional Lithuanian Pantheism in confrontation with the changing mores and attitudes. "The oldest of the elderly men in the village," a legendary figure mystically united with nature, he is pitted against the new breed of more utilitarian peasants who "no longer respect the holy woods." Kreve, author of an epic novel-drama on the biblical world and of stories on Buddhist themes, demonstrates convincingly that the Lithuanian village, too, can be the stage for sublime drama of great import. In a parallelism typical of the Lithuanian folksong, Lapinas dies when the ancient linden tree is felled; a whole world goes under. Kreve's art redeems what had been an unknown backwater and transfers it to the map of universal literature.

The pace of "Veronika" by Antanas Vienuolis (1882-1957), another classic of Lithuanian prose, may seem too relaxed and the descriptions of nature too expansive for some contemporary readers. But nature here does participate as a significant agent in the clash between the protagonist of the title and the dark underside of the patriarchal village, its cruelty bred by misery and ignorance. In externalizing Veronika's emotions in the myriad forms of nature, the author underscores her attractiveness in counterpoint to the forces of doom. Veronika never questions the patterns and rhythms of village life woven from the ancient seasonal rituals or the newer Christian beliefs, because they all invest her life with order and meaning. Then, in an ironic stroke, they become her prison as well. When she turns to the world of nature for solace, the rye whispers to her a reply of dark omens, snatches of folk songs reiterate the verdict. Because Veronika was so full of life, she must die.

The fate of Peleksas in "The Misfit" by Vaizgantas (1869-1933) resembles Veronika's destiny. He perishes because he does not fit into the prearranged narrow scheme of things, a crime for which his father brands him an outsider. The story is suffused with claustrophobic fatalism but the author saves it from becoming unbearably morbid by refracting his subject through the prism of an eleven-year old's vision. The boy is the only one who notices Peleksas' "sky-blue eyes that expressed such joy and longing" and sheds his tears when the outcast dies. It is the same capacity to discern "joy and longing" in the most dismal of circumstances that characterize Vaizgantas as a writer. Although his verbal exuberance and dexterity never found an appropriate structural framework, his sprawling and densely peopled canvas of Lithuanian life during the 19th and early 20th centuries still exudes great warmth and vitality.

The stories of Kreve, Vienuolis and Vaizgantas harbor the substructure that will be reiterated by those who follow in their path and that will affect even those wanting to escape it. Vaizgantas' portrait of his own mother vividly shows how this symbolic universe was conveyed to the artist as a child:

> "At night, when she gave thanks for the blessings of the day, she would fall prostrate on the ground, embracing it and kissing it devoutly, and address herself directly to the earth: "Black Earth, Holy Earth, I humbly kiss thee, I thank thee, I thank thee for bearing me, sustaining me, and giving me joy . . .'

For her, nature was full of the Almighty Will. She would not suffer anyone to speak ill of the good earth; she would use only the purest water, drawn straight from the well, to put the fire out..."

Antanas Vaiciulaitis (1906-   ), perhaps the outstanding stylist of Lithuanian prose, shares Vaizgantas' radiance and feels very much at home in his world. Steeped in French literature, however, he exemplifies the new aesthetic aspiration of the independence period. His mellow tales such as "Noon at a Country Inn" are imbued with Christian humanism and glide gracefully between reality and fantasy. The cataclysms of war and exile were not powerful enough to leave even a scratch in his canons of symmetry, simplicity and lucidity.

Another stylist of note is Vincas Ramons (1905-   ), in whose "Captain Boruta" man's decay is outlined in a series of sharply etched images.

Petras Tarulis (pseudonym of Juozas Petrenas (1896-   ) was one of the leaders of the literary avant-garde movement, *Keturi Vejai* (Four Winds) in the 1920s. His story "Blue Trousers" reflects some of the aims of the movement: the imperative of simplicity, the "cleansing" of the old vocabulary, the challenge to the heritage or romanticism and symbolism. Preoccupation with the past and with rural life were now to be replaced with a cult of technology and with Futurism. The cruel, unpredictable sea and the cosmopolitan crew in "Blue Trousers" are perfect antidotes to the habitual rustics and reliable good earth heretofore dominant in Lithuanian prose.

Keturi Vejai died out in the late 1920s and experimentally inclined writers of the next decade generally applied new narrative techniques to the traditional milieu, as witness the montage of cinematic images in "Seven Swords" by Juozas Kralikauskas (1910-   ), resembling the modernist treatment of fok art motifs in painting. The story, with its truncated sentences and Expressionist devices, skirts mannerism but is held together by a genuine lyrical sweep. The promise held by "Seven Swords" in the author's first collection of stories (1937) was amply fulfilled in his daring novelistic recreations of Lithuania's archaic past, written during the years of his Canadian exile.

The cosmopolitan scene and sophisticated playfulness, qualities totally absent from Lithuanian prose at the turn of the century, are served with *panache* in "The Red Shoes" by Jurgis Savickis (1890-1952) and in "The Ordeal of Assad Pasha" by Ignas Seinius (1889-1959). Diplomat by profession and esthete by vocation, Savickis deftly sketches the trail of an imp—the imp of seduction in thought—amidst the brittle elegance of pre-diluvian Europe of the late 1930s. The story of Seinius who spent most of his life abroad, is an example of the great range of his writing. One of the first Lithuanian writers to assert the primacy of art, a seminal experimenter, and author of one of the earliest European satires on Nazism* he unfolds here a modern fable of the Orient like a connoisseur slowly and lovingly opening an ornate carpet. As a citizen of a small country that had to rebuild itself from the shambles of imperial domination, Seinius may have found it easier to sympathize with the people of an underdeveloped Third World State and to steer clear of condescension that often mars such stories.

Most of the stories in this volume were written after the great divide of 1940. That year marked the end of Lithuania's independence and cut short the cultural flowering generated by the end of foreign domination in 1918. The Lithuanian nation and its literature were absorbed into the totalitarian realm, the universe of Auschwitz and of the Gulag Archipelago. About two-thirds of the Lithuanian writers went abroad in the middle 1940s—probably the largest such exodus in history. For some West Europeans or Americans, the word "exile" still evokes images of vindictive Bourbon emigres, or Russian counts chauffeuring Parisian taxicabs and gnashing their reactionary teeth as they dream of return and revenge. None of the Lithuanian refugee writers owned latifundia and their debts probably exceeded their bank holdings. They fled in an instinctive move of self-preservation because they sensed that the word would be the prime target of the Soviet system.

Mass exile added yet another bizarre dimension to the already frenetic development of Lithuanian letters. Children of an earthbound literature, intertwined as few others with its *genius loci*, they were scattered all over the world. Tragic figures and inheritors of a supreme sorrow in their own eyes, they were often seen as

---

*Rejuvenation of Siegfried Immerselbe.

grotesque strangers by the natives of their new countries. A single leap catapulted them from a literary organism of which they were purposeful members into the vast and atomistic land of modern letters, whose authors wrote of exile and displacement within their own lands and hearts. But it would be inaccurate to equate exile with loss and mourning alone. As that astute chronicler of Lithuanian refugee writing, Rimvydas Silbajoris, has expressed it:

> The holocaust of war blew down the walls of home, making us both naked and free. It was a tragic liberation, but it did open new horizons, new countries, new civilizations, new ways of perceiving things. Some writers refused this challenge and remained safely inside the walls of what they persist even now in believing is their home, although it has lost all material substance . . . Other writers, however, decided to face the new reality as well as they could and to search for new forms and ideas which would make their work meaningful in terms of the new situation . . .

The work of Antanas Skema (1911-1961), better known as dramatist and novelist, is one of the most eloquent examples of an exile writer determined to face the new void, the Hemingwayan *nada,* naked and without traditional supports or illusions. Not surprisingly, he found the Existentialists and Absurdists very congenial. While most Lithuanian readers in exile craved soothing reassurances and wanted their writers to provide them with dioramas of familiar landscapes and values, Skema saw their attitudes as a plastic cocoon and chose instead to become the "destructive element" in Lithuanian letters. His characters bleed in torture chambers, haunt the air-raid sites where they were killed once, and go insane inside the elevators of New York hotels without any assurance that their sufferings or death would acquire meaning within some scheme, human or divine. The theme is already announced in his early story, "In the Hospital." Smilga, the daughter of displaced persons who are trying to cling to normalcy in a world gone mad, is contrasted with little Wolfgang, perennially starved and never able to hold his food, a tiny postwar Sisyphus caught in the unending cycle of vomiting. Surrounded by the suffering children, Sister Rose intones the evening hymn to truth and harmony.

The bitter ironies of Germany at war are explored in "Counterbalance" a self-contained excerpt from the novel, *House Upon the Sand* by Jurgis Gliauda (1906-   ), one of the most prolific of exile prose writers, with a special interest in moral questions. A German civilian kills a French prisoner-of-war, another "displaced" person, the eternal scapegoat—although he had liked him as an individual. The prisoner must die so that the German's own son's death at the front can be rectified and the "cosmic balance" restored.

Does exile almost invariably reinforce the trend toward abstraction? "Elena" by Stepas Zobarskas, (1911-   ), known also as anthologist and publisher, is a good case in point. In contrast to his earlier stories, suffused with uniquely Lithuanian shapes, smells and colors, "Elena" inhabits a semi-abstract ground; the author's concern is not with concrete time or place but with the geometric combinations of love and passion, resembling musical variations on a given theme.

Several of the exile stories are set in the United States. The American, a rare and exotic creature in the pre-diaspora Lithuanian prose ("The American . . . you should see him; with a watch and galoshes," "Veronika"), has now become a next door neighbor. Once translated, the stories with an American background exist not only as esthetic objects but also enlarge the body of American immigrant literature" whose map, despite the singular achievements of the Jewish-American writers, still contains many gray spots. (For instance, even in the hands of a master story-teller like Flannery O'Connor, the Polish immigrant in "The Displaced Person" is a flat character, whose inner life she does not penetrate, in contrast to her most primitive Southerners.) Such Lithuanian stories thus lend faces and voices to people whom both prejudiced WASPS and "progressives" interested only in fashionable minorities blithely consign to the category of "hard hats" or "Archie Bunkers."

Among the writers on American-Lithuanian themes, most of whom immigrated to the United States in the late 1940s, Antanas Tulys (1898-1977) stands out as the chronicler of the earlier, mainly pre-World War I, wave of Lithuanian immigrants. In his

"The Three Knots," he views the two women mired in the moonshine era as a detached observer, in the manner of Naturalism, a school with which the writers in Lithuania did not feel much affinity.

The old refugee in "The Brink of Madness" by Aloyzas Baronas (1922-   ), an immigrant of later vintage, has resigned to his humdrum existence in the strange new country as the lesser of two evils. What crushes him before his time is the inevitable relativization of values that exile brings. His victory in defeating temptation and upholding traditional values turns out to be his defeat; his stubborn honesty earns him the scorn of his neighbors and hastens his death. It is against the same relativization of values, deeply felt but dimly understood, that Adele wages a losing struggle in "The Heavens Are Full Again" by Algirdas Landsbergis (1924-   ). Her familiar heavens are swept clean and then refilled with new gods.

The heroine of Vytautas Alantas' (1902-   ) "The Crown Prince Needs Blood" feels "Lithuanian" at her parents' home but becomes "American" as soon as she steps out into the street. She describes herself as "wavering between two forces, like a reed whose roots are deeply embedded in some sunken continent." Biological survival, cultural survival—remote textbook phrases for some, matters of life and death to others. The author arrives at his desired solution by marrying biology and mysticism and conjuring the imperatives of the "collective subconscious" through a dream.

Kazys Almenas (1933-   ), the youngest writer of the diaspora in this volume, provides a different vantage point. His position may be summed up in the words of the narrator in his story, "The Yellow Buick": "I nodded my head significantly, though to me the war was but a hazy childhood recollection." Almenas is not suspended between the old world and the new, like other exiles, nor does he roam the fields of nostalgia. In tracing the disintegration of the young Slovak Vladzhio, victim of his "greenhorn" fantasies and of the American success mystique, the author surveys from a critical distance both his young contemporaries and the immigrant communities caught in the process that sociologists, with their unfailing ability to devise tortuous abstractions, have defined as acculturation.

The experience of exile has made it easier for some of the writers to embrace the techniques of modern literature. The spiral or the linear plot progression, for example, seemed quite appropriate at home and in times of peace, when continuity was the very essence of being. But in the exile's upside-down wonderland the old linear plot may appear fantastic, and realism may be discovered in structures resembling complex metaphors, or in webs of flashbacks. Glimpses of home, refugee wanderings, daydreams mingle in the "Queen Mother" by Kazys Barenas (1907-   ), a writer of decidely realistic inclinations. The scene in this segment of a novel strung together from twenty-one stories is England, where the refugee heroine settles, reviews her past and concludes that "you cannot go home again."

Some refugee writers have damned exile and have sequestered themselves in replicas of the past, like brokenhearted widows in rooms redolent of faded weeds and yellowing photographs. Others again have grasped the opportunity provided by displacement to acquire a focus and a new sense of form in order to recapture time and space lost, as Adam Mickiewicz had done in his masterpiece *Pan Tadeusz*.

"All this came from my heart and my experience, which the years of exile have matured and ripened in a particularly plastic manner and have given form to things that were scattered and loose at home," wrote Pulgis Andriusis (1907-1969), the author of "He Was Not Allowed to See." Displaced almost as far as Mars, to an Australian cityscape, he recreated a universe of Lithuanian flora, fauna, and feeling with what Ivar Ivask has accurately described as "Joycean verbal density." This, he accomplished by remaining true to the nature mysticism of his region of Eastern Aukstaitija, where "the grass, trees, fish, insects, clouds, even stones are not merely a linguistic embroidery or stage props, but brothers, sisters, life's companions with equal rights, with the same care and joys as we."

Marius Katiliskis (1920-   ), whose present home is the Illinois prairie, manifests the same uncanny ability to recreate rural Lithuania. When, in "The Midsummer," a shotgun-marriage story with a twist, he wants to convey to his readers the girl's unusual popularity, he does it by means of a physical detail, one of thousands surviving in his memory with complete clarity. ("The old man could no longer keep the gates in order, for the men and the lads of the village would lean too heavily against them, thrusting them out of place.") Elemental and baroque, where Andriusis is whimsical and lyrical, Katiliskis has demonstrated in his other stories that he is not limited to his native habitat but can portray the American Midwest as well—the city workers, the drifters and, especially, the hillbillies, those other "displaced persons"—with precision and empathy.

Liudas Dovydenas (1906-   ) has tried to go back home from exile by returning to the wellsprings of Lithuanian prose, the folktale, "Petras" is one of such recreations, close to the spirit of the original and congenial to his own narrative vigor. Folklore harbors for Dovydenas the magic formulas and guarantees of continuity and permanence amidst the essential impermanence of an exile's existence.

The tale of Dovydenas also reveals the earthbound concreteness of the Lithuanian peasant's mentality ("two pairs of shoes, a bucket of sausages and two wooden spoons" are the protagonist's supreme desires addressed to the higher powers) that coexists with the mystical side of his nature.

Julius Kaupas (1920-1964) draws the sustenance for his lucid tales from different sources: the fantastic elements of the city, Christian morality, and German romanticism. Even when he ventures into a basically realistic subject, as in "Organ of Kurkliskes," his provincial scene of cobblestones, chickens, and gasoline fumes seems to hover on the verge of dissolving itself into moonlit unreality.

The blend of legend and realism in "The Thorn" is typical for its author, Nele Mazalaite (1907-   ). She places the events immediately after World War II into a setting in which the older Christian and the new national symbols retain an unquestionable validity; life as in the medieval universe, is an allegory from which a distinct moral can be derived.

"The China Bowl" by Jurgis Jankus (1900-   ) is an object that stands as the central symbol of the story. The breaking of the bowl not only interrupts one of the favorite situations in Lithuanian prose—the affectionate interplay between grandmother and grandchild—but also causes a crack in grandmother's own self, through which she suddenly perceives destructive evil, an "alien presence" of which she had not been aware. The themes of evil and subconscious motivation, intimated here, are prominent in Jankus' psychological novels.

Icchokas Meras (1934-   ) occupies a special place in this anthology as both the newest member of the Lithuanian writers' community in exile and as another participant in the 2000-year-old Jewish diaspora. He now makes his home in Israel, where he arrived in 1972 amidst the recent wave of Communist anti-Semitism under the guise of "anti-Zionism" that since 1968 has sent abroad large numbers of East European writers and intellectuals. His writing represents an interesting and fruitful blend of the Lithuanian and Jewish traditions. "The Old Woman with a Green Pail" on the surface a plain episode from the life of recent immigrants in Israel, is really a tantalizing parable that calls to mind Walter Benjamin's words of Kafka: "Each gesture is an event—one might even say, a drama—in itself." From these gestures and from the seemingly casual glances and remarks, the reader must try, as in the case of many modern short stories, to reconstruct the meaning of action.

Several stories in this anthology were written by authors who grew up and matured as artists under Soviet Russian rule. The Marxist-Leninist view of literature lacked the refreshing bluntness that characterized the Nazi attitude toward culture during their brief occupation of Lithuania (1941-1944), as exemplified by one of the poetic flights of the SS magazine, *Das Schwarze Korps,* which declared that Lithuanian culture was destined to vanish like a drop of water on a sizzling hot stone. The Soviet Russians, whose tenure in Lithuania turned out to be much longer, saw literature as a useful tool that had first to be cleansed of earlier impurities and then used as an instrument for the transformation of mere bourgeois mannikins into Soviet men. This conception of literature has room both for the view of the gendarme who would shut anybody up who dared to step out of line, as well as for the Jacobinist-Utopian vision of a language qualitatively altered and thus redeemed. Literature, as in other East European countries was to be made useful, churning out proper fictions and thus constructing the crystal pavilion of appropriate myths corresponding to those spun by the Great Leader or, at other times, by the Party's Central Committee. Lithuanians, with their historic memories, did not take long to discern behind the trappings of that Great Utopian Dream Machine the all too familiar features of Great Russian Messianism and self-adulation. What happened was that just as the tsars had imposed the Cryillic alphabet on the Lithuanian language 100 years ago, the commissars are now inflicting the peculiar agonies of Russia's history and culture—the legacy of censorship, the distrust of the aesthetic, the Leninist politicization of all art—on a literature whose organic development, needs and shapes of imagination have been quite different. Lithuanian literature must now observe alien limits and suffer through a foreign malaise. The Soviets are fond of using the term "cultural colonialism" with reference to the French or British cultural high-handedness in Africa and Asia, but the term fits their own actions like a glove.

One of the critics active in Lithuania today, V. Zalatorius, has described the postwar decade in Lithuanian prose as one in which:

> "one-sided ideological allegiance was demanded from the writer, and any newer, more modern form was regarded with suspicion . . . contacts with the trends of world prose were weakened."A (partial) list of taboos included: "Doubt, inner turmoil, solitude, continuous transvaluation of values, self-irony, secret suffering, destructive passion, romantic longing, pantheistic links with nature . . ."

The sacred formula to describe and justify all that was "Socialist Realism," a method that Maxim Gorky once hopefully defined as the capacity to view the present from the vantage point of the future; it turned out, alas, that the shape and needs of the future would be determined by bureaucrats, censors, hacks and policemen, while the artist's imagination was to be held in extreme distrust.

What better proof of the vitality and resilience of Lithuanian literature could one find than the fact that it not only survived the bleakest period of such "cultural colonialism," but that it also raised a whole generation of talented young writers, and even enlarged its frontiers? The reasons for this seemingly contradictory victory-in-defeat are too complex to be recounted here in detail. To put it briefly, Stalin's death and the ensuing turmoil in the Empire have presented the artists in Lithuania, as elsewhere in East Europe, with an opportunity to expand the limits of the permissible and reassert the demands of art. The inherent contradictions and dialectical tensions within the hybrid Marxist-Leninist esthetics provided the artists with additional space for maneuvering. Official lip service paid to the tenets of humanist socialism could sometimes be claimed as the artist's birthright. Even the inundation with Russian literature turned out to be a double-edged sword because among the classics, at least, the reader found an emphasis on truth-seeking and moral obligation. The pressure of Russification and of the ideological leveling boomeranged by strengthening the resolve of non-Communists and some Communists alike to preserve the national heritage and create genuine literary works, instead of producing copies of master designs. When the strictures were partly relaxed in the period 1956-1958,

> Lithuanian prose turned into the groove followed by story writers and novelists of all lands . . . stylistic patterns of the stream of consciousness . . . associative images, free interpretation of space and time . . . absurd situations (A. Zalatorius).

By choosing this path at the earliest opportunity, Lithuanian writers again demonstrated that they considered tnemselves as belonging to the world, rather than merely to a narrow sect of letters. The new formal diversity of the short story has been causing much concern to the Party supervisors of literature who suspect the indirections of the "plotless" or "artistic" story and have expressed their preference for a "well-made" story with an obvious conflict and message.

Despite the alleviation of the literary atmosphere in Lithuania, there is still a large price that must be paid by those who refuse to prostitute their writing. The list of forbidden subjects and styles remains formidable. The totalitarian apparatus of art control, although reduced, has not been put into mothballs. On the contrary, since 1968 that apparatus has been employed again at near-capacity in a new ideological campaign designed to narrow the boundaries of literature. But even in this dismal situation, there is cause for guarded optimism. Lithuanian literature did not go under in the late 1940s and early 1950s when the Party used Stalinist terror against the cowed older writers and tried to mold the dewy-eyed youngsters; it is even less likely to succeed today when it dares not return to the old methods and when it faces a large body of mature artists tempered in the fire, only few of whom have compromised themselves irretrievably. Or, to quote, the dramatist and short story writer Juozas Grusas: "Each stomach digests meat, some stomachs even digest bones, but there is no stomach that would digest the spirit."

Formidable as the efforts of the Stalinist "engineers of the souls" have been, Lithuanian prose has preserved a continuity and a common sensibility beneath the varieties of technique and message. It is a sensibility informed by restraint (a northern version of the Mediterannean *Mesure*), strongly imbued with lyrical and contemplative qualities, and nourished by humanism.

Juozas Grusas (1900-   ) in a sense personifies the continuity of Lithuanian prose during the period covered in this anthology. Through these difficult times he tried to remain true to his art and to his personal philosophy of humanism—not of pollyannas or of unitarian coffee hours, but a humanism similar to that of the modern Czech writers, tested in the extremes of inhumanity, acknowledging man's extreme capacity for destruction, and yet retaining a grain of hope in man's regeneration. In "The Heavy Hand," we are shown that committing evil is doing what comes naturally: ("Their souls shuddered momentarily, not longer, however, than the human body does upon immersion into a cold bath"), but we also perceive that even the most destructive among us can have an epiphany: ("His heavy hand dropped down and came to rest on the woman's shoulders"). The progress of evil occupies the entire story except for this last sentence—Grusas' grain of hope.

"The Striped Trolleybus" by Romualdas Lankauskas (1932-   ), a versatile short story writer and novelist, exemplifies one of the important trends in recent Lithuanian prose—the striving for honesty in writing through extreme simplicity and matter-of-factness. The trend, partly coincidental with the influence, and for a while almost a cult of Hemingway in the Lithuanian prose, is also discernible in other East European literatures, notably among the Czechs (Kliment, *et al.*) The star of Hemingway though has been eclipsed by the discovery of Faulkner in the late 1960s—a generation-long lag is the price one pays for enforced cultural isolation.

Vytaute Zilinskaite (1930-   ) has the distinction of being the outstanding humorous prose writer in a country with a rather underdeveloped literature of humor. As her two short stories indicate, she has already gone beyond the anecdotal feuilleton and is staking a claim in the territory of Zoshchenko and Mrozek. In her wry and wise parables one encounters the typically East European convergence of the most ordinary and the fantastic.

The story of Juozas Aputis (1936-   ), which furnished one of the opening images for this introduction, concludes the anthology. Tractor-driver Gvildys of the "Wild Boars" and the herdsman Lapinas of "Grainis' Linden Tree" link hands across 50 years of Lithuanian short prose; both are sick at heart, because for them, in Yeats' famous line, "Things fall apart; the centre cannot hold . . ." The contrast between the tongue-tie of Gvildys and the importance of the transformations around him is not merely a routine irony ploy by the author but a direct expression of man's inability to explain "absurdity" and mortality. In the same way, Aputis' sytle deliberately eschews grace and fluency; the absence of connectives in his syntax directly mirrors his protagonists' disjointed groping.

The questions and challenges in the stories of both Kreve and Aputis go far beyond conservative nostalgia or the yearning to preserve some quaint rusticity. They amount to a radical questioning of reckless modernization and of the blind cult of technology, a questioning that is more deeply felt and more pertinent than the chic fatuities of, say, "The Greening of America." The two stories attain universal validity while remaining unmistakably Lithuanian. The reader will hopefully find more such rewards in this anthology. Whatever the limitations or inadequacies of Lithuanian prose, one should open this book not because one feels obligated to contribute to some sort of UNICEF for little-known literatures but because the stories here offer pleasures, insights, a fresh vantage point, and since this collective body of prose reveals that personal trials and national calamities can be transmuted into art.

An anthology of this kind is, by definition, incomplete. A host of most deserving short story writers had to be left out lest the volume burst its covers. The only reason, apparently, why anthology editors do not shrivel away in frustration at a tender age is that in the midst of their despair, they are already planning new anthologies, as this editor is probably doing, in which they will try again to accomplish the impossible.

Fairleigh Dickinson University

BIBLIOGRAPHY

Kazys Bradunas (ed.). *Lietuviu literatura svetur 1945-1967*, Chicago: Laisves Fondas, 1968.

Rimvydas Silbajoris. *Perfection of Exile.* Norman: University of Oklahoma Press, 1971.

Albertas Zalatorius, *Lietuviu apsakymo raida ir poetika.* Vilnius: Vaga, 1971.

Albertas Zalatorius (ed.). *Tarybine novele.* Vilnius: Vaga, 1969.

by R. Kalpokas

Vaizgantas

VAIZGANTAS

One of the most beloved Lithuanian writers, and an outstanding national figure, VAIZGANTAS was born in Malaisiai, Lithuania, on September 20, 1869. A Roman Catholic canon, a university professor, the author of some nineteen volumes of novels, short stories and critical essays, Vaizgantas was, above all, a champion of political independence and cultural freedom. His profound humanity, optimism and understanding of human nature have made him the most influential individual of his generation. His talent found its most suitable form of expression in his sketches and short stories. His major work, *Pragiedruliai* (Clearing Skies) 1918/1920 is an epic novel filled with dynamic characters and unfolds a panorama of Lithuania at the time of the National Awakening. Also outstanding are his short story, "Rimai ir Nerimai" (The Rimas and Nerimas Families), 1914, and the novella *Dedes ir Dedienes* (Uncles and Aunts), 1929. He died in Kaunas on April 29, 1933.

VAIZGANTAS

(1869-1933)

The Misfit

THERE HAD NEVER been such a hot spell; even dusk brought no relief. Men and beasts dragged their feet, feeling barely alive. The grasshoppers alone kept showing how alive they were; their liveliness even seemed to be increasing as the draught grew worse. And who had provided them with gadgets, charper than awls, to pierce men's ears? Yet the piercing and pricking of the insects brought no pain. It only made one dizzy and awakened a longing for summer. But there was no time for dreaming in the midst of the busy season.

"The bloody bugs, how come they don't dry to dust," our hired man was muttering as he entered the gate and tipped his cap before the tall wooden cross. He was passing a dense guelder-rose bush from which the grasshopper seemed to be teasing the poor workmen.

It was already dark inside the cottage. In the summertime, when days were long and nights short, lighting a lamp seemed indecent. Eating could be done in twilight and the light of the kerosene lamp could only disturb the sleepy weariness that seized a poorly nourished body after its physical exertion of the day. Their meal finished, the men could hardly lift their hands to make the sing of the cross and, ghostlike drag their feet to their flea traps for a deathlike sleep.

Three horses, their heads hanging listlessly, stood tied to an osier in the middle of the yard. Their paunches were empty and the way they were behaving suggested that they were hungry. The horses dozed as they waited in vain for someone to lead them out to pasture.

"Eh, what's going on?" the master, my father, realized belatedly. "Who'll take the horses to the pasture, now?"

It was not the thing for him to do, the man in charge with a family of at least ten. The women had already slunk into their storehouses and bolted their doors tightly.

My elder brother was silent. He seemed to be totally vanquished by work although he was still rolling a cigarette, having collapsed on the bench on the way to his bed.

The hired man got the message. "It's up to me, of course. Who else? One verst there, another back, and it's midnight. And then getting up at four with the sun just beginning to rise—and fifteen hours of work. How can a man survive?"

He began putting his arm into the narrow sleeve of his jacket although he did not need it in such heat. "Do as you think best, Master, but I refuse to tend horses during summer harvest time."

It was true. One simply could not use a hired man for such purposes. Father was silent. He was evidently going to ride the horses himself.

I was still half-awake. Although sleepiness and fatigue had overcome me, I enjoyed listening to the grasshoppers and watching the poor workmen and sympathizing with them.

"Daddy, please let me take a night ride, at least once. I'll sleep until breakfast."

I assumed that my father would not allow me to do this. I was was not even allowed to tend the cattle during the day. I was the youngest and they pampered me and hired a shepherdess so that I would not have to do any herding.

I was nearly eleven and was quick as a pepper, although small and frail as a cricket. I had already managed to roll myself upon a horse when barefooted. To accomplish this, I needed to use the big toe of my left foot. I would push myself off from the horse's knee where, as luck would have it, there was a bump; then mercilessly tearing at the mane, I would finally mount the animal. The horse suffered patiently through all these exertions and then obeyed as I rode even when I forced him through beating, to pretend that he was rushing into an all-out gallop. The "gallop" of the old creature was more like an aged crone's dance if anything, but it was enough for me; I prided myself on having galloped and was sufficiently excited by it.

Father contemplated my offer awhile, took a large whiff of tobacco, looked at his littlest one across his shoulder and, with considerable contentment, said, "Well, why don't you ride for the night? And what do you lack to be a true night rider? You can hobble them, you can take off their halters, And at night, we've got the horseherd. In the morning, one of the older ones will help you manage."

I leaped with joy and boasted like a grownup, "That's small stuff, hobbling and halters . . . and I'll ride back properly."

What pleased me especially was that my mother did not hear any of the plan, and the next day I would be able to tell her about everything after it had happened! This meant that, for the first time, I would appear to her as capable of participating in farm work.

All three men felt a surge of joy, too, knowing that their life would now be easier. The disgruntled hired man suddenly became very cooperative and hurried to untie the horses. My older brother immediately snatched a huge fur coat and threw it over the horse, telling me in a consoling voice, "Here, bundle yourself up from head to toe like a little caterpillar; you'll sleep in a bed that's warm as a dumpling!" Then he flung me on the horse as though I were a sheaf of wheat.

I spread my legs wide and stretched out my arms like a gingerbread man. "Giddyap!" I shouted excitedly in my thin boyish voice and swept the horse-lock over their three backs.

The horses burst into a speedy trot but I did not stop whipping them since I wanted them to gallop. I yelled and screamed so that the entire village could see me riding out that night. But the villagers did not see me since everybody was in bed, sleeping. The night herdsmen had all ridden out already, and even the dogs failed to do me honor. Not a single one of them barked at me from in front of the granaries. They must have assumed that one of their own was making all this noise.

The horses began trotting lazily as usual, but under the whip they broke into the gallop I desired. When we made the turn past Peciura's cottage, the last one in the village, they whinnied, as if in agreement to a drove of horses dimly outlined in the distance, and showed that they could gallop properly.

For the first time, I realized with astonishment how great the difference between forced and voluntary labor was. The horses were giving all they had, even flattening themselves to the ground, as the saying here goes. They seemed to have grown smaller and the earth appeared to be closer to my feet. Hopping off would have been a very easy thing to do. But there was not time for that. The wind was rushing past my ears. The manes of the horses' necks, stretched in a cranelike fashion, spread out along their withers. The hair of their flying tails whistled like a whip. All at once, I became frightened. "Steady, horses, steady . . ." I muttered, nearly choking on my words. But they did not listen to me any longer. There was no more time to pull in the reins—I had to hold on to my horse's mane with both hands because my legs were hardly touching the animal's flanks and I was almost propelled into the air. If only I hadn't taken that coat! With its fur side out, it was sliding up and down on the slippery hair of the horse, and I could hardly hold it down with my legs.

"I'll fall . . . I'll kill myself . . ." The thought terrified me and I did not realize that I was squealing like a piglet.

A narrow bridge over a muddy stream loomed in the darkness ahead. It was laid over with loose boards that were wide enough for a one-horse carriage on a very straight course. The boards rattled like organ keys when the organist is giving them a nimble workout during mass, and they tended to tip over. It was possible to cross the bridge with a pair of horses if they pressed their flanks closely together. But with *three* horses one had to wade through the stream.

My three chargers never stopped to give the matter a thought. In their wildness, they were probably not inclined to do any thinking at all, the only thing on their minds being how to reach that distant drove of horses. The boards thundered from their heavy hooves, and then the outside horse splashed into the stream, the middle one stumbled on a protruding board, and the animal I was riding fairly jumped across the bridge. I did not fall off, however, and I completed the ride to the edge of the marsh with two horses.

As we approached a group of horses which stood slightly apart from the rest of the herd, my mounts whinnied again. The other horses neighed in friendly response, and suddenly we came to a stop beside a man who was kneeling in the soggy grass. He had just about finished hobbling the last of them.

"What kind of a witch has come flying here with such thunder and squealing?" he asked, deeply curious.

I was still glued to the horse and felt half alive and half dead. Frightened and swooning, I clutched the animal's mane spasmodically and my tense fingers would not let it go.

"Who's here? Could that be Juzukas?" the man asked, coming closer. "Why did you go out riding? Come on, get off that horse! Where are your hobbles?" he asked as he eased me off the horse by my armpits.

There were no hobbles in my hands, no cap on my head, no fur coat on the horse, and the outside horse was still missing. In the next instant, however, it came snorting by, all covered with mud.

"Dashing . . .everything got scattered . . ." I started muttering, my jaws feeling as if they were locked stiffly in place.

The night herdsman understood. "Let them graze unhobbled for awhile," he said. 'We'll go and gather your things."

That was not difficult. I knew the route I had taken. We found the things scattered on both sides of the stream. Back at the meadow, we hobbled the horses, found a dry place to sit down and started chatting.

Or, rather, I did all the talking, breathing nervously into my neighbor's ear about the terrors and dangers I had just experienced.

Although I exaggerated the dangers, I was truly convinced that if I had fallen off the horse my body would have broken to pieces, or, if I had slipped off the bridge with my horses, my back or spine would have cracked on the spot. It had seemed to me that each jump of the horse I was riding dealt a blow to my chest, pressed as it was against the animal's back. My chest still felt sore and I reclined on my side in order to rest and, if possible, to elicit more sympathy from my audience.

Peciura's Peleksas believed everything I said and managed to calm me down. He praised me for not falling off the horse and said it was time for both of us to go to sleep.

By now the other herdsmen had finished their work. Some were stretched out on the ground, their heads covered with short jackets to get quick warmth from their own hot breath. Their bare feet had been left unprotected, and they curled them under trying to get them to fit beneath the cover. But soon the feet would slide into the cold air again. Misery's own children they were, these men, like savages without roofs of their own.

Others continued to talk. Their speech was short—a few words here and there. Mostly, they kept turning and stomping their feet like dogs who turn and twist until they finally settle down on bare ground.

I was met with contemptuous smiles. The chief horse tender, bundled in "two's," which meant a woolen overcoat stuffed into a fur coat, and with his belt tightened to the limit, seemed to be prepared to drive to the forest instead of being on a night watch. A thick sweater reached above his ears. All of this was in anticipation that the warmth of the late evening would give way to cold for a couple of hours before sunrise.

"Come now, they wouldn't be sending us such a horse tender for the night. Just the right fellow to guard us from theives and wolves . . ."

"And what would you do here? . . . Why should you get your wages if we need another watchman?" Peleksas growled. The horse tender shut his mouth and plunged into the darkness to check the horses.

I was expecting those who were still awake to surround and question me in awed and fearful voices as to how I had managed to get there at a full gallop without losing my head. But nobody asked me anything; for them, galloping and bouncing along on a horse's back was quite an ordinary affair. So I started telling the story myself, without being asked. Yet even this made very little impression on them. The only thing that interested them a little was the fact that one of the horses had fallen into the stream.

"How come his weight did not pull down the others?" they asked me.

"Some luck . . . You'd have been as handsome as your horse!"

It seemed that the whole story would simply end there. But it had really only begun.

"What kind of fakery is this? Our gray mare has become dapple-gray!" The words greeted me as I rode into the yard.

"Was she stuck in the mud somewhere; did you have to pull her out?"

I did not answer, making matters worse. The entire village was already buzzing with rumors of how I had drowned my horses in the stream and lost my head in the bargain.

People started voming and inquiring, while I snored peacefully in a warm bed in the drawing room until it was almost lunch time.

The farm hands' lunch was brough to the field. I did not see them. In the afternoon, my mother kept glancing through the window and, having noticed Peleksas passing by, invited him inside. She made him sit in the place of honor and brought him a heaping sacuer of buttered cream—twice as much as the sacuer was meant to hold. She asked me to help him finish it. We ate and ate but mroe than half was still left. I was full and Peleksas shied away from eating too much in someone else's home. What would people think? Yet for a healthy, strapping fellow such as he was, a whole pitcherful would have come in handy!

Mother kept urging Peleksas to eat and was constantly nudging his hand toward the saucer of cream as if her were paralyzed, and inquiring about what had happened to me during the night.

"Oh, nothing. The horses made their run and the one on the outside slipped off the bridge. Nothing else, Auntie."

"And Peleksas helped me gather up the scattered things. Then he helped me ride back."

"Thanks to God for such an end! And here, people were concocting all sorts of stories. My son wouldn't tell me anything when he came riding home . . . Well, you know he wants to tend the horses at night, but he's still a cricket—not big enough yet to catch a horse and too small to hobble it. You, Peleksas dear, you are a grown up and steady lad. Couldn't you take our boy around with you when the others may need his help, at least during the busy season? They get tired, you know. How can they go on with their drudgery without sleep! And our Juzukas can get his sleep during the day, when he comes back."

"Will do," Peleksas replied and, having kissed my mother's hand, he started for the door. He was opening it when my mother caught up with him and stuffed a sizable chunk of her special barley bread in his pocket. "I'll send more of that to the field," she promised, raising her forefinger in a conspiratory gesture.

Peleksas had become very kindly disposed and was impressed that such a grand housewife had showered him with hospitality and promised him more tasty treats. But he began to feel somewhat like a bribed man.

In our parts, if a neighbor shows you hospitality, it amounts to your borrowing from him; you have to pay him back in kind or reciprocate in some other way unless you want him to think badly of you.

Such had been the circumstances which had brought me and Peleksas together. We made an odd couple, though. He was eighteen or nineteen—and I was not yet eleven.

II

We were the last family on the slope; Peciura's farm was the last one on the hill. We could never get together with this, our most distant neighbor. During the summer, there was no time and during the rest of the year, the street was impassable. One might have gotten there past the barns, but the high fences of the gardens provided formidable obstacles. And on top of all that, Uncle Peciura Peleksas' father, was a man who struck terror in our hearts.

He was handsome to look at, of medium height, clear-faced and endowed with a nose that sported a little aristrocratic hump. His children were even handsomer. Fair-haired, they had such light complexions that even during the summer they did not get the faintest shade of tan. There were so many red cheeks in the family that, as someone said, you could shave at night if they were around. This saying was aimed mainly at the Peciura girls because what fellow would stare at other fellows, especially in the darkness! Peciura's brood was so large that people in the village could barely remember the older children who had grown up and left home. But there were still plenty of them left at home. Peleksas was the youngest of them and almost a man himself. Meanwhile, Uncle

Peciura was still in his middle years and had not even started to turn gray yet, as if he was ready to produce twice as many more offspring. However, he had too many worries about his brood already: to find husbands for his daughters, to marry certain sons to farm heiresses, to buy farms for tohers. And there was only so much property.

Night after night, Peciura would lie in bed without being able to fall asleep. Hands constantly seemed to be reaching out to him, demanding: for me, and for me, and for me! Uncle Peciura would turn on his side angrily and spit out his usual comment through his teeth: "May a bolt from the blue sky take care of you right now!" But even that tid not help. His worries about how he could assure a good (which for him meant a rich) future for all his children simply refused to disappear.

This may have been the reason why Uncle Peciura became crafty and sly (unless he was born that way). His children were also sly, crafty and conniving, following in their father's footsteps. However, they were all loyal to their family and to the village.

Peciura's farmstead sprawled on the richest soil of the village. It was loam: not the red, sour variety, but the light-red loam that resembles wheaten dough because it has been mixed with a little sand.

Apple trees had a special fondness for that loam. Planted on a slope by Peciura himself, these trees "went crazy," according to the old saying, as they burst forth in ever new branches and foliage. Their leaves were almost as big as a man's palm, and the apples themselves seemed to have been molded by craftsmen from the purest wax. White, with a shade of pink they were unbelievably fair and completely spotless. And they were as huge as a sturdy man's fist.

The orchard was long and had at least three dozen trees in it. It would have been quite expensive to build a good fence around it, so all that surrounded it was a horizontal fence to protect it from animals since the enclosure for the cattle of the entire village was right next to it. As for people, anyone could easily have entered the orchard and taken his fill. Neverthless, no thief, large or small, was ever known to have dared step across Peciura's fence, night or day. If some young pranksters would have ever thrown each other's caps into Peciura's orchard, they would probably have given them up rather than attempt to jump over the fence, such terror had the frightening Peciura struck in the hearts of the young of the village by his guarded malice and watchfulness.

No one could imagine Peciura's drawing room, which faced the orchard, without Peciura himself standing behind the window. And even if he happened to be absent from the window, one envisioned him there or imagined he could see his face in the galss. Peciura was guarding his orchard. And that gave rise to a strange image of a huge eye—Peciura's eye—inside the glass—as large as that "eye of Providence" painted on covered posts by the wayside to remind everyone that God is watchful and alert, that He sees everything, no matter how one might try to hide it, and that He instantly administers severe punishment for any evil deed. The people of the village no doubt applied the idea of God's Providence to Peciura's watchfulness over his orchard and all his fields.

Peciura's homestead seemed to have been built especially for him, the keen watchman. The only place one could not really see him from his farmhouse was the village itself, which was dense with trees. Peciura had a perfect view of the three other directions whenever he wished it: He could see whether his horses and cattle were properly tended, whether the boys had let the geese in their care wander into the summer corn, or whether the swineherds had fallen asleep and let the pigs loose to root up the meadows. The fact that the shepherds and herdsmen were watchful and cautious was due mainly to Peciura's ability to observe and his readiness to promptly grab the wrongdoer by the collar, throw him down and give him a merciless beating with that well-known stick which, although not thick, was by no means a mere rod. The stick was not a bone-breaker but, pliant as it was, it could wind itself around the body contours of the object of Peciura's wrath in order to inflict more pain.

Uncle Peciura never beat anyone, large or small, outside his own family. He lived in peace with his neighbors, without any squabbles or quarrels; he would attend their christenings and funerals and would invite them to his. As for his shepherd boys, he would frequently present them with luscious apples, reserving the biggest one for the naughtiest boy, saying: "Watch my little orchard, so that nobody will do any harm to it. Some ignorant dolt will want to pluck one apple only but in his fear and haste, he'll break a whole branch. It won't do him any good but it will do a lot of damage to the orchard, There will be ten apples less next year. Besides, never you mind, I see and punish everyone who deserves it, so you can tell others about this!"

The shepherd boys melted with fear as Peciura spoke. And the most ruthless poacher of gardens and orchards would wave his finger in front of the noses of the children and threaten them: "Don't you dare put your foot on Peciura's land!"

Uncle Peciura never raised his hand against most of his own people, either. But all his children were afraid of him and tried to oblige him, joining in the fun with him whenever they felt that they would profit from it. Peleksas alone, the youngest of the children, seemed to have been hatched by some hobgoblin. He was totally unfit for farm work or for village life.

Peleksas was not unpleasant to look at, however, He had his father's nose, although he was not of the usual fair complexion. As healthy as the other children in the family, he was nevertheless unusually lanky, and skinny as a sapling crowded in a thicket. He had black hair and handsome sky-blue eyes. Nobody saw their beauty, though: not his parents nor his brothers and sisters, not even strangers. Peleksas never looked at anyone directly, only downward, at his feet, as if he were jealously guarding that treasure of his eyes, Even when he was sitting in a close circle of companions, he would direct the words of his answer (he rarely asked questions himself) to the bridle in his hands, to his pipe, his whittling, or to whatever he happened to be holding in his hands at the time, and never to the person who was addressing him. And his reply was always curt. He would twist his upper lip to the left and to the right, then pull his nose, in his father's manner, and stare at his knees again.

Nobody had ever seen Peleksas playing with other children, running with them across the silken meadow, turning somersaults or engaging in other childish fun. The people of the village noticed Peleksas only when he started taking the horses out for the night. But that had happened almost ten years before and he had not changed any since then. Peleksas did not seem to fit anywhere else; he was Pecuria's permanent horse tender and nothing more. He had become quite an expert at his trade but, as time passed, his father began to value him less and less, even as a horse tender.

Peleksas used to spend half of the year out-of-doors, most of the time reclining on his side at the foot of some hillock. His nights were spent turning and twisting on the same bare ground and in the same sweat-soaked fur coat. Such routine boredom had a soporific effect on Peleksas. He slept at night, whatever there was of it, and did not wake until breakfast. He could doze off instantly, at any time, and sleep as long as he was allowed to, as if he was in a state of lethargy. He slept and snored with such abandon, it was as though he wanted to make up for several days of carousing. He would sleep undisturbed in a group whenever he was in a common tent, knowing that others would protect his horses from any harm.

His face would puff up from sleep, especially his upper lip. The Peleksas was ugly to behold, as though he had some kind of swelling disease or had been stung by bees. This would send the horse tenders into gales of mirth and mockery. They would dance around him and sing:

"What a lip, what a lip."
"Oh, that lip, lip, lip!"

Sometimes, having waited in vain for Peleksas to leave the tent and surmising that his lip had swollen to a proper size, they would tie his feet with a rein, attach a halter to the rein and, shouting encouragement to each other, would pull him out of the tent in the same manner that one drags wet sedges from a bog to a dry place: "Oh-ho-ho! Oh-ho-ho! Drag, drag! Pull, pull!"

Frightened and half-awake, Peleksas would fearfully grope for the ground, turning over and over until he realized what a team of horses were dragging him. He would not explode in anger or curse his tormentors or try to pick a fight with them. Peleksas never became involved in any quarrels. He would simply loosen the bands on his feet, yawn broadly and with studied indifference, stuff his pipe. As for his friends, they had no intention of abusing or denigrating him. He was quite a regular fellow, otherwise, brimming with brawn.

The men who tend the horses at night play their tricks on anyone, whether they are asleep or awake—even on those who resist being given a forcible ride by their feet! Some of these men would even try to creep into favor with Peleksas and ask him for a puff from his pipe. But he usually rebuffed such flatterers, and they had no choice but to go away and leave Peleksas alone.

Peleksas was always the last one to ride away and ride back home. He was somewhat detached from the group and would become blanketed in a cloud of dust raised by those who rode in front of him. Yet he never stayed completely apart from the crowd. Even during herding, he would sit somewhat apart from the group although not far enough apart to miss any of their conversation. He did not drop out; he participated in the group despite his silence and sham indifference. Nobody bothered to find out what Peleksas was thinking in his solitude; and nobody cared anything about what he felt, what things delighted him or what he found disgusting.

It was the same situation at home. Peleksas would sit down at the table and quietly do as he was told. He never quarreled with his parents or his brothers. Nevertheless, they all felt that Peleksas was not quite like the other members of the family; he was almost completely alien in his own home. He did not care about either the present or the future, about what he would do when he became a man or how his brothers and sisters would fare. He merely lived; and he lived not as a candle burns but as a stick smolders. Peleksas was not a member of Peciura's farmstead or of the village—he was a misfit, that's all.

Old man Peciura worried about him, too. And his ire grew unchecked when Peleksas turned out to be neither farmer nor craftsman nor singer nor even a party-going rake! He was neither fish nor fowl. And Peciura began to think that Peleksas alone obstructed his efforts to insure a good future for all the members of his family. Things grew worse as time went on. The old man developed a passionate hatred for his youngest son. He felt like kicking him whenever he passed by. If he failed to do that, he looked for an excuse to find fault with him and give him a painful beating.

After doing that, he would quiet down for a week. Then, again devoured by bitterness, he would look around, at home and in the fields, to see what Peleksas was doing. Finally, he would swoop like a buzzard to the edge of the marsh, knowing that he would find Peleksas asleep there, and would relieve himself of his anger by thrashing his son's hide. Peleksas was a nimble youth and whenever his father would surprise him unawares and start beating him painfully with his cane, he would slither like an adder trapped between his father's arms and legs. But the old man was also quite agile and would manage to seize some end of his son and beat him until his wrath was spent.

In the market, Peciura came upon a thin and flexible but strong cane, and started bargaining for it. A neighbor who happened to be passing by wondered why he needed such a cane. Was this not something young gentlemen carried on their idle walks? What farmers needed was a solid stick, good for attack and defense.

Peciura answered firmly, "Just the thing to thrash Peleksas with."

"What for?" the neighbor asked.

"Ah, he's a misfit, that's what for."

III

The following day when I rode my team of three horses to the edge of the marsh, Peleksas had already let loose his three good horses and had returned to the dry land, the black patches of his wet knees indicating that he had shackled his team while kneeling in a wet spot. Seeing me, Peleksas seemed to perk up from head to toe. He stopped my horses by the bridle and wanted to help me down, but this touched my most sensitive spot and I slid down from my horse on my stomach and without any help.

The two of us and our horses found ourselves some distance from the others, as usual. Later, we joined the group again. Meanwhile, I considered it my duty to remind Peleksas that he had been bribed by my family and was therefore like a servant or a slave.

"My mother gave you a treat yesterday and I promised to

give you wheaten bread; so you'll help me gather my horses tomorrow!"

"Will do," Peleksas agreed as he removed the headstalls of the bridles and threw a handful of them at me. They had to be arranged neatly, as one arranges a long rope, and be tied with one headstall to prevent them from being scattered all over the place and lost in a pile of others. When the herders went to sleep, they put them beside, or even under, their heads.

We found a crowd of night herders getting ready to go to sleep. They were arguing about the arrangement; nobody wanted to be situated at the edge of the group. And there was good reason for that: Should a wolf or some other creature of the dark grab someone, who else would it be but the fellow at the end of the row?

"I won't lie down—I won't . . ." I seized Peleksas' hand fearfully.

"Don't scare yourself. There's nothing to be afraid of. There are no wolves or bears here and no forest where they could live. And as for the ghosts, they're hiding inside the castle mounds. You know what? Let's lie down by ourselves. We can use my coat as a sheet and yours as a blanket and we'll be warm on all sides."

We did exactly that. One fellow immediately plopped himself down next to us, then another, and then another—and a latecomer was stuck at the edge. Thus, we solved the problem of positions for the night.

I found myself at Peleksas' side, just as I had, long ago, found myself at my mother's side in a feather bed. I felt warm and happy. I clasped Peleksas' neck and hugged him and he tucked me in carefully to make certain I would not freeze because of some little gap in the coverings.

We woke up at sunrise and I lifted the edge of the fur coat and peeked out. The whole world glimmered and glowed in joyous sunlight. It was getting warmer and the soil was sweating in big dew drops and then drying instantly. It would be a clear day. I knew that I should get up but this was not easy to do at sunrise. At that hour of day, most living creatures are drowned in sleep and find it virtually impossible to rouse themselves. Even if one found a real wolf at one's side, one would simply offer the animal an opportunity to join in the slumber.

When I awakened for the second time, I felt like a caterpillar wrapped in a huge fur coat while Peleksas, wearing only his shirt, had taken pity on me and had not pulled out his two coats from under me. Rather than disturb me, he risked freezing in his shirt. I understood that and felt that it was improper for me to take such advantage of my friend's thoughtfulness.

"Peleksas, you'll freeze to death. Why don't you get your clothes?" I asked.

"The sun will warm me. Look, it's rising higher and higher—sending more and more rays and more and more warmth. After a little while, it will be so warm we'll have to take a dip somewhere."

We sat down together on the slope. I could not recognize Peleksas. He was gazing around, his eyes wide open, fixing them now and then on some spot. I saw, for the first time, what beautiful eyes he had. With those sky-blue eyes that expressed such joy and longing, he now looked straight at me. I was even more astonished by Peleksas' unexpected loquacity.

"Juozas, dear, wouldn't you like to cross all the marshes now and get to the bluff of the highest valley to watch the sunrise from there?"

"No. What good would that do?"

"But I would like to. And then go from that peak through other marshes to that distant hill . . ."

"And what will you find there?" I asked.

"It's far away . . . and then even farther. To go and go . . . very far . . . all by myself along nice dry highways—or even better, not along the highways but across the hills and meadows and along the rivers . . ."

"And what for?"

"Just like that—without worrry or fear of being followed . . . And that's what I'll do when I put my mind to it."

"And your father? He'll snoop and search and run around and scream . . . And when he finds you, he'll give you a licking." As I spoke, I was suddenly seized with fear that his father would start beating a lad who had turned out to be so adult and so handsome.

Peleksas did not answer at first. He was still not sure about his plans.

"I need to know," he said finally, "to know a lot: who, where and how? Then, even my father won't find me. But how will I find out if I don't go to these places?"

"I've already finished half of my primary schooling," I bragged. "And I got on the honor roll, too!"

"But what do you know about our land?" Peleksas asked with intense curiosity.

"Well, nothing really. I read and write and do arithmetic... and I'm memorizing the catechism. That's about all."

In reality, I was as unschooled as the other children, just as Peleksas was, too.

"But my father didn't teach me anything," he said. "He taught everybody to read except me."

"Why?"

"How do I know? He doesn't want me to be like the others or like him. He sleeps as long as he wants to, but he forbids me to do the same. Instead, he beats me, saying that sleep is bad for me. He puffs his pipe whenever he feels like it and as much as his heart desires but he forbids me to smoke and he beats me again, saying it's bad for me. Whatever's bad for me seems to be good for him. He downs a glass or two during holidays, but he scolds others who drink. He's hellbent on making a profit, but if anybody else tries to do the same, he calls him a Jew. I don't know what I should do—what's good and what's bad. Perhaps it's something I should decice myself."

We sat there for a long time after our conversation, gazing around at the beautiful countryside. Peleksas kept training his sights on more and more distant things, while I rejoiced in little things close to me. I found the greens alongside the marsh and the small meadows enormously pleasant. Here, I was comfortable and felt that I was myself. But when I gazed at that boundless horizon, I felt that I was nothing, a mere nothing. Peleksas evidently felt just the opposite.

It was Sunday and we lay for a long time in the sun, feeling warmer and better all the time. But Peleksas was restless. It seemed that he wanted to contribute something of his own to that harmony of summer, the violin or clarinet would have suited him well if he could have played it softly, as softly as if nature itself was making those sounds. But Peleksas was incapable of that, either.

"You know what? You stay here alone (it was as if he did not see the others who were a short distance away), look after the horses and I'll run home and bring back some breakfast for us."

"Why should you go? We'll have to be returning home soon anyway and a good breakfast will be waiting for us."

"No—definitely not! I'd rather stay here." With that, he dashed off on his long legs and was back in half an hour. He was carrying a pile of soft rye pancakes wrapped in a white kerchief, and a small jar or butter.

We were naturally quite hungry. Nevertheless, I felt somewhat uneasy. "Peleksas," I asked, "did my mother give you all this?"

"No, she didn't see me," he replied.

"How did you get it then?"

"I came in from the garden past the barn."

I would never have dared to help myself to the pancakes, not to mention the butter, without having first asked my mother. But Peleksas did not share my scruples.

"Here, eat!" he said, offering me the tasty pancakes and butter. Overcome by hunger, I took some and enjoyed them, even though I was aware of my participation in the theft.

Peleksas felt happier with every minute. He ate with relish, scooping the butter and swallowing the soft pancakes without bothering to chew them. He twisted his mouth in all kinds of ways, deeply inhaling through his nose as he ate.

Having finished our meal, we got our horses together and rode home . . . to breakfast. I just couldn't eat any more, and everybody wondered why. But I would not explain. I felt no scruples any longer.

Why did Peleksas do it? I think that probably he had to—that he could not help doing it. He simply had to treat himself.

Suddenly Peleksas changed completely. He began looking straight into other people's eyes—not only mine—and sometimes, out of the blue and without being asked he would say, "Your mother gave me a treat . . ."

Peleksas watched over me like a nursemaid. And he had no secrets from me. I don't recall how long this juvenile idyll lasted;

I only remember how it ended—and I shall never forget it.

Greed had taught us, children and grownups alike, to snatch as much as we could from the common holdings. The pasture, for example, was for common use. But the especially solicitous tenders fed their horses by hand. They would take a quick look around and then lead their horses to where they thought the grass was more abundant—as though the horses themselves did not know where the grazing was best! Moreover, the horse tenders actually interfered with the grazing by their continuous criss-crossing from one spot to another.

Soon, this manifestation of greed became infectious and everybody started doing the same thing, including myself. Peleksas was the only one who refused to adopt the practice. And, to tell the truth, his horses were better fed than the rest.

Once, when the horses were grazing contentedly and Peleksas was snoring on a hillock, Uncle Peciura suddenly emerged out of nowhere and started beating Peleksas for neglecting his duties. He struck him wildly and with such fury that we became nauseated. It was then that we started hating Peciura with all our hearts and stopped calling him "Uncle." Only our terror of him prevented us from slinging mud at him.

Another time, Peleksas was busy at the foot of a hillock, making a wooden form for the bottom part of a pipe bowl which he was eventually going to cast from tin. I am sure that he devised it himself since nobody would have shown it to him. He brought a fragment of glass to smelt the tin, lit a fire and was about to complete the carving of his form without releasing his pipe from his mouth. We were sitting around and following with greatest interest what would result from Peleksas' craftsmanship. So we did not notice Peciura again emerging right next to us as if he had come out of a hole in the ground. He wrenched the pipe from Peleksas' teeth and then the unfinished one from his hands and broke both in pieces. Then he started thrashing the craftsman with his cane for puffing "that stinking pipe." "Oaf and whippersnapper," he called Peleksas. "Hell and damnation!"

That incident was the final straw and Peciura's reputation became extinguished before our eyes. We all sympathized deeply with our friend and were, at the same time, astounded by his failure to avoid his father's blows.

Peleksas remained sitting although he had been struck at least five times in the same place on his back. His face completely expressionless, he just stared with his big eyes at the beastly rage of his father and refused to budge. The blank look on his face was terrifying to behold and Peleksas: father noticed it, too. He spat angrily on the ground, flung out one more thunderous curse and left for home in a hurry.

After that time, Peleksas stopped looking directly at people again. He stopped all his activity and seemed to be interested only in sleep. He would cover only his head and sleep day and night—or perhaps he was only pretending to be asleep because he was not interested in looking at the world any longer. And nobody ever thought of mocking him for his continual sleeping, or of playing tricks on him.

We also stopped sleeping apart from the others. Peleksas began to complain that his thins were disappearing. Everybody wondered how Peciura could miss such doings under his very nose. Peciura had noticed the change in Peleksas and followed him. With the help of some other men, he seized a Jew who was selling brandy secretly. They found Peciura's missing objects in the man's place and forced him to divulge who had brought them. The Jew betrayed Peleksas.

Peciura roared back home with the men and, with their help, brought in reins, horse collars, a plank and sticks. Peleksas, his face as white as a linen cloth, was sitting by the stove. Nobody showed him any sympathy and even his own mother was aloof.

"Well, get him!" Peciura screamed, and two men seized Peleksas.

Peleksas did not resist. He merely looked around with his ghastly eyes and warned the neighbors, "If you're going to beat me, then beat me to death. Otherwise, I won't forgive you. First, I'll fry my father alive in his own house; and then I'll get to you. Father, I stole because I wanted to revenge myself. I decided to pay you evil for evil. All my life, you've tortured me. If I'm a thief, then you're *all thieves:* you, and you, and your sons. Search the Jew's place; you'll find more stuff there . . . Where will you start, you animals . . .?"

Peleksas' words sent his father into a frenzy. The neighbors became infuriated also. They beat Peleksas with all their strength but stopped short of torturing him. And they never saw him again. He vanished, leaving the villagers in a terrible fear.

"He'll burn us down, the freak!" Peciura worried. So did the neighbors, all of whom felt guilty.

"why did *we* have to get involved? Peleksas stole from Peciura and Peciura should have meted out the punishment. Did Peleksas harm *us* in any way?"

For a while, the villagers scarcely slept at all. Two watchmen made the rounds each night and would raise an alarm sometimes, but in vain. Peleksas never appeared again. The summer passed and then fall and winter went by.

In the spring, rumors reached the village that, in some distant village, a horse thief had been caught and killed and that his murderers were now in jail. The dead thief was a certain Peleksas Peciura, a vagabond without any documents. Previously, he had been loitering in several other districts.

The village thanked God for the disappearance of the spectre. Peciura, who always used to complain: "What a son has God given to me; may hell take him," was suddenly silent.

One Sunday, Peciura's wife came home from church where she had bought a Mass for Peleksas' soul. As she was handing the money to the priest in church, she wept bitterly and told him the whole story, between sobs. The priest listened to her but did not offer a single word of consolation.

"Let us pray," he said. "As for Peleksas, you, his own parents, ruined him yourselves. You saw that he could not be a land tiller, so you should have taught him some craft or sent him to school so that he could have become a normal human being."

When the Peciuras went to bed that night and the old man exploded in his usual manner about his wife being so jumpy and restless, she bluntly told him, "The priest says that we, Peleksas' parents, have destroyed our son." And she repeated the conversation.

Peciura cursed the priest but he, too, spent the night turning and tossing without being able to sleep. He never complained to anybody about Peleksas again. However, he did not go to the place where his son had died, nor did he confront Peleksas' murderers.

When I heard all that had happened, I timidly pulled my mother aside and asked, "Have you heard! . . . that Peleksas was murdered?"

"Yes, I heard," she replied sadly. "May he rest in eternal peace. He never harmed us in any way."

"He never harmed anyone . . ." I began. "If you only knew what a good person he was, how gentle . . ." I burst into tears, unable to continue. And mine were probably the only tears that were shed for the misfit Peleksas.

Translated by Algirdas Landsbergis

by J. Pencyla

Vincas Kreve

VINCAS KREVE

Considered by many as Lithuania's foremost writer, VINCAS KREVE, was born in Subartonys, Lithuania on October 19, 1882. He studied at the universities of Vilnius, St. Petersburg, Kiev, Vienna and Lvov, receiving the degree of doctor of philosophy in 1908. Following his return to Lithuania in 1920, he was a professor of Slavic Languages and Literatures for the next two decades. Appointed Foreign Minister and Deputy Prime Minister in the "People's Government" in 1940, he traveled to Moscow to protest Soviet policies that were endangering his country's economic welfare and independence, only to be told by V. Molotov that Russians intended to incorporate Lithuania into the Soviet Union. Kreve's resignation from his post was accepted only after the mock-elections to a new parliament were completed under Soviet military occupation. Withdrawing to Austria in 1944, he was invited in 1947 to the University of Pennsylvania, where he served as assistant professor of Slavic Languages and Literatures until his retirement in 1935. He died on July 7, 1954.

A prolific and versatile author, Kreve wrote historical dramas, collections of folklore, short stories, sketches of village life, novels about contemporary problems, and tales based on Oriental themes. For some forty years he was engaged in writing *Dangaus ir zemes sunus* (The Sons of Heaven and Earth), an epic work in biblical style, the first part of which was published in 1949. The second part and fragments of the unfinished third part appeared only after his death. His other outstanding works are the dramas *Sarunas, Dainavos kunigaikstis* (Sarunas, Prince of Dainava), 1912, and *Skirgaila*, 1925; folkloristic tales, *Dainavos salies senu zmoniu padavimai* (Legends of the Old People of Dainava), 1912; short stories, *Siaudinej pastogej* (Under a Thatched Roof), 1922-23; *Raganius* (The Sorcerer), a novella, 1939; and many others. A collection of his short stories appeared in English under the title, *The Herdsman and the Linden Tree*, 1964, and his novella, *Pagunda* was published as *Temptation*, 1965.

VINCAS KREVE

(1882-1954)

The Herdsman and the Linden Tree

I

TWO ANCIENT ONES there were in the village of Pagiriai: Grainis' linden tree and the herdsman Lapinas. As long ago as I can remember, both had always been the same: one—green with numberless widely spread branches, the tallest of all trees in the vicinity; the other—vigorous and, though short, sturdy as a moss-grown stump of an old oak with its roots deep in the soil, long-haired, full-bearded, gray, like an apple tree in bloom, and the oldest of all the elderly men in the village.

The enormous boughs of the linden tree bent in the wind every day, its green, luscious leaves whispering and rustling. Waking on an early summer morning, after rubbing the sleep out of my eyes, the first thing I could see was the tranquil movement of the branches, and the first sound I could hear was the subdued tinkling of its leaves, which brought my senses fully awake and joy into my heart, as the very top of the tree flamed with the rays of the rising sun.

But I would never have had these glorious experiences if the herdsman had not wakened me every morning with the sound of his horn and the cracking of his whip.

The linden tree was always populated with birds of all kinds that visited its branches and filled them with song! There, the boisterous sparrows celebrated their noisy weddings; the golden orioles sounded their warning to Eva, telling her to keep her flock out of the meadow; the thrushes, guests from a shady forest, whistled; the jay himself, that restless vagabond, the eternal traveler speaking a dozen languages, was a frequent visitor here, always on the point of departing for strange countries, and never arriving there. The owl, too, liked to come and sob at night in the green branches, complaining, poor girl, that nobody wanted to marry her.

The herdsman could be heard at a distance as he set forth early in the morning. Wherever he turned up, children shouted and dogs fought. Lapinas loved them both equally, though with a peculiar, herdsmanlike love. He was amused to see the dogs at each other's throats, and he took pleasure in making the children tussle and brawl like so many sparrows on a dust heap.

As he drove the herd home, the children met him at the very edge of the woods; as he herded out, they followed him as far as the heath itself. In the spring he carved whistles for them and made little flutes out of the willow bark; or he would let them crack his whip or blow his horn. How he laughed as he watched a child huff and puff with all his might, his cheeks blown to the bursting point, without getting a single note out of the formidable ram's horn!

The herdsman told the youngsters how the foxes sat on their eggs, how the wolves hatched their young ones high up in the trees, how the orioles milked the hares to feed their little ones, and how the hawks suckled their hawklings. He told them about the fairies living in the farmers' bathhouses who, after sunset, washed their linen cloth at the edge of the marshes; how they made sacks, caught little children and dumped them into the bog— especially those who lacked respect for their elders. He gave them detailed descriptions of *miskinis,* the bogeyman, who lived in the swamps and wandered through the woods, who liked to confuse the traveller and lead him into the marshes making him lie down on a hummock so that he believed he was lying at home on a warm clay oven.

Lapinas would stuff their little heads with so many hair-raising lies that the children would be afraid to walk home to the village, especially if there was a bog or a bathhouse along the way. As dusk fell, they would become really miserable. Even while sitting on a bench at home, they would be afraid to let their feet hang and would refuse to sit by a window; they would crouch all evening with their feet tucked beneath them since at any moment a hairy monster might stick its head in through the window, grab them and carry them to a bog without their parents ever noticing it; or a *naminis,* a bogeyman of the domestic kind, might snatch them by their feet, drag them under the stove and strangle them there before father and mother could rush to the rescue.

However much the parents tried to send a child out into the yard on an errand, he would never obey. He would accept a spanking rather than an encounter with a ghost. Actually, it was not as bad out in the yard as it was terrifying to walk through the dark foyer!

Lapinas also used to tell the children about the gigantic forests which grew in the neighborhood in the old days, about the dense pine groves, the muddy swamps and the abundance of wild beasts, now no more to be seen: the wolves, the elks, the bears...

He told them about the ancient people, how strong and brave they had been. Old Luksys, for instance, the great-grandfather of little Petriukas had once come home riding on a bear he had caught and bridled out in the forest, when the bear had tried to stop him on his way. And old Dundis had singlehandedly clubbed to death a whole pack of wolves one winter as they fell upon him on his way from Rudnia late at night.

Nobody else knew as many fairy tales, nobody else could invent as nimbly and no one could lie as convincingly as Lapinas. Often, it was not the children alone that he led by their noses, but the grown-ups as well. The latter spat angrily on the ground, then laughed at their own credulity, and then they would listen and believe again.

So the linden tree and the herdsman both grew merrily older, though the people complained that the tree was useless, that its shade was damaging the kitchen gardens, and that the old herdsman was weak in the head.

Lapinas lived at the far end of the village in a chimney-less one-room hut, alone with his wife, who was as old and light-headed as himself. Since they had no children every year they raised a couple of piglets as chubby, contented and well-fed as two babies. People would laughingly maintain that old Lapinas' wife bathed them every week in a wooden trough as if they were children, and then combed their bristles.

Whether this was true or merely a joke, no one could tell, but everyone in the village knew that if you called one of the young pigs, saying: "kookut, kookut," it would come running over to you and follow you around whining until you gave it a crust of bread or a boiled potato.

Nobody really knew, or cared, how Lapinas made his living. Every summer he herded the cattle of the villagers, while his wife gathered berries and mushrooms in the woods, which she carried to the town nearby and sold to the Jewish merchants. In the winter Lapinas made fishing nets or, in the absence of orders for nets, knitted sweaters for the village women, while his wife spun cardings of flax for the farmers.

Thus did the old couple live year in and year out, both happy and cheerful, especially Lapinas. Seeing this, the villagers envied them.

"See how easy they have it? They live like some gentle folks."

"Do they overwork themselves, do they ever get tired? Why shouldn't they be happy?"

"That's right, little man, and does anybody earn his living as hard as we do, we tillers of the soil? Always on the run, and never to catch the other end, and still have nothing . . ."

Whether Lapinas had anything nobody knew, nor did it interest the villagers.

But there is no enduring happiness in this world. One winter Lapinas' wife died, leaving him a widower.

Thereafter the old herdsman sat no longer in his hut making fishing nets. He wandered around in the village from house to house, waiting for the woods to spread their leaves, impatient to get out there with his herd.

People teased the old man and taunted him as they only knew how, some out of boredom, others on simple impulse. But Lapinas never became angry or felt offended.

"Little Uncle, when are you going to get married again?" some joker would ask the herdsman.

He would glance about, think for awhile and scratch his head.

"I haven't picked out my bride yet, little child. Can't find another like the old one used to be."

People never understood whether he was joking or talking seriously.

II

The pine forest had the spicy fragrance of a farmer's orchard full of beehives. You had only to open your mouth and inhale and you felt as if you had been eating honey.

The heat had been simmering all day long, like a boiling pot, and only toward the evening did it cool off a bit as the horizon became shot with a hazy mist.

I was returning from town, jacketless and barefoot. The trip was not long, only about two miles, and the road led through the woods.

Some years ago, a deep forest had stood on both sides of the road—shady, luxuriant, and as dark as the night. The firs soughed mournfully, pines swayed their branches in silence, the green, knotty oaks whispered mysteriously. As you entered the forest, you found yourself in an entirely different world, so secret and sinister that a cold shiver ran down your spine. There was silence and gloom, as if it were some haunted palace. The trees stood motionless, like village elders who had seen much in their lives; not a leaf rustled, not a whisper anywhere, not a single twig moved. You could hear a little bird flit from one branch to another and a gray squirrel scramble up a tree trunk. Then, all at once, the forest sighed as from a distance; the sound swelled as it approached, it grew to a mighty roar, and the leaves began rustling overhead, and the boughs moved, and the tops of the trees dipped and soared as though someone were manipulating them—and then once again, silence and calm fell on the lofty pine woods.

I used to walk in this forest when I was a boy. Then, the sunshine seemed warmer to me, and the world appeared in gayer colors, and everything was transfigured before my very eyes by the mysterious voices and rustlings.

Several years ago, as the forest, covered with white snow, dreamed in its deep winter slumber, people came with axes and saws. The giant trees tumbled with a crash, the pine forest cried and wept. As trees went down and the forest was cleared, new trees were planted and one could hardly penetrate the seedlings and underbrush. Since neither cattle nor horses were allowed to graze on the plantation, the grass came up to a man's waist, rank and firm as the willow bushes. As soon as I entered the plantation, I heard Lapinas shouting loud enough to make the woods echo on every side.

"Sarka, Sarka, let the wolf get you! What a dumb beast you are! Pretty Head, where are you going?, Can't you find enough grass without straying away? Jonuk, Petriuk, don't you just stand there like two hoopoes! Run to the lakeside and make sure the cows don't get into the oat field."

A whip went crack, crack, and I saw Lapinas emerging from the underbrush. He sat down on a tree stump by the roadside.

"Little Uncle, aren't you afraid of the forest keeper, to make such a noise in the plantation?"

"The forest keeper has gone to visit his father-in-law," explained a voice, speaking in the bushes. I glanced around and saw Mykoliukas crashing through with a cupped leaf full of wild strawberries in his hands. The herdsman sat without a word, snorting like a young colt. He appeared to be angry. What had happened? I had never seen Lapinas angry before.

I sat down on another stump and began putting on my shoes. It was unsafe to go through the woods barefoot since you might step on some thorns or get stung.

"It is not good what you are doing now, Little Uncle," I said as I busied myself with my shoes. "The cattle will damage the seedlings, and you will be in trouble with the forest keeper."

"Why, not good?" asked the herdsman harshly. "Is it bad only because the forest keeper or some other fool forbids it? The grass is a gift of God; it belongs not to man alone but to the little animals as well. Those who forbid are the evil ones; not me, who is letting the animals graze. Is there any reason whatever why the grass should go to waste? Now I am going to let my little cows stuff themselves with it," he added, softening a little, his face clearing. "They'll give more milk, and the housewives will make my gruel whiter with it."

"Yes, but how many of the young plants are your cows going to break?"

"Why, in the old days when no one was seeding or planting the forest, it kept growing all by itself and stood like a wall; nowadays, they plant it like cabbages, but still the forest is disappearing. What woods used to grow around here! My heart aches at the very thought of it. I often regret living to see people lose their love for their forests. They no longer respect the holy woods."

"They do love them, if they keep replanting; but they also need the timber."

"Stop talking nonsense to me! The forest doesn't need to be planted. It needs love. But who is cutting down the trees? The merchants, devil with them all! They make a good living anyway. Look into their houses, more beautiful inside than a priest's. The other day while shopping at the store, I opened the door to Berka's dwelling and had to spit on the floor, I was so surprised! For what devil's sake do they destroy our woods?"

"Our people would be making timber themselves if they had the money. Who doesn't need lumber these days?" observed Mikas. He sat down on a nearby stump, poured the berries into his cap, pulled a slice of bread out of his pouch and broke off a piece in preparation for a repast.

"Please taste some of this," he invited me, proferring his cap with the strawberries.

"And how depraved the people have become, God save us! They aren't human beings any more. I don't know what to call them. Would I hire myself to the merchants to help cut down the woods?"

"No one would go, if the merchants didn't pay. And people like us need money. Last spring, my father promised me a pair of shoes but he still hasn't come around to buying them. No money," complained Mikas.

"What if they do cut them down?" I persisted. "After replanting, the forest will come up young and even more beautiful."

"Now, don't tell me that. I understand more than you do, even though you're educated. What do you know? Only what's there in the books, while I've lived so long that I've even forgotten how old I am, and I spent my whole life in the forest, from the time I was a little child."

"Were you herding the cattle of Pagiriai all that time, Little Uncle?"

"No, I herded at Gruzliai for a few summers. But I didn't like it there; no woods in Gruzliai. Grazing in the open all through the summer; only occasionally some bare little marsh or a scrubby hillside. That was all the pleasure to be had there."

"But it seems to me it's much easier to herd in the open; you don't have to worry about losing cattle, and you can see a lot," said Mikas.

The herdsman only smiled.

"What's so good about that? The sun broils you there, like in a frying pan, and when the rains come, you have no shelter. On the other hand, how could it be good anywhere where there is no forest? Man is miserable without a forest. Here, the pine tree sings for you and the aspen leaves tinkle, and the little birch tree whispers to you as she is putting her braids in order . . . And all the birds . . . No, without a forest it's no good anywhere, even in America itself. Since the gnomes are even running away from there, it means there's no forest any more, either; so, it's no good there."

"No gnomes ever existed, Little Uncle. They were invented by superstitious people," I said, to enlighten him.

Hearing this, the old man sputtered like a potful of soup splashed on live coals.

"People of olden times who saw gnomes with their own eyes, were wiser than you! How would it be if no gnomes existed! It doesn't pay to argue with your kind, you young wiseacres!"

He made an impatient gesture with his hand, as if chasing away a gnat, and turned his back on me. Pulling out of his pocket a tobacco pouch and pipe, Lapinas filled it, tamping down the tobacco with his finger.

"I do love the gnomes and fairies myself, Little Uncle, and I'm sorry to see them leave the forest and hillsides of Lithuania, to see them die and disappear like the forest itself," I said, hoping to mollify him.

The old man took a pull at his pipe and spat on the ground without a word, as though he had not heard me.

"The uncle is in a bad mood today," said the shepherd boy. "He went to the priest yesterday to have his banns published, but the priest sent him away."

"The banns?" I asked, surprised. "Is it true, Uncle, that you want to get married again?"

"Why not? Why shouldn't I? My late wife has left two rolls of linen cloth, five bunches of carded flax and about five pounds of linseed. Why should it all perish? And I have my hut. And I'm not going to die soon."

"How do you know, Uncle, that you're not?" Mykoliukas asked.

"If I say so, it means I do know. Once, when I was a child, a gypsy woman saw in my palm that I would die at the same time as the linden tree of Grainis. The linden tree is still strong. It will outlast every other tree around."

"Why, Little Uncle, that tree will live for several more centuries!"

"So will I. Why shouldn't I live that long? If they don't destroy all the woods, I can go on herding cattle."

"But why did the priest send you away? Was it because you were too old?"

"No, child, it was because I didn't know the catechism. I went to him, true enough, and he asked me how old I was. I said I didn't know exactly but that I could be over a hundred. He said nothing in answer to this, but then he asked me whether a man's soul could die. I answered that it probably could. That was why he sent me away."

"How does it happen, Uncle, that you, who've lived so long, don't know that man has an immortal soul?"

Lapinas drew vigorously on his pipe a couple of times, making the fire inside crackle, then he raked it with a little screw that dangled on a string from the mouthpiece.

"How could I know? Am I a priest? When I was a little boy, nobody taught me things like that. All I knew was how to serve my master. I was a serf. And my master had an ill temper. In those days, priests didn't ask questions from the catechism."

"He will accept me the next time. Now I know that man's soul cannot die. I'm going to tell him so right away."

"But he's going to ask you something else this time, and you won't know again," I warned. "Do you know, Uncle, how many gods there are?"

The herdsman stuck his pipe inside his belt, thought for awhile and scratched his head.

"There you've got me, child. That I don't know."

Then, after some thought, he added, "There are, I guess, three."

Mikas guffawed;

"See, see! And you should hear him pray!"

"Ha, you may well laugh, since you were taught your prayers as a little tot. Our masters were only interested in making us work. There was no time to learn anything; many a man couldn't even make the sign of the cross."

After awhile, he added, "And still, the people were better than nowadays. Probably even wiser."

"Wise they were! The masters whipped them, and they kept still about it!" said the shepherd hotly. "I'd like to see someone try it now!"

"And what would you do about it? They not only whipped us, they bartered people for hounds."

"Whatever happened, I wouldn't have let them get away with it," continued the boy teasingly. "And wise they really were! My grandpa, an old man like you, Uncle, would not go alone past a bath house after dark for fear that a fairy might drag him inside and tickle him to death!"

"And why couldn't it happen? Isn't it true?"

The boy laughed again.

"Laugh, laugh! You'll see what this laughing will bring down upon you."

"But, Uncle, there are no fairies whatsoever, they exist only in fairy tales," I said.

"No fairies, no fairies . . . How do you know there aren't any fairies? What a life it would be for man if there were no fairies, no *miskinis,* and no gnomes!"

"The priest, too, says they don't exist, Little Uncle," said the shepherd. "Aren't you going to believe a priest?"

"Priest, Priest! What does that young priest of yours amount to? There used to be priests in the old days, and what priests! All from the gentlefolk—and what gentlefolk! What is a priest nowadays? A few years ago, little Janka of the farmer Makstys was my swineherd, and many a time I measured his back with my whip—and today, he is a priest and women kiss his hand! A priest can only know as much about these things as any other man. If he knows everything, let him tell us what that is," Lapinas continued, pointing with his hand at a distant rainbow. "He won't be able to tell you at all. But the ancient people knew everything."

"I can tell you this even without asking the priest: the rainbow is made by the rain."

"Not by the rain at all. Don't you lie to me. If rain made it, we'd see the rainbow every time it rained. See, you don't know either although you're educated."

Lapinas continued to snort angrily for a long while. The shepherd and I kept silent, curious to hear what he was going to say next.

"If you don't understand, don't talk about it!" pronounced Lapinas finally, as he stood up from the stump and, without saying good-bye, disappeared into the bushes.

III

No other holiday is as good and happy as Pentecost. When it comes, a man awakens as if from sleep; and not people alone; the trees, too. Their leaves spread more in a single day on the eve of Pentecost than all the earlier days of spring, so that man may make his dark and gloomy abode more cheerful by adorning the walls with green twigs and branches.

On the second day of Pentecost that year, Valainis had a merry and noisy christening feast for his first-born son, whom he had expected and for whom he had yearned so long that he had become quite old in the meanwhile. Five daughters had been born to Valainis, but of what use are girls? Many daughters, many troubles. Once you have several of them, you might as well lie down and die.

Although he complained, Valainis obstinately kept hoping for a boy.

"Should I have no son? No, this cannot be! Even if I get ten or eleven girls, the twelfth must be a boy, and that's that!"

The neighbors laughed as they heard this, but Vilainis did not give up hope.

At long last a son was born to him. He arrived after Easter

but Valainis kept putting off the baptism until Pentecost so that the feast could be better prepared and enjoyed.

It was an uproarious party, as noisy as a wedding. Except for the absence of dancing, one could have believed it really was a wedding. Vilainis had a messenger invite his neighbors. He invited the entire village. Seeing these goings-on, some people scoffed, others wondered.

"The man is going out of his mind."

Valainis asked the curate of the parish himself to be the godfather, and for the godmother he chose the wife of the village mayor, Alksninis, who had more than a hundred hives of bees. God alone knew why Alksninis was so successful. Some people said he knew some kind of charm; they even called him a sorcerer. Others whispered that once, upon receiving Holy Communion, he took the Host out of his mouth, brought it home, and placed it in a beehive. Lapinas said he had seen with his own eyes a chalice in the hive, exactly like the one in church, but made of wax.

Alksninis sent a whole jar of honey, containing ten pounds, maybe even more, to the feast.

Besides the villagers, Valainis also invited his entire kin. Everybody knew that he belonged to a distinguished family. He was not one of those men who had made their fortunes in America. His quality reached back to ancient times. Thus, there came to the christening, among others, Cepulis of Rudnia, whose son was a priest; Dumblis of Pakelmiai, who had built a brick house for himself, like a nobleman or a city-dweller; Kozulis of Pagilse, the wisest man in the whole parish, who often dined at the rectory and could not be spared when it came to singing the Supplications after the High Mass; and Dundis of Parsedai, who had over three hundred acres of land as black as coffee-grounds—he was the richest man in the parish and no one addressed him other than with "Sir." Some lower class folks even went so far as to kiss Dundis' hand. Although rich, he was a good man; he did not put on airs, he was not proud or haughty and he did not ape the ways of the gentlefolk. Many other famous men came with their wives, and some with their children.

Now all were making merry. Their laughter and shouting could be heard at the other end of the village. The old women, after a beer or two, or with the help of a tumblerful of *degtine,* became so gleeful that they soon started singing the *dainos,* the ancient songs, not the stuff that was being sung nowadays. The men raised their voices and told stories to one another without paying much attention to what was being said.

A real wedding, nothing less!

As noon drew near and the sun stood in the zenith, twang, twang, twang went the horn of the herdsman in the distance. The swine were already in sight, their tails upturned, galloping at full speed, each eager to beat the others in being first to run around all the corners and reach the goal line.

Lapinas was returning from the early morning grazing. The housewives left the feast immediately. The herd must be taken care of, the cows milked, the pigs fed and shut up so that they would not get into someone's vegetable patch. It could not be expected on a day like this that someone else, a daughter or a hired girl, would do all this for you. The girls had left at daybreak: Some had gone to church, others had rambled off to the meadows. The holy day of Pentecost draws people out to where there is green; no one can resist it.

Only the men now remained at Vilainis' house, and they did not sit inside. Some went into the yard and others into the orchard, while still others, standing on the street by the gate, discussed this and that, mostly things of no significance.

The godmother led the women guests into the other end of the house to make preparations to take the baby to church. Valainis himself was busy with the carriage in the cart shed, putting on new wheels and greasing the axles so they would not creak. "Asking for a drink," as the saying goes.

Lapinas appeared.

"How is your health, old one? Still creeping around?" asked Kozulis of Pagilse.

"As you see, Sir. Why shouldn't I be creeping around?" said Lapinas as he approached and put out his hand. "And how does God keep you in His protection?"

"I am getting old, that's all. But you, yourself, you're the same as you've always been; not getting a bit older. When are you going to die, old one? Or are you aiming to outlive us all?"

"Man, why are you talking about death?" Cepulis asked, smiling. "He's thinking of marrying again but he can't find a suitable girl; all are too old for him!"

The men laughed boisterously at this. An old hen who was taking a sunbath under some currant bushes, became frightened and ran off, cackling loudly. Lapinas did not like to be made fun of in this manner. He was used to teasing, but not in front of strange people from other villages.

"Now, man, it's a good thing you reminded me of something," he said, turning to Cepulis. "I had forgotten all about it, talking here to you nice people. You're having a good time, while out there at the end of Valakai, at Miegakuline, those two boys have most likely already killed each other. We had a lot of trouble pulling them apart as we drove the herd by. Both of them bloody, their clothes torn, pounding each other with rocks! We just managed to save Antanukas; Macke was slugging him to death."

Cepulis could not tell whether Lapinas was telling the truth or lying and poking fun at him. Everyone knew, though, that the two Cepulis brothers, Juras and Levanarda, who had recently divided their father's property, were getting along no better than a cat with a dog and that their sons, Antanas and Macke, fought with each other even more bitterly than their fathers had. As soon as Levanarda's wife, milking a cow in the neighboring yard, heard this, she started to yell at her husband.

"Let the god Perkunas strike him down, the murderer! Levanarda, why are you standing there like a doorpost? Are you deaf? Don't you hear what the man is saying? Run along, quick. Your child is probably done to death already!"

Levanarda scratched his head, still hesitating.

"Aren't you lying to me, old one? You're surely lying."

"Why should I? Believe me, if you like, or don't believe me, if you don't like. I told you, that's all. Go ask the swineherds."

Lapinas turned away to another man, asking him some trivial question, as though entirely unconcerned about what Cepulis would do.

"All right, all right, I'll show him! He'll know how to start a fight!"

And pulling his cap down over his ears, Levanarda spun on

his heels and ran across the vegetable garden.

Juras' wife, learning the news and seeing Levanarda scurrying over the gardens to Miegakuline, called her husband and sent him in all haste to rescue their son, whom the murderous brother-in-law might have been killing by this time. Juras, a hot-tempered man and the younger of the two brothers, threw his homespun jacket over his shoulder, pulled a stake out of a picket fence and ran after Levanarda.

"Those two fiends quarrel and fight like dogs, but why should they break my fences?" sighed Slaminis, seeing this.

Meanwhile, the two sisters-in-law, milking their cows in the adjoining yards, kept up the flow of abuse as best they could, calling each other a witch and a thief. As old Lapinas listened, he kept adding a word or two to make things flame up again, as one keeps loading firewood into a stove.

"I really did brew some gruel for those people!" He laughed with satisfaction rubbing his hands.

"May the gods punish you, old one!" shrieked the men through the laughter, hugging their bellies. "The way he invents things!"

"The mothers are ready to fight, while the fathers are probably slugging it out in the field. This time, it won't be the parents."

"What a liar the old one is, what a liar! He spreads it so thick that you can never make it out!"

"His equal couldn't be found in the whole district. Though you know he's lying, you always believe him, and that's that!"

The men guffawed again, and Lapinas seemed delighted, as if they were praising him for some good deed.

"I see you've not forgotten your old tricks," said Dumblis of Pakelmiai village, where Lapinas had herded the cattle for two or three summer, laying his hand upon the latter's shoulder. "As you were then, so are you now. Let's go inside, old man, and have some beer."

The men led Lapinas to the house and poured a glass of beer for him. Lapinas drank it in one gulp, then, wiping his lips on his sleeve, he broke off a piece of cheese that Dumblis had pushed over to him, and began eating. A second drink soon went the way of the first; a third followed close behind. They poured *degtine* into his glass. The old man downed it without making a face. He drew a bowl of meat to himself and began working at it so diligently that beads of sweat stood out on his forehead.

The herdsman became jovial; his eyes shone as he started to crack jokes. Everybody laughed without a word of praise or blame. Lapinas told them how he had deceived this one and angered that one, how he had lied to still another. The men's belts were slipping down from their waists as their sides shook with laughter. Kacingis alone sat serious.

"I think, men, that you're wrong in abetting him so," said he in his deep, trumpet-like voice. "If he had lied to me as he boasts he's done to others, I wouldn't respect his age, I'd pull his hair off. Once a man is old, he shouldn't be acting like a little child."

However much Kacingis was distressed, no one listened to him.

Lapinas went so far as to tell them about how he had gone with Juzia to have his banns published and how the priest had sent him away.

"What a girl you found for yourself!" exclaimed the men, laughing again. "You couldn't have found another like that with a candle! But what's Vanka going to do without her?"

Juzia was an old maid of more than fifty. She lived in the house of Vanka, the Ruthenian, an old bachelor of her own age who had drifted in no one knew when, how, or from where, and who lived at the end of the village in a hut that he had bought from some poor cottager.

"What now? Without the catechism no priest is going to publish your banns, and without the priest no girl is going to marry you, not even Juzia."

"That's nothing, my little man, I'll learn. I already know a lot; Mykoliukas is teaching me now."

"Fine times you, old one, have lived to see. The children are teaching the old people. Would you ever have believed it?" asked Dundis, himself an old man.

"Oh, children today aren't like we were in our time," said Dumblis. "I'm not a very old man, but as I recall my childhood, I was no match for our own little ones!"

"I remember," said Julius Naujelis, "how our uncle used to scare us. He would tell us the swamp was full of wolves, and that they catch children to fatten their youngsters on. We would be afraid to go out of the village, not to mention the swamp. Just try to scare children that way now, if you like!"

"Well," bragged Lapinas, "I can put holy fear into them even now, and what fear!"

"We are no longer young, any of us here," observed Kacingis meanwhile. "Most of us have gray hair already, but we were no taller than this, and ran around without our little pants on. You, Lapinas, must be no less than a hundred and you're still strong. Could anyone else like that be found among men today?"

"I might be a hundred already," agreed Lapinas, munching his bread and cheese. "Already a hundred or more, maybe a lot more."

"What, a hundred? He's probably two hundred already," put in Valainis' wife as she busied herself about the oven. "Who can remember him as a young man?"

"There is someone older than I."

"Who could he be?" wondered the men. "No, there's nobody older than you. You're not living your own life any more; you're living someone else's life."

"I'll tell you: Grainis' linden tree is older than I," laughed the herdsman. "And I'm going to live as long as that tree."

"Why, little man, it will stand a few more centuries! However long you live, you can't last that long!"

"I will, I'm telling you! Why should I be in a hurry to die? There's plenty of time. Don't I have it good down here?"

"If that tree were mine," said Valainis' wife to Grainis, "I would have cut it down a long time ago. How often have I cursed it, and you Grainis for keeping it! Half my vegetables die in the shade, nothing grows around that tree."

"It's good that God didn't give horns to the pig!" said Lapinas vehemently. "What an idea, to cut down a tree like that! Did you plant it yourself, or what?"

"And do you think I get much profit out of my vegetable garden?" said Grainis to Valainis' wife, paying no attention to Lapinas. "Mostly nettles and offshoots."

"Why don't you get rid of it, then? What's the use of its standing there?"

"A beautiful tree, it would be a shame to cut it down," said the other men.

"Why do you listen to her?" cried Lapinas with wrath. "Men plant trees around their homes to adorn them, while she says: 'Cut it down, cut it down!' What do you think this linden is, a fly? Slap, and it's no more, ha? You should be ashamed, old woman, to talk like that!"

"What should I be ashamed of? Some day the storm is going to shatter it or uproot it, and the tree will crash down on the stalls and crush the animals."

"Uproot it, uproot it! Listen now, you people. The linden has stood there for hundreds of years, and now the wind is going to uproot it! You're full of beer, little woman! Cutting down such a tree is the same as killing a man."

Grainis' face suddenly flushed.

"Well, and what if I do cut it down? The tree is mine, who's going to stop me? I can do what I like. I can cut it down or let it stand."

"The tree is yours? Why, did you plant it? Did you make it grow so that you feel free to destroy it? Or is it yours only because it happens to stand on your property? The linden tree does not belong to you, Grainis. It belongs to God and to the little birds!"

Furious, Grainis pushed away the table and stood up from the bench. "Just look at the old man, how eloquent he can get! A real lawyer, when it comes to defending a tree!"

"Now, old one, watch out. Grainis is going to cut it down," teased the men provokingly, "and you'll have to die sooner than you expected!"

"The tree is mine and I will cut it down. I'm going to cut it down tomorrow. I want to see the man who's going to stop me," repeated Grainis with drunken obstinacy.

"No, you're not! The tree is not yours. Your hands will wither away, and your legs are going to break. What do you think that linden tree is, a little pine out of the forest? Are you going to chop it into firewood and burn it in your stove? What is becoming of people today! Our ancestors, in the old days, did what they could to have trees around their dwellings. The villages rustled like a forest and there were swarms of all kinds of birds everywhere; now, some snotty fellow, not much higher than the ground, starts hollering, 'I will cut it down, I will cut it down!' jeered Lapinas sarcastically.

" 'The tree is mine,' he says! You should have tried to talk like that in the old days. You would have been stretched out on the threshing floor and have threescore rods counted out on your backside! You would have known better, then."

"I'm cutting it down, and that's that! The linden is mine and that's the end of it! If it weren't for the holiday, I'd go chop it down right now!"

"Tfu," spat Lapinas on the floor. He gathered his whip, his horn and his cap and left without saying good-bye.

The men guffawed and their laughter followed Lapinas into the street. They, of course, believed that Grainis was pulling the old man's leg, that he did not even think of cutting down the linden tree.

IV

The sun was approaching the zenith. Although the heat shimmered in the open fields, it was not so bad out in the woods where it was cool all day long. Lapinas, however, noticed that gadflies were milling around the cattle in steadily increasing swarms, and little flies were getting into his nose and mouth. The cows were trying to sneak away into the shade of trees. Lapinas walked out in the clearing to take a look at his shadow and see whether he could step over it. He made a mark on the ground where his shadow ended and his foot went beyond the mark. It was close to noon.

"Let the cattle go home, little children."

The shepherds were already waiting for the signal. They surrounded the herd and, cracking their whips, drove the cattle as fast as they could go.

"Don't chase them, now! Don't chase them! You're not on your way to church, no need to hurry!"

But the boys did not pay much attention to the herdsman.

One buzzed in imitation of a gadfly—buzz, buzz! Another buzzed too, and after him all the shepherds started buzzing, in all sorts of voices, as loudly and as shrilly as only they could. The cows listened attentively for a few seconds, then turned up their tails and started off at a run. Those who were lazier or heavier than the others got a taste of the whip on their sides.

What a frolic! The trees stood motionless, voiceless; the sun was baking the earth; the birds alone let themselves be heard here and there. chirping and then suddenly stopping, as if frightened by their own song. How beautiful and joyful is the world of God, especially in the middle of the woods!

As the swineherds saw the cattle come out into the open, they immediately started off their pigs.

"*Udziu home, Udziu-dziu ho-ome!*" they shouted with all their might. The swine were remembering the troughsful of tasty, soft, succulent leaves at home and started rolling along like so many balls, with the sheep following at their heels, although the latter had nothing to expect at home. Seeing the swine running, the sheep also starts running, although not to any purpose it knows.

Having gotten rid of the pigs, the swineherds sat around on a hillock by the pond, waiting for the cattle to catch up. The herd rushed to the water and began drinking; some cows waded in up to their bellies. As they filled themselves, they took on a new and better look; they became rounder and fatter.

Then came the herdsman's helpers. One was toting several bathing-besoms made of birch twigs, another—a new broom, the third one—a fluffy oven-duster made of pine tufts. Of course, they were not the ones who had made all these things; it was the herdsman himself.

Finally, they arrived at the village.

"Aunty, hey Aunty!" shouted Lapinas. "I got the medicine herbs for you."

A woman, still young, but sickly in appearance came out of the gate. The herdsman pulled a bunch of roots out of the pocket of his russet coat and put them into her hands.

"Hold your apron, now, there's more coming. I dug out a lot so they would last longer."

The woman held out her apron and Lapinas filled it with the

roots, turning out his pockets.

"God load you with His gifts, Little Uncle! I don't even know how to thank you. I don't know anything about plants, myself."

"Not at all, little wife, no need to thank me. It's no trouble to me. Only thought it would help."

"Step into my house, Uncle, as you go out to herd in the morning. I'll give you a piece of hard cheese to nibble on in the woods."

"I sure will, I will, little woman, why not?" promised Lapinas driving the herd on.

"Motiejus' wife, hey, Motiejus' wife!" he called out to another woman who was crossing her yard over to the cowshed, with a milking pail in her hands. "Were you the one who asked me for an oven sweeper?"

"Yes, my little heart, I was the one. My old duster is nothing but bare stalks."

"Yes, little woman. Now I've bound together such a one for you that's going to last you all through the summer. Like a tuft of grass."

"Oh, that God should always keep you in good health! I'm going to bake for you, Little Uncle, a nice millet cake. Such trouble was I having with the old duster!" chattered the woman, taking the oven duster from the herdsman's hands. "I could sweep and sweep and half the coals would stay in the oven. And do you think I could get my men to make a new one?"

"What would you all do if you lost old Lapinas?"

"Uncle, as you drive past the gate again, look in, and I'll put a boiled egg into your bread pouch. Don't forget."

"Good, good, Little Aunt, I'll come. Why should I forget?"

The herdsman contined on his way along the village street. The children beset him on all sides like a swarm of flies.

"Little Uncle, did you bring me a basket?"

"A flute for me?"

"Did you carve a trumpet for me, as you promised?"

The herdsman put into their hands a basket, a flute and a trumpet. There was even a beautifully carved staff, which went to the smallest child.

"Make sure, now that all of you steal some tobacco from

your fathers' pouches; and you," addressing the little owner of the staff, "you must bring me at least ten matches. Otherwise, I'll take the staff away from you and give it to Jonukas. He's going to bring me a whole handful of matches. Won't you, Jonukas?"

"I will," laughed Jonukas, his eyes shining. "If you'll make me another one like this, and with a crook on it."

"All right, all right, I'll carve the most beautiful shepherd's staff for you; only make sure you bring me those matches tomorrow. A whole handful, do you hear? And now, take these bathing-besoms and give them to your mother, I promised them to her the other day."

The boy took the besoms, carried them through the gate and dumped them on the ground.

"Petre, take these to your Mom, quick!" he shouted to his little sister who, with a switch in her hand, stood guard over the pig's trough to make sure the swine did not push away the piglets. The boy himself climbed the fence, and perched on a post like an owl.

"If you sit on the fence, a tail will grow on you," warned the little girl.

"Don't worry, it won't," replied Jonukas.

"For whom, Uncle, is the broom?" wearily asked the boy who was carrying it.

"I'll give it to my housewife, she'll make my gruel whiter."

"Uncle, Uncle, look! Grainis has cut down his linden."

The herdsman looked up. It was true, the tree was no longer there. Incredulous, he rubbed his eyes like a man wakening from sleep, and peeled them as wide as he could, but still he could see no linden tree. There, beyond the cherry orchard, above Valainis' cow shed, it had stood, the tallest and shadiest of all trees, and now, there was only a blue gap in the sky.

The old man took a few steps into Grainis' yard and looked into the garden. He saw the linden tree stretched out across the entire vegetable patch, over the potatoes and onions. Its green boughs were sticking out like so many upraised arms. Its leaves still rustled in the breeze as if complaining against their fate. The little birds, whose nests covered the branches, now kept flying around, chirping sadly, as though they wept over their destroyed homes: chirrp, chirrp, cheet . . . They flew to the tree, crawled in between the twigs, and again rose into the air, flinging themselves back and forth or perching in a row upon the fence.

Grainis stood beside the tree, his axe in one hand and scratching his head with the other, bewildered by what he had done. The vegetable garden was ruined. What was he going to do now, with this mess? And why had he cut down the tree?

Oh, if he could only stand it up again and put it back on its stump . . . But you can't stand it up, you can't make it live again.

That morning Grainis had awakened late, with a headache and a bitter taste in his mouth, filled with disgust as though after a dose of wormwood. He went into the yard to begin his chores but his head felt as empty as a pot and everything kept falling from his hands. He started fixing the plough and broke its handle; he began thinning the scythe and hit his knuckles with the hammer. Grainis dropped the scythe, flung the hammer under the granary floor and spanked his child who, playing on a heap of chips, had gotten underfoot.

What to do now? Grainis stood in the middle of the yard, scratched his head and looked around. He then remembered how the day before, at Valainis', he had promised to cut down the linden tree. Grainis glanced at the tree, turning his head first toward the sky, then toward the tree again. Such a resentment seized him at the sight of the swarms of birds flying around and twittering in the branches that he fetched an axe and walked into the garden.

"You won't be making noise here any more; you won't be ruining my corn and stealing my cherries, you bunch of good-for-nothings! I'm going to smoke you all out of here, I'll drive you away!"

Grainis came to himself only as the tree crackled, trembled and leaned to the side; at first, slowly, then, faster with loud cracks until suddenly, it crashed down across the entire garden.

Lapinas stood by the fence, saddened and downcast, looking at the children who had swarmed there from the entire village to break the branches and pick out the nests. He shook his grey head.

"Man, man, you have no heart, nor any fear of God, to have destroyed such a tree . . ."

"Go on, go, old one, go your way if you don't want to taste this ax-handle!" Grainis jumped angrily. "And you, you little vipers, are you going to trample my vegetables?"

He attacked the children, who scrambled over the fence or raced into the adjoining gardens. But in a few moments, they again were crouching around the tree.

The herdsman sank his head and walked away, mumbling to himself: "If the people have no heart for a tree like this linden, they won't have pity for anybody. It is better to die than to live in times like these."

He walked tiredly to the house where it was his turn to eat that day. The beet soup tasted sour and the gruel was insipid. Lapinas dipped the spoon a couple of times and stood up.

"Why are you so sad today, Little Uncle? Are you sick?" asked Dziangis' wife, who was used to seeing him always merry. "Or is the food not good enough?"

She was afraid Lapinas would make fun of her cooking before the entire village. With this in mind, the housewives always put more milk into Lapinas' gruel than into that of the members of their own families and made sure that he got more fat in his cabbage soup.

"No, the food is good. I'm getting old, that's it, woman. Time to die, that's what it is!"

And throwing his russet coat upon his shoulder, forgetting his horn and whip, which he had never done before, Lapinas went home.

Once at his hut, he did not go inside but sat down by the wall, filled his pipe with tobacco and pulled at it again and again. As he sat there, he felt nauseated. Drawing at his pipe, he looked over the barns and sheds to where the linden tree had once rustled. Nothing but the sky. It seemed to him that the sky itself was getting bald with age.

Lapinas spat on the ground, put his unsmoked pipe out with his finger, stuck it inside his belt and walked over to the little flower garden where stood his single tree, a wild pear. He spread his coat on the ground, laid himself down, turned on his side and went to sleep.

His dreams were heavy. Lapinas tossed and moaned in his

sleep. He dreamed that Juzia had come to him, but she was altogether unlike the Juzia he had taken to the priest to have their banns published and who did not know the catechism any better than he did. She was now young and beautiful, prettier than she had ever been even in her youth; she wore a wreath on her head and flowers in her hair. She was wearing a skirt with innumerable flounces and a black bodice with two rows of white whalebone buttons, clothing that nobody wore these days any more. The seamstresses had even forgotten how to make them.

"Get dressed, quickly! The bridesmen and bridesmaids are waiting for you already. And the priest, in his vestments, is standing before the altar."

"What priest? What bridesmen and bridesmaids?"

"Why, our wedding party! Have you forgotten how we went to have our banns published?"

"But what am I going to do with you, the way you're now? People will laugh at an old man like me marrying a young girl!"

"Who said you were an old man? Take a look at yourself!"

Lapinas ran to a bucket full of water that was standing on a stool under the shelf and looked at his reflected face. From the bucket, instead of a grey ancient, a blond-haired, pink-cheeked bridegroom was looking back at him, just as he himself had been many years before.

"Am I bewitched?" gasped Lapinas with astonishment. Standing in the middle of the floor, he looked himself over. His clothes, too, were not of the usual sort. He had on a long greatcoat with a dozen flounces around the waist, its borders trimmed with black velvet. As he turned to the side, the flounces rustled. When he turned back, the flounces rustled again, just as the greatcoat of the late Antanas Gaidys would have rustled!

On his feet he had a pair of high top-boots with brass ornaments and brass heels. But Lapinas did not have time to admire himself to the full. A team of horses neighed outside, and on the threshold appeared old Jurgaitis whom Lapinas had served as a swineherd in his youth. He was then getting ten *auksinas* and twelve *skatikas* a year, as well as a woolen russet coat, bordered with black ribbon, and a pair of good cowhide footwear. Such farmers as Jurgaitis did not exist any more. He was not like the masters of today; he did not talk much; if you broke the rules, he would lay his belt along your backside adding, in more serious cases, a few strokes with the buckle, and that was enough. Also, you could not hide from him in the hemp field, or anywhere else.

"Why should I be chasing you, you stinking rogue?" Jurgaitis would shout after some wrongdoer who ran away from his belt. "You'll come to the house sooner or later, and you'll get twice as much, then!"

This man now stood in the door, glowering at Lapinas in his usual sidelong manner. Lapinas remembered that Jurgaitis had died long ago and an icy chill ran down his spine.

"You animal, why do you make people wait for you? My team is tearing the lawn to pieces! Hurry up! Or do you want to taste the buckle of my belt?" And Jurgaitis began fumbling at his waist. Lapinas turned around quickly and without a word, went to the other end of the house. As he walked, he could feel the eyes of old Jurgaitis following him.

The room at the other end was filled with guests. There sat Mocius Grainis, the grandfather of the present Grainis and Juozas Cepulis and Antanas Kacingis. They had all been dead for at least forty years. There also sat Cesnulis of Randamona who had a badger skin pouch across his shoulder which meant that Cesnulis was not an ordinary guest, he was the matchmaker himself, whom everyone present must obey. And if you did not obey the matchmaker, he could order you to be locked in a pigpen.

Now Cesnulis put his hand on Lapinas' shoulder.

"Now, now, the groom! What kept you so long? Take your bride by the hand, it's time to lead her around the table."

Lapinas looked around for his bride. She was standing with Jurgaitis' wife. And, O my gods, how she was dressed! A green wreath of rue on her head and what an abundance of ribbons on her shoulders—long, reaching to the ground, red and green and every color imaginable! And she, herself, she was not Juzia any more; she was Jurgaitis' daughter Munia, whom Lapinas had so admired as a boy, when he had tended her father's flock.

He remembered now that Munia Jurgaitis, too, had died long, long ago; her sons and daughters were also dead—only her grandchildren were still living.

"Hey, what are you gaping at?" shouted Jurgaitis again.

Lapinas shyly approached his bride and took her hand. The girls struck up a tune he had heard more than once but he could neither remember nor understand the words. Everyone began throwing oats at the two of them.

Lapinas led his bride around the table but he had scarcely taken a few steps when the girls stopped singing and everybody began shouting at him.

"No, no, the other way, the other way! You mustn't go against the sun, not with it!"

"You snotty one, you're bringing a calamity down on your own head!" roared Jurgaitis, and Lapinas became aware of the belt buckle hitting his back. Such terror seized Lapinas that he let his bride's hand go and crawled beneath the table. He saw that his bride was crawling after him. Now she was no longer a young girl but an old, toothless woman, her back as crooked as the branch of a tree, and she was covered with moss!

"She's not my bride, she is not!" cried Lapinas, pushing her away. "I don't want to marry her!"

"Why don't you, you fool?" shouted the guests with indignation. "Are you blind? Don't you see it's your linden tree?"

"Kill me, but I'm not going to marry her!" cried Lapinas as he pushed and pounded her with his fists. But the linden tree clung to him; she grabbed him tightly and put her arms around his neck. Lapinas tried to escape but his feet caught in the footrail, he tripped and fell, turning the table upside down. The guests roared with laughter and began stoning him; they threw dust and ashes at him. The old woman, the bride, did not let go of his neck but squeezed it so that Lapinas could hardly catch his breath. Meanwhile, everyone kept flinging at him whatever they could lay their hands on. Finally, he saw young Grainis himself, the man who had cut down the linden tree today, standing at his side and aiming an ax-handle at his head. Lapinas screamed as loudly as his lungs would allow and woke up.

He saw that he was not lying in the shade any longer: the shadow of the pear tree had crept away and he was baked by the sun. Strangely enough, Lapinas felt chilled, and the side on which he had lain was aching.

This was the first time he had ever slept outside in the yard.

Lapinas got up, went into the hut, climbed onto the top of the baking oven, where his bed was, and lay down. However thoroughly he covered himself with his sheepskin coat, he was still chilled and shivering and feeling pain in his bones.

"Old age," mumbled the herdsman, pulling his old, tattered russet coat over himself. He warmed up a little and then dozed off.

"Uncle! Uncle! Get up! Time to herd out!"

It was Petriukas and Barnaska calling him, the biggest among his shepherds who helped him with cattle in the woods. Their parents had sent them to find out why the herdsman was so late that afternoon.

Lapinas sat up. It seemed to him that he had just closed his eyes and that he had not even gone to sleep. But one glance at the window showed him that the sun was halfway down; it was dark and gloomy inside. Usually, he left in the afternoon as soon as the sun hit the rim of his little table. He was very late today.

Lapinas felt hot in the face, his temples throbbing with fever. As soon as he left his bed, he began shivering again; his head buzzed and swam, his bones seemed to be breaking, and the room was heaving before his eyes as if the hut were afloat.

The old man got dressed, nevertheless, hung his bread pouch across his shoulder and began looking around for his whip and horn. Only then did it dawn on him that he had left them where he had lunched.

Lapinas went over to the door, staggered and almost fell; he sat down on the bench in the corner, under the shelf. Having rested there awhile and recovered somewhat, he lay down on the bench with his clothes on.

The shepherds, meanwhile, sttod in the middle of the hut, waiting for him.

"Uncle, are we going to herd out this afternoon?"

"Go by yourselves, today. Seems I've done my share already . . . Time to rest before the trip . . ."

The boys stood there for a few more minutes; then, seeing that the old man was breathing hard and did not try to get up, they left.

That day, the herd was driven out late and by the boys alone, without the herdsman.

V

The following day, too, the boys herded alone. The housewives were distressed. They had become well aware, the night before, what the absence of the herdsman meant to them and to the cattle, The cows came home as thin as so many bean pods and a few did not come home at all. They were found only late, in the oat and millet fields. How much searching there had been, how much running around, how much moaning by the women that the milk was going to spoil.

"Now, you're going to lose cattle again, you impudent ones! What's ailing that lazy herdsman? He kept the cattle in the stalls yesterday till evening, and he's not herding out today," whined the women.

"The herdsman is dying, Aunties! We tried to wake him up but we couldn't, he opened his eyes, looked at us as though we were strangers, and mumbled something to himself. He must be delirious," explained the shepherds.

The news soon spread throughout the village that Lapinas was on his death bed. A few of the more tender-hearted women ran over to visit him. It was true. They found Lapinas very weak; the herdsman was complaining of chills, of pains in his bones and of an aching side. He would talk reasonably for awhile, then his mind would wander off.

"The old one doesn't know himself what he's talking about," the women whispered among themselves. "You'll see, he's going to die."

"And high time for it . . . Much younger men have died long ago. God has told him to go, too."

"But, still, one feels sorry for a living man . . ."

The women busied themselves about the ailing herdsman. One ~~bourght~~ him a piece of boiled chicken; another, a pound of butter; a third, ten eggs. They made a fat egg-dish with butter and medicinal herbs but Lapinas had no appetite; he complained of fever.

"Taste this, little heart, you'll see how it will make you feel better," coaxed one and another.

Lapinas fended them off as though they were so many flies.

"Leave me in peace. I can die very well without your advice."

"Why should you die now, Little Uncle? You'll certainly get well, you'll see how soon you'll get well again. You must have caught a little cold—it makes itself felt in your bones."

"Who is going to herd our little cows if you, Uncle, want to die already?"

Thus, the women tried to console him while, at the same time, they pressed their husbands:

"You should at least bring a priest here to him, you shameless ones. The man might die unshriven!"

The men were in no hurry for the priest, although one or two of them went to Lapinas' hut.

"What, Uncle, getting ready to go home?"

"Why shouldn't I? There's nothing for me to do here any more. That men should dare to cut down the trees their ancestors planted for their own profit..."

"Never mind, little man—if not today, then tomorrow we're all going to die. All of us will have to take the trip..."

Hearing such talk, the old herdsman would turn to the wall and only mumble under his nose. So many times he had heard these same words. Why do people not tire of babbling like parrots?

"The old one doesn't want to die yet," snickered the men. "But, brother, whether he wants it or not, when the time comes, you can do nothing!"

"The man has already lived long enough, but still he hates to leave..."

"Look at me. I'm carrying my sixth cross already but it still seems to me as though I were born only yesterday, while the skull and bones is already behind my back," sighed the third one.

Seeing how fast Lapinas was losing his strength, they became convinced of the seriousness of the matter and, teaming their horses together in a carriage, they went to fetch the priest.

The womenfolk, meanwhile, prepared Lapinas' hut to receive the Divine Guest in a fitting manner. They swept the entire yard and even the street in front of the gate. They washed the benches and the table, and covered them with bright-patterned cloth. Then they placed a crucifix, the most beautiful one in the village, between two holy candles set into candlesticks made of turnips, in the absence of genuine ones, and adorned the table with sprigs of rue and myrtle and other evergreens. They knew that the young curate loved plants and flowers.

They did not neglect the old man himself. They washed his face, put a freshly laundered shirt on him and spread a new coverlet over his bed. Then they waited in respectful silence for the arrival of the priest.

Lapinas alone was troubled. He felt shy and was afraid the priest might ask him the catechism again.

The curate was soon there. The people met him in the manner that God decreed for the reverence of His servants. Lapinas made his confession and the priest calmed his fears, consoling him so much that the old man wept with joy. After the administration of the sacraments, the curate talked with the men of framing, crops, and of the sick man.

"You should bring him a doctor as well."

"We were little children when he was already gray. We are getting ready for death ourselves; it has been so destined by God for him."

"He is old, that's true," admitted the priest, "but he's still strong. He might get well."

The men made a semblance of agreeing, although, of course, they had no intention of bringing a doctor.

"You know those educated people: 'The doctor, the doctor!' "

"Too bad we forgot to ask the priest whether the old one is ready to die. He knows it well," said Valainis.

"Of course he does!" answered a little woman who happened to overhear the conversation. "The Blessed Sacrament shows him. If a sick person is going to die, the Holy Host turns upside down in the priest's fingers. That's how the priest knows it in advance."

"Ha!" laughed Kacingis. "Who can tell the difference between a woman wagging her tongue and a hen flapping her wings. Whoever told you that the Holy Host turns upside down? Have you seen it happen yourself?"

"You always know better, you shameless one!" All the

womenfolk fell on him. "You, who are impudent enough to argue with the priests themselves!"

Kacingis made a deprecating gesture with his hand and went home. The men stood around the gate in a crowd for awhile, talking of this and that, scratched their heads, and scattered.

As soon as the priest left, Lapinas fell asleep.

"He is resting before his journey," whispered the women. And, true enough, toward evening, Lapinas became very feeble. He groaned, tossed in his bed and continued his delirious arguments with the linden tree.

Soon he calmed again. Meanwhile, the women began bickering over who should keep the night watch. As they began cackling aloud, like so many boisterous hens, Lapinas opened his eyes.

"Go home, you crows, all of you. Let me die in peace at last. I don't need you at all."

He turned away from them with some effort and then became silent. The women noticed his eyes suddenly turn glassy. They hardly had time enough to light a holy candle and place it between his fingers.

Soon, there was no Lapinas any more. He died like a tree felled with an axe.

Translated by Albinas Baranauskas

Photo by Prof. Buhe

Vienuolis

VIENUOLIS

VIENUOLIS ("The Monk," pen name of Antanas Zukauskas) was born in Uzuozeriai, Lithuania, on April 7, 1882. He studied in Grusinia, where he fell in love with the nature of Caucasus, and at the University of Moscow. His participation in the revolution of 1905 cost him a prison term. An ardent traveler, Vienuolis traversed most of Europe and some Asian countries. He died in Anyksciai on August 17, 1957.

His collected writings, in seven volumes, 1953-55, contain numerous omissions and have been retouched in parts by the Soviet censorship. His short stories and novellas are considered his supreme artistic achievement. "Paskenduole" (The Drowned Girl, or Veronica in the English version), 1913, perhaps his most popular work, has inspired a movie, a play and an opera. The stories "Inteligentu palata" (The Intelligentsia Ward) and "Vezys"(Cancer) are on a similar artistic plateau. His novels include *Viesnia is siaures* (The Visiting Lady from the North), 1932-33, and *Kryzkeles* (Crossroads), 1932. He also wrote plays and legends, and his memoir, *Is mano atsiminimu* (From My Memories), 1957, ranks with his outstanding literary works.

ANTANAS VIENUOLIS

(1882-1957)

Veronika

VERONIKA was tired and upset when she came home from church that Pentecost Sunday. She ate a hasty lunch consisting of leftover beet soup and sour milk. Then, instead of lying down or going to the neighboring dance, as she usually did on Sundays, she grabbed a milk pail from the fence and ran into the fields to milk the cows.

The sun was still high when Veronika came near the pasture. She did not continue but stopped in the meadow which bordered a field of rye, and looked around. Then she hurled the pail among the rye, sank to the ground, and cried out, hiding her face in her hands: "Dear God, oh, dear God!"

She had been to town today, she had gone to church and to the post office; she had also gone to visit an old woman whom she knew to be a great help to girls in trouble.

Although she had felt out of sorts for some time, Veronika could not believe it, but today the old woman had finally convinced her—she told her definitely that she was going to have a child.

Besides advice, the old woman also gave her some coarse powder, for which Veronika paid ten *auksinas*—although she had tried to bring the price down to five.

For two months now Veronika had been going to the post office every Sunday in vain. Before leaving for America, her beloved Juozelis had promised to send for her and to mail her a ticket as well as one hundred rubles to cover traveling expenses. The days passed but the ticket and the money did not arrive.

It was the post office as well as the old woman that made Veronika so miserable that Pentecost Sunday.

Veronika lay on the ground awhile before she drew the small brown paper from her pocket. She opened it and smelled the white powder inside—picking some up with the tip of her little finger and tasting it. The powder looked like salt—but it tasted a little bitter perhaps, a little more sour, with a strong, unpleasant smell.

"And after boiling it in rues I have to drink all of this terrible stuff," moaned Veronika twisting the paper in her hand and remembering the old woman's instructions.

"If it can save me, fine, but if not?" A stab of pain passed through the girl's heart. Quickly she folded the paper and put it back in her pocket. Then she stretched out on her back, and closed her eyes.

> *On the hill grows the rye, in the valley—the wheat.*
> *And a mother is calling her daughter:*
> *My daughter, come home, my young one, come home,*
> *Your father has promised your hand to a tailor....*

A young girl sang as she herded her geese near the rye field.

Long lay Veronika in the meadow, tossing and turning, listening to the song of the goose-girl, and her trouble, the terrible misfortune about which she could not think without shuddering while she still was chaste, stood out clearly before her eyes as if it were alive.

> *Home I never will go, I won't marry him, no.*
> *Wait, wait my fair young man, my will is not yours yet.*

The young girl's song again interrupted Veronika's thoughts. Slowly she opened her eyes: above her, embracing the whole earth, were the heights that no one had ever reached, the deep blue sky where the gay swallows cut the air with their wings, and the little insects danced in the air, and the larks trembled and warbled as if they were hanging on invisible thread. The air around her was heavy with the smell of honey and clover. The rye surrounded the meadow like a golden wall, which swayed to and fro and seemed to whisper: "Veronika, Veronika, what shame has befallen you, what misfortunes await you...."

> *My daughter, come home, my young one, come home,*
> *Your father has promised....*

The herd-girl did not stop singing, and Veronika once more closed her eyes.

"Could it be that he will forget about me and won't send me the ticket or the money?... The lord God would never forgive him for my young days...." Veronika relaxed and tried to recall his loving words, his caresses, his wonderous tales about Liepaja, Ekaterinoslav and America. He had long planned to go there—and finally he went away. She remembered now: it had been a Sunday, too. They had sat in the very same meadow. Juozelis talked to her, his eyes following hers. He had squeezed her hand gently and snuggled up to her, placing his head on her lap. At times, when they had run out of conversation, he would become lost in his thoughts and would play with a grass-weed, drawing it across her face and neck. Sometimes she would be annoyed by this, sometimes she smiled. Without any resistance on her part Juozelis had grown bolder. . . . There was no use to talk about it now—neither the night nor the bright moon knew what had happened—only she and Juozelis and God—they only knew everything and saw everything.

Veronika cried out and sat up quickly: no one was around. The same swallows and lark; a lady bug was hurrying along her neck, tickling her. For a moment she thought it had been Juozelis and his grass-weed. And she still heard the whispering of the rye:

"Veronika, Veronika, what shame has come upon you, what trouble awaits you?"

Finally Veronika rose from the meadow. The sun was beginning to set now and caressed the rye with its fading rays. From every farm the milk maids hastened to the meadow and a group of them had already gathered beneath the shrine on the main road. They waited until they were all together, so that they could sing as they went to the pastures.

Veronika hid in the rye field until her friends had passed. She felt like a thief. She did not dare show herself to the rest of the girls. She felt that everyone would guess what was the matter with her—what shame and trouble had befallen her.

*   *   *

A few months ago Veronika had been very different. For three years she had worked for Kaikaris, one of the wealthiest farmers in Shepechiai, and she made so many friends among the villagers that she felt as though she had been born there. And lively she was, the Veronika of old, first in everything, were it a dance, a festival, or what have you. She often sang and had a good voice. She knew every quadrille and every polka—and so many songs that it would have taken more than two mowing seasons for her to sing them all.

She could weave simple cloth as well as complicated patterns. And according to her mistress, household chores simply melted under her hands.

Aside from all these accomplishments, Veronika was beautiful, and if she had not been a mere dower-less servant girl she would have had the bachelors at her feet long ago. Whenever she put on a new dress woven by her own hands, and tied her braided hair with a red ribbon, heaven only knew what went on in the heads of many a youth. On such an occasion even the son of the richest farmer was ready to marry her, dowry or no dowry,—if only his parents would let him.

Whether in church or out of church or anywhere, Veronika was never alone.

"Veronyt, we'll be at the party in Shepechiai tonight, see that you meet us there and be a nice hostess to use," the young men from Bukonys would say to her after church.

"I will, providing you bring nuts and candies and at least a couple of bottles of wine!" answered Veronika without a single thought.

"Veronyt, my little heart, when are you going to sing the 'sad song?' Mother and I waited for it till midnight yesterday," spoke her childless uncle Anupras from the neighboring yard; he kept teasing her that he would adopt her as his daughter.

> *Through the cabbage, through the beet,*
> *To the girls for a night's sleep,*
> *Ri tai, ri tai, ri tai tam....*

sang out Shaltenis' farm-hand, as he met her in the middle of the village street; he was making a wry face and accompanied his song on the harmonica.

"Now, who's going to take care of the pigs if you oversleep tomorrow, and won't the herdsman beat you up?" answered Veronika laughingly.

The boy, crushed, walked away, scratching the top of his head. "She really put me to shame, that little snake!"

"It was as though she had covered the boy's head with a sack," the neighbor Butkis told Kaikaris the next day, while they were watering their horses at the well.

Whether it was winter or summer, Sunday or Friday, she was always gay and she could hardly sit still. And what a lively imagination for tricks she had!

In winter time, she would run across the village: sneak into someone's house and steal a spinning-wheel, for instance, then loading it on the shoulders of the first lad who happened to come by she would tell him where to bring it; then she would go to another friend and grab her flax, or untie the band, take off the spindle or remove the spool; to those who knew her well she would only give a signal through the window or make a gesture with her hand, and the same evening, all the village girls would gather to some house with their spinning wheels to have a party.

Having fed their cattle, the lads would follow them. Some of them would spin the fetters, some would make bast-shoes, the others would spend the time by talking nonsense. And the merry shouts and gay songs resound in the village all through the night.

There was one thing that Veronika lacked—devotion, and the village women scolded her in vain and threatened her with terrific tortures after death; even if some of them had impressed Veronika for a moment, it never lasted long.

Even at the May prayers or on Sunday, as she was saying her rosary, Veronika would take a look at some dozing young lad, or at the God-fearing little old woman who moved her lips soundlessly, and she could not help but burst out laughing, and the others would follow her.

And then, as aunt Juozaponis put it, would begin "the glory of the devil."

"God forbid such a prayer," aunt Juozaponis would cut her shortly. "Are you obsessed by the evil spirit or what? What is it? . . . The second mystery. Mary's visit to Elizabeth. Our Father who art in heaven. . . ." and she would continue to say her prayer.

The girls would pinch themselves, they would bite their lips, trying to revive in their minds the tortures in purgatory, until one way or the other they would calm down. But as soon as Veronika's turn came to say the mystery, she would begin to act as though she had forgotten her prayer, or as though something had stuck in her throat and she had to cough; and look, here and there some girls, trying to hold their faces as innocent as they could, pushed their kerchiefs over their eyes and dashed out of the devotion.

"Tri-tri-trili, tri-tri-trili," a herdman blew on the trumpet in the pasture, to tell the girls where the herd was being tended.

Veronika jumped from the grass, took the milk pail from the rye field, fixed herself up and walked to the path.

The girls were already far away, only their kerchiefs were visible out of the rye and their song was heard in the distance.

"Tri-tri-trili, tri-tri-trili," the herdman blew his hoarse trumpet more forcefully when he heard the girls singing.

"Look, even Veronika comes running!" shouted one of the girls, as she looked back.

"It's Veronika, all right. Where was she till now?" added another one.

"She's probably still bored and longing for her Juozelis."

"You just wait until he marries her, poor as a church mouse that she is. Don't you think he'll find someone more beautiful and richer than she is? . . ."

"Veronyt, where have you been all this time?" called the girls in one voice. "We were looking for you at the party, and at home. The aunt said: 'Who knows where she is, she took the milk pail from the fence and walked out through the barn.'"

It seemed that no one had yet guessed the reason for her hiding.

"You know, girls, what happened today?" Veronika began to explain, blushing and confused, and yet pretending to be calm and merry. "In the morning, I put the wooden milk pail on the fence to dry, and I forgot to take it off, before I went to church. It swelled up again.

"You found time to lay it in the water," scolded Onute Baltakis, pretending to be angry, then, friendly again.

"You know, Veronyt, the lads of Bukonys and Paberzhiai arrived, and they brought two harmonicas and a violin with them. Boy, we'll be dancing tonight!" chattered the party-goer Katriute.

"The American Samuliukas came, too. You should see him: with a watch and galoshes!" whispered Maryte, the daughter of Juozas Slizhys.

"So let us hurry, girls, if we want to go back with the sun," urged Veronika, although she did not care anymore about the lads or the dances: she had a constant urge to disappear somewhere among the fir-trees, far away from people, and think over her misfortune.

"Veronyt, drive your red-brown black-headed cow here, we'll do our milking next to one another," said Maryte Slizhys, who would not leave her alone; she was in love with Samuliukas, and apparently wanted to tell her something more.

Those who finished their milking first came together in a group and waited for those who were still behind. They were all dressed today, in their Sunday best, merry and gay, and many a girl was dreaming of meeting her loved one and having a chat with him in the *kletis*, the store-room.

When they finally walked to the highroad they began to sing:

When my mother brought me up while I was little girl,
No one would ever recognize me in the world,
No one would ever recognize me in the world....

Veronika sang the lead, and her pleasant voice, although very sad today, stood out from the other voices with its timbre and note, echoing in the meadows and pastures.

When my mother stopped rocking me,
Then a cuckoo began to call,
Then a cuckoo began to call....

sang the girls as they walked along, and in the village, at the dancing party, the lads cut them down:

When I grew up as a young little lad,
I was calm and free as a flower.
I made myself merry as long as I wanted to,
And I did not know what worries were....

When Veronika had strained the milk and finally joined the dancers she found all the young people of the village there; only Juozaponis, the one who always read the lives of the Saints on holy day was missing, as well as several children of "good" and "God-fearing" parents.

God, how long and boring the dancing party was to Veronika! Although the music was excellent, the boys were handsome and the girls beautiful, there was not a trace of her usual gaiety left.

She was tortured by the thought of Juozelis who had given her no word for such a long time. She was disturbed by the woman doctor's medicine and by that atrocious sin which shows no pity and punishes humanity in body and soul forever.

Whether she was dancing with some young fellow or chatting with him in the *kletis*, it seemed to Veronika that her dreadful misfortune was following her and seeing to it that she could not hide anywhere or forget her plight for an instant.

Every time she finished dancing or escaped from the arms of a young lad, Veronika sat in a remote corner, among the herdboys and younger girls, and gazed from the distance at her happy and healthy friends. And as she looked at them, self-pity and envy began to choke her.

She probably would have had to suffer much longer there if it were not for a small incident: Jonas Slizhys' wife waited too long for her Maryte to return, and at dusk she came with a long switch to chase her home. When she found her daughter in the group of youngsters she began to whip her with the switch over the shoulders and head. Maryte did not know where to hide herself from shame and dashed from the yard. Slizhys' wife turned towards the party-goers to curse them and their hosts. Finally, feeling that she had performed a good deed by chasing the young dancers away and threatening to tell about it to the priest, she left.

There was a big commotion, and Veronika was the first to slip away. She did not go to bed for a long time yet, she only sat in front of the *kletis*, thinking.

She woke up early the next morning and was the first one to rush into the pasture, to milk her cows. When she returned home she lit the oven and put on the pots.

While everybody was still sleeping and the farm hand had not yet come back from the night-watch, Veronika hurriedly picked two handfulls of rue in the garden, brought out the powder which she had hidden in the *kletis* yesterday, and boiled it as she had been told. Then she poured the whole thing in the glass and drank it down.

The liquid was so bitter and unpleasant that it made her shiver.

Spitting and coughing, she began to work around the oven with increased speed.

Soon the farmer appeared from the *kletis*, and his wife began to cough in her bedroom, and Veronika still kept on fussing around the oven and spitting.

She was about to bake pancakes, when she realized that she was drenched with perspiration. She felt so bad that she could barely catch her breath.

She had hardly had time to cross the threshold of the hall when something gave way in her brain and pressed down on her heart; she tried to hold on to the rail but missed and fell down.

Kaikaris and his wife hurried out of the house. Veronika lay in the middle of the yard as though she were dead, green foam oozing through her clenched teeth.

Without waiting another moment, the farmer spilled two pails of water over her and his wife began to burn blessed herbs over her

Veronika soon came back to life, although she still was trembling and shivering.

The other village women rushed in. They smoked her with *devyndrekis,* a magic grass, gave her a piece of St. Agnes' bread to swallow, then made her drink some herb tea. Finally Veronika got up.

As it was a holiday and the old women had not much to do at home, they thought it was a good idea to summon a priest for the sick girl, but they could not do it, simply because the Kaikaris farm-hand had gotten drunk somewhere and did not drive the horses back until late in the evening.

In two days Veronika completely recovered, and there was no need to bring a priest or to have an exorcion performed; only from that day on the innocence of her face and the gaiety of her disposition were gone forever. No one ever saw Veronika laughing or singing again. Misfortune took her over, conquered her, mingled with her blood and poisoned her thoughts, her nature and her entire life.

* * *

The medicine did not make it any easier for Veronika. And time was flying away.

The mowing season arrived, and the people began to cut the hay at the edge of the rye field.

Every day, here and there, among the fields and in the little meadows, wagons of green hay sprouted and grew larger, and as if they moved by themselves. Creaking and tilting they headed towards the village.

"Dzim—dzim, dzim-dzim," one heard the sharpening of scythes, the clank of hammers, the people's gay voices. Their songs and laughter echoed everywhere, and the girls, dressed in their lovely home-spun dresses, flocked together like the storks in the fall. One could see the gaiety and the importance of the season. It was as though the people were awaiting some great and distinguished guest, for the whole village and the road were covered with the verdure of green hay.

The fields and villages rustled in the distance, and the young people's songs echoed all over.

* * *

Next to the big road in the thick wood, stood an old, leaning cross made of oak.

Not even the oldest people of the neighborhood knew or could remember when and by whom it was erected. Nevertheless, everybody venerated it and considered it an act of great sanctity to visit it in their distress.

When the Cross holidays came, the neighboring village people did not miss the chance to come to this cross and to relax in the shade of nearby oak trees.

In the spring, when the grass first began to sprout and the earliest blossoms appeared, the people would adorn this cross with flowers and cover it with garlands, and the girls would bring the first sweet briars, green rues and new blossomed lilies from their gardens.

Even while the snow was still melting, early pansies and yellow cowslips were already withering on the cross; later, its trunk would be covered with white cottage-cheese-like branches of birch-cherry, and the white and bluish elder blossoms would attract the eyes of the passers-by.

Here and there, stuck behind the wreaths, one could see wilting bouquets of daisies, sprigs of mint and a few ears of rye. Dahlias would adorn the cross in the fall. They were frostbitten and soon turned back, as though nature itself were in mourning. They remained during most of the winter, rattling in the icy wind which blew the snow around the trees in the woods making the pine trees moan, and the oaks wave their naked branches threateningly. Yet the frozen flowers still clung to the cross. And it seemed to anyone passing by that these shriveled blossoms still dreamed of the sun, of silent star-lit nights, serene, blooming gardens, and of the lovely maidens who tended them. It was hard to believe that when the spring came again and nature awakened once more, these flowers would not smile at the sun anew; that a flower in this world blooms only once, and when it is picked it withers and dies....

Under this very cross the rebels had prayed before they went into the woods... here, too, their wives and mothers wrung their hands, as their breadwinners were being shipped to Siberia.

In this very spot Aunt Adomas screamed wildly when her husband was fatally injured at the mill; here wept a mother, having buried her last son; here, too, cried the neglected orphans. Many tears had been shed at the foot of the cross and many heartaches revealed.

It was midnight when Veronika approached the cross. In one hand she clutched a rosary, in the other a wreath of flowers.

The woods lay in uncomfortable silence, interrupted only by the sporadic rustle of unseen animals under the dry leaves. Occasionally a frog would leap up, and here and there glow-worms flickered in the darkness.

Veronika jumped every time she heard a rustling noise or a snapping twig, and clutching her rosary tightly, tried to disperse the frightening thoughts that would leap into her head.

The trees rustled above her and a mysterious shadow darted across her path. In the depths of the woods two trees collided.

"For the souls suffering between the two trees, Hail Mary...." whispered Veronika, making a sign of the cross in the direction of the noise.

She recalled that there was a lake not far from the woods about which many strange stories had been whispered. She remembered the burial ground of the hanged nearby. She remembered that not long ago in these woods a beggar had hanged himself.... Her heart began to freeze and her knees shook. The blood was pounding in her head. In the dark the pine trees began to resemble monsters, the bushes had suddenly acquired arms and legs. Tree stumps turned into bears and wolves. Above her, from the pines, dangled a corpse, and mysterious shapes pressed against her from every side, following her every step.

At long last the trees became more sparse and she could see the large gray road in the distance. Veronika stopped and began to breathe easier. She looked up and down the road to make certain that no one was around, then she slipped out of the woods and ran towards the cross.

When she saw it leaning among the trees, spreading its mournful shadow on the ground, her heart became heavy and tears flooded her eyes. Unconsciously she dropped the rosary and the flowers, and crumbling at the foot of the cross she embraced it with both arms. The tears, heavy and sorrowful, rolled down her cheeks unto the cross. Her misfortune was so great and painful that she could hardly find words to pray with. Yet she felt that the Crucified Who hung above her and looked sadly down saw her tears and knew why she had come, what she was asking....

Finally, after her tears were all cried out, Veronika remembered that it was not sufficient to ask God's favors with tears and the heart. She moved away and found the rosary which she had dropped before. She took the wreath, wound it around the cross several times, and began to walk around it on her bare knees.

At first, the pebbles and twigs cut into her knees and tore her flesh, but soon her feet were numbed. A cold sweat drenched her body and there was a bitter taste in her mouth.

She felt so weak that she had to rest every few minutes and wipe the perspiration from her brow. When the rosary had been said and after she had walked around the cross many times, Veronika leaned against it and for a long time sat motionless. The moon had already set behind the trees, but here and there one could still see its diminishing rays filtering through their branches. The horrors of the night disappeared, unseen animals no longer rustled under the leaves. Only the trees refused to be silent and whispered something foreboding to mankind.

Veronika stared into the darkness of the woods, thinking. Her knees burned fiercely and her head was spinning—she had no desire to rise from the foot of the cross.

A bird began to wake in the bushes, a bat fluttered by overhead and far away, from the other side of the woods, came the faint cry of a cock. Then everything was still once more. Veronika would have liked to pray a while longer, but when she heard the cock crowing she stood up and limped onto the road. The shadows had disappeared. The sky was getting lighter and the air was clear. Even the trees were whispering more pleasantly.

Going through the woods she frightened some small animal. It darted under the leaves and ran away.

When she came to the end of the woods Veronika stopped short. She could see the village on the other side of the lake. It was surrounded by fog-blue and smoke-like. Above it in the sky hung two white clouds—like linen put out to whiten by God. Over the pastures, as though trying to hide its shame, hung a pale and melancholy moon. Smoke rose from the surface of the lake, and it seemed to Veronika that someone had poured hundreds of pails of hot water into it during the night. The morning star twinkled among pink-tinted clouds, now glowing brightly, now almost extinguished, like a candle burning in the wind.

Veronika could see one of the sheet-like clouds unfold across the village, the other turned towards the east and begin to glow in the first rays of the dawn. And the morning star still burned and died like a candle flickering in the wind.

Only once before had Veronika seen another such beautiful morning. But that was long ago when she was still a small girl herding for the neighbors. It had been the morning of her mother's funeral, when, after having sat all night with the coffin, she was led from the hut into the morning air. There had been the same blue sky then, the same pale moon, the same strange clouds and the same beckoning, pleasant morning star.

Veronika remembered her mother as she lay with a white kerchief tied around her. She recalled her wax-yellow wrinkled face and quietly folded hands. She remembered how her mother used to visit her on Sundays when she herded in the neighboring village. She would stroke her head, kiss her face and sing softly to her. On Sunday evenings she would accompany Veronika as far as the cross and bid her good-bye, kissing her and pressing her head against her breast....

And sad tears rolled down Veronika's tired, unhappy face.

*   *   *

After a few days had passed, Veronika went to the cross once more. She did not feel any better, and the trouble under her heart grew bigger and more painful every day.

In vain did she walk those three miles to the wake of St. John, and the liquid presented by a certain Hungarian doctor did not help her either. She had changed considerably, she had become thin and sallow, and she had completely lost her patience. She began to hide herself from people. She could seldom sleep at night, and during the day, when she had to work, she could hardly keep her eyes open.... Finally, when she saw that neither medicine nor prayers were of any hel, she decided to visit an old and respected woman, one Juozaponis, and open her heart to her: perhaps she could give her some advice, console her, make her feel easier....

Veronika knew Mrs. Juozaponis was a God-fearing woman who belonged to various church groups and who went to confession every Sunday and fasted three days a week. She also knew that every priest who happened to come back from a sick bed had never passed by the Shepechiai village without stopping at Juozaponis' house, for she herself had a son who was going to become a priest.

When Veronika entered the Juozaponis' yard, the mistress was sitting on threshold and with sleeves rolled up to her elbows dyeing wool.

As she approached the "aunt" (as she was respectfully known to the village), Veronika hailed Christ and wanted to kiss her hand.

"Oh, Veraniote, how are you?" cried aunt Juozaponis, after she had given her a casual glance, and she offered her elbow to be kissed, for her hands were covered with blue dye.

"Well, my daughter, have you been to Benediction?" aunt Juozaponis began to question her, plunging the thread into the pot.

"No, I've not been yet," answered Veronika meekly, with a sad and dejected voice,

"And why not?" asked aunt Juozaponis as though she were astonished and angered by the girl's disobedience, and looked sternly at her.

"Aunty, I couldn't . . . I . . ." and not knowing how to explain, Veronika pushed her kerchief over her eyes and began to cry.

"Oh, God, my Lord, what has happened to you, my little daughter?"

The "aunt" softened to Veronika. She dried her hands on her skirt and took the girl into a half-darkened pantry which smelled of mold.

"What is it, my girl, tell me, what happened?" Aunt Juozaponis tried to tear the kerchief away from Veronika's face.

"Aunty, my dear, oh, how unhappy I am!" she leaned against the barrel and plunged into tars.

"Oh, my good Lord!" Juozaponis hunched her shoulders as she finally realized what had happened; she became angry not because of the girl's misfortune but because of her own stupidity. How was it that she, who knew all the news of the parish, had missed up till now what was going on under her own nose; she should have realized it when Veronika had fainted that Pentecost Sunday.

"Who's responsible? How long have you been that way?"

Veronika told her all about it, trying to clear herself.

"You just wait until he marries you now!" the old woman snapped angrily.

"Did you go to confession? Have you told the priest about it? Did you do penance?" she rushed question after question, getting angrier with each word.

"And how come that thunder has not yet struck you? How could the holy earth bear you yet, you low woman! Such a mortal sin, and she has not even yet gone to confession! Oh, why didn't you die the other day when you drank all that dirty stuff, and perish with your soul and body for ever? Oh God, my Lord! What will the priests say once they learn what has happened! You'd better rush to confession and reveal everything and pray, do your penance. You see, Veronika, didn't I tell you that the good Lord would punish you because you used to laugh at the May prayers or at the rosary? You see to what ends you have gone? If God abandons somebody, the devil rushes after him. . . ."

She scolded her for a long time, and Veronika stopped crying; she only listened to the old woman's words, still leaning against the barrel, now and then drying her eyes and cheeks with the fringes of her kerchief, and dark thoughts, one worse than the other, crossed her head.

"Aunty dear, don't tell anybody about it!" Veronika prayed as she kissed her hand, ready to leave.

"Silly head, even if I kept my mouth shut, how long do you think you'd be able to hide your secret? You can't hide a cat in a bag," ironically finished "aunt" Juozaponis as Veronika left the pantry.

Now Veronika had another problem, and as she walked home she shivered from the thought what would happen if she died before Sunday, before she could go to confession; if she died suddenly she would be damned forever.

She wanted to say a prayer against unexpected death, but then she remembered the aunt's words that God never listens to anyone who is in mortal sin, and she stopped. She had now realized why the Lord had not taken pity on her when she prayed at the cross and had not performed any miracle for her.

On Saturday evening Veronika asked her mistress to let her leave early the next day to go to confession; before she went to bed she brought in enough water and put wood in the oven, and very early the next morning, while everybody was still asleep, she left for church.

The sun had just risen above the night-dark pine forest, and large drops of dew began to sparkle on the weaving ryes and grasses.

The lake slowly evaporated, and slowly began to warm in the sun. At the edge of the meadow a few horses stood around lazily holding their heads down, having eaten their fill during the night. Two lapwings walked slowly through the grass. A man from the neighboring village was tossing his net into the lake.

Calm and silence lay all around, and it looked as though nature herself were celebrating Sunday and relaxing together with the people.

"I'll go to confession, I'll tell all my sins. I'll take my penance and everything will be all right," thought Veronika as she walked along the dewy path and lightly brushed the heads of rye with her hand.

"Afterwards, I'll go to the post office; the letter and the money must be there today. Am I not a silly head, indeed! America is not behind Kovarskas, it is far over the seas, much farther than Liepaja, and even in America people don't get handfuls of money at once, that's why Juozelis could not send a hundred rubles to pay my voyage, and of course, he's ashamed to send a letter without any money.

"There's no need for me to become sorrowful and to grieve. . . . If I get the money today, I'll be going to America next Sunday. I'll leave the money with aunt Juozaponis or even better, I'll sew it in the sleeve of my blouse and carry it myself," and again a gay wave of life flowed into her heart. In such a way sometimes, on a gloomy day, a ray of sunlight shows up from the clouds very unexpectedly, brightening the fields and filtering through the woods, giving a sparkle to the lulling brook and making the flowers seem to laugh, and then hides itself behind the clouds as unexpectedly, never to reappear.

It was very early when Veronika entered the town. Aside from several beggars who were sitting in their benches and singing the rosary, the church was deserted.

Veronika knelt humbly, bent her head and said three "Hail Marys" and sprinkled herself with holy water; then she walked straight to the Jesus Chapel, her new shoes clattering at every step.

"Blessed art thou amongst women and blessed is the fruit of thy womb, Jesus," the beggars' voices echoed in the empty church, and it seemed to Veronika that they were not really singing the rosary but merely imitating each other.

After she had finished reading the prayers for Confession, she examined her conscience once more very carefully, and with the help of her fingers counted her sins. She wondered which priest she should go to. She had always gone to the young one, a priest with an angel face who never looked into any woman's eyes, and when men approached him would listen to their confessions outside. But now she felt ashamed to go to the angelic one, and decided to confess to the rector himself instead.

"He's older, and I won't be so ashamed to tell him everything," moaned the girl, even though an invisible force was pushing her towards the younger priest's confessional.

Veronika recalled how she had once been in love with the young priest, how she tried to meet him, to see him, to kiss his hand. Whenever she was kneeling in the church she would try to put her face close to his cassock and touch his surplice, and a strange feeling of happiness filled her heart. She would begin to burn with love and fervor from the sweetness of her mysterious heavenly dream. She would dream of becoming the priest's housekeeper, washing his laundry, cleaning his rooms just to see him every day, even from a distance. She remembered one holiday when she had brought two rubles to the young priest and asked him to say a mass for her mother's soul; he asked her who she was, where she was working. And when the time came to bid him good-bye, she kissed his palm. The young priest presed her face to his hand so strongly that she lost her balance and stumbled with her head against his chest. Suddenly she felt a warm- tea-smelling breath close to her face, and she felt his lips on her neck; the blood rose to her face, her heart beat faster, and her head began to spin. Then the young priest took her by her hands and pushed her away.

God knows how she would have gotten herself out from such an embarrassing situation if it hadn't been for the rectory housekeeper who came suddenly into the room and announced that lunch was ready.

The rest of that day Veronika burned with the strange feeling which she had experienced for the first time in her life. She was plunged into mysterious thoughts, still feeling the hands of the young priest, his warm breath that smelled of tea, and it clung to her heart like a bright thorn bush, blooming and blooming forever. . . .

During the night, when she went to bed, her imagination wandered so far that afterwards she had to confess her thoughts to the same priest. . . .

For a long time Veronika knelt in the church. The beggars had already finished saying their rosary, and the people began to gather around the confessionals.

*"Hail be the bright dawn,
Thou art the joy of mankind. . . ."*

the organist began to sing with his vibrating voice; the organ accompanied him with a pleasant roar, and Veronika felt so calm, forgetting her awful confession and her misfortune, that she began to sing in tune with the organ.

> *Blessed Virgin Mary,*
> *Mary most Holy,"*

chanted the organ above her, and Veronika, her eyes filled with the music, bowed her head and remembered that early morning when the morning star burned and shone in the sky.

The organist finished his song and the young priest arrived. Veronika was beginning to feel sorry that she did not go to him when she heard the rector clearing his throat. Her heart began to beat faster: she was the first one at the window. Soon the rector appeared in the chapel. But as he approached the confessional he tripped over the shoes of a small boy kneeling on the floor and stumbled. He lashed out and kicked the boy's feet in anger. An old woman who had grabbed his hand and wanted to kiss it, became frightened and fell on her knees as though someone had struck her over the head.

Veronika's heart sank, and she wanted to move back from the rector's confession line, but then she heard a knock at the window and a hoarse voice:

"What are you doing, sleeping?"

Veronika knelt at the window and was about to start the introduction to her confession, when again the rector shouted roughly:

"Why did you cover this side? Cover the other side with your kerchief!"

Frightened and upset, Veronika could not distinguish which side was right and which was left, and again she covered the same side of her head. Enraged, the rector leaned out of the confessional, grabbed her by the hair, tore off her kerchief, pulled her braids and showed her how to cover herself.

Veronika felt the priest's hand on her head and heard the fall of the pins on the floor. She felt as though she were dead, unable to say a single word.

"Why are you silent?" the priest breathed in her face.

Veronika wanted to start from the beginning, but the rector cut her down:

"I heard that before. Now tell me your sins."

"Tuk, tuk, tuk, tuk," her heart was beating, the perspiration rolled over her face, and her hair loose under her kerchief crawled into her mouth and eyes.

Afraid even to move, so that she would not leave the spot in which the rector had placed her with his own hand, she began to tell him mere nothings at the beginning, then she pronounced her capital sin, and was silent. The rector was silent too. When Veronika, with her lips trembling, wanted to continue her confession, the rector suddenly interrupted her:

"Where do you come from? What's your name? How long have you been that way?"

Veronika answered all these questions.

"You loose woman! You strumpet! Do you want to spread filth in my entire parish!"

Veronika began to sob.

"Stop it!" shouted the rector so loud, that most of the people turned their eyes towards them.

Veronika could no longer follow what the priest was saying, how he was threatening her. She was not even able to hear what penance he had given her. After he had stopped shouting for a moment, Veronika began to explain to him that she probably would have to go to America and that on the voyage she might die or drown, but the rector again interrupted her; showing his teeth and leaning over the window he said in his whistling and hoarse voice:

"Fall on your knees, you whore, there won't be any absolution for you, I'll only bless you now."

Veronika knelt down, bowed her head and did not know what to do: whether to beat her chest and say, "God, have pity on me, a sinner," or something else; soon, however, she heard the priest's signal to move away. She rose from the bench, blushing and covered with tears; her kerchief slipped down, and the remaining pins fell on the floor. She fixed her hair a little bit and wanted to kiss his hand, but the priest drew it back angrily. The girl, even more ashamed than before, crept away.

All heads turned in her direction, and all eyes followed Veronika: to her it seemed that all had guessed her sin.

Everything was confused in her head. Once she had bowed her head, she was afraid to raise it again, for she thought that everyone was staring at her and waiting for a chance to look into her eyes and to revile her.

At the gospel, when everyone was standing, she slipped out as though she had stolen something, and headed towards her village.

She only stopped at the cemetery. Still only half-conscious, she entered through the gate, passed the chapel of the big landowners; having reached the grave of her mother, she cried out:

"Ach-ach-a-a-ahaa!" and fell prone on the ground. She pushed her face into the grass, dug her hands into the sand and began to cry like a little child.

It was still in the cemetery: there were no people, no noise, no commotion. Crosses stood quietly around the place, and scattered here and there were the mounds of earth where the miserable ones, once alive, now rested; the trees were green, the flowers were in bloom, and the bees buzzing mournfully kept flying from one blossom to another. It seemed as though they were telling everyone how poorly the dead had lived in this world, how hard they had worked and how many troubles they had seen; some of them suffered in this vale of tears because of misery, some suffered from sickness; some were mourned for a long time, others were soon forgotten. The bees told about a dead mother who had left her little orphans alone, and about a young maiden who never knew what love was, and about a young lad who lost his life in a strange land. . . . They flew around, buzzing, and told all about those who lay there in eternal peace, and the trees and flowers and leaning crosses listened to their talk, until finally the bees would sigh, fly around for a second and then disappear into the blue sky. . . .

Listening to the bees, Veronika, too, became silent; still keeping close to her mother's grave she calmed down; only now and then her shoulders would shiver, her back tremble, and her hands would dig deeper into the sand.

Church services were over, and the people began to flock homeward, the wheels of their wagons rattling as they passed the cemetery. Here and there some women and men stopped at the gates and came inside to say a prayer for their parents, brothers or sisters; here and there one could hear a loud cry, a moan, a sorrowful word. There was a mother crying for her little daughter, before another tomb a daughter was in tears praying for her mother. In front of a new grave which had not yet overgrown with grass wept a young widow, and next to her sat an old woman saying silent prayers for her grandchildren. In the shade of the chapel, a few women were sitting and eating their bread and cheese; they had finished their prayers and now exchanged opinions about their bad daughters-in-law, their fathers and sons. . . . In another place, two sisters who had been separated by distant marriages and had not seen each other for a long time, now opened their hearts to one another. In a word, this place was not for passing gossip, but a place where one could cry, tell one's troubles and remember those who had gone.

After a while most of the people had left the cemetery, but Veronika still kept crying at her mother's grave.

"What are you crying here for, my little daughter?" a strange old woman approached her and began to shake her gently by the shoulders. "Are you grieving for your dear mother or father? Calm down, daughter, be silent. His is the holy will, and He knows what He's doing. Here lie three of my own, too: my father, and my son, and my daughter. Say three 'Hail Marys' for the souls suffering in purgatory and go home. It is late now, and you know there are some chores to be done at home."

"Oh aunty, I'm not grieving for my mother!" cried out Veronika with her lips full of sand. She raised her head from the grave. Moved by the sight, the old woman understood; she opened her kerchief and taking out a small roll handed it to her.

"Eat it, my little daughter, perhaps you have not had anything in your mouth since breakfast; eat it and go home. Crying won't be of much help now. His is the holy will, and He must know. . . ." The old woman dried her tears and walked away.

* * *

It was almost evening when Veronika returned.

Passing the vegetable garden, she noticed that the yard and house were filled with people, mostly women and girls.

"Is is possible that they have already learned about it?" thought Veronika. "Would aunt Juozaponis have told them all? No, maybe they only gathered for an evening song."

But when they saw through Veronika coming back, all of them rushed away: some slipped through the door into Butkus' vegetable garden, the others through the backyard as thought they were hurrying home; aunt Juozaponis herself tumbled over the wooden fence into neighbor Lukshy's yard.

"What happened to you, Veronika, you didn't even come to eat on time and now you return with the last heifers?" said Kaikaris nonchalantly, not looking at her and pretending to fix something on the fence.

"I was delayed in town for a while," answered the girl.

"Oh, Veronika has come back," spoke up the mistress from the store room, shaking he rskirt. "So let us hurry, men, take your seats at the table. I'm hungry."

When everybody was sitting at the table, the mistress, still not looking at her, asked:

"Did you go to confession, my little daughter?"

"No, I didn't," answered Veronika, not daring to raise her eyes, and bowing her head. "Did they see me? Did they know about it already? Had aunt Juozaponis revealed my secret?" Questions rose in the girl's head one after the other. She could not be mistaken: all of them knew not only about her troubles but also about the priest's refusing her the absolution, his scolding her, and pulling her braids. Now they also understood why she had fainted the other Sunday.

"Who'll be its god-parents?" asked the farm hand Anicokas, who sat opposite Veronika. He prolonged word after word, and his voice was low.

"This is not your business!" the farmer cut him down roughly. "I'll hit you on tne head with my spoon for it!"

Everybody kept silent; Veronika tried to swallow her piece of bread but it stuck in her threat; she put her spoon aside, pulled the kerchief over her eyes and began to cry.

"I also say it's nobody's business!" added the farmer's wife while she was pouring some soup. "She sinned and she will suffer for it."

For the last few days it had seemed to Veronika that her misfortune was dangling above her on a thin thread, and now Anicokas had cut it down and the misfortune fell on her with all its weight.

"What shall we do, Veronika?" the farmer began after dinner. "You may leave us some day, and the rye harvest season is coming soon. I'll need a strong worker. You wouldn't do me any good, even now you seem to be walking in a daze."

Veronika said nothing, she ran behind the oven, sat down and began to cry.

Walking towards the door Anicokas glanced at her and became confused: he had never seen the girl so beautiful, so sad and so dejected as she was now; her large eyes were filled with tears, her eyelashes wet—her pupils sparkling and pale cheek with rosy spots on them made her extremely lovely and interesting. He came back to drink some water at the door, and again looked at Veronika: she was still attractive and charming.

For no apparent reason he broke a branch from a lilac tree; for the same reason he slapped the horse which was grazing at the edge of orchard; and when he entered the barn he sat down on the wagon and began to think. He felt sorry for Veronika, and he felt bad that he had insulted her—such a pretty and sad maiden.

While he was watering the horses at the well, he saw Veronika enter into the little *kletis* where she slept. His first impulse was to leave the horses, step inside, embrace Veronika and caress her as gently as he had never caressed any girl before. He wanted to ask forgiveness and to soothe her, but he noticed his mistress looking through the window, and her husband standing at the threshold, and he lost his nerve. He only shouted to a colt, "Go away, you frog!" mounted the horse and dashed away for his night-watch.

That evening Veronika spent at home; once she had finished her chores, she locked herself in the little *kletis* and began to say the penance which the rector had given her.

She said her rosary, then she prostrated herself cross-like on the floor; suddenly she heard the cry of a harmonica somewhere in the village, and young laughter and voices which came closer and closer to her. Some of the boys were singing about a housewoman who had enough milk to make his soup light but that she wouldn't give it to him, neither did she give him any bacon to eat. As they passed Kaikaris' yard, Shaltenis' farm hand played a few notes on his harmonica, then he sang a newly composed song about her:

> *Ver-onyt, V-e-r-o-n-y-t,*
> *Why are you so crying?*
> *Are you sorry for your rues,*
> *Are you sorry for your worries,*
> *Waiting for Juozelis?*

When they had passed by and everything was quiet, at last she heard a noise outside the little *kletis*. Something rustled, someone gave a short laugh. There was a slap and a whisper to shut up. After a moment, an artificially sweet tune imitating an old mother's voice mocked the girl's misfortune as he sang out:

> *Veronyt, my little daughter,*
> *Who has opened the door of your kletis?*

The other voice imitating a young girl answered him:

> *My dear little old mother,*
> *There was a cat who was chasing a mouse.*

The first voice continued:

Veronyt, my little daughter,
Why is your bed . . .?

A big stone banged at the little *kletis* door and fell in the gooseberries. Then everything was silent once more, except for the fading whoops of the young men and the laughter that echoed in the village.

"You good-for-nothings, you scoundrels! I should catch one of you by the hair and grind your scalp!" Farmer Kaikaris walked out of the other *kletis* and began to shout.

"For heaven's sake, now we won't have a single, quiet night. That's what we get for keeping a whore in the house. Running around with cigarettes in their mouths, they may set a fire." The mistress agreed with her husband as she appeared at the window of her bedroom.

"Of course they can set a fire. It will never end now once it has started. I'd better tell her father next Sunday to come and take her to his hut: she's not much of a worker now anyway, and its only a disgrace for the house to keep her here."

Veronika was afraid of everybody now, but most of all she was terrified of her father. She still remembered how he used to beat her mother, kicking her with his foot and tossing her on the ground by her braids. He used to beat Veronika, too, if she would start crying. A hot wave crossed over her as she began to think what would happen when her father learned about this.

In spite of the insults and weariness, Veronika could not fall asleep; she tossed and turned in her bed, trying to find a way to be comfortable. She even tried lying on two pillows, then on one. She stretched herself out and coiled herself into a roll, she covered herself with a blanket, then tossed it away, but sleep never closed her eyes. An unexplainable burden pressed her whole body.

Closing her eyes hiding her head under a pillow, she tried to keep away the thoughts that hounded her. . . .

. . . In a barn, a pig was rubbing itself against the wall. In front of the little *kletis* a dog was shaking and scratching itself. The dawn, breaking the fog, was beginning to rise from the lake. The little town was filled with smoke. . . .

"In the Holy Scripture it is said that such a woman should be stoned to death," spoke a priest in Veronika's ear.

"Oh, dear God, what a burden for me to hold; if only I could get a little bit of sleep," whispered the girl, rolling over on her side.

Again everything was quiet. The dog still scratched itself in front of the *kletis*. At the very ceiling, the rye was rustling in the wind.

> "Hail be the bright star of Dawn,
> Thou art the joy of mankind. . . ."

sang the organist in the attic, but the rector rushed to him and shouted: "Be silent, you fallen woman!" Veronika woke up again.

It was growing light . . . In the cemetery, the bees were buzzing around. . . . Somebody began to take away the pillow from under her head. . . . Someone had opened the door of her bedroom, walked in and stopped at her bed.

"Are you asleep, my beloved daughter?"

"I'm asleep, my dear mamma, I'm asleep. I went to confession and I grew so tired."

Her beloved mamma came closer to her bed, bent over her and keeping her waxen hands crossed on her heart, said:

"I have sewn a little white shirt for you, my darling daughter."

"Oh, my mother, how small it is! I won't be able to fit in it. I am not a little herdgirl any more, you know, I'm a maid."

"Now now, my beloved daughter. This little shirt is not for you, it is for your baby."

"Mother, I shall go to America now, I've received a hundred rubles from Juozelis."

"You can't cross the seas, my daughter, after having committed a mortal sin; if you drowned you'd perish with your soul and body forever. You'd better come to me."

"But how can I come, mamma, the rye has not been harvested yet?"

"You're not a good worker any more, only a disgrace to the whole house. You'd better come to me!" Having said that, her mother began to grow, to expand. Her white veil disengaged itself and wrapped itself around the floor and ceiling; and her calm wax face began to wrinkle. . . .

"Veronika! Veronika!" her mother leaned over and suddenly began to shout and bang the walls with her fists.

"Veronika! Veronika! Do you hear me, get up! Veronika! Veronika!"

"I hear you, I'm getting up," shrieked Veronika in her dream, and instantly she sat up in her bed.

"What happened to you, one can't even wake you up any more. Are you getting up?" It was farmer Kaikaris who banged the walls of the little *kletis* with his fists.

Frightened and shivering, Veronika arose, but she could not make out whether she had really spoken to her mother, or whether it had only been a dream.

"Go to the swamp to rake some hay. Anicokas will cut and you will rake it into a basket and bring it to a ry spot. Be sure to bring the cord basket with you from the barn," shouted the farmer and again lay on his warm bed.

"Oh, Jesus!" Veronika shrieked as she opened the door. She leaned back against the wall. The door of the little *kletis*, the jamb and the gates of the flower garden were smeared with tar.

As though she were jumping from a fire, Veronika dashed out of the *kletis*, grabbed a pail of water and poured it on the door, to wash the dirt away, but the water only rolled down over the tar and even made the door look dirtier.

She poured a few more pails of water on it until she was convinced that this would not do her any good, then she began to rub the door with a brush and scratched with the fingernails. But the black water mixed with tar seemed to spurt from the door, like black tears, and there was no way of scrubbing them off.

While she was cleaning the dirt, the farmer appeared, and when he saw what had happened he began to shout:

"You stupid one, you idiot, why do you wash it with cold water? You need hot water water, and you have to rub it with sand."

Not even half-an-hour had passed by and the whole village knew about the wicked mockery against the girl. And everyone found a reason to pass Kaikaris' farmstead and stop for a while in his yard.

*   *   *

Hard days arrived for Veronika; frightened and ashamed, she tried to hide from everybody; she avoided people whenever she could, walked with her kerchief over her eyes and her head lowered. And yet, she still had a spark of hope that Juozelis would soon send the money for her voyage.

She worked hard during the day, and at night she said her rosary and lay cross-like on the floor; at the end of the week, the girl became so lean and so sickly that any God-fearing village woman would have pitied her if she had not hidden her eyes under her kerchief.

Sunday came again, and Veronika went to church, looking around cautiously, afraid that someone might follow her, and making sure that no group of fellows was sitting at the roadside. It seemed to her that everybody had a right to insult her, to call her a fallen woman and to smear her.

In the church, she knelt in the farthest side under the stairs, and soon after the sermon was finished, without even waiting for vespers, she slipped away before the people began to walk out; she hurried to the post office in vain, and after staying in town for a while, made her way home.

She did not cry any more, only her head was lowered, and she constantly pulled the kerchief over her eyes. She stopped in the rye field to take a rest.

* * *

"Veronika, are you going out?" shouted Kaikaris when he saw her walking through the door.

"Of course not, where could I go?" answered Veronika, looking at her feet. She walked into the little *kletis*, covered herself with a large kerchief, sat on the bed, laid a prayer book on her knees, and gazed at the barrel which stood in front of her.

"Be sure not to go out; we'd like to have a talk with you," said the mistress as she stepped in, to make sure that Veronika had no intentions of going anywhere.

Veronika realized that this conversation would not do her any good; without even stirring a little, she remained in the same position she was before.

An unusual commotion began in the village the way it does when a priest is expected to come to a sick man or to pay his usual visit before Christmas. The homes of two neighbors of Kaikaris swarmed with people: men, women, and herdboys—all, except Veronika, knew that Kaikaris was expecting her father that day; they saw Kaikaris buying a drink for Veronika's father and asking him to come over and discuss his daughter.

"He's coming! He's coming!" shouted the gooseherds as they ran through the Butkus yard, hardly able to catch their breath.

Everybody ran out and stood in the yard, looking at the man who walked through the village, carrying a cane in his hand. Although it was midsummer, he was wearing a short, patched fur coat, a torn brown cap and instead of a belt he had a rope tied around his waist. From a distance, he looked like a man who was ready for anything.

The villagers could not stand any more, and the whole crowd of them, like a herd of animals, invaded Kaikaris's yard.

The old man walked erect with fast, long steps, keeping his eyes straight, not saying a word to anybody. As though he did not even see the gathered people, he walked straight through the yard into his daughter's little *kletis*.

Veronika was sitting in the same position as she sat right after the dinner, with her prayer book open on her knees and her eyes staring at the barrel.

She started as she saw her father, jumped off the bed, cried out "Daddy" and fell down at his feet. But her father dealt such a blow to his daughter's back that the cane broke in half. With the shorter end he continued beating Veronika over the shoulders and back and sides. . . .

When the girl, scared to death, tried to escape and hide under her bed, her enraged father grabbed her by the braids, lifted her from the ground and continued to strike her with his fists over her cheeks, and head, and breasts. . . .

Who knows how it would all have ended, if it had not been for the farmer's small daughter and a stranger who happened to come to Butkus. The little girl began to scream and ran across the yard as she saw Veronika hanging in the air by her braids. The stranger answered the little girl's scream an hurried into the little *kletis*. When he saw what was happening, the stranger grabbed the old man by his sheepskin coat and threw him behind the barrel. Once on his feet again, the old man was about to fight the stranger but then Kaikaris and his wife entered the little *kletis*, took him out and asked him to come into their room.

No one knew what they were talking about, for after the stranger came into the picture, the whole crowd disappeared. Only the herdboys and children remained in the yard. They were the only ones who heard the old man's angry remarks as he had left the Kaikaris' house:

"She can even do it at the foot of the fence, I'm not going to accept her in my home."

.   *   *   *

No one had called Veronika for supper or for chores that evening, she still lay on the floor as her father had left her.

At eventide, Anicokas came home from the town drunk; having learned about Veronika's beating, he again wanted to go into the little *kletis* and talk to her, but he could not wait until the farmers went to bed, so he began to sing and curse, and walked out for the night-watch.

The sun had set and it began to grow dark. Mysterious shadows drifted from the woods and extended through the fields. An evening star twinkled in the sky. The glow in the West started fading and moving towards the East. In the Northeast the red glare of fire rose up, and the moon appeared slowly, timidly.

The water of the lake glittered, and its surface looked frozen. The reeds and grasses fell asleep, and the crosses from the cemetery of suicids seemed to gaze downward.

In some gardens, between the mints and sages, a grasshopper began to chirp; the night beetles and butterflies were rustling and moving among the leaves, and the bats flitted around the houses.

The air was fragrant with honey, nasturtiums and blossoming fields. A sad and sorrowful silence filled with moonlight and nostalgia reigned over the sleeping village.

It was midnight, when Veronika rose from the ground, walked out of the little *kletis* and stopped in the middle of the yard. The full moon shone straight into her eyes and threw a grotesque shadow on the grass.

It was calm, and peaceful and mysterious everywhere, only at Galai she could hear Anicokas singing his song and the chirping of the little grasshoppers in the garden.

A dog saw her, crawled from under the porch, wagged his tail and began to sniff all over the yard.

Veronika grew so tired and weak that she could hardly stand on her feet; she walked towards the porch and sat on a stone.

The dog rushed to her, put his forefeet on her lap and began to lick her bloody face and swollen eyes. He licked her hands and hair and whined as though he wanted to speak to her.

Veronika embraced the dog's neck with both hands, pressed him against her, and holding her chin on his head, began to cry more bitterly than she had ever cried before.

She did not cry because of her own troubles, of her shame or because she had been beaten; she cried because all the people who had been so close to her heart, all these uncles and aunts, her girl friends and sweet boys who seemed to care so much for her, who seemed to love her, now derided and humiliated her; they had pushed her away from themselves forever as though she were dirt. Forgotten by God and abandoned by the people, still not knowing what her crime was, Veronika cried bitterly, and the mournful light of the moon and Anicokas' song, mysterious and low, sadly echoing in the foggy fields, seemed to cry with her like a beautiful and hurt little orphan.

She remembered other nights, the handsome young man, his sweet words, love, hope, wonderful dreams. . . .

Veronika pushed the dog away and stood up, strong and healthy, and full of pride; she climbed over the fence into the vegetable garden, and from there she headed along the rye field. . . .

"Is she out of her mind, that girl—to walk alone in the fields at midnight!" thought the moon, which appeared for a little while, but then, always busy doing something, it disappeared behind another could.

And the girl, bareheaded, with her braids loose, walked on to the lake with small, determined steps.

The sleepy rye fields whispered to her as though suggesting something, beating their heads against her uncovered neck and trying to tickle her. But she paid no heed to them. She walked erect, with her head held high and shoulders thrown back with pride. It seemed that she was trying to make up for all the times she had cowered with bent head and the kerchief over her face.

Occasionally some small bird would flutter excitedly from the path; or an animal would make a rustling noise among the rye. At such times the girl would stop and gather her strength—holding her head even higher than before. . . . She would clench her fists and defy the unseen enemy, as if saying, "Come out in the open if you dare—I have no more patience with you. I dare you to come out . . . just try and we'll see what happens." But nothing ever showed itself. And so she continued on her way, more proud than ever, walking to the lake with her small, firm steps.

Several times the dog caught up with her, whining and wagging his tail. He didn't know whether to follow Veronika or to go back to the farm which he had left unguarded. But seeing that the girl paid no attention to him, he sat on the pathside and began to howl.

When the journey was ended, Veronika stopped for a moment and let her eyes encompass the silent expanse of the lake—the stars sparkling in the water, the submerged crosses, the sleeping village on the hill. . . . She looked and she knew that she was already a stranger in this beautiful world. No longer would she be coaxed by the moonlight, no longer would she dream her innocent maidenly dreams. She knew that now she was alone in the world . . . her portion would only be hardship and abuse.

Suddenly she clutched the rosary around her neck and with a hoarse cry pulled apart the chain. The meadows and fields answered her cry, as it echoed beyond the lake. They answered but did not come forth . . . and Veronika slowly waded into the water.

The reflected stars began to shiver, the reeds shook with fright and one after another little wavelets, as though running, formed circles around Veronika.

When the moon appeared again the water was still once more. The reeds were sleeping peacefully and the stars shone brightly on the glittering surface.

Her body was found the next morning, but it lay on the bank for a day, until the authorities came from Ukmerge and finally ordered some of the men to make a coffin and bury the girl.

Veronika was buried near the lake—on the hill of the suicides. There was no mourning—no one cried for her or said prayers for her soul. The grave was dug quickly, and no cross was put over it. The people went back to their homes in silence.

* * *

Many years have passed since poor Veronika drowned herself, yet even now the people claim than on moonlit nights one can see a spectre with a small child rising from the graveyard on the hill. Surrounded by a white mist, she walks through the rye fields picking cornflowers, or she wades among the reeds gathering waterlilies. But most frequently she wanders along the edge of the lake searching for her scattered and wasted rosary beads.

Translated by Nola and Stepas Zobarskas

IGNAS SEINIUS

IGNAS SEINIUS (the pen name of Ignas Jurkunas) was born on April 3, 1889, in Seiniunai, Lithuania, and studied in Kaunas, Moscow and Stockholm. From 1923 to 1929 he was Lithuanian minister to Finland, Norway and Sweden. While in Lithuania he took an active part in the country's life as editor, counselor and delegate to the National Red Cross organization. Having escaped the Soviet invasion of 1940, he returned to Sweden. He died in Stockholm on January 15, 1959.

His early prose works—especially *Kuprelis* (The Little Hunchback), 1913, and *Vasaros vaises* (The Feast of Summer), 1914, played an important role in the modernization of Lithuanian prose. He also wrote an anti-Nazi satire, *Siegfried Immerselbe atsijaunina* (Rejuvenation of Siegfried Immerselbe), English version in 1965; stories, memoirs, and two novels in Swedish. One of them, *Den roda floden stiger* (The Red Flood Arises), a day-to-day account of the subjugation of Lithuania, had a strong impact on the "neutral" Scandinavians.

Ignas Seinius

IGNAS SEINIUS

(1889-1959)

The Ordeal of Assad Pasha

I

"NOW what's happening?" Assad Pasha began to wonder, when he realized that the Shah's adjutant was not going upstairs but was leading him unsteadily along the corridors of the seraglio to the far side, where the orchard was.

The adjutant's steps were unsteady because the corridors had been polished for the approaching ceremonies, but the carpets had not yet been laid. Assad himself had to proceed cautiously, one foot at a time, to avoid slipping. Neither of them spoke, although they were close acquaintances and had both shed blood in the struggle that overthrew the previous regime. They were aware that on the way to an audience with His Most Illustrious Majesty silent contemplation befitted both the guest and the guide. They had respected this rule on the not infrequent occasions of the last few weeks, when Assad Pasha, the Minister for Home Affairs, had visited the elderly Shah Hussam-Eddin on public business or, more often, to play chess. Chess was His Most Illustrious Majesty's favorite relaxation from the monotony of state affairs, and Assad Pasha, whose portly figure carried his forty years well, was a skillful player, given to bold moves with his castles and his knights. The invitations usually came in the afternoon, but sometimes in the middle of working hours.

This time it seemed unlikely that the Shah had suddenly decided to try out a new defence against Assad's flank attacks. Something was wrong.

As he walked down the long corridors, the effort of keeping his balance made Assad's arm ache. He had been wounded in the elbow two months before, when he led a battalion in the attack on the Palace, where the Cabinet was on guard. The Ministers had gathered to consider measures for suppressing the rising. Now the recollection of those glorious hours made the pain in his arm vanish like dust blown away by the wind.

When they reached the orchard, the adjutant turned back. Ancient usage demanded that the Minister for Home Affairs should find his own way for the rest of his journey. In the past he had often had to solve his problems unaided.

Assad had never been in the royal orchard before. He knew about it only from the tales told by army officers and from the secret map kept in the Ministry. Somewhere among the buildings, large and small, was the Shah's Chamber of Meditation. It was very old, and the Shahs of Namiristan used to retire there alone in times of crisis.

Assad Pasha had no time to guess what might have made the Shah withdraw to a place that was a relic of old ways. Hussam-Eddin's penetrating intellect had been nurtured on Western education; he had learned to think quickly in every predicament. Assad knew that he must make haste.

Speeding his progress was no easy task. Alone in the orchard he felt as if he were lost in a green sea, where slender palms mingled with the stout trunks of lofty paullinias, gigantic teak-trees and spreading planes. Countless bushes were in full bloom after the showers of the past week and the first warmth of spring. There were flowers in rectangular beds and bordering the paths, flowers that had sown themselves among the bushes and other growths in the shade between the trees. The scent of magnolia and jasmine hung heavily in the peace of the orchard. Yet the place was far from silent; the ear was continually assailed by the call of birds, that kept repeating their song, by the shrill cry of peacocks and the hum of bees and insects.

All this was nothing new to Assad. He had an orchard of his own, though it was neither so large nor so overgrown. He might not have noticed the heady scents or the contented sounds, but his awareness was sharpened by the oppressive necessity of choosing his way.

The paths wound through the orchard; in places they led steeply up artificial hillocks and little hump-backed bridges. They had been laid on purpose to compel the Shah to slacken his steps, if he should feel obliged to withdraw from his counsellors; he must be restrained from excessive haste.

Assad stopped for a moment, looked around and asked himself anxiously whether he was going to arrive too late. Perhaps he ought to ask one of the sentries the way. He himself had supreme command of the guard in the orchard and the seraglio, and his men in their British uniforms were standing singly where the paths crossed, or proceeding to and fro with measured steps in British fashion up the inclines and down the valleys. Yet it was not right that the officer who had ultimate responsibility for security should present himself to his subordinates with a request for help, even though every one of them looked a model of discretion. Suddenly he saw and recognized his commanding officer from afar.

The pain in his elbow returned. Hot and ill-at-ease, he felt as if his feet were too big for his open shoes, made of white canvas in the latest style. In the humid warmth of the orchard his loose-fitting white suit seemed tight at the armpits and elsewhere.

Presently the sense of discomfort compelled Assad to stop. Beads of perspiration dropped from his brow and rolled beneath his nylon shirt. He had lost his way.

As suddenly as in a fairy-story he saw in front of him a narrow dome of emerald green tiles that were beginning to need repair. It stood on a hillock shaded by palms on the far side of a waving expanse of plane-trees. It was the Chamber where the Shahs had made so many decisions, wise decisions and others.

There was new vigor in Assad Pasha's footsteps as he set off directly on the circuitous route that would lead him to His Most Illustrious but, perhaps for the moment, uneasy Majesty.

Assad wondered why he had been sent for. No Shah had ever invited anyone there before, not even from among his most loyal adherents. Besides, why had he been chosen? Did some unforseen peril threaten the internal peace of Namiristan? Yet as far as could be ascertained, all the reactionaries had been rounded up and were awaiting trial. The resumption of relations with the Western Powers had brought about a perceptible recovery in the country. In Debridan negotiations about trade and munitions supplies were proceeding satisfactorily with a Delegation that had arrived by air from the United States. How could anything untoward occur now that Nirsan, the Shahpur and heir to the throne, had bowed to his father's will and agreed to marry Adile, the Shahsenem and princess of reactionary Idaristan? His decision meant that no danger need be expected from Idaristan, even though the sectarian outlook which predominated there was fertile ground for chauvinistic and aggressive tendencies. No, something serious and unexpected must have occurred just at the time when the whole country was busy with preparations for the wedding.

Assad's reflections were interrupted by the sight of a group of peacocks, crowding together in the shade near the door of the Shah's

Chamber. He paused to consider whether to take his shoes off. The custom of removing the shoes on visiting the Shah had been abolished early in the reign of Hussam-Eddin. Nevertheless, Assad sat down on the steps and took off his shoes. He could not do otherwise, when he saw the ancient green tiles of the Chamber and the dreamy fragility of its dome. Besides, his feet were swollen and moist with the heat.

Leaning back against the door-past, Assad sighed with relief and rested his feet and his whole body. A moment later he stood up, collected himself and pushed very gently at the door, which gave a loud creak.

"Hurry up and shut the door, or you'll let the flies in!" a deep voice called from inside.

Although Assad Pasha was a man of powerful build, who never lost his self-control or allowed his gaze to falter, he started as he came inside the Chamber of Meditation. The Shah was crouching among brightly-colored cushions, which were scattered in the middle of the circular floor; his bowed head was shrouded in a turban of green silk, and his bent form was wrapped in a loose robe of brown velvet. He had not shaved since the day before and he had not slept. He was deep in thought and, without raising his eyes, he pulled hopelessly on a hookah. Assad had never before seen His Most Illustrious Majesty Hussam-Eddin dressed in such a way, sitting on the floor in a fashion that had been superseded and smoking a hookah instead of a cigar. A mere two days had aged the Shah by many years. If Assad had had time to direct his glance upwards, he would have noticed cobwebs hanging heavy with trapped flies from the narrow turquoise dome. They were a relic of the nationalist regime that had been overthrown; its slogan had been the preservation and restoration of the holy traditions of Namiristan. The cobwebs also illustrated the inefficiency of the new Minister for Palace Affairs.

Assad regarded the Shah with unfeigned consternation. He took two steps forward and bowed in the traditional way.

"My Supreme Lord, Shahanshah!"

"Take a cushion and sit down." A fatherly smile lit up the pale fae of Hussam-Edin, as he pushed the hookah to one side. "Where've you been all this time, my son? Couldn't you find the way?"

"The engine of my automobile was nearly boiling in the heat," said Assad in apology, as he sat down and curled his legs under him. He dared not admit that the duties of the Home Ministry might be too much for him.

"I saw that you've a new automobile. If you haven't time to spare, let someone else run it in. I've another problem to make your head ache."

The Shah spoke in dull, steady tones.

"Has something unforeseen happened, my Lord?"

For a moment the Shah scratched his head in weary silence. His eyes, full of wisdom and experience, looked straight at Assad Pasha, whom he held acountable for domestic affairs.

"My beloved son, the Shahpur Nirsan has changed his mind. He refuses to go to Idaristan and marry the Shahsenem Adile. But both the Idari and the Namiri have completed their preparations for the wedding."

It was as if the walls of the Chamber had burst open and the broad, heavy carpet had risen and floated away with Assad and the Shah on an inscrutable journey. Assad leaned forward, resting both arms on its smoothly woven surface. Already he could almost picture the inevitable consequences of the Shahpur's decision, but like a responsible statesman he tried to comfort the Shah. What else could he do?

"Even so, we must understand the Shahpur Nirsan's point of view," said Assad. "For a man who has had a good Oxford education it would be a terrible sacrifice. It would mean accepting a woman he has never seen as his partner for life. Of course, she comes of a good family, but what difference does that make? A good family doesn't always mean good looks. Besides, her country is so backward, as if Allah had forsaken it."

"My son, you talk about Oxford as if it were a source of enlightenment. Surely a man who has had a good Western education and experience of the world must realize that you can only get to know a woman after marriage?"

"But if only you've seen her before, when you eventually get to know her better at least you understand the origin and nature of your disappointment."

"That's small comfort. You're an Oxford man yourself and you used to talk differently before. I myself have seen you tell the Shahpur that for a man whom fate and duty call, his partner in life is a secondary consideration, even if she were like an oasis to the traveler in the desert or a bright star at night."

"I remember, my Lord."

"You said that a true monarch finds the deepest joy and the meaning of his life in the hazardous pursuit of political and military victories."

"Yes indeed, I did."

"You said that, when the monarch has time to spare, he may subtly modify his wife's character, even while amusing himself and her. He can remould her to his heart's desire. Always provided that she has not already been spoilt. But we all know that the Idari do not spoil their womenfolk."

"No, the Idari treat their women too strictly."

"I knew at that time, my son, that you were a loyal Minister and your object was to help me. You must help me again now. Otherwise the Idari won't forgive us; they will regard the refusal as a deliberate affront, and as the situation deteriorates, the Americans will lose interest in negotiating with us."

Assad did not know what to say. The smooth carpet and the Chamber with all its contents seemed to be floating anchorless in the air.

"What a disappointment for the people here and in Idaristan, after all they've done to prepare for the wedding!"

"Yes, there may be serious consequences."

"Now I can see that you're talking sense again."

"The Shah and his minister understood one another. They felt once more that they stood on the firm ground of reality, however many pitfalls there might be in their path. She Shah began to pull at the hookah. Assad suggested that they should send for Nirsan, who was, after all, the heir to the throne, and talk the matter over with him calmly; in two and a half days it would be time for him to go to Idaristan.

"My dear Minister, do you perhaps have some premonition of the present whereabouts of the Shapur?"

"Unfortunately, not at this moment."

"I should imagine that he is in hiding with some beautiful woman who has bewtiched him. She has enticed him away from his duty and cast her spell on him just at the most critical hour of his life."

"Very likely, my Lord."

The Shah pushed the hookah to one side.

"Pasha, I give you the task of finding the Shahpur. You must carry it out in person, without relying on intermediaries. If the Shahpur—may Allah preserve him!—if the Shahpur does not yield to persuasion or will not let you bring him here ... then do as was done in Namiristan in former days. And do not deal with him alone; you must attend to the temptress as well. If anything happens to him, it will be described in modern times as an accident. I, the Shah, give you my word of honor in this holy place and with this sacred covering on my head."

This time the walls of the Chamber seemed to burst apart in front of Assad. He felt as if he were hanging all alone in the air, without even the carpet to support him; gusts of air whirled him around, leaving him breathless. But after a while his sense of responsibility returned to him; once more he felt himself a man and a Namir.

"I will do my best, my Lord. Even—Allah preserve me!—even if something should happen to me."

II

When Assad returned to his car, which was parked in the shadow cast by the plane-trees and the wall of the seraglio, he looked around and pondered before taking his seat. He had something to think about.

The seraglio and the orchard stood on a hill, girded by two rivers that flowed together on the far side. Assad could see the city of Debridan stretching beneath his feet like a string of beads. His shoes had ceased to cause him discomfort. There were modern buildings in the streets and the declining sun cast a white light on their rectangular shapes. For three whole years the previous regime had spared no effort to give the city a national character. It had added ornamental cornices and beams of native workmanship; it had even equipped the new public buildings, banks and bazaars with towers and turrets after the fashion of minarets. But these new sections of the town with their eccentric improvements were almost lost to view in a grey sea of narrow, winding streets and somber huts of baked clay. Washing had been hung out to dry on the roofs, and it swayed in the breeze, white, patched and many-colored. The dull expanse was pierced in places by minarets that rose straight upwards in hues of bright blue and bright green. These were real minarets, which had withstood the changes of many centuries; the delicate lines of their walls were varied with Moresque ornamentation in tasteful restraint.

Like desert flowers that never wither, they feared neither heat nor drought, but raised their blooms towards heaven amid the endless toil, hopes and illusions of mankind.

Assad let his gaze wander over the city, which rested like a picture in its frame between the valleys of the two rivers. To the north and the east the splendid villas of the upper class climbed the terraced hills. To the west, separated from the seraglio by one of the rivers, stood row upon row of red-painted barracks. The squalid, irregular huts that formed the poorer quarters of the town stretched southwards as far as the eye could see, till they were lost in the desert. Whatever the direction of the wind, there was always a smell of sweat and garlic from the south side of the town.

Which way should he go to begin his quest for the vanished Shahpur? Girls of more than earthly beauty were to be found not infrequently in the poverty and filth of the southern part of the town, like flowers that grow from beneath a rock and blossom in a desert tortured by heat and frost. They shone before the eye like minarets; they fascinated men as inevitably as mountain-deer lure the huntsman. Previously, when the region of Hussam-Eddin had inaugurated a new era, their very existence had impeded the enforcement of the law of monogamy, and now that reaction had been overthrown a second time, difficulties were still to be expected. Girls from the south part of the town worked as sales assistants in the modern bazaars and as typists and secretaries in public offices. Naturally, they were also employed in beauty parlors.

The only problem was to discover who had captured Nirsan's fancy; seducing him from the call of duty and of his country. Who and where?

Since the revolution Assad had had some experience in solving complex and tortuous problems, but this one was too much for him.

Only one thing was clear to him: in spite of everything, the Shahpur Nirsan was a man of firm character and strong will, fully aware of his social standing. The charms of the feminine sex would never decoy him into any breach of good taste. He would not be tempted by a mere typist, even if she were the loveliest flower in the southern part of the city.

Assad wondered whether to have a talk with the senior officers of the police force. They knew all about the favorite pursuits of the best society in the capital. He could approach them cautiously, without mentioning the Shahpur, and then he would know better where he stood.

But such a course would be dangerous. He could not allow any shadow of suspicion to fall on the Shah's family.

He decided to consult his wife, Kassiri. Her advice had often proved to be the best. A young woman of her beauty and intelligence had many contacts and a wealth of information. Women liked her, and she was popular with men of influence and understanding.

Assad sat down in his copper-colored sports car, drove away from the patrols of picked sentries guarding the seraglio and turned northwards into the street of Ahmad the Great. His villa was about ten miles from the town.

The sight of his own plot of earth, clinging to the south side of a green slope, gave Assad new confidence. It had the same effect on every visitor or traveler coming from the city. The white villa had not long been built and stood in the shade of phoeniz palms. Trees of many species grew in the orchard, which was surrounded by an avenue of poplars. A clear stream flowed down the hill-side through the orchard and continually changed the water in the enormous swimming-pool. In the evenings and at night there was a cool breeze from the blue mountains, which rose in lofty splendor in the distance.

Assad drove into the orchard and stopped in front of the garage, that was half hidden by spindle-trees. A group of peacocks beneath the ripening cherry-trees looked up at him, as if they wanted to ask: "Why are you so early today? The Shah must have lost the game very quickly—didn't he want his revenge?"

Assad went indoors into the vestibule, but his Negro servant John did not come to meet him. Usually John took his hat and his gloves and told him what Madam was doing. Apparently Kassiri did not expect him back so early and had dismissed the servants for the afternoon. No doubt she had withdrawn to the cool and elegant harem (which they kept as a secret between them) and was deep in a French or English novel. She would be sitting by the open window, where she could hear the rippling stream in the orchard and the shrill song of the crickets. Kassiri had been educated in Switzerland and she enjoyed good imaginative literature.

Assad took off his shoes, which fitted him so badly, and put on a pair of soft slippers made from kid-leather. He would creep in silently and surprise his beloved Kassiri by his unexpected return. She was his faithful wife, his third wife, but he had given up the other two. To him she was a star in the depth of night, the queen of his desires, a Shahsenem without peer. He had learned to know her well before choosing her for his own, and he had never regretted his choice.

Borne on the wings of love, Assad glided in his soft slippers over the soft carpets, like a shadow flitting from room to room.

The doors did not creak. The hinges had been properly oiled.

The bedroom was furnished in Western style, as befitted the new era, but beyond it lay the harem, a small room designed for his only wife. No expense had been spared on the Kashmir rugs for its floor and walls; it was scented with jasmine and at night it was lit by concealed lights.

Assad drew aside the curtain, which served instead of a door, and raised his hands in joy. But in the same moment his raised hands froze in the air; his breast seemed to turn to stone, and he could not breathe.

Kassiri was wearing light clothes, clothes a little too light even for a warm day. She was reclining on one side in an engaging posture amid the bright cushions. She was not holding a book in her hand. With both her hands she was stroking the form of a man. He was lying at ease with his face towards her. His gaze was fixed on her. He was lying very close to her. He was the Shahpur Nirsan.

Assad Pasha's quest was at an end.

Assad's hands dropped feebly to his sides, as if they had been cut off. All at once his body felt very heavy, as if he could scarcely carry his own weight. He did not step forward or speak; what could he say? Instead, he began to withdraw slowly, walking backwards, like a soldier who comes face to face with a wall of mountains, or an insuperable obstacle. As he retreated, Assad bumped against the bed and the chairs in the bedroom and he could scarcely find the door in the dining-room, but he did not make any noise, not the slightest sound.

Still walking backwards he reached the vestibule and sat down rigidly in the first chair he could find. If the well-trained John had seen him now, he would have asked in some consternation:

"A glass of cold water for my Pasha?"

Assad would have murmured to the Negro:

"She never looked so beautiful, so fantastically charming before!"

Assad had no need to hide his most intimate experiences from John. He could talk to him, not as to a stranger or a servant, but man to man.

But now Assad was alone in the vestibule. There was no one to see him. His heart was bursting, his head was splitting. He needed air and space.

He grabbed the shoes that were standing tidily where he had put them. He took off his slippers. He put on his shoes.

When he started the engine of his automobile and put it into reverse, the peacocks stopped hunting for cherries, stretched out their necks, and tilted their heads to one side, as if to ask: "Are you going back already? So soon?"

The car set off on the road back to Debridan. But what was the point of going there?

Assad's hands grew hot, as he grasped the steering-wheel. The old wound in his arm began to ache again.

He wondered whether he could report to the Shah where and how he had found the Shahpur Nirsan.

But the Shah's instructions had been brief and clear. His orders were to persuade the Shahpur of the error of his ways.

What means of persuasion could be used, when the heir to the throne was discovered in a situation so extraordinary, so unexpected and so unpredictable?

The Shah had given him the right to punish the criminal with his own hands, in accordance with the ancient custom of the Namiri. The Shah had also given him the right to punish the wanton, the partner in guilt, the unspeakable reprobate Kassiri. All the circumstances har been perfect for an "accident" to happen.

Why had he failed as a man and a Namir? Why had he betrayed the trust that the Shah placed in him? Why had he crossed his Lord's will? He had made no attempt to fulfill his task.

He thought of going back. But he was already half-way to Debridan.

When a man has once run away, he cannot turn back, least of all if he is a Namir and a Pasha.

Even so, Assad slowed down his automobile and wiped his brow. He began to think more calmly.

Perhaps it would be best to adhere strictly to constitutional procedure.

He could suggest that the Prime Minister should summon a Cabinet meeting and there he could explain everything.

The very idea made Assad shudder. He would be a laughing-stock to his colleagues in the Cabinet. He would be a laughing-stock to the whole country.

The only solution was to go straight back to the seraglio and make a report to the Shah. It was for Hussam-Eddin as the father of Nirsan an head of state to make the decision. Or he might choose another agent for the task.

But this idea was so desperate that Assad's automobile stopped of its own accord.

"It doesn't bear thinking about," said Assad to himself, as he tried to control his thoughts and a cold sweat broke from his brow. "It would only make the confusion worse."

After waiting a little and gazing vacantly through the windshield, Assad realized what he must do. He put the automobile into gear and drove on with slow determination.

III

Assad did not stop in Debridan. He drove straight through the town from north to south. Like an exemplary patriot and Minister for Home Affairs, he acknowledged courteously the salutes of the traffic police and stopped for the lights at every intersection, even though in Debridan, as in the rest of the country, motor vehicles were far from plentiful.

His goal was the Oasis of Destiny. It was the first oasis to the south of Debridan and about thirty miles away. In earlier times it had been the haunt of lions, tigers and other wild animals of the desert. They were attracted by the shade and the refreshing water of the springs. Besides, they developed a taste for the criminals of the capital and its neighborhood, who used to be brought to the Oasis on foot or in carts. Harder times began for the four-legged habitués of the place when Hussam-Eddin introduced democratic principles into the penal code, but their fortunes took a turn for the better with the growth of tourism. When foreign visitors brought them morsels of food, lions and even tigers learned to eat out of their hands and to pose for photographs. Enterprising businessmen set up refreshment-stalls and sold ices and soft drinks. When reaction regained the upper hand, the Oasis of Destiny became, as before, the rendezvous for criminals and wild beasts.

As he traveled south from the city, Assad noticed that the road to the Oasis was being thoroughly repaired and leveled. A concrete pavement was being laid to prevent dust, and at a short distance on either side, wicker fences were being erected to shield the road from sand-storms. Patently the Treasury expected a new wave of tourism to draw visitors, even from the land of the dollar. Indeed, if the negotiations at present in progress reached a successful conclusion.

Americans would certainly form the majority of the tourists.

Many of the officers in charge of the repairs and some of the workmen recognized Assad Pasha. They supposed that the Minister for Home Affairs was anxious to see whether their work was approaching completion; it would have to be finished before the wedding of the Shahpur.

Assad stopped by a bridge that was almost ready, and although he did not ask, one of the engineers came and assured him that the repairs would be finished in time. Assad believed him; although there still seemed to be plenty to do, he saw that the road was already passable throughout its length, provided that he drove with care. He expressed his appreciation of the engineers' efforts and took an interest in every detail.

It did not occur to anyone who saw or spoke to Assad Pasha that he did not expect to return from the Oasis.

He was determined not to turn back. He had failed in the task which the Shah had entrusted to him; he had proved himself incapable of defending the national interest or even of inflicting on the Shahpur and his temptress the accident that they deserved. All that he could do now was to meet with an accident himself. It was the only course open to a Namir, a man of duty, a man whose honor had been offended. Assad Pasha would be true to himself to his very last moment.

He no longer noticed that his elbow hurt him whenever he gave the steering-wheel a sharp turn. He did not notice how the heat of the day and of the engine made his feet swell till his shoes squeezed them. He removed his tie and unbuttoned his collar. His movements were automatic, like those of a man preparing for the decisive act of his life.

Presently he could see the Oasis. The spreading tops of the palms became visible beyond the deep sand-dunes. The Oasis enticed him like an island of tranquility amid the towering waves of sand in the raging sea of the desert. But the sea was stilled; only above the summits of the dunes the evening breeze raised a veil of sand like a transparent crest, sometimes pale blue and sometimes pink, as the setting sun filled the sky with golden light. Not far from the Oasis as the automobile drove up an incline at the end of the road and its tires crackled over a thin layer of sand, the shadows grew longer and ever darker in the valley. They were the shadows of Destiny and of Assad's last hours, that stretched their cool lengths over the burning sands.

Assad had no time to think about the shadows. He felt as if he were going into battle. It was not the first time in his life, but this time he already knew what the outcome would be. Yet he was resolute and prepared. He longed to know what would happen to him, or at least how it would happen.

He drove across the broken ridge of the sanddunes. Thickets of osiers with narrow, slivery leaves began at the bottom of the slope. The road followed them in a bend to the left; here the pavement was in good condition and free from sand. Grey thistles grew on mounds on the other side of the road and beyond them were teasels with dry leaves like blades of metal. The thistles had bright red flowers like fresh blood; the flowers of the teasels were a somber blue.

Assad drove slowly and carefully, as if the road were crooked or full of potholes. He was on his journey into the unknown. He passed the long expanse of osiers and entered the Oasis. The ground rose in gentle hillocks covered with tall, shining grasses, and sank away again in shallow valleys, where the verdure was richer. Here and there slender palms stood singly or in groups and the foliage at their tops swayed and rustled in the breeze. In places there were clusters of young palms, that raised themselves upwards with their long leaves resting on the ground.

Without pausing to contemplate the beauty of the scene. Assad stopped the automobile and climbed out. He showed no more concern than if he had come in his official capacity to determine where applicants should be allowed to set up refreshment-stalls and sell tea and cold drinks.

Then he noticed something. Another automobile was parked not far away in the shade of some low palm-trees. It was a two-seater sports car, like his own, but painted in an attractive shade of dark green. Assad had no desire to delay; but once he met his lion or lions, he did not want a third party to intervene and save his life. On coming closer he saw that the automobile was empty; the owner had left neither possessions nor weapons in it. The only relic was the Stars and Stripes waving silently over the bonnet. Some American from the Trade Delegation must have come fearlessly and without companions to visit the most famous oasis in Namiristan.

Assad made his way towards the main pool; there, when the sun was setting and the muezzins from the minarets summoned the whole country to prayer, the lions used to come to drink. They came in hope of food, too. Assad strode noiselessly through the grass. He could hear his heart beating violently in his breast, as if it wanted to hold him back.

A lioness was resting on the trampled grass of a slope that led down to the pool. She kept licking her lips and blinking her eyes, as she listened, contented and half-asleep, to the rustling of the palms. Her three cubs, not yet a year old, were playing by themselves in the grass. One of them was sitting up on his haunches and struggling in vain to pull his head out of a white topee. He threw his head from side to side and tugged at the topee with both forepaws, but he could not get it off. Another cub was tapping pensively at a broken camera and examining its interior. The third had entangled himself in an endless roll of black, shiny film; happy in his predicament, he ran about in the grass, leaping and biting at the crackling band that trailed after him.

There were other recent remains to be seen. It was obvious that one or perhaps two Americans had beaten Assad to his goal. Possibly that had not been their intention.

The only thing left for him to do was to continue on his way into the depth of the Oasis in hope of meeting a hungry lion. When the lioness saw a human being go past between the palms, she rose lazily to her feet, gave her cubs a commanding glance and withdrew to one side where the bushes were thicker. The cubs followed her. The one with the roll of film had ensnared his feet in it and another cub tugged at it from behind to tease him. The cub with the topee had more trouble than his brothers; it was hanging from his neck and kept banging against his legs.

Suddenly Assad heard a hushed whisper above his head; it came from somewhere in a half-grown palm that was bent. It changed at once into a broken whistle. Very much against his will Assad stopped in his path and looked up. A pair of female legs was hanging from the bent palm. They were alive. They were clad in elegant nylons and a tiny pair of shoes made in Western style. Although Assad's thoughts were already in the next world, he noticed that they were a shapely pair of legs and made a charming picture with the slender trunk of the palm in the background.

A girl's round face poked itself out between the broad leaves of the palm. It was pale from terror but at the same time lit up with unutterable hope. The eyes were already shining to greet their rescuer.

"Mister Sheikh! Mister Sheikh! I just can't hold on any longer! My hands are numb!"

"Jump down," said Assad in a dry tone. "You can see the lions have had their fill."

"But I can't! I shall only fall. Do be a kind Sheikh; hold out your arms and catch me."

Assad stood directly beneath the palm and held out his arms. He forgot about the weakness in his left elbow. He had suffered so many blows in one day that another would mean very little to him.

This was how he used to meet Kassiri on his return home in earlier days, before he suffered his wound. She would jump from the raised porch of their villa straight into his arms. The American girl felt just as soft and warm and she clung firmly to his neck just like Kassiri, but she was taller and heavier. Assad took a deep breath and was on the point of putting his burden on the ground.

"For Heaven's sake, don't put me down! My legs are stiff and I shan't be able to walk. Carry me back to the automobile."

What else could a Namir with an Oxford education do? He set off carrying the American girl with her arms clasped tightly round his neck. Selflessly he summoned up all his remaining strength for the task.

The path back to the car seemed to have grown longer and more uneven. Assad's feet bumped against mounds of earth, became caught in tufts of grass, and sank into potholes. His elbow ached and smarted, his legs bent and his feet stumbled, but he did not give up. At times he began to think that he was already in the next world, and that as a reward for his services to his country Allah had given him an American houri, a girl of paradise, to carry in his arms. Thanks be to Him for not fulfilling the Koran's promise of several!

Sometimes, when the long grass wrapped itself round Assad's feet and compelled him to stop, his thoughts returned to this world. He became sufficiently conscious of his surroundings to save himself from falling. A married man at the head of the Home Ministry could not afford to fall with a strange woman in his arms.

Perspiring and red in the face, Assad at last reached his journey's end and prepared to deposit his charge in the nearer of the two automobiles. It was the one with the American flag.

"I can't drive after all I've been through today," said the girl. "Would you be so kind as to take me in your automobile? That other one is yours, isn't it? Perhaps you could take the late General Peacock's automobile in tow?"

Assad Pasha set the girl down on the bonnet of his car and looked her straight in the eyes. The pallor in her sunburnt face and the terror in her blue, tearful eyes told him what had happened. Now it all became clear to him. The topee which the lion-cub had carried off and the broken camera had belonged to General Joe Peacock. Certain other pathetic human remains had been his too.... He was the head of the United States Delegation to Namiristan; he had an excellent record of service in the World War II, but now the lions of Namiristan had disposed of him, while the Minister for Home Affairs was occupied with personal problems rather than attending to the safety of distinguished visitors. Personal affairs were of no great significance in comparison with Assad Pasha's public responsibilities. But at least his shortcomings were not unique; at this very moment Namiri of even higher rank were neglecting their duty to the state. They were bent on satisfying their personal and, indeed, physiological needs.

Encouraged a little by the new turn which his thoughts were taking, Assad raised his heavy and aching head. The girl's eyes were still fixed on him, and although full of sorrow and distress, they had begun to regain their clarity and charm. Already, by the judicious application of aids to feminine beauty, her face had recovered its allure.

After a short silence the girl smiled a smile of resignation and began to speak with naive sincerity.

"I guess Joe meant to ask for my hand today. Maybe it was because of my tolerable appearance, or maybe he was affected by the preparations for the wedding of the heir to the throne. Everybody's talking about the Shahpur Nirsan and the Shahsenem Adile; the newspapers haven't room for anything else. I don't mind saying that in men's eyes I'm not just an ordinary girl but this year's Miss America, Her Majesty the Beauty Queen of the United States. At college I studied Middle Eastern languages, so they hired me for this Delegation. That's why I'm here."

This new wonder in a day of surprises took Assad's breath away. He was utterly at a loss what to say and how to behave. He stared at the Beauty Queen, who had fallen from heaven or from America, and waited to see what more she had to tell him.

"I guess Joe wanted to choose a real romantic spot for his confession," she continued. "But even when we'd arrved here, he kept putting it off and waiting for the perfect moment, like the dear, silly boy he was. When he saw the lioness with the cubs, he just had to go and take a photograph. I warned him, but he insisted on going as close as he could. He wanted to show off a bit in front of me, that he was so manly and courageous. The lioness didn't like it."

There was nothing more to add. Her story was only too clear. Lowering her head, she paused in recollection of the man for whom she had worked and whose shy affections she had perhaps aroused; he had been alive such a short time ago! After a little while she began to feel more grateful than ever for being alive and for the womanly instinct of fear, to which she owed her preservation. She realized that she must express her appreciation to the stranger who had rescued her from her alarming and uncomfortable refuge at the top of the palm. She stretched out both her hands towards him and said:

"I thank you with all my heart! My name's Daisy Harrington."

"And I am Ben Nahim Assad Pasha, Minister for Home Affairs."

"You have very efficient security in Namiristan."

"Firty-fifty. Precisely fifty-fifty, Your Majesty. The rescue of Miss America may perhaps make amends for certain shortcomings."

By this time Assad Pasha felt very much better. He was in command of the situation once more, and was beginning to recognize the possibilities it held for the Minister for Home Affairs. Without saying anything more he made ready to lift Miss Harrington chivalrously from the bonnet and carry her to the seat of his automobile.

"Thank you, Pasha, I don't need help this time." She jumped down with graceful agility, straightened the pleats of her skirt, which had become creased in the palm-tree, and took Assad Pasha by the arm.

She was leading him to his own car. It was extraordinary! And he could do nothing about it; he did not want to do anything about it. She went on talking in steady, uninhibited tones, and he could hear the grass rustling beneath her footsteps; he could hear her plum-colored skirt rustling as it swung lightly about her legs. His arm touched her side and he was aware of the brisk, youthful rhythm of her gait. He was aware of the supple, tempting undulation of her breasts. Without seeking to draw comparisons, he became acutely conscious of the difference between a living body and a corpse. A man has only to accept life and he will find new experiences and new creative opportunities.

Everything might have turned out differently, if he had been aware of himself as a living being when she jumped from the palm-tree. Shocked and terrified, she had put her arms round his neck and her blond hair had mingled with his own black locks, but he had not noticed it. He had not noticed what he carried all the way back to the automobile. Had he realized, he would have tumbled to his knees in the grass from delight.

Now Assad's eye took in her whole form, although he did not look at her directly. She was a Shahsenem of beauty, charming in her build and in her movements, a woman whose presence blinded the intellect and set the blood on fire. Although they only walked a few steps together, this was enough to make the Namir of the old order come to life again in Assad. He would gladly have returned to tradition and confined her in his harem. He would have confined himself there with her Kassiri could know, for all he cared.

The thought of Kassiri roused him from his dream, reminding him of the events of the day, the national crisis and his own heavy responsibility. With a shudder he pictured what had happened in the Oasis; he imagined what Miss Harrington had lived through and he admired the queenly fortitude with which she hid her feelings.

When they reached the car, Assad Pasha gallantly freed his hand from her arm and opened the door.

"No," said Miss Harrington. "I'll help you tie Joe Peacock's automobile to yours. We'll do it quicker together."

Her words captivated him still more, setting a new harmony in his thoughts and his feelings.

IV

After sunset a cool, refreshing breeze blew from the mountains in the north-east. It filled the sunbaked and perspiring town with the smell of southern woods, magnolias, yellow rhododendrons and ... wild onions. Rather than stay stifling indoors, the inhabitants came out into the open air. They floated into the streets and the bazaars, bringing new vitality into the city's preparations for the great festival. Electricians in blue overalls climbed tall red ladders and fastened colored lights to doorposts, windows and cornices in the main streets, and on public buildings and the houses of eminent dignitaries. On the balconies men were trying out rugs to see which ones to hang for the wedding; their movements were slow and many of them wore beards. In place there were crowds of spectators, of whom some could pride themselves on their good taste. Pickpockets mingled with the crowds, and from the side-streets came beggars in clothes that had been reduced to rags by time or on purpose. Presently policemen, some mounted and some on foot, followed in the tracks of the beggars. They wore uniforms of British style, and they urged the beggars to bear their lot in patience without showing themselves in the streets for the next few days; they no longer beat them, as they used to when the reactionary regime was in power.

Approaching from the south, a copper-colored sports car drove into the street of Serabd the Conqueror. It was towing another car, which was dark green and empty, except for the Stars and Stripes on the bonnet. The leading car was open and the Minister for Home Affairs in person sat at the wheel. By his side was a foreign woman with blond hair and a fresh complexion.

A murmur of interest and bewilderment crept along the street of Serabd the Conqueror from one end to the other. Citizens of Debridan, who had come out on hasty errands or merely to converse and take the air, stood still at the edge of the sidewalks. Old-fashioned women drew their veils a little to one side to get a better view. The electricians and the men with the rugs turned round from their work.

What could have happened? What had happened to Assad Pasha to make him drive through the heart of the city with an American woman at his side? Had this protagonist of monogamy taken a second wife? Or, if bent on such a step, was he still merely paving the way?

Consumed with curiosity, the Namiri watched the automobile as it drove slowly past; they looked at its two occupants and then at one another. Those lacking Western refinements scratched their heads or their beards. They admired the girl's beauty, even if they did not know that she was Miss America, and she for her part waved her hand to the people on either side; it was not the first time that a crowd had greeted her with a standing ovation. A smile of triumph and satisfaction beamed from her face, as if she had not been won as a second wife but had herself won a second husband or a third. The Namiri were still more puzzled in spite of their more or less slight acquaintance with Western customs. They did not know how to greet the Minister for Home Affairs or the unexceptional figure of the foreign woman or the police, who appeared in growing numbers at the corners.

Not far from the Ministry for Home Affairs Assad Pasha stopped his car near where a mounted policeman was on duty. The policeman rode up, dismounted from his black Arab steed and saluted. Cupping his hand to his ear, he listened to Assad Pasha's instructions. Then he rode away at a smart trot to the Central Police Station.

Assad turned into the street of Ahmad the Great and drove on as slowly as before, as if he wanted everyone to see his beautiful foreigner. He was making for his residence.

"He's bringing his second wife home," people whispered to one another. "No, she's not his second wife; she's his fourth. Not a bad wife either, with an automobile of her own. But what will Kassiri have to say about it? She's been a protagonist of monogamy too, and she's a woman with a will of her own."

Assad Pasha turned into the drive of his villa, jumped out and helped Miss Harrington out of the car.

"Behave as if we were the closest of friends," said he to remind her of the agreement they had made on the journey. "Behave just as if we were in love."

"I'll do my best; you can rely on me. I'm beginning to wonder what this day will lead to."

Lights were shining in the drawing-room of the villa, but there was still no sign of the attentive servant John. Assad conjectured that Kassiri was still entertaining guests whom the servants were not to see. She herself had not come to meet her husband, although she could hear him coming home almost at his usual time. Apparently the Shahpur Nirsan, having made the most of his conquest, was in no hurry to go home but was resting and enjoying the company of another man's wife. He must be out of his mind to think that he could do as he liked. He had no respect for his father, the Shah, no thought for the danger he was bringing upon the state and no consideration for the Minister for Home Affairs, the officer responsible for law and order.

These thoughts made Assad's blood boil. Even so, he offered his arm with perfect restraint to the ally he had won by his selfishness, and together they went up the steps into the vestibule. As she pressed his arm, Daisy Harrington sensed the emotions in her rescuer's breast, but after the experiences of the day she was not afraid of anything.

Kassiri and her guest were drinking tea in the drawing-room. They were sitting face to face, heedless of the world around them. A plate of sweetened Oriental fruits stood between them. Nothing fell from the hands of either of them, when they saw Assad come into the room. They had expected him and were ready for him. Yet they could not have expected him to return arm-in-arm with a girl who might have been dropped from heaven, a girl of considerable allure and obviously in love with him. How could they have imagined anything like this?

The Shahpur Nirsan was the first to rise to his feet, although his superior rank would have allowed him to remain seated. Kassiri could not stand up quite as quickly, as a good hostess does to welcome a visitor. She was in some confusion.

"I've something important to tell you," said Nirsan to the master of the house. He preserved his composure with an effort.

"I'm sure you have," replied Assad without much subtlety. "But first allow me to introduce Her Illustrious Highness Daisy Harrington, Beauty Queen of the United States."

The Shahpur Nirsan smiled and clicked his heels like a candle catching fire of its own accord. The shell that his rank and education gave him was not resistant to feminine charms.

"Welcome, Star of Beauty from distant America!" he exclaimed and added, mndful of his representative function: "Your visit is an honor to my country."

"Your Royal Highness," said Miss Harrington with cool reserve, as she leaned affectionately on Assad's arm. "I've had a very mixed welcome from your country. But for Ben Nahim's foresight and heroism, I should have been eaten by the lions of Namiristan."

"Kassiri, go and prepare a room for our guest." Assad spoke to his wife as men did in earlier times.

"Miss Harrington needs to rest here in your care and recover from the terrible experiences she has had."

"Very well, I will," said Kassiri, bowing her head. Her spirit was already bowed by her own unexpected experiences.

She felt as if she had sunk through the floor to her knees. She was feebler and smaller than the foreign woman who had appeared from nowhere. The husband whom she had deceived and who deserved to be deceived was taking his revenge with an American Beauty Queen. The Shahpur Nirsan, who had spread his whole kingdom at her feet and refused for her sake to marry the Shahsenem Adile, was now all on fire for some artificial Queen, whose reign could only last a year. But she herself was a woman rooted in the ancient civilization of the East; what could she do but obey her husband, however much she hated him at this moment?

In the doorway Kassiri met John. Now that he at last put in an appearance, he announced the arrival of new guests. There were a great many of them.

Soon the drawing-room was half-full. The guests included the United States Ambassador with the First Secretary, the Chief of Police of Debridan with his staff, and a host of reporters and photographers from Namiri and foreign newspapers. The American Ambassador expressed his surprise and appreciation on finding that the first to congratulate his fellow citizen on her rescue had been the Shahpur Nirsan, even though His Royal Highness would shortly leave for Idaristan to bring home his bride, the Shahsenem Adile.

Kassiri followed the last of the visitors into the drawing-room. Even in the depth of her chagrin, irresistible curiosity compelled her to come.

Daisy Harrington was a woman of good education, and in America she had grown used to the officiousness of photographers and the importunity of newspapermen. She told her story briefly, in simple and graphic words, while she leaned gracefully on the arm of her rescuer, as if, after all she had undergone, she still needed the unflinching support of a strong man. Besides, she wanted to display her gratitude to one who had behaved so chivalrously at the critical hour.

"I guess I don't have to go into all the details," she said. "General Peacock wanted to take advantage of a pause in the negotiations and show me the Oasis. He'd been there before. I thought it would be fine on such a hot day to go for a ride in the sports car with the Chief of our Delegation. In the Oasis we saw a lioness with her cubs, just like on a coat-of-arms. General Peacock reckoned he'd take a photograph to bring back home as a souvenir. At first the lioness seemed quite tame and full of curiosity."

Assad Pasha confirmed that Miss Harrington had told him exactly the same story in the Oasis.

The United States Ambassador, a tall gaunt figure, took two steps forward.

"It's very sad about Joe Peacock," said he. "He was a brave man and a great officer. But as of now we've plenty of generals in America and we're very proud of them. We only choose one Beauty Queen of the United States every year. On behalf of all my fellow citizens I express my most sincere gratitude to the Honorable Assad Pasha for saving the life of Miss America."

Unanimous applause greeted the Ambassador's well-chosen words. When it was over, he went up to Miss Harrington and invited her to stay at the Embassy. He promised that he and his wife would give her every attention and comfort. Daisy Harrington turned to Assad.

"What shall I do?" asked she. "I've already accepted your invitation, Ben Nahim."

Kassiri, who was standing apart from the others, heaved a deep sigh and sat down on the nearest chair. She hid her face in her hands.

Assad Pasha's glance fell on his wife and on the Shahpur Nirsan. He took Daisy Harrington by the hand and said:

"Exceptional beauty carries with it obligations and binds you more closely to your country. You must follow the customs of your country and obey its demands. You'd better go back with the Ambassador."

Daisy Harrington took both her rescuer's hands in hers and squeezed them. Then she linked arms with the Ambassador and went out of the room with him.

The police and the newspapermen left. Kassiri withdrew; perhaps she went to see the last visitors depart. She was shaken and humiliated.

The Shahpur Nirsan and Assad Pasha were left alone. The two men had something to tell each other.

But although they had been waiting for this moment, each still needed a little time to think over what he had to say.

The Shahpur Nirsan was stocky and broad-shouldered, always swift in thought and quick to act. He looked out of the window. He took his time before turning round and resuming his seat. Such an eminent guest sat on the best settee.

"Have you anything to smoke?"

Without a word Assad Pasha opened a silver box of Egyptian cigarettes on the table and offered them to the Shahpur. Then he took one himself. He offered his eminent guest a light. He lit his own cigarette and sat down facing the Shahpur. They were ready to talk as man to man.

After drawing once and again on his cigarette, the Shahpur Nirsan broke the silence.

"Perhaps the goings on I've just seen were a little comedy that you planned for the sake of its effect on me. Ministers for Home Affairs in Namiristan have always had their little jokes."

"You can think whatever you like."

"But . . . one action of yours had a very great effect on me. When you came home the first time today and opened the curtain into the . . . er . . . I saw you."

Assad gripped the edge of the table and looked hard at Nirsan

His gaze was not that of a humble subject or an obedient servant; it was the gaze of a judge.

"Then I realized how much I had sinned against you and my loyal friends. You showed self-control."

"Don't talk about that."

"All the same I ought to be as capable of self-control as you are."

The Shahpur stood up.

"I shall go and fetch Adile, curse her! My old father will be pleased and the interests of the state will be safe. We Orientals can't allow women to determine our actions."

"You're doing right." Assad Pasha began to unbend.

"For your part promise me one thing: don't punish Kassiri. Behave like a European this time. There are not many women like her. Only, to take care of her, I'd advise you to employ a eunuch. An armed eunuch."

Translated by Raphael Sealey

Jurgis Savickis

JURGIS SAVICKIS

JURGIS SAVICKIS, born in Ariogala, Lithuania, on May 2, 1890, studied law at the University of Moscow. When Lithuania became independent, he joined the country's diplomatic corps and spent most of his life as an envoy to various European countries. He also served briefly as director of the State Theater. Following the occupation of Lithuania by Soviet Russia, he was relieved of his post as envoy to the League of Nations in Geneva. He then moved to Roquebrune, southern France, where he died on December 22, 1952.

    Savickis made an impact on Lithuanian letters as a stylistic innovator. He published three collections of short stories, *Sventadienio sonetai* (Holiday Sonnets), 1922; *Ties aukstu sostu* (Beside the High Throne), 1928; and *Raudoni batukai* (Red Shoes), 1951. He also wrote the novel *Sventoji Lietuva* (Holy Lithuania), 1952, and four travelogues under the pen name of J. Rimosius. His last book, *Zeme dega* (The Earth Aflame), a panoramic memoir, was published after this death.

JURGIS SAVICKIS

(1890-1952)

The Red Shoes

JUST look what the spring does to people! They become excited. Take me, for example. I'm not young any more, and yet some devil makes me whirl. My blood begins to boil, as though I were a youngster who had put on his student's cap for the first time. What courage I have! And how many ridiculous things I do! Things that look brave, logical, and essential, yet they only make other people laugh. Because I am young.

Today, for example, is Sunday. Instead of going to the drugstore, where my wife and the doctor have sent me to have my varicose veins attended to, I am walking on Kaunas street, following a lady who is a complete stranger to me. She is wearing a tailored suit; and I believe that she is a true Sunday "widow."

If I didn't go to the drugstore I should be going to church. When I attend Sunday services I go to the cathedral, because it's more interesting there; the priest delivers his sermons a little better than do priests in other churches. After church, I generally have my breakfast and dinner at home.

I am a practicing Christian, and that satisfies me. But I'm not a fanatic. I respect the creeds of other people. So, as you see, I'm quite a carefree fellow. Once in a while I like to be merry. I have in mind the cultural amusements, of course. Coming back to the ladies, I do not seek any "occasions." I'm married.

But after my wife went away, I was alone and free. Not free in a bad sense. The city intrigues me today, as a toy intrigues a child. Otherwise I am quite a serious-minded man, and an executive of no small rank. No one would believe it! If one looked at my tie and coat, one would say I am like the rest of the people, in a Sunday mood. But, actually, I'm vice-director of my department!

Keenly, I scan the street. I feel as though I were again in Paris, back in the good old days when I used to walk along those deserted Paris streets on Sundays during the summer. I seldom reminisce about Paris and my days at the Sorbonne. Remembering Paris is not one of my duties now. I have enough work of my own at the office, where I'm noted for my zealous attitude; I enjoy talking to people, and now and then quite a few subordinates of mine have to stay with me after office hours. I sometimes believe that if it weren't for me, the whole machinery of the state would stop moving. However, the employees are not angry with me; they feel that I give them extra work for their own good.

I see the "widow" talking to a man with a car. Cars are not abundant in our town, which we call "the temporary capital." And each of us knows almost all the owners at sight. She doesn't talk long. He gets back into his machine and drives away, leaving her alone. Being all by herself, she stops at a store and gazes at the fine things in the window. There is nothing so wonderful as a morning in the city. It is full of mysterious waiting and hoping for the coming day.

A stylish gray little skirt stretches over her pillow-like buttocks very nicely. The swish of her silk skirt can be heard as she walks. Her well-shaped legs are covered with fine stockings. What can be more beautiful than a woman's pretty legs, so full of temptation, so deliciously dangerous! That is, when one is ready for everything. She is tall and her profile is enticing. Two silver fox skins are lying heavily on her shoulders. That can convince any man and give her a *raison d'etre.* The woman walks on, and her white blouse under her suit is half open. And so forth, and so on.

"You're beautiful, no doubt about it." Now she will probably buy a loaf of bread and walk home to have breakfast.

"Greetings!" She does not say it with words, she says it with her eyes. But it is as if I heard her voice. Without even turning her head, she passes me by. She must have noticed that I was looking for "Paris," and that I am not quite in complete control of myself.

"Who is she? Do I know her? Is she a client?" She has behaved seriously and kindly toward me. Now I'm not sure whether I may have met her at some social function, or at the Ministry. But she walks away. As I have nothing better to do, I keep following her on my swollen legs. I do not answer her, not even with a smile. I keep walking, as if it were a punishment of God. Even the lady is distracted because of me. She walks a little faster, and hurries to get out of sight.

"Who is she? Could she be a woman of easy virtue?"

There are some men who mistreat that kind of woman. They

don't pay them what they are supposed to, and otherwise insult them. They also try to be impolite. Not I. I am always polite with everybody. I think that men like those others should be beaten. Sometimes they are men of high rank. They should be beaten with canes, burned logs, or anything at hand.

My goddess has disappeared. I get sentimental and start lecturing myself, as a priest would do to me. A peculiar religious Sunday mood tries to take me over.

I buy no medicine. The reason: the drugstores are closed. I walk back home. But I'm full of thoughts, as if I were about to write a story. I'm off balance. Should I go to the Ministry today?

All the women look well-dressed today. Because it's spring. It's lighter and lovelier everywhere. As if in this society everything were already regulated, and life easy. There won't be any rain today. Crowds of young people are moving out of the city—that is, everyone who is able to move. Some of them are riding their bicycles, others are walking. They are all gay and noisy. The day will long be remembered by everybody. Some, especially women, will remember it for the rest of their lives. Some of the women apparently cannot travel to the suburbs. They are probably waiting for their escorts. But all of them are smiling silently, and their hair is fixed carefully, because today is Sunday. Their clothes caress their flesh, and they all look happy and satisfied, and interesting. How do they know how to display what should be shown and especially what should not? They probably learned it at school, and that covers their education. This eternal coquetry!

I'm all by myself at home. My wife went abroad a few days ago. "To get away from family life,"—she said. Although we live very soberly. But, in any case, one needs gleams of light. Furthermore, she said, she had to do some shopping. Everybody knows that one spends money much faster abroad. She will have enough time to begin to miss me. But she did not know then where she was going. She had not yet decided. It's a usual thing with women. Until she meets some grandma on her way and arranges a definite schedule for her trip. Once she's back, I'll be pacing the floor in my department, as usual, and she will resume arranging her charity teas and social gatherings with the other Kaunas ladies, and they will necessarily be called "five o'clocks." And we will both be successful. I will become old. I may become a secretary general, and that ranks higher than vice-director and even director; sometimes it is on the same level with minister. Although I have some political connections with the conservative elements, I am not interested in politics. I do not care ever to become a minister. That's how I feel today.

But something has happened, and all at once I must, I must go abroad. The Ministry is sending me to Lausanne, to a special Social Help Conference. The conference, as I see it, has been well organized. There will be plenty of guests. Even from the Far East. From India and elsewhere. I will prepare myself well.

It's a pleasure to travel. No one knows who you are. Like some kind of Lord Halifax or Dundendron van Housen, you're bumping over the foreign roads. Only that devil spring, that got into me while I was in Kaunas, still does not want to leave me alone.

Am I bidding a farewell to my youth? Who's going to beat whom? What a tournament, a kind of game! The majestic game that everyone has watched. I look deeply at women's eyes in "Mitrope," as I pace the coach. I irritate the other men on purpose. Sometimes I put a rosebud or a nice spring flower into the buttonhole of my coat. The deuce with it! What do I care! One can afford to do so when one is over forty. I travel by myself. Young, curious and rich. And deep inside, I keep thinking: even if I remain vice-director until I retire on my pension, I shall be satisfied. There would be fewer worries, for I know my work. I have saved enough money and have made no debts. I haven't a big estate, either. When land reform came to the Republic, I did not purchase a single piece of land, as some of my confreres did. Now they're going crazy because of it; they sit in their comfortable chairs at the Ministry, and try to manage their farms by telephone. All these friends of mine are eating dry bread at home. They cannot afford to go any place, and, with all their estates, they have never had peace. They have fallen into debt up to their ears, and they look so funny to me. They don't love their soil, they don't plow it. Either you yourself work on the farm or you leave it. Once in a while, I can at least leaf through a book. And I can help out my older sister, the teacher who has remained on the farm. Let her enjoy her old age there. The other day, I even put in a new stove for her. I ask nothing in return. We have never argued over what belongs to whom. What do we care? I have no children. My wife and I live well. What more should I want?

The women intrigued me while I was coming back from the congress. Although it was midnight, I decided to walk to my hotel. I felt so gay and carefree.

I have noticed that people pay more attention to the congressional parties and their meals than to the congress itself. The bigger the congress is, the more fun they have. This seems to be the goal of all such meetings. Women are very eager to make new connections and create friendships. They probably are in the same good mood as I am, and they all want to enjoy themselves. With their newly purchased clothes and carefully chosen moods. For abroad all people appear as if "they were not the same."

A young woman, some journalist, I suppose, the one who brought a large volume for us to put our signatures in, dominated the congress at the beginning. I told her that I could only write verses in the ladies' albums.

"*Eh bien! Dans ce cas là—de la poésie!*"

"Don't you think this is a little out of date? *Un petit peu démodé....*"

Next to my name I made an anchor. It meant "Hope."

That lifted my lady friend's mood even higher. She now completely forgot my promised verses. She herself grabbed my anchor —the one I had launched.

"More! More!"

"What more?"

"About your country, of course."

I write—"Lithuanie." But because I want to appear patriotic, I add in Lithuanian—"*Lietuva.*"

She asks me again:

"Since you're such a good writer, let me have a motto, a motto."

"But I have no motto in my life."

I looked at an official paper in my briefcase and was about to copy our White Knight, which actually is very handsome and militant, into her album, but there were so many people jostling me. They pushed me away from her.

Glad I did not do it. It might have ended the same way it had in Vienna's Prater several years ago, when I drew a crown of laurels in a restaurant guest book. It has two ribbons around it, and was held by two doves. Underneath one I signed my name; underneath the other Mme. Deveikis signed hers. That was a lucky coincidence. I had met her in a strange land, and I thought it was only patriotism on my part to try to make the way of a fellow Lithuanian easier.

When I came back home, my wife met me at the door and looked at my face suspiciously.

"Well, well, how was that supper with Mme. Deveikis?"

I was stunned.

"And what did those two doves mean?"

"That—is a regional custom."

When I glance occasionally at the lady journalist,—those stolen glimpses,—I notice that she too is observing me. Well, well! One can read her eyes easily: she is so serious and I—so frivolous. It was only for a moment. But, in life, such moments are frequently very significant and endure for a long time. Already she has disappeared among the other guests. Now I notice that there is something of the sea about her. Her hair is pulled to one side. It is a little reddish, and it ripples over her head. And she prances about like an Arabian horse. She betrays herself in her actions and language. And I am not sorry that I had mentally used such a word as "horse." After all, Lithuania is an agricultural country.

A delegate from Switzerland with a stomach like the stump of a tree, a celebrity and an expert on international social questions—that's probably why he wears that long heavy beard—has noticed that I was paying attention to the lady organizer of the congress.

"She's our most prominent poet."

How poetic everything is today!

Later, there was a performance on the stage. The folk dancers from the village were invited to show us their local dances. Other people sang. There was plenty of applause and an abundance of drinks—and speeches. Oh, those speeches!

If I wanted, I could probably sneak out with this lady to a park or to some small restaurant. We could surely find a common language.

But I do not invite her, and I don't even try to start a conversation with her, although I would like to deepen my knowledge of modern Swiss poetry with her help. She smiles at me during the lectures and lets me know that she likes me.

"Where would you put her, you old wolf! You might be crying afterwards. Let her fly around the fire and roam with other men, according to her Bohemian tradition." As a serious-minded fellow, I begin to think about my wife, even if she is not as young as my charmer.

To enrich its social studies, the congress was invited to take a boat ride on Lake Leman and to see the fireworks at night. I declined and instead went to bed, as is proper for a well-bred citizen who is one of the pillars of the fatherland. And I always think about my wife. I leave "night studies" to the others. Still, how can a man who is not very old, though not too young either, decline the fireworks and bright lights of the city? . . . Fireworks . . . spangles . . . the night! And the flashes of lightning in women's eyes! Wherever I go, a red-headed lady, whose face looks a trifle dusty, gazes at me tenderly, and she offers me a glass of beer.

Walking on the street, I meet again a lovely Japanese girl from our congress. She's slender, with attractive feminine lines, and eyes like slits stretched upwards. They are good and naive, those Japanese women—to walk all alone at this time of the night. A Mexican and a New Zealand woman catch up with her. They are probably hurrying to their hotel. I could catch up with them, too. If I became acquainted with them, I could extend my knowledge of life. It would be pleasant to get acquainted with such a lovely Japanese girl and exchange opinions on various matters—even after one o'clock at night. Where do they all live? I don't know. We are all dispersed throughout the city hotels. I bow in a courtly manner to them—we all happened to come back to the same hotel, all of us. But my favorite is the slim Japanese with her intelligent and smiling eyes, so child-like. How wise can those Japanese women be, like this one. For, as one can see, she can control her husband through the attractiveness of family life, through fidelity, humility and feminine poetry, of which she has an inexhaustible spring.

I'm at home, in the hotel. But there's such a turmoil in my head. It is as if I were still listening to the last chords of a Strauss waltz. It's calm. The way it has always been after balls, when you have seen an old and exciting cancan.

I've put a bandage on my swollen leg, and also some compresses. I could fall asleep any moment now. I've also put my shoes outside to be shined—they had led me a long way through the strange city.

But to put your shoes outside in a big city hotel is not an easy matter. It's quite an operation, especially when the people in the hotel do not know each other, or don't want to know each other, or are looking forward to getting acquainted.

All manner of shoes are standing in line: Alpine shoes, even those of women. How can a woman wear such clogs in the summertime? They probably belong to some excursion group. A little farther, I see family shoes, good-looking ones. But in front of my own room—stands a pair of red shoes. A real contrast to the other shoes, elegant, with holes cut in front. They're standing in good order. That means that the lady is respectable, not sloppy. And all these shoes are waiting for tomorrow.

They are—Japanese shoes.

If I walked in, she probably would be a little surprised, but she would not become hysterical. She'd be wearing her silk pajamas, of course, with white large ibises. But it would be embarrassing if she started screaming in her Samurai language, which nobody understands here. More likely, she would only look calmly at me, suspecting nothing, and ask:

"*Vous voulez—?*"

She's not asleep yet. What if I tried to reach her by phone?

And if she is asleep—what chastity!

I stroke my forehead so intently that my shoes, which I had intended to put outside to be shined, fall from my hand. And again I walk to bed. I cannot forget the Japanese girl for a long time.

It was strange that I dreamed only of mothers and fighting devils that night.

The next morning, I again remembered legs. This time—my own. They hurt me. There are wrinkles under my eyes. I certainly miss my wife. Where is she now? If she could only have come here! But no woman has ever joined her husband while he was at work. I really should stop using the word "work." And my wife's not "old"—who has ever said that?—and she would look quite elegant among the others.

It's morning. In company with other guests I kill time in the exquisite lobby of the hotel. We do not know yet how to start the day. We are all congress people. And look how many of them! They're all preparing themselves for something important, and they look so very busy.

One woman appears, stocky and short. It looks as if God had too much clay left and He put it on her in abundance. As if God had had nothing better to do. Or as if an artist, who was tired of making a statue of clay, had thrown together the handful of leftovers, not giving a damn where they might fall. He made such a bulbous nose on her face. Blapt! Take that! A large hamburger of a nose. And she looks more like a man. She has heavy shoulders and very short legs. But her hair, which is neatly combed, gives her a tender, feminine touch.

I have seen her in the congress before, only I can't remember which country she comes from. She's busy preparing for the coming day; she is leaning over her foreign papers, handbooks, and her school notebook, in which she has scribbled many lines. I don't see any more men around. Some of them have gone to the city, and some of them are still asleep. The ladies are alone. Before I came here, I decided to follow the congressional work methodically; therefore, I do not avoid the women. One never knows where one can get an inspiration.

To the other lady who is sitting in the lobby a servant brings some water, to wash down her morning medicine. She looks awfully pale, but she's tall and stylish. She, too, is working on her morning correspondence; maybe she's writing out her checks. Her face looks hard and she too gives an impression of being a man rather than a woman. Does she have a heart? Although she does smile graciously at the servant.

"Could one of the two ladies wear that pair of red shoes? No!"
"I would not like it if either did."

The short and stocky one is wearing real masculine shoes. The other, with the checks, the slim one, keeps adjusting the embroideries on her bosom which are slipping because of her lean bones. She's a genuine Englishwoman. She orders tea and milk—as is becoming to a good Englishwoman. Her face is sunken; perhaps she was in an auto accident, or maybe she fell when she was skiing. She might have lost a lot of blood in the snow. And all this because she was learning the sport of skiing while her feet were not strong enough. Probably she does not participate in any sports now. Her face looks tired, although the operation has obviously been successful. Her breast is hollowed, otherwise she looks quite elegant. Not bad at all. Would she be the Cinderella of this pair of enchanted shoes? Ah! She's wearing a different pair. Simple and comfortable ones. She certainly would not know what more to seek in life. She looks sad in an English way. She might be an interesting conversationalist. No! It is not this one!

The Japanese girl comes into the hall. She is tall and radiant. She smiles at everybody. Just as she did yesterday, when she was escorted by the Mexican and New Zealand women. What a pleasure to me! I rush through the wide hall to greet her. What do I care about the others.

And bonjour, and how are you—without end. Oh, those woman's eyes! I'm delighted to be acquainted with her; the Japanese intrigue me a lot, and she herself is very anxious to learn more from me.

"You see how easy it is to come close to the Far Eastern world," I say to the lady, beginning to believe in my own super-human might.

New Zealand and Mexico got lost—they had to do some shopping in the city; now we were alone. After we had gone through the Lithuanian and Japanese geography, through the structure of the house and family, and politics—we kept talking fast and without any system—my Japanese friend set her heart upon going out to do some shopping, too. But I would not go with her. To walk from one store to another with a woman degrades a man.

But those shoes! I was convinced that she had them on, without even bothering to make sure. Of course it is she! But as I watch her crossing the street, I see she's wearing modern shoes, not red ones.

She was not my Cinderella, that chaste princess.

Every time I started thinking of something, I always came back to that mystic pair of shoes. Like a detective. I had to find that Cinderella.

I remain in the hall. There are very few people around.

The second day of the congress has begun. Here I see another woman. She's holding a newspaper as if she has nothing else to do. She takes a bite of some food now and then as she reads. She's wearing a suit, a very stylish one, and she has two fine fox furs on her shoulders. She is well built, but her face is hidden. As is becoming to a director, I tactfully approch this interesting lady who keeps on holding her morning paper and who, no doubt, has some interest in politics.

"Ha! The red shoes!"

"How could it be?—It is she!"

"At last."

And what a divine pair of legs. Shoes are shoes, they are not so important. But what on earth could be more radiant than a woman's well-shaped legs? Wonderful! I flatter myself on my studies. Although this is the city, spring puts its nose into each shop-window and expresses itself in every inch of the street.

"Oh, those red shoes!" I am satisfied with my nose. I rub my hands joyfully. "This is a reward for my honest work." I feel like a detective who has finally caught a criminal.

I must look for the same paper she's reading. As an important member of the congress, I need it badly.

"Zeal justifies means."

My search for a newspaper was a zealous one. When the lady noticed a strange man so persistently making noises at her side, she pushed aside her paper and gave me a cold glance. What was I doing here! She happened to be a very beautiful woman. For a while I stood speechless, with my mouth wide open.

She was my wife.

The lady spoke up:

"At last, I found you." Now she threw her paper on the floor.

"You're here! And I thought—a Japanese."

"A Japanese! I have always said that those congresses are not good for men."

"But how is it you're here?"

"Well, I'm here, as you see."

"That 'as you see' does not explain much."

"You're very tired, my congressman."

She came closer to me. I was also very happy to see her.

"What Japanese are you talking about? What Japanese? Do I look like a Japanese?"

"No, I thought—the shoes. . . ."

My wife looked at her shoes.

"Do you like them? I wonder why you have become such a gallant man. In Kaunas, you would never notice even if I bought a dozen pairs of shoes."

"But these are so uncommon."

"Do you really think they're extraordinary? But they're nothing particular." This news made her happy. Moving here and there and raising her pretty skirt over her knees, she kept looking at them. I felt a bit embarrassed.

"Be careful. The people."

"What people? I'm showing you my stockings. And the things I have bought. Every honest husband should take an interest in his wife's legs. And in her shopping."

"But these legs belong to you."

"All right, so what have the other people to do with them?"

My wife had much to say about the advantages of buying things abroad. I did not argue with her; I still kept dreaming about the lady with the red shoes. There was a real *chanson sans paroles* in my ears, but it could have turned out a tragicomedy.

"How did you happen to come here?" I still could not get it out of my mind.

"It was very simple. I took a taxi and drove here."

"No, I mean here—to Lausanne."

"I took a regular second-class train from Leipzig. I am sorry, I did not take a regular plane."

She was playing with me. She felt that she had to use a more frivolous and easy tone, as is fitting for a tourist. One cannot talk seriously with women.

"I had an impression at home that you wanted to go somewhere else."

"Oh, Alfred! There is no life without my Alfred."

"But how did you find out that I was in Lausanne?"

"Well, even the Ministry sometimes gives away its big secrets, and informs the wives of their employees when they go abroad to a congress. One needs only a little talent to find out. They all send you their best regards and ask you not to hurry home once the congress is over. It looks as if they're sick and tired of you."

I could not calm down.

"And you had to choose the same hotel?"

"That was sheer coincidence."

"And the shoes. . . ."

"Well, that was a risky business, to expose my shoes in front of my husband's door. But you should be happy that there was only one pair, not two."

The government was satisfied with my work at the congress.

Translated by Stepas Zobarskas

Photo by Vytautas Mazelis

Petras Tarulis

PETRAS TARULIS

PETRAS TARULIS (pseudonym, Juozas Petrenas) was born in Utena township, Lithuania, on March 19, 1899. He was editor of various Lithuanian periodicals, including *Keturi Vejai* (The Four Winds), the organ of a literary avant-garde group with Futurist leanings. His collection of stories, *Melynos kelnes* (Blue Trousers), 1927, was an attempt to embody the theories of *Keturi Vejai* in prose. He published another collection of stories, *Zirgeliai padebesiais* (Dragonflies Skirting the Clouds), 1948, in Germany, where he spent several years as a refugee. Emigrating to the United States in 1949, he served as editor on several newspapers and worked for Lithuanian fraternal organizations. His novel *Vilniaus rubas* (The Garment of Vilnius) appeared in 1966.

PETRAS TARULIS

(1896-   )

Blue Trousers

THE SEA.
    Night. A storm.
    And in the very thickness of that storm, two sea wanderers––tightly crumpled, very old, frightening from afar. Two ships drunk on sea wind, on a peculiar odor made of a hundred odors, on the sweat of exhausted, angry people.
    Into the monotonous course of these ships the free storm of the sea suddenly tangled. The old steamship, battered in all the harbors of the world, with its beautiful, beguiling name. And the deserving sea laborer, the sailboat; its name a self-mockery.
    "Brave Pioneer."
    Their trade was common: hauling herring, the sweet fruits of warm countries, costly furs, human brawn for newly opened mines, silver pieces, secretly captured women for industrial centers, little mirrors, rosaries and, finally, syphilis for our wild brothers.
    It was so terrible a storm as sailors tell of in the most terrible of their tales.
    The old sailboat suddenly pitched forward, crackled in all its joints and––as though carrying out some whim of its own––began to sink, slowly and awkwardly, bow first. The old ugly rear rose disgracefully above the water.
    Duty. Hard, essential duty. The duty of lifting heavy boxes, of dragging dazed friends. The duty, if necessary of plunging silently and unobtrusively to awesome depths. All this is duty for the sailor.
    Cold and weariness. Their brains grew numb, objects fell out of their hands. They no longer understood one another. Their pale, no longer intelligent faces, their watery eyes! Waves were stealing them from the steamship, but still they tried to save friends on the sinking sail-sieve. Bouts of fever were now crushing hapless men's bodies with flax-brakes.

The blind waves, like old, disheveled, toothless women——witches howling as they grab with wide jaws at the still-eluding steamship. The lantern dying, now only the vast emptiness of the waters remains. The lantern blinks and, for a moment, pale human faces appear within a multitude of shadows——strange flowers swaying on long stems.

The multitudinous shadows are angry, full of strange smiles——madmen winding an eerie ring around the lantern. A meaningless dance moves in ever closer to the lantern that knows not where to vanish.

The enraged wind, caught in tight, wet ropes, howls and tears.

Right by the lantern, a figure stands straight and peaceful, like a dry tree——the captain. His gray beard glistens for the sailors like a lantern.

* * *

Nobody noticed when a small Chinaman crawled into the steamship. He was quiet and lean. His face was fearful, as though it had often been battered, and it was old. The Chinaman seemed very contented, as though he were in a marketplace of his own country. He glanced about vacantly and uttered something in a scream that only he understood. It could have been an expression of pleasure or eerie fear. He did not seem to comprehend anything that was transpiring.

But when everyone grew quiet and focused on the rare spectacle, the steadily sinking ship, the Chinaman suddenly shuddered all over. Then, as though performing a circus trick, he jumped up and screeched. He flung himself about, going through contortions and yelping like a puppy. Then, hastily and alertly, like a monkey, he glanced about and, snatching the small light-green, wind-tossed lantern, he began to run with tiny steps. His black braid was reminiscent of a sea rat's tail. This Chinaman pushed his way through the crowd and with sure, if trembling hands grabbed the wind-tossed rope ladder. One man, then another grabbed him and tried to hold him and bring him back but he was agile and escaped from them all. With a rage nobody understood he tore himself away from the hands of those who tried to stop him. He screeched, he yelped, he even bit someone's finger. At last like a wild apple nobody needs, he rolled down in the sinking ship.

Meanwhile, the ship sank deeper and deeper. Already, waves were overpowering it. Already, the awful whirlpool was near.

The tired, muted voices of the seamen could be heard:

"Where are you? Back to back!"

"What does he need there?"

"Look, he's going down into the ship."

"He'll drown, the yellow devil."

"What is the Chinaman looking for?"

Suddenly, a huge wave engulfed the steamship in its hungry maws, silencing everyone.

Darkness and foam.

"Where is the Chinaman?" someone slowly recalls.

"May the devil take it, don't worry," a voice counsels sternly.

"Didn't he stink, though! We wanted to leave him in the harbor but when we got out to sea we found him under some sacks," explains the mate who had been rescued from the sinking sailboat.

"Well, it's all right. There wouldn't have been enough food," someone answers his own question.

Suddenly someone shouts:

"Look, there's the Chinaman, carrying something in his teeth!"

"Listen, take my basket, too. There, in the corner. Everything left behind."

"Quiet, aren't you ashamed?"

"And what's the matter with you?"

"He'll drown, even without your basket."

"He's climbing, he's climbing," several voices called out. Everyone seemed suddenly concerned with the Chinaman.

"He'll crawl up, the devil."

"Agile like a monkey."

"Listen, you toad, grab with your left hand."

"But what's he dragging in his teeth?"

"Don't you see? His blue trousers!"

"Oh, those same ones he so proudly displayed walking in the streets of Liverpool."

"Those pants are his only riches."

"Look, he's climbed up high already!"

"What are you aiming at? Filthy creature. Through stupidity, he'll feed the sea."

"Here, here, closer!"

"Quiet!"

Suddenly everyone shrieks with fright: "Wave, wave!"

"Careful! Hold on . . ."

So terrible were the jaws of that wave that a cry rose in the steamship that was neither human nor animal: "A-o-o-o!"

But the sea's sarcasm suddenly and mercilessly cuts off that shrill cry. All details disappear simultaneously in the sea. Only after a while does the lantern again blink timidly, like a thief behind a shelter.

"Curses. I couldn't get any air," someone says, shaking himself.

"That's nothing, child. We old sea wolves say it's washing the milk from prickly jaws," another voice answers.

"Salty, huh?"

"Right, and where's the Chinaman?"

"Shine it over here, closer."

"Look, aren't those the blue trousers?"

"And the Chinaman's not in sight?"

Close by, a shy, trembling voice inquires:

"Who knows where we'll drift to?"

"It's all right. The steamship is old, it knows its own way."

"I had quite given up hope."

"Well, be glad. You're saved."

"And your wife, is she young, pretty?"

"It's a year since we've been together."

"Oh. . . . I would have let you go with the Chinaman," someone jokes obscurely, flatly.

"I'm so grateful, I'm so grateful," someone else is explaining with all his mobilized emotion.

"What for? For the rescue?" sacrilegiously cold comes the reply. "All right, now, all right. You'll treat us with a cigar in the next port.

Meanwhile, the quiet sailor stands apart. His whole life has been on the sea. He has long ceased being surprised by anything. Many times he has been in the process of drowning. He has seen friends drown by the tens. Yet now his yellowed, wrinkled face, dry like a maple leaf in autumn, has for some reason smoothed out. His little eyes, which have seen the entire world, blink a couple of times unnecessarily, hidden under grey brows. His legs are crooked and spread but he stands surprisingly steady. He stands there and unbeknownst to himself, a quiet smile shyly flashes across his features——a rare guest on this face. The old sailor forgets the terrible waves for a moment, he forgets the eerily tossing ship on which he himself is swaying, he forgets the wind which touches them all with the coldness of a dead man's legs. He gathers a multitude of wrinkles around those eyes that are so used to gazing into distances, and pursuing his own distant thoughts and without knowing why himself, like an echo he repeats the just-spoken words:

". . . . blue trousers."

Impossible to guess the path or direction of his numbed thoughts.

In the gigantic body of the sea, the last trace of the sailboat has now vanished before their eyes.

The sea has now ended one minor event, which would be worth perhaps one line in a newspaper story.

Translated by Rasa Gustaitis

ANTANAS TULYS

Born on April 6, 1898, in Seduva, Lithuania, ANTANAS TULYS immigrated to the United States in 1913. He studied at the University of Valparaiso, receiving his degree in pharmacy in 1924. Since 1946 he has been running a hotel in St. Petersburg, Florida. His stories have appeared in Lithuanian and American magazines and periodicals. He has published the story collections, *As buciavau tavo zmona* (I Have Kissed Your Wife), 1936; *Tuzu klubas* (The Club of Aces), 1956; and *Inicialai po tiltu* (Initials Under the Bridge), 1956. He has also written and translated plays. He died on January 15, 1977.

Antanas Tulys

ANTANAS TULYS

(1898-1977)

The Three Knots

I

BLONDE LIFTED HER HEAD. Once more she wondered whether to escape from Westville into a larger town where nobody knew her. She was tormented by the thought that her body was beginning to lose its gracefulness, that it was growing stouter, and that the lithe outlines of her figure were fast disappearing into a shapeless mass. Soon, no one would want her any more. Besides, another anxiety had begun to disturb her. She was worried about her daughter Rozale. The girl was already seventeen years old and almost grown up and Blonde was aware of the temptations around her.

If Blonde went to Chicago or another large city, she would find herself a husband. As long as he was rich, it would not matter if he was old and ugly. Then Rozale could take a course, or find herself a job and get to know a nice circle of young people. The only future that awaited the girl here was her mother's career. Of that Blonde was certain.

"Rozale, we're going away," the woman said to her daughter, who was standing and looking through the window into the empty street.

"Mama's beginning to talk again. And in half an hour's time she'll start drinking and singing sad songs while I'll be left to gaze through the window at this desolate little street."

"No, I'm not just talking this time. I'm telling you what I'm going to do. We're going away—really going away from here. This is no place for you any more, Rozale. Men come to visit me and we talk ... and you are grown up enough to understand how your mother makes her living. God forbid that you should learn from me ... Suppose some wretch was to catch you one day. It only has to happen once and then its goodbye to your name and everything."

" I don't see that that's anything to worry about. Nobody calls me by my name, anyway. I'm just Blonde's daughter to them. Besides, having a man near you doesn't leave a mark on a girl's forehead. You've left this all too late, Mama, to begin worrying about my future and what I shall be," Rozale replied and she turned her face toward her mother to see what effect her words had had.

"What do you mean, it doesn't leave a mark on a girl's forehead? Who taught you to speak like that?" Blonde was astounded.

"Oh, a man said it to me once."

"Look at me, darling. Take a good long look at me. Don't you see what little there is left of my beauty and I'm not quite forty yet?!"

"But you can't expect to stay the same all your life—as you were fifteen or twenty years ago. You're still young and beautiful. Much lovelier than lots of women your age who live with their husbands."

"Yes, I know. But I'm not like the young women."

"But Mama doesn't take enough trouble with her appearance, and she drinks too much, and she's always falling into those fits of melancholy. Why, I never saw you as drunk as you were yesterday."

"My men are like that and I'm like that. Maybe I'll die that way, too. Only, I don't want you to be like me."

"You could easily have been a high class prostitute. You'd have had men who wore fine clothes and washed every day. And they would have paid you well because you were a very beautiful woman. And you still are. Your figure is still as sexy as ever."

"What are you saying, Rozale? How can a girl your age talk like that?"

"Oh, I've been thinking like that for a long time. Actually, I must have been only eleven when I began to think about such things."

Blonde was distilling her home-made spirits that morning. Now she noticed that the whiskey was not running smoothly and that the liquid was barely trickling into the pot. She had been making whiskey for twelve years, and for once she did not know what had gone wrong. She examined the retort from all sides and was angry with herself for always having to live this way.

There was always a jar placed in a corner of the room with the liquid fermenting or distilling. The stench of whisky hung about the house, and pots and barrels of spirits stood against every wall. The furniture was shabby and the rooms neglected, and there were holes in the roof. Blonde herself had long since ceased to dress properly and went on existing as if without hope. Sometimes, she thought she ought to go to church on Sundays. At least it would make her wash and dress properly once a week. And she would get some fresh air, too, on her way there and back.

Meanwhile, Rozale had moved away from the window and gone into her bedroom to put on a new dress which she had just shortened the day before. Then she powdered her face and painted her lips and her eyelashes. She had heard that Albertas Cibulis was coming to see them that day.

"Hell! I've done everything right but it isn't coming through properly," Blonde moaned.

"Take a good look. There may be a hole somewhere," Rozale called from her bedroom. Then she went straight over to the retort.

"Rozalyte, I've only just noticed how tall you are and so very, very pretty. A king would give up his throne for you, and you've grown into such a lovely girl. And there's not a prettier face than yours in the whole of Westville. Your voice and the way you speak are pleasant, and you're such a sensivle child. Soon, you'll learn how to cook . . ."

"You might as well add that there's no one quite worthy of me in the whole of Westville," Rozale remarked drily.

"Yes, you're quite right. We must move to Chicago or St. Louis, and you'll have no difficulty in finding yourself a husband."

"That's where the trouble is," Rozale said, pointing to a broken place in the rubber tube which was resting in a bowl of cold water. "Your moonshine is pouring out on the floor, and you haven't noticed it."

Blonde changed the tube and the whiskey began to run smoothly, as it had for the past twelve years. Still, she felt restless and dissatisfied for she kept thinking about the past. There had been a time when she was young and beautiful, just as Rozale was now. She was not afraid of anything then ...

"Rozale, I began to live like this because I had to. You were only a baby when your father died. I was left to take care of us both. I had to do something. I was young and good looking, and the men liked me. I began living with one of them, then with another, and so it went on. I taught myself how to make moonshine so that we could make some money. But what's the use of all that money lying in the bank if we have to go on living like this? I'm a witch, I know, but not one of those, thank God, who cares only about what she earns. And in my case, my time's coming to an end here. A girl will come one day from somewhere and she'll take all my men away and put me to shame. There's no future here for you, either, Rozale. We must go away ..."

The door opened and Albertas Cibulis walked into the room without knocking. He was a stout man in his early fifties, of small stature, and the biggest idler in the town. He lived in a four-room cottage, which he owned, but when it rained the water came pouring down into three of the rooms. So he confined himself to the one dry room. Into it he had brought his bed, his chest of drawers, his table, his stove—everything, in fact, that he possessed. Soon, the other rooms were not fit to enter because the floors had rotted and the boards had given in from the rain.

Cibulis was in a hurry to sit down. As soon as he had seated himself, he began to feel his leg with his hand. He looked quite stylish this morning. His suit was well pressed, he had put on a clean shirt, and he had taken the trouble to polish his shoes. He wore a bright tie and he had bathed and combed his hair. His face looked brighter and younger, and his eyes were not as red-rimmed as usual.

"I was just telling Rozale how lovely she is," Blonde explained to Cibulis, suspecting that he might have overheard their conversation as he was coming in.

"They say you'll find the sweetest smelling flower far away in the woods where few people pass by," remarked Cibulis.

"Yes, in the woods. When she gets to Chicago, she'll be out of the woods then. She'll find work there, and when the time comes she'll make a good match for herself. But if she stays on here, some scoundrel will sidle up to Rozale, rob her of her name, and what then?"

"Oh, there's not much robbing to be done. There's no need to be afraid of that," Cibulis said, laughing.

"And what do you know about a girl's fair name, Cibulis?' Surely, no such bliss has ever come your way?" remarked Blonde cheerfully.

"Maybe it has and maybe it hasn't. Is there ever a man who can think he's been that lucky? He can boast though, and that's all."

Cibulis had broken his leg three months ago in the mines, and this morning he had come out of his house for the first time. He was in high spirits.

Suddenly, Blonde noticed that Rozale had been listening attentively to their conversation.

"Rozalyte, why don't you go out of town for a while? Let people see you in your new dress," she said to her daughter.

"Why must I be off to town? You never minded before," replied Rozale.

"Why are you all dressed up, then, if you're not going anywhere?"

"I want to stay home. You can go to bed, if you want to."

"First, before we begin, I want to settle my debts. That's why I've come," Cibulis put in hurriedly.

Blonde at once forgot all about Rozale.

"You do owe me a great deal. So much that I'm afraid to tell you. I'd never have given anyone else so much credit. But let's have a drink to start off with, and then we'll get down to business," Blonde suggested in her other, her gentleer voice.

"Pour me a glass straight out of the barrel without any water," said Cibulis.

Blonde had worked out her own system for recording the debts of her clients. They were illiterate people, just as she was herself, and they found her method clear and acceptable. Ninety-five per cent of them spent their fortnight's pay the same day they received it. They would settle their debts and buy the absolute necessities, but they would then spend more money on drinking and by the end of the evening they would have only a few cents in their pockets. They would then buy everything on credit for the following two weeks.

Cibulis was an exception this time but only because he had had the bad luck to break his leg. He had received no wages but was to be paid a sum of money as a compensation for his injury. For almost three months now he had been sending for whiskey. Cibulis would thrust a scrap of paper, the size of a postage stamp, into the hand of a friend and say, "Be off to Blonde for half a quart, there's a good chap."

When Blonde had drunk three glasses straight from the barrel, she began to feel drowsy. To wake herself up, she put her head into a bucket of cold water. Then she shook her hair, brushed away the water from her face with her hand and said, "So you want to pay me, do you? We must count it all up."

She opened a drawer in the commode and took out a cup that was filled to the brim with small pieces of paper. She turned the cup upside down on the table and counted the pieces of paper. Then she counted them a second time and exclaimed, "Three hundred and thirteen chits. I don't know how you could have drunk that much whiskey in three months and still be alive."

"No, I haven't drunk quite that much," Cibulis objected.

"You must have, if there are that many chits here. You're welcome to count them for yourself."

Cibulis was an improvement on his old self today, not only in his attire but also in his manner. Rozale took several sharp glances at him and thought to herself, "He'd be a handsome fellow if only he were a foot taller. His head, his hands and his waist are like those of a large man, but his legs are too short. But who cares about a man's legs anyway? They don't matter in bed."

"I don't know how to count up to three hundred, but we'll see," declared Cibulis.

He sat down at the table, spread the papers before him and began to examine each one in turn. When he had looked at several of them, he separated them into two groups. A full half-hour went by before he came to the end of his task. Then he took the smaller heap of papers in the palm of his hand and laughed out loud.

"I've drunk that much and that much only," he said to them

and showed them what he held in his hand. "And I want to pay for it at once. You can do what you like with the rest—that isn't my signature."

"What do you mean? They all look alike to me," said Blonde in astonishment.

"They may seem alike, that's all," replied Cibulis without offering to explain.

"Well, show me how you can tell them apart."

"Come here, sit down and I'll be glad to show you. I'm just as illiterate as you are, Blonde, a man without education, but all the same wise enough to get along in the world."

Cibulis selected one piece of paper from each pile and said to her, "Examine them closely and tell me what you see. They look alike, don't they?"

Blonde stared at each scrap of paper in turn but could see no difference. "They're both yours," she exclaimed at last.

"No, look here." He pointed to the corner of one piece of paper. "Do you see a hole here made with a needle?"

"Yes, I see it now," Blonde reluctantly agreed.

"Look at each piece of paper in this heap, then. You'll find a hole in every one of them. But not in the others . . . And that is my signature—the means by which I've chosen to defend myself. No, I'm not a learned person . . ."

Blonde drew the larger pile toward her and then began taking up paper after paper, scrutinizing each one carefully. Quickly, she began to separate them into two groups. When she had finished, she pushed the smaller group toward Cibulis and said, "These are yours, too, Cibulis. They have the mark of the needle on them."

Cibulis examined them, counted them and said, "Yes, they're mine; all ten of them. I must have overlooked them before. My eyesight isn't as good as it used to be. It means that I've drunk exactly one hundred half-quarts of whiskey, but not three hundred and thirteen. And I only intend to pay for my hundred."

Water was still trickling down from Blonde's hair onto her face, neck and shoulders. From time to time, she brushed the glistening drops away with the palm of her hand and shook her head impatiently. But now she rose, walked to the corner of the room, seized the first rag that came to hand and rubbed her hair with it vigorously. She wiped her face, her neck and her shoulders and came back to her place beside Cibulis. A long argument followed between them because of the two hundred pieces of paper which were not to be paid for.

"You can go to the devil, if you won't pay for them!" screamed Blonde in exasperation. "Don't ever dream of coming back, d'you hear, if you won't settle for them. No, you won't have me nor my moonshine."

"Please don't talk like that," said Cibulis softly. "I've been coming to see you for the last twelve years. You've been almost like a wife to me."

"Mama, you've said enough," Rozale put in hurriedly. "Cibulis knows what he's talking about." She got up and stood very straight before them. There was anger and determination in her face.

"Oh, all right, all right. We'll leave the papers until next time," agreed Blonde. "D'you want to pay for the knots now or later? You broke your leg on the last day before your wages were due, remember? So you were prevented from coming to see me then."

"Count them up and I'll pay you," said Cibulis.

Blonde opened the drawer again and drew out of it a skein of cotton threads which were fastened together at one end. Each color represented a different client, and there were knots tied on the thread close to one another. One knot stood for a half-quart of whiskey—two knots for the bed. There was a small gap left in each thread at two-week intervals. The knots that had already been paid for were tied over in double fashion in order to avoid confusion. Blonde was a good accountant. She had never made a mistake in her career, nor had there ever been a misunderstanding in the last twelve years.

"Mine is the dark blue one," observed Cibulis.

"Yes, yours is a shade darker than that of Prosketis. It's this one isn't it?"

"Yes," and then he added, "Do you ever come to tying . . . a double knot . . . for him these days?"

"No, not very often. He's got himself a lovely wife, they say—passionate, too."

"You must have a very good memory, Blonde, to remember

which thread belongs to whom. I daresay you've at least two hundred threads there. Or maybe more?"

"Almost two hundred. And it's not hard to remember when you've been using the same color for the same person for years. I only have to see the thread to recall the person it belongs to—as if I saw him in the mirror, almost." Blonde counted the knots on the dark blue cotton and continued, "There are twelve knots here and four double knots. Wait a minute—twelve knots, three double knots and a triple one. How did the triple knot get here? I didn't tie it. I've no use for triple knots in my profession."

"Never mind," Cibulis said hurriedly. "I'll pay for the triple knots as well. Twelve knots at a dollar each, three at two dollars, and one at three. It all adds up to twenty-one dollars, doesn't it?"

"No, I don't want your money if I don't know what I'm taking it for. But I do want to know how that triple knot got here."

Blonde fell silent and brushed away the drops of water which were still running down from her wet hair.

"It was *I* who made that triple knot," Rozale said quietly. Cibulis knows. Let him pay for it."

"You tied it? And what did you tie it for? Does it mean three dollars, then?" Blonde opened her eyes wide.

"Yes, it means three dollars," Rozale said in an even tone.

"Rozale, you must tell me all about it."

"It would be better for you not to know, Mama," said the girl.

"Rozale," Blonde demanded in a rising voice, "You have never hidden anything from me before. Tell me, why did you tie that knot there?"

"Don't you two start a quarrel, now. I'm ready to pay for it, isn't that enough?" Cibulis said, interrupting them.

"You be quiet, Cibulis," Blonde shouted. "Rozale, I must know what the knot stands for."

Rozale rose to her feet slowly, moved her large blue eyes up and down and examined her conscience. She found no trace of sin or transgression in her heart, and what she had done had left no scar in her feelings. For a moment it occurred to her that perhaps she was more competent now than her mother to decide what was right and what was wrong.

She stood very erect before them, with her head held high. Looking straight at her mother, she said in a firm voice, "It was like this. One morning when you'd gone out to town or to visit somebody, Cibulis came over and asked for you, Mama. So as not to let a dollar slip by, I took him to bed with me. Besides, suddenly I felt that I wanted to embrace a man. And when it was all over, I tied a triple knot on the thread—not a double one as you do, Mama. I explained this to Cibulis and he agreed. And that is all there is to it. And please don't let's say any more about it."

"Where was your head, Cibulis." Blonde screamed at him.

"I would certainly have been without one if I had refused such bliss," Cibulis replied.

"Which of you started it?"

"I did," said Rozale quickly.

"It was neither," explained Cibulis. "We merely looked at each other and went quietly to bed."

"He's quite right, Mama. When we got there, I told him that this was the first time for me and that I was afraid. Cibulis said that there was nothing to be afraid of and that having a man near her did not leave a mark on a girl's forehead. And it hasn't. Nor in my heart, either!"

"Rozale, you're the loveliest of lovely young girls and only just seventeen. What in heaven's name made you do such a thing? How could you have given yourself away to such an old man? Where was your taste, I ask you?"

"I've done what I've done because I love him." The girl turned her eyes toward Cibulis.

"*Love* him? You don't know what you're talking about!" Blonde seized Cibulis's shirt near his throat and went on in a threatening voice. "You hooligan, you thief, I'll fetch the flatiron and beat you till you can't walk!" She turned about and grabbed for the iron but Rozale placed herself in her way.

"You mustn't hit him, Mama! I won't let you hit him," said Rozale in a determined voice.

"I'm going now," said Cibulis. "I'll come another day when you two have made it up." He hobbled out into the street.

"Where are you going, Cibulis?" shouted Blonde. Cibulis did

not answer and soon he was out of sight.

Blonde turned to her daughter. "Take a good look at me, Rozalyte, and you'll see how horrible I am. You'll be like me, you know, in twenty years' time if you live the way I do. And twenty years go by in a flash—just like that." She spat at the side of the barrel and pointed with her finger. "Just like spitting."

"Well, I'd rather live the way you do, all the same, and be known by everyone, than exist like just any other woman in Westville. The village is full of them and there's nobody to care if they're alive or dead."

"But they have a *name,* Rozale."

"Yes, and who knows it! Whereas you, Blonde, are famous in the whole of Westville, and not only among the Lithuanians. The men and the women all talk about you."

"I see that we're not speaking the same language," Blonde said to her daughter and went over to the corner of the room to attend to her whiskey. She hummed a sad tune under her breath as she moved among her pots and pans.

After awhile, Rozale went over to her mother and asked her to listen to what she had to say. "As from now on, Mama, I intend to solicit men for myself. I'll keep a book for writing down their debts. Soon, we'll be able to move to the other side of the railroad into a lovely house with a bath and running water. We'll buy some new furniture, and the garage will be a good place for making moonshine."

It terrified Blonde to listen to Rozale. It was not so much the thought that her daughter intended to go into business that frightened Blonde but that she would be taking all the men away from her. From now on, it would be Rozale and not Blonde.

"I won't let you entice my men away from me!" she shouted to her daughter.

"I have no need for your men, Mama. Young fellows will come to see me from the other side of the railroad. I'll only take Cibulis from you," Rozale said in a soothing voice.

"I won't let you have Cibulis!" Blonde retorted, raising her voice for the last time. Soon afterward, she felt that she must have a good bath, wash her hair and dress herself properly. And without wasting any more time, Blonde began to heat the water and pour it into the tin bath.

Translated by Danguole Sealey

JUOZAS GRUSAS

Born in Zadziunai, Lithuania, on November 16, 1901, JUOZAS GRUSAS graduated from the University of Kaunas in 1930. He achieved acclaim for his satirical novel, *Karjeristai* (The Careerists), 1935, demonstrated his skill as a craftsman of the short story in the collection, *Sunki ranka* (The Heavy Hand), 1937, and made his dramatic debut with the well-constructed psychological play, *Tevas* (Father), 1942. After World War II he wrote mainly for the theater: *Herkus Mantas,* 1975, a tragedy dealing with the extinction of the Old Prussians; *Meile, Dziazas ir Velnias* (Love, Jazz and the Devil), 1967, an expressionistic play on youthful nihilism; *Barbora Radvilaite,* 1972, an historical drama; and others. In his new collections of short stories, *Rustybes sviesa* (The Light of Wrath, 1969, and *Laimingasis tai as* (I Am the Happy One) he experiments with novelistic themes.

Juozas Grusas

JUOZAS GRUSAS

(1901 -   )

The Heavy Hand

ON THE FAR END of the parcelled-out land of Noriunai village, in a clearing, there once lived a thief. He was much talked about and hated like the very devil. Still, by some arrangement of fate, he went on living in spite of everything. He had a wife, two little brats, sixteen acres of marshland, a nag, a cow, and two scabby sheep. Dolieba (such was his last name) did not till his land—his piece of mossy bog, bought from the count, was left for the snakes to use as a breeding ground.

Although nobody knew the state of Dolieba's conscience, he was held responsible for every theft that occurred in the vicinity. He was called a horse thief and he actually served a jail sentence for stealing a horse.

A peasant's hatred and vengefulness is a thing to wonder at. He will have a drink with a traitor to his country provided the latter foots the bill, but the only way he wants to see a thief treated is with a rope and a branch of a tree. If the peasant has no opportunity to tan a thief's hide with his own hands, he will have no satisfaction. A grudge will gnaw at his heart like a worm at a tree.

Dolieba was just such an object of the peasant's hatred. After every theft in some neighboring village, he was cursed bitterly. The villagers had long been waiting for a good chance to vent their wrath on him.

When the Germans left Lithuania in 1919, such an opportunity presented itself at once. In Noriunai, as in the other villages, the so-called "honorary militia" was formed—a loosely organized, poorly controlled temporary force in charge of public safety and order.

Hard times came followed by all thieves and their helpers. The farmers, jealous of their bit of hard-earned property, decided to rid themselves for good of the thieves and their breed. Dolieba's cabin was surrounded with a great uproar, but in vain; the host did not wait to welcome his guests. Whenever the men attempted to catch him at his lair, they would only find his frightened wife and two children bedaubed with potato mush. This vexed the militia beyond endurance.

Somewhere they captured a comrade of Dolieba named Rukas whom they duly "examined" and put in "prison"—a farmer's corn-kiln, dark and sooty, standing alone in the middle of the fields. The poor wretch could not bear it; he hanged himself.

Still, fate continued to plague the self-styled guardians of law and order. A couple of days later, two horses disappeared, the last of those the Germans had overlooked. And most important of all, they belonged to an honorable milita member himself! This was too much! Dolieba must be given a resounding lesson, even if he had to be dug out of the very earth. What a tumult ensued!

Someone whispered that Dolieba was returning by night to his wife, leaving again before daybreak. Well, this time he would not slip away!

"Let's keep watch throughout the night!"

So it was done. Four of the smartest fellows were assigned to the job; they prepared themselves as if for a bear hunt. As dusk fell, they stealthily waded through the snow and encircled Doleiba's cabin on all four sides. Crouching in the bushes, they watched the little house set in the midst of a white field as astronomers watch a new planet. Looking about, they waited for someone to sneak up to the cabin. Nobody appeared. Only a yellow light flickered in the little windows throughout the evening, filtering into the blue emptiness outside. The men were greatly tempted to peep through the windows but the cabin was guarded by a dog. Every noise had to be avoided.

The light went out and the cabin showed no sign of life. It just stood there in the dead of night, humped like a hayrick.

Not a soul anywhere. The night was calm. There was such stillness that the frost itself could have been heard.

And what a cold! Such cold only increased the sense of emptiness and frustration. It stung the men's ears. It made their noses burn. It put gooseflesh up their backs. This waiting business was agonizingly tiresome, a torment! But this torment would be paid for.

The men began trampling the snow underfoot. They swore silently but with conviction. They angrily beat their sides with their fists as they grew more and more impatient. The dog overheard them, growled, and, its suspicions confirmed, started to bark.

The whole strategy was spoiled.

Januska waded through the snow to his neighbor.

"There you are! How foolish to freeze here . . ."

"What are we to do, then?"

"What to do . . . Let's arrest the old hag. After a good thrashing, she'll tell us where her husband is."

Januska was surprised at his own ingenuity. Great things take shape in an accidental way. Why hadn't such an excellent idea come to their heads earlier? This was wonderful! They could march the old lady over to the village and give her a real scrubbing over there! Their blood simmered at the very thought of it. All four were delighted. Now, they no longer felt the cold. They became lively and warm, they began shouting. Their pent-up energy had found an outlet. A single idea, a random thought had opened a new vista before their eyes and breathed new life into their enterprise, which was about to lose its meaning. It did not matter any more whether this would help to catch the real thief. The men anticipated the pleasure of vengeance. That was enough for the moment.

They headed excitedly over to the cabin and, increasingly boisterous, began pounding on the door, several fists at once.

"Let us in!"

"Don't you hear, you thievish blackguard?"

There was a rustling inside; somebody fumbled around the cabin for a long while. Finally, a light appeared and a squeaky door opened into the fore-room.

A weak, tremulous woman's voice was heard close to the outer door.

"Who's there?"

"The militia!"

"Open up, and no questions! Or the door goes to the devil!"

A wooden bolt slid away with a clatter and the door, pushed

from the outside, gave in with a bang. Four husky men tumbled into the fore-room. An undersized woman, wrapped in a shabby overcoat, retreated into the cabin. Her pale face was changed by fear; her eyes, glassy with surprise, gazed fixedly at the unexpected guests.

"Get dressed!"

"This very instant!"

"You're taking a trip to the village!"

"Woman, you're in trouble!"

They did not bother to ask her about her husband. The intruders went at Dolieba's wife as though she herself were the thief. They acted as they did less from disappointment than from eagerness to satisfy their thirst for vengeance. Somebody must get a drubbing—so long had they been making themselves ready for it, such pains had they taken, so long had they waited outside in the cold, so many curses had they uttered in their impatience.

The woman glanced about her. It was dawning on her what this business really meant but she still kept silent unable to make a decision.

"Going to make us wait?"

"Didn't you understand?"

The men were in no mood for parleying. They were as though steel. They would wait only as long as it took them to look around for any criminal evidence.

The woman started fumbling among some rags. Her children woke up (one was seven, the other nine), and the younger one began crying.

As she listened to the weeping child, Dolieba's wife became nervous and alert. She turned this way and that, like a cat beset by dogs. She said that she had no shoes and no warm clothing and asked what they wanted to arrest her for. Finally she began crying herself. Her boys, seeing their mother in tears, hollered with their mouths wide open. But the men were adamant.

Dolieba's wife took a long time to get dressed. She tried to forestall, as long as she possibly could, the disaster that was sneaking up on her like a black shadow. She knew these fellows well.

This irksome business was brought to an end by several pairs of hard hands which dragged her out, like a bird from its nest, and pushed her ahead across the field.

Having marched her to Januska's farmhouse, the men threw their weapons, old shotguns and clubs into a corner and noisily surrounded their victim.

"Now, old woman, you'll remember the day you were hatched out."

She retreated into a corner and waited there in anguish for the first blow.

How could they best instill the greatest fear in the shortest time? An interesting problem. The men did not consider themselves accountable to anyone; they could do whatever came into their heads. They were kings. Oh, how pleasant it is to afford to balance one's accounts in full without forgetting the accumulated interest!

Their leader was Januska himself, a sturdy chap about thirty years of age. He opened the proceedings.

"Tell us where your husband is or you're going to turn cold!"

And, without waiting for an answer, he struck the woman on her jaw with all his might.

She reeled and, without an "ah" or an "oh" collapsed on the middle of the floor.

The preliminaries were disgusting. A shiver ran along the men's spines, as though cold water had been thrown on them. But this was only the first moment, just the first impression. Their souls shuddered momentarily, not longer, however, than the human body does upon immersion into a cold bath. The initial trembling, the sudden shock only invigorates and increases one's energy. The loathsome introduction put more fire into their spirits. Their eyes began to shine with an evil glow.

The woman lay on the floor, shrunken and limp, like a heap of rags. But she soon moved her head a couple of times, sat up, looked at the men with haggard eyes, and stood up automatically with unexpected nimbleness. She looked at the men once again, her eyes wide with terror, and screamed as though she were losing her reason.

"Don't hit me!"

She screamed several times in a voice that now expressed

only consternation and dread.

Her eyes suddenly caught sight of a crucifix standing on the window sill. She sprang over to it, seized it with both her hands and began kissing it.

"I swear . . . I swear . . . I know nothing . . ."

Januska wrenched the cross out of her hands and threw it back onto the window sill.

"No snivelling here. We're not priests!"

The old mother of Januska woke up in the next room and thrust her sleepy head inside.

"What are you bothering the woman for? Beasts!"

The men exchanged glances.

"A wet hen . . ."

But now they felt constrained. They became nervous; their sense of vengeance, gone into full swing, was being thwarted. Like frightened hawks with prey in their claws, they had to look for a more convenient spot.

One of them proposed to take Dolieba's wife to the "prison." All seriously agreed. They tied the woman's hands and feet and then locked her temporarily in the maid's bedroom, while they assembled in the outer room to decide what to do next.

Januska brought a huge pitcher of beer.

"Let's have a drink for more guts . . . guests' health!"

"Your health, Januska!"

"Have another, boys. Dealing with women, you know . . . Sickening business."

"Ha!"

"Hell . . . That's nothing."

As they drank, the men became more and more talkative and excited.

Each of them was busy proving tht Dolieba's wife must know where her husband was. Impossible that she shouldn't know. No, that was an affront to the honorary militia. Whip her! She, too, must have had a part in the thefts—no doubt about it. They weren't little children to be fooled. And, anyway, after so much effort and trouble . . . That woman is cunning! Like the devil himself. All thieves are cunning. But the guardians of law weren't idiots, either.

Let's march her over to the "prison" and give her a proper

going over there . . .

They drank as they talked and they reached an agreement.

They marched the little, ragged woman through the snow-drifts, over the fields, for about half a kilometer. Stooped and sighing, she walked ahead of the men, wading through the snow with short, slow steps. Two men accompanied and guarded her while the others carried the lanterns, guns and clubs, calling out commands regularly.

"On the double, old woman!"

"Turn right!"

"Keep straight ahead!"

"Forward march!"

They were in a military mood and swore often.

The night was cold, empty, senseless—the sky remote and calm . . .

The corn-kiln was dark. Cold and terror lurked within its uninhabited dirt walls.

The woman's eyes froze and became like ice; her face turned blue with an unnatural pallor. She kept as silent as the earth itself, waiting for something dreadful to happen. She did not part her lips because she was overpowered by a black, sickening hopelessness. There was no pity to be expected, no pity . . .

"Think it over, now—either you tell us of your own accord where your husband is, or . . . cross yourself. If you don't tell, you won't ever get out of here," Januska said firmly and with cold callousness.

It was an ominous, harsh moment. There remained no dilemma any more—just grim necessity. The woman could scream, she could summon the very angels of heaven down to her, but it would not help her—some inexorable power had already pronounced sentence. She stood trembling before her unseen black cross, looming as large as the immensity of the night itself.

"You're not speaking up," rang out the iron words.

She remained silent.

A heavy hand, clutching a piece of tightly twisted rope, rose into the air, and the blows started raining. A strong man kept hitting the woman on the shoulders and head with all his might and without as much as blinking his eyes. Dolieba's wife screamed, raised her shaking hands, staggered but recovered her balance again.

The tired hands sank down.

Now, the woman's entire body was shaking, as though she had been thrown into a wintry stream, and she softly moaned,

"Ahhh . . . Ahhh . . ."

"Speak up!"

"This very moment!"

The words fell like so many sharp-edged bricks.

"I don't know . . . know . . ."

Such was her whispered answer.

A short pause.

"She feels nothing because of her sheepskins. Let's take 'em off."

The men tore the woolen scarf from her head and pulled off her sheepskin coat. The woman remained with only a blouse on now and with a white linen scarf over her head. She was thin and tiny, like a neglected, starved child.

The militiamen groped about for the rope ends and other instruments of torture, shouting and reeling in a kind of drunkenness. They felt giddy and hardly knew themselves what they were doing. Their hands trembled, they spoke haltingly and made uncoordinated movements. Some force had overpowered them and was casting them about. The men obeyed insensibly, like a stream of burning lava hurling down the mountainside. Now they fell to striking the little childlike body.

"Tell us, tell us, tell us!"

Their "tell us" served only as a rhythm for their blows. The torture was no longer a means, but an end in itself.

The woman fell to the dirt floor, whimpering and writhing like a mud-fish thrown into salt. The blows burned her like molten lead. She felt all aflame. Her scarf came down upon her neck, and her black braids spread undone on the soil.

There remained only a continuous suffering in her.

Suddenly she grabbed the feet of her executioners and told them in screams that she would speak, would tell them right away, would tell them everything they wanted to know . . .

They were all, both the woman and the men, in one of the circles of hell—unaware of one another, blind to one another, all seized by madness, dizzy and forgetful. Half the building could burn down before they would have noticed it.

"Tell us!"

"Tell us!"

"Tell us!"

"I'll tell you. He went . . . he went . . ."

"Where did he go?!"

"He went . . . I don't know . . . he beat me . . . he's gone."

"Let's burn her soles, the monster!" shouted one of the men. "See how she's cheating?"

It was an inspiring thought.

Instantly, they put a rope under the woman's armpits and hung her—limp, dishevelled, no longer a human being under a rafter. One of the men twisted together a handful of straw and set it on fire. Another quickly pulled an old pair of man's shoes and a pair of socks off her feet. They began a torture of the kind that calls for vengeance to high heaven itself. The woman jerked, kicked, quivered, stiffened in a convulsion, whimpered with her choking breath, and lost consciousness intermittently. When they finally loosened the rope, she dropped to the floor as though she had no bones. She could not stand up on her feet. She cried and moaned like a cruelly beaten child, and now there were tears in her eyes again. She was saying that she could not tell them. She embraced their feet, she named the places where her husband might be hiding, she contradicted herself, then she told them again in screams that she knew nothing, nothing at all.

"Let's shoot her!" shouted Januska. He seized the woman, dragged her over to the wall and tied her to a couple of hooks.

"You'll soon be cold."

He began aiming at her with his old double-barreled shotgun. He meant only to scare her.

Januska raised his gun slightly and fired. The grapeshot went into the wall and roof above her head.

The loud bang of the shot sobered the men a little. Januska's wild pranks made them a bit uneasy.

"Aren't you going to tell us now?" shouted the man angrily,

and he cocked his gun again.

The woman tossed about, quite dazed. No one could understand what she was muttering.

"Put down that rusty junk of yours—you're going to set us on fire," warned one of the men with unexpected sobriety.

Januska meekly stood his weapon in the corner, among some discarded lumber, not having the presence of mind to set the gun's safety latch.

Meanwhile, the woman was again groping for place names, trying to guess the whereabouts of her husband. The delighted "examining magistrates" overwhelmed her with questions, but Dolieba's wife became confused and contradicted herself, no more conscious of what she was saying.

"See? Again you don't know."

Januska reached for his gun. He grabbed it by the barrel and pulled it out from among the old boards full of protruding nails.

Suddenly, the second barrel went off.

"Jesus! Holy Mary!"

After the fearsome bang, a hollow scream from Januska was heard. He grabbed at this head with one hand and lifted the other, trembling, high in the air. Standing in this posture, he shook himself a few times, then staggered and fell with a muffled thud, his entire length sprawled out on the dirt floor. Blood was oozing from his head and neck.

The men were not prepared for this. They seemed to be waking from some horrible dream. They felt as if they had been hit on the head. They were petrified, like so many pillars of salt, and had no idea what to do. Soon, they all crowded around Januska.

"He killed himself!"

They felt hot lead in their breasts as though they themselves were shot. Their hands and feet trembled like the leaves of an aspen tree.

The wounded man tossed his bloody head and gasped for breath.

The men were too stunned to do anything.

"Take me home," Januska said weakly.

But there was no cart and no horse there, and Januska's farm was half a kilometer away. The men flung themselves about as though the place were on fire, but no one did anything to help the wounded Januska.

"Ahhh... take me home... ahh... home!"

Two men ran around the kiln looking for a cart although they knew well that none was there.

"Tie up his wounds!" someone shouted, and they all busied themselves looking for some first aid material. But they found nothing suitable. They were all wearing sheepskins and had only woolen scarves around their necks.

"A priest! Get me a priest!"

The wounded man was drenched in blood, he tossed about and kept shouting. He was not even aware of any pain, he only saw a black coffin before him, while his life flickered like a candle about to go out. Poor man, he was shouting for help against death itself, a sudden and eternal death...

"Get me a priest right away! I'll die...I'm dying...I hanged Rukas!"

His soul cried for help; in the absence of a priest, he confessed to his friends. His friends were to him like straws to a drowning man. Januska pulled himself together, tried to get up and fell back again.

"I told you, his wounds must be tied up!" shouted one of the men again, though not telling with what.

Finally, they noticed the white scarf of Dolieba's wife. They grabbed it and tried to pull it off but the scarf was down on her neck and tied with a double knot. The men could not untie it with their shaking hands.

"Come, lady, tie up his wounds... You know better how to do it..." begged the men, even calling her "a lady," as they untied her ropes in a hurry.

She was soon free to move, but could not walk on her burned feet. She could hardly keep herself erect, leaning against the wall.

"Come, lady, come..."

The woman stepped forward, staggering, putting each foot down with pain, stopping, and, at intervals, losing her strength.

"Get her her shoes! Don't you see the woman can't walk barefoot?"

Her shoes were instantly picked up and the men crowded around to put them on. One knelt at her feet while others held the tortured woman in their arms.

"Make haste, lady, make haste . . ."

Every second was a matter of life and death. The shoes only made her feet hurt more. Finally, she reached Januska, knelt at his head and, without a word, began to tie up his wounds.

What a surprise! She had even brought dressing material with her.

The men tried to make themselves useful and carried out her directions like the most docile children.

The wounded man stared at her with the greatest hope, unable to say a word. His heavy hand dropped down and came to rest on the woman's shoulder.

Translated by Albinas Baranauskas

VYTAUTAS ALANTAS

VYTAUTAS ALANTAS was born in Sidabravas, Lithuania, on June 18, 1902. He studied literature and art at the universities of Kaunas (1923-1924) and Montpellier (1925-29), was director of the Lithuanian press agency Elta (1930-34), served as editor-in-chief of the daily Lietuvos Aidas (1934-39) and was manager of the Vilnius Theater (1941-44). After five years in Germany as a displaced person, he emigrated to the USA in 1949 and lives in Detroit, Michigan. Collections of his short stories include *Artisto sirdis* (The Artist's Heart), 1931, and *Svetimos pagaires* (Under Foreign Banners), 1954. Some of his novels, such as the controversial *Pragaro Pasvaistes* (The Glares of Hell), 1951, and *Sventaragis,* 1972, deal with Lithuania's ancient past. Nine of his plays have been collected in the volume *Dramos veikalai* (Dramas), 1963. His recent novel, *Amzinasis Lietuvis* (The Eternal Lithuanian), 1972, and a collection of short stories, *Nemunas teka per Atlanta* (The Nemunas River Crosses the Atlantic), also 1972, deal with the life of Lithuanian emigres who came to America after World War II.

Vytautas Alantas

VYTAUTAS ALANTAS

(1902-)

The Crown Prince Needs Blood

I

THE STEREO SHRIEKED its last beat and the dance was over.

"It's more than time," Laima thought; she was sweltering and the touch of her underthings on her body was unpleasant.

Vytenis raised her hand to his lips and, without letting it go, guided her to the bar in the corner of the cellar-and-game room. Her father, Antanas Jovaisa, still brisk at the brink of sixty, with intelligent features, was in charge behind the bar, his sleeves rolled up professionally.

"Steve never kisses my hand," she thought again as she was settling with her partner on the high stools. "Daddy, will you pour me a Tia Maria on the rocks?"

"Cognac for me, please," Vytenis lit a cigarette.

The guests were not many, all selected by her. She wanted "select" company for her birthday, as she told her mother. The invitations went to her fellow students––Lithuanian and American, several young doctors and engineers and, of course, to the main guests: the Daugvydases, old family friends, with their son, Vytenis, and the young doctor, Steve Stone, and his sister, Patricia. Vytenis and Steve, both university graduates and independents, were her old friends.

Vytenis was tall and fair-haired, a good athlete (Laima's steady tennis partner) and a music lover. He himself played the piano fairly well. His partners were not well-to-do but they sent their only son to the best schools and he had graduated in architechture at the top of his class.

Steve Stone came to the bar and sat down next to Laima.

"The next dance is mine," he said giving her a sideways glance.

"Have they made any arrangement between themselves?" Laima gave each of them a quick glance. They were both very serious that night and sitting between them, Laima felt as if she was in the path of an icy draft.

"Scotch on the rocks, please," Steve asked Jovaisa.

Steve was the exact opposite of Vytenis: stocky, even-featured, with a shock of coarse black hair. During their long friendship, Laima had never seen him angry or excited. He was always cool, reserved and withdrawn, although she felt an extraordinary masculine power and intellectual aspiration behind that mask of fake or genuine emotionlessness. His father was of Italian origin, his mother Irish. The old Stone, now retired, was a famous physician. She had visited the Stones' suburban home more than once and was dazzled by its luxury. She had never seen any comarable home. After the old Stone's death, a large portion of their fortune would go to Steve. His sister, Patricia, was Laima's close school friend; it was through her that Laima had met Steve.

"Rather stuffy here," Vytenis said in English, wanting to interrupt the uncomfortable silence, but Steve kept resting his elbows on the bar gloomily and did not seem inclined to keep up the conversation.

"You must have had heatstroke, both of you, or did your tongues stick to your palates? Have another drink, wet your gullets, perhaps then you'll be able to say something," Laima tried to jest.

"I don't intend to entertain that gloomy-eyed fellow. He seems to carry his nose so high that he'll knock the lamps from the ceiling," Vytenis said in Lithuanian.

Laima burst out laughing.

"What is the mason chattering?" Steve glanced at Laima. He sometimes mocked the architect by calling him "mason."

"The mason is chattering that he will build a special lab for you where you'll be able to mix potions against boredom," Vytenis answered him in English.

Laima laughed again. The male duel was fun.

"Just be sure that you don't build by mistake a church tower that looks like a telephone pole," Steve answered, still cool and composed, without raising his eyes from the glass. He aimed his shaft at Vytenis' love for modern architecture.

"Doctors do even funnier things," Vytenis retorted sharply without hesitation. "When they're unable to pinpoint the patient's sickness they diagnose it as witches dancing in the stomach." Vytenis smiled in satisfaction, as if he had made a good return of a tennis volley. His smash was aimed at Steve's book on witchcraft.

Laima surveyed the cellar. All was peaceful and proper. Some guests were trading jokes in little groups; others were sipping their drinks by the wall, and nobody surmised that a fierce verbal duel was in progress at the bar. Laima noticed no change in Steve's expression. The duel had not even ruffled his composure. Then she turned a concerned look toward Vytenis. On the surface the architect looked calm but from time to time he would impatiently stroke his thick, blond hair with his long, thin fingers and she knew that he was nervous. The fun was over and she began to fear that their dialogue would go too far and her friends would start quarreling. But then the music was heard again and she went to dance with Steve.

"What does that mason want from me?" he mumbled, displeased.

"And what do you want from him?" she looked coolly and straight into his eyes because his tone seemed insulting.

Steve did not answer and for a while they danced in silence. Laima felt pleasure in giving herself away to the rhythm of the dance in a strong man's arms. Then Steve asked: "D'you know what day it is today?"

"My birthday, of course," she answered carelessly.

"And our second anniversary. Remember? Patricia took me to your birthday party two years ago. That's a very memorable date for me. I wanted to say that this may be the last time I call on you, unless, of course, things take a better turn."

"Last? Why last?" Laima was surprised.

"In exactly a week, I'm going on a vacation trip to Europe. I'm not sure yet but I might spend a longer time abroad: I want to get acquainted with Europe's best laboratories and hospitals. What's definite is that I won't be returning to this city any more; I've got an invitation to work in the Mayo clinic."

"But what about your father's practice? Haven't you taken it over?"

"I don't care to dawdle with patients——I'll be transferring my practice to my colleagues. Scientific research, that's the only thing I want to do."

"This is quite a surprise to me——you've never shared your plans with me before."

"Is that so? I'm twenty-eight already, it's time that I put family matters in order. I've never hidden my plans from you—— quite the opposite. I talked to you about them several times. I'm sorry to be saying it but I must confess I'm a bit tired of knocking endlessly at the door of a woman I love who refuses to say yes or no. You know that I love you, Laima, and if it depended on me alone, we would have left for our honeymoon a long time ago. Frankly speaking, it's not too late even now. A word from you and we'll transform your birthday into an engagement party. And we'll go to Europe together."

"I get you now. Since I cannot make up my mind, you're running away."

He pretended not to have heard her and went on.

"There's something else, too. I'm the peaceful, sedentary type, and I want peace and harmony in my family. In short, I need a serious, educated woman for a wife. I think we two would be an ideal couple of scientists. You've completed biology and you could work as my assistant. I'll admit it, I don't like to chase women. Love, marriage are, for me, a mutual agreement, friendly and sincere, and not some storming of castles . . ."

"You mean, you wouldn't go through fire and water for me?" Laima threw back her head and flashed her remarkably white teeth flirtatiously.

"Of course I would——but only if you were my wife or fiancee. As long as it's not yet the case, I don't want to singe my hair or get my feet wet. I repeat, this is my last visit and I want to hear your word. Yes or no?"

"An ultimatum?"

"Not at all. You're an intelligent and mature woman and you realize yourself that all this can't go on forever. Finally, it seems to me that it's positively improper for a serious woman like you to lead two serious men by the nose," he concluded somewhat preachily.

"You bore me tonight, Steve," she tried to jest. But although she did not like his pedagogic tone, she realized that the time for jesting had ended and that this entanglement with two men had to be resolved.

"I simply can't understand you, Laima," Steve added after a pause. "Sometimes, it seems to me that you're deliberately escaping from yourself, so that you can avoid making a decision. As a doctor and logician I can't believe that you can be in love with two men simultaneously. Or perhaps you love neither of us, but simply can't decide which would make a wealthier match?"

"If wealth mattered to me, you know very well that you're much richer than Vytenis," she answered icily, almost insulted. "Marriage for me is not a multiplication table."

"Then would you favor me with an explanation——where's the rub?"

"I don't know, Steve," she turned aside. "But you're right, I must make up my mind . . ." She wanted to say something else but fell silent when her eyes caught the large Lithuanian doll on the little table in the corner, the doll her mother had made and which her father had christened Queen Morta for some unknown reason.

When the dance was over, Steve did not return to the bar. He reminded her once again that he would be waiting for her answer until tomorrow. Then he said his farewells, and left. Laima returned to the bar where Vytenis was waiting with a notebook page in his hand.

"Take a look, Laima, how do you like it?"

She looked at the sketch of an attractive house.

"It's a handsome house, and the pool looks like a lake, but why that turret in the corner? The house is modern, but isn't the turret gothic in style?"

"Why, you ask? From where, then, would we look at the castle of our happiness on the moon?" he laughed.

"You're the eternal builder of sand castles," Laima smiled respectfully.

"Once man stops longing for beauty, he will suffocate!"

"It's easy to long for beauty when the stomach is full."

"Laima, dear, you're beginning to sound like Steve!"

"I've got my own mind, thank you," Laima pretended to be slightly insulted.

"Of course you do, but everything was different before that Aesculapian crossed our path. Aren't our parents old friends? Haven't we almost grown up together?"

"He's leaving for Europe in a week and he won't be coming here any more."

"That's the best idea he could have had!"

"But he may change his plans if I agree to marry him."

A long silence descended upon the bar. Vyetnis downed his drink in a gulp and pushed his glass at Jovaisa for a refill.

"You're both my dear friends," Laima spoke cautiously. "Sometimes it seems to me that I'm wavering between two forces like a reed whose roots are deeply embedded in some sunken continent. Father told me," she glanced at her father, "that the ancient Lithuanians believed in Destiny, that Destiny was like a god to them. Who knows? I may be waiting for an omen from that Lithuanian Destiny. Do I go to Europe for a honeymoon with Steve, or do I move with you into your new house?" She laughed.

"Laima makes a lot of sense!" Jovaisa filled his own glass and raising it, exclaimed: "A happy journey to Lithuania!"

II

In her bedroom, Laima slipped out of her party dress, took off her girdle and put on her nightgown. She was dizzy, perhaps not as much from the liquor she had drunk as from the amorous glances of the two men that caressed her throughout the night.

The large dressing-mirror reflected the young woman's dazzling beauty: her thick, chestnut hair, her firm and attractively rounded shoulders, her suntanned arms. Her beauty blended harmoniously with her health. Whenever she looked at herself in the mirror, she thought proudly and gratefully that, in creating her, mother nature must have had the ideal woman in mind. Her offspring would be healthy and strong. As a biologist, she was quite aware of that. Among her friends, she stood out by her boldness combined with elegance, and by her independent mind which despised empty display. She felt that she looked at life soberly and openly, and anything that smacked of romanticism was, for her, simply "games immature people play." She became twenty-three tonight, she had graduated from the university and she would start teaching next fall.

Laima again stretched her limbs on the spacious bed. She felt tired, yet it was not the tiredness that drives one to bed and shuts the eyes, but rather a fatigue caused by the spilling over of youthful energy demanding to share her body with a man's. Laima felt ripe to begin that most important stretch of life for a woman called motherhood.

"I'm ripe to be a mother. I want to be a mother. I'll be a mother!"

She smiled, watching with shining eyes her body brimming over with the sap of life. "All I need to do is flick my little finger," she thought, "and I'll become Mrs. Daugvydas or Mrs. Stone! They're fighting over me like lions, but if the lioness won't respond to their call, the lions will run away to look for others," she laughed.

Although she tried to jest about it, a tiny alarm pressed her heart slightly like an iron ring. What if she loses both of them with her clever fun and games? They're both dear friends to her, but, as Steve said, she could not lead them by the nose any longer. She must choose, but which one? They're both young, handsome, strong, educated men. What else does she need? Her mother and father, just as Vytenis' parents, were trying to persuade her to marry a Lithuanian, but this was silly. She won't be living with a Lithuanian or an American, but with a man.

Deep inside her soul there was some strange block, a cover, preventing her from making up her mind about who she was. She never concealed the fact that she was Lithuanian, but did not treasure her origin. Lithuanian history and culture were of little interest to her, just as she paid only as much interest to American history and culture as they demanded from her in school. Sometimes, she would think with a smile that under her father's roof she felt Lithuanian, but once she went out into the street, she became American. She would draw the conclusion that she probably was a "straw" Lithuanian, and not a much better American. She was something in between.

An imaginatively inlaid jewel box stood on the night table next to the mirror. She opened it and took out a splendid necklace of large amber beads, Vytenis' gift. She felt their weight as she raised them in front of the mirror and felt the coolness ripple along her entire body after putting it on her neck. The necklace drooped halfway down her breasts and glittered with a palely cool and mysterious color in the mirror's reflection.

Her father's stories about amber left her with a nebulous impression that the so-called sun stone was somehow linked with Lithuanian destiny and that it harbored a particle of the Lithuanian soul. She found it somewhat ridiculous and yet she was not able to shed that impression. And she remembered how Vytenis, placing the necklace on her, remarked in jest, "In olden times the people believed that amber had magical and healing power. It chased evil spirits away and restored health."

"Spare me the old wives' tales, I'm as healthy as a lioness and I'm not afraid of any evil spirits!" She had dismissed it then as a joke.

Laima remembered her father telling her about the famous medieval physician, Avicenna, who lived somewhere in the Middle East. Avicenna proclaimed the magical powers of amber to gladden an aggrieved heart, strengthen the spirit and keep heart disease away. Another Aesculapian, the Egyptian Seraphin, asserted that a piece of amber next to the sore was of great help to the patient. In the 14th century, Pope Clement's doctor, Arnoud from Villeneuve, used ground amber in his compound designed for rejuvenation.

But Laima's favorite item in this amber lore were the words of Dante in the 24th Canto of the Divine Comedy where, speaking about the legendary bird Phoenix, he said: *"During its life it feeds on neither grain nor herb, but on incense and liquid amber..."*

"How beautiful!" she sighed. She always remembered this passage after Vytenis had recited it to her.

Laima opened another exquisite jewel box and took out Steve's gift, a golden bracelet inlaid with diamonds. She clasped it on her wrist and looked at the mirror: the amber necklace and the bracelet were in perfect harmony. Patricia told her that Steve had spent a pile of money on that bracelet.

"They're both in love with me, but which one of them do I love?" she asked looking in the mirror. "Maybe neither one? Obviously, I love Steve more: he's so masculine, intellectual, his sister is my close friend and wants me very much to marry Steve, he's rich, we'll both be able to do research, money will never be a headache for me. And what would I gain by marrying Vytenis? I'll have to slave in school and we'll have to skimp until we'll improve ourselves materially some day. What does it matter that he's Lithuanian? I'll have to live with a man, and not with a Lithuanian. And as a man Steve is more attractive to me. She recalled how she felt safer and more intimate while dancing with Steve than with Vytenis who would sometimes give her a wild twirl.

The thought of calling Steve immediately flashed across her mind, but she remembered her parents' gift and took the folk costume in a plastic sack from the closet. She held it in front of her and modelled it before the mirror, taking enormous delight in the harmony and elegance of the patterns and colors. Laima liked the folk costume and felt that some mystic meaning was concealed in its patterning and color scheme. For her name's day she would always receive a Lithuanian gift from her parents: an amber bracelet, a Lithuanian painting, a book. A reproduction of a painting by M. K. Ciurlionis hung on the wall of her room. This year her parents had mentioned that they had decided to pay for her trip to Lithuania for her next name's day. She knew that they would be ready to spend their last penny, if only she could see Lithuania, and especially Vilnius.

Laima replaced the folk costume in the closet and went to the open window. A rose bush was spreading right underneath, illuminated by pale amber moonlight. A gentle, pleasant aroma invaded her entire body. Bending to the roses, she inhaled deeply and a mixture of pain and passion undulated in her limbs. Determined to go through with it, she went back to the night-table and began dialing Steve's number but that instant she heard a knock at the door.

III

Down, down into the dungeon she descends by a narrow spiral staircase. There seems to be no end. The guide, who had just shown them the opening in the corner of the castle ruins, has vanished from sight and so have all the other tourists with whom she had climed the hill. She steps cautiously from stair to stair, careful not to dirty her dress against the moist walls and not to hurt her head against the low ceiling. The smoldering torches attached here and there aginst the wall make the air in the dungeon smell of tar and mold. When the staircase suddenly ends, she finds herself in a spacious hall lit by torches. On the walls she sees portraits of Lithuanian rulers, warriors, bishops and nobles. Placed around the hall were richly ornamented coffers.

It seems to her that as she walks slowly past those portraits they follow her with their eyes from inside their frames, very concerned, as if waiting for something. She recognizes them all. Her father had described all the rulers of ancient Lithuania in detail with the exception, perhaps, of King Pukuveras, about whom historic sources are almost silent. She stops at the portrait of Queen Morta who, strangely, is in a mourning dress and seems to be very sad. A sudden thought flashes through her mind that the entire dungeon is drowning in sadness, in some strange expectation.

As she keeps stopping, the nobles seem to step out of the frames of their portraits, place them against the wall, surround her and stare at her. Queen Morta comes to her and says, "I am Queen Morta. My son is ill with anemia. He is gravely ill. He needs blood. Give him your blood and he will be well. Without blood, he will die! I will give you a chestful of amber."

And when Laima keeps silent, not knowing how to answer, the queen adds, "I will give you my golden crown for a single drop of your blood! My son is the crown prince. He will inherit the throne, and if he dies, our line will die, too. Here, take it!" Then Morta takes the crown off her head and offers it to Laima.

"Our line will die out! Our line will die out! We will have no king!" She seems to hear voices from a multitude of throats echoing along the dungeon's vaults.

Laima can see distinctly thousands of eyes fastening themselves on her——begging, pleading, and even demanding. And again, something unheard and unseen seems to happen. The entire throng of nobles seems to fall down on their knees before her and, their arms raised, exclaim in supplication:

"Blood, please, the crown price is dying! Without your blood the crown prince shall die and the race will vanish into nothingness! Don't begrudge a drop of your blood. Make a gift of your blood and the crown prince shall live!" They seem to implore her thus, on their knees, as if reciting a litany.

She seems to waver and is at a loss what to do. She is sorry for the crown prince and his mother but she is afraid that if they get her consent, they might suck all her blood. Besides, how will they remove her blood? No medical instruments here, no vessels . . .

As though she were reading Laima's thoughts, the queen takes her by the hand and says, "Let us go!"

And suddenly Laima finds herself in a splendidly appointed laboratory where her mother, a nurse by profession, is waiting for her dressed in a white coat and holding a syringe in her hand. Through the open door she sees a huge hall with a wide royal bed in the middle. The crown prince is on the bed. He is pale beyond description, resembling a corpse rather than a living being. His eyes are closed and he does not move, as though he hasn't the strength to raise an eyelid. And somewhere in the distance a sad throng, burdened with a majestic sorrow keeps vigil along the walls.

But what astonishes her the most is the perch hanging from the ceiling above the crown prince's bed. A huge diamond-feathered bird resembling a griffon is perched there, holding in his beak a golden chain with a large piece of amber attached to it dangling above the crown prince's chest.

"That's Phoenix, of course. Or perhaps the Lithuanian House-Demon-bird," she thinks, recalling her father's stories of the House-Demon transforming himself into a golden bird and flying high in the skies.

But the queen disrupts her train of thought by saying, "See, my son is so weak that even amber does not gladden his heart any more."

"Lie down on the table, dear daughter, and I will take some blood from you," her mother seems to be saying.

She resists no more and lies down on the cleanly covered table, stretches out her arm and the prick of the sharp syringe is as distinct as though it were real. She sees the syringe fill with dark red blood and instantly everything around her begins to change. She sees the pallor slowly vanish from the crown prince's face and rosiness replace it. Life's joy begins to sparkle in his eyes. The hall now seems to be filled with the same nobles who had stepped out of their frames. But now the crowd is larger. The walls seem to open and waves of people stretch as far as the horizon. Nobles mingle with peasants, craftsmen, soldiers and workers. They all seem to be greeting her jubilantly and her name resounds from horizon to horizon. She has the sudden thought that it was her blood that had awakened them all from lethargy.

Queen Morta embraces her and giving her a motherly kiss, says, "You saved our line!"

The crown prince jumps nimbly out of bed and, down on one knee, as she had seen in a film about the Middle Ages, kisses her hand, saying, "You saved my life and I'll take you home on my steed!"

The nobles surrounding them lift her respectfully and put her on a saffron leather saddle. They gallop along the caves but the thought strikes her suddenly: How will they get to the surface on that narrow path? Seized with terror, she sees the opening approaching.

"Stop! Halt!" she shouts in panic but the rider does not listen to her and keeps galloping on.

Terrified and screaming ever louder, she wakes up, jumping up from her pillow.

Dawn filters through the open window. The coolness makes Laima tremble all over. In the mirror, she sees her dishevelled hair and her eyes still frozen with fright.

"I'm returning from the caves of the Vilnius castle. What foolishness!" she mumbles to herself. She jumps out of bed and closes the window. Then she collapses back into bed and falls into a peaceful, deep sleep.

Waking up late in the morning, Laima lays on her back for a long time, watching the ceiling and reliving her dream with all the details. She had read somewhere that dreams were more real than waking reality. She did not believe such nonsense, of course, but it occurred to her now that last night she might have glimpsed what was hidden beneath that block, behind that cover floating in the halfways of her soul and preventing her from taking a clear look at the future.

Her father had said that everybody was a hunchback in his own way. But she never agreed with him. Not everybody! "I always considered myself a positive woman," Laima thought to herself "And I liked to take potshots at the romantics. But haven't I become a hunchback in a single night? Phoenix, the House-Demon are legends; the amber's curative power and the particle of the Lithuanian soul concealed in it——that's sheer mysticism; the anemic crown prince is a dream. But I can't understand why, in this irrational world, I don't feel myself a stranger. Could it be that I didn't really know myself until now? Wouldn't it be absurd to believe that in a single night I could have regained my senses, found myself again and learned that a dream may sometimes be more real than reality itself? Or could it be that it was the sinking continent of my nation surfacing from my subconscious? If you want to find yourself, lose yourself, said some sage. Maybe this is the same as leaving your slippers by the door on entering a temple. Legends, visions, dreams glow and glitter somewhere beyond the boundaries of reality. But what light is there, what beauty, and who knows, they may be the true reality. Vytenis may be right in saying that we would suffocate if we ever stopped longing for Beauty! If the crown prince has such great need for my blood, let him have it. I don't begrudge it. Especially if my blood can save a life!

Laima dialed Vytenis' number and invited him for breakfast.

Translated by Jeronimas Zemkalnis

VINCAS RAMONAS

Born in Trakiskiai, Lithuania, VINCAS RAMONAS studied Lithuanian and German literature and pedagogics at the University of Kaunas. He taught in high schools in Lithuania and, after his retreat to Germany, in the displaced persons camps (1945-46). After spending a couple of years in Australia, he immigrated to the United States in 1950 and settled in Chicago. His first collection of stories, *Dailininkas Rauba* (Painter Rauba), 1934, was followed by two novels, *Dulkes raudoname sauleleidy* (Dust in the Red Sunset), 1943 and 1951. and *Kryziai* (Crosses), 1947, which generated considerable controversy. He also published *Miglotas rytas* (Misty Morning), 1960, a collection of three novellas. His *Crosses* appeared in an English version in 1954.

VINCAS RAMONAS

(1905–   )

Captain Boruta

TODAY HE PAID a sum of money to Dr. Wagner, the venereal disease specialist . . . . Now, he saunters through the yellow barracks' park, taking pot shots at the sparrows in the trees. The still-warm form of one of them lies in his hands. He examines its black, membrane-covered eyes. The legs are stiff; one wing is shattered. The wind tosses gray feathers about the park.

In the dusty square, several soldiers are playing tunes on harmonicas. Others toss a football, shouting. A group has gathered around the barracks' cat––black, sleek, dear to all the men. The soldiers compete for the animal's affection. They smile and stretch forth their hands to caress it. And the cat is so intelligent, so soft and warm! Their hands tremble as they stroke its fur. They cannot quite understand what that gentle warmth recalls to them––here among the barbed wire and the cold bricks.

Captain Boruta approaches the group. The soldiers move aside respectfully. The captain's eyes are fixed on this spectacle––cold, gray eyes––impenetrable, like the panes of hospital windows. He stops smiling and begins to glare at the soldiers. His brows start to twitch nervously. The fingers of his right hand tighten around the dead sparrow's wing. The sound of laughter can be heard in the distance. The captain hurls the sparrow to the ground and trudges angrily away. The soldiers stand silent, casting fearful glances at the cat.

Beneath a portrait of Napoleon stands a table covered with red velvet. A sword, a helmet and a grenade rest on its surface. In one corner of the room, in front of a mirror, is a statue of Venus de Milo on a black pedestal. Someone has placed a white skull beside her feet. Violets have been inserted into the eye sockets of the skull and doused with perfume. Blue eyes. Silence––except for this one chilling joke of death, whose morbid laughter permeates the mirror, the silence, the room.

He stands before the mirror, combing his brittle, receding hair, and rubbing cologne into his temples and on his cold frequently trembling hand——hands traced with blue veins that have popped to the surface. He examines these veins and wonders what yellow, putrid fluid flows through them. He sprinkles on more cologne and continues to stare at the mirror. Probably brought about by the cologne, he thinks, regarding the yellow, pimpled face which looks back at him. The eyes have receded into dark hollows; the moustache is sparse, the lips wrinkled. How that mirror distorts one's face!

He collapses into an easy chair. Outside the darkening windows, branches begin to rustle . . . the voice of autumn mourning in those branches . . . the dark blueness of the sky . . . the moon glistening on the rooftops. That moonlight has become a torture to him . . . that sighing wind . . . that mournful, violet sky.

He is alone. His friends are celebrating at the club, drinking and gambling. He is afraid to go there. He cannot go where people drink. At times like this he would like to take a grenade and pull the pin . . .

The branches whistle. Desire and silence . . . autumn. The oak leaves in the Japanese vases are beginning to decay.

*   *   *

A letter lies on the table. He takes it, turns it over several times and replaces it. Cradling his head in his hands, he seems to be staring somewhere in the distance. Her image appears in the darkened window pane. Her immense, blue eyes——clear as the tears of a beloved woman. Boruta begins to tremble. He shuts his eyes. He is unable to face those eyes in the window pane . . . that smile. He feels like a criminal who is confronted by his mother's loving face. He clenches his teeth and shakes his head.

Long ago there was joy. A small manor. On the hill, white birches that etched themselves across the sky. The day when Kristina became serious.

"You . . . are . . . dear." That was all she could say, at first. She was trembling all over. That day, her uncle looked at her and smiled knowingly, shaking his gray whiskers with satisfaction.

And he had colored, abashed. How childish it was——and how sweet! Even now, he would give anything to relive that day——to see that knowing old man's smile, to blush childishly, to feel the frantic palpitation of his own heart.

It had been Whitsuntide and everything was adorned with birch branches, everything was green. Then . . . the military academy . . . the waiting. Then . . . the officer's uniform and a certain night spent in red rooms. Brimming glasses smashed on the floor . . . the dark-eyed woman . . . that terrible kiss! He remembered everything as in a dream.

And then the whole world had changed. But today, strangely enough, that letter still had the power to wound his heart.

He met her unexpectedly yesterday. Kristina seemed shocked.

"How horribly you have changed!" And she was still the same. He could not abide her merriment. He stared at her in silence, as though beset by fear.

"Why have you become so withdrawn? Why do you avoid your friends?"

Friends! What would he discuss with them? The price of shoe polish? At that moment he became as coarse as the material of his army coat. He knew that he would say something repulsive should she being to reminisce about the past. But Kristina had remained silent.

And now he must see her again. He had accepted the invitation thoughtlessly . . . an invitation to celebrate her engagement.

*   *   *

He sits in the armchair, thinking. How lovely she has become! A vague feeling of envy and regret engulfs him as he recalls the sweet, healthy womanliness of her glance, her breathing, her every motion. She reminds him of the marble statue before the mirror . . . Venus de Milo. Suddenly, his thoughts stop, the memories vanish. A slimy wave drags him under. Now, her person becomes repulsive. Those breasts . . . that tempting beauty . . . become merged with memories of the dark-eyed woman from the red rooms . . . with memories of *that* night.

Hatred fills his being and his face becomes distorted by it. He takes the revolver into his withered hand and fires. The statue shatters. A frightened servant rushes in.

"It's nothing, you idiot. Bring my overcoat!"

* * *

In town, he notices women at every step——happy, well-dressed women. And he detests them all. He can visualize them completely naked before him. He examines them with his dim, knowing eyes——eyes that have been poisoned by a woman's naked body.

A woman gazes solemnly at Raphael's Madonna in a gallery window. The captain notices her and smiles in disdain.

A ragged beggar squats on the corner by the tavern. The captain glances at his bandaged head and fiery nose. He thrusts a bill of large denomination into the beggar's hands.

"He'll waste it on drink, I know. But what of it? He, too, is acquainted with misery." The captain climbs back into his automobile and drives away.

* * *

Kristina is smiling, aglow with happiness. Her gaiety warms the captain. For a moment he forgets his problems.

"That light-haired man . . . her fiance, no doubt," he decides calmly. He is not impressed.

Kristing asks him to dance. He looks strangely at her, but nevertheless bows and takes her hand in his. She smiles into his eyes as he desperately tries to escape from her galnce.

"How are you these days?"

"Please——don't inquire."

"Do questions about yourself displease you?"

The captain shudders.

"What's the matter. Aren't——weren't we friends? Truly, it's very difficult to recognize you," she remarks, again scrutinizing his face.

The captain grits his teeth. Suddenly, he feels very ashamed of his features and of his wizened hands. Hatred begins to engulf him. What special thing was there about her? She was, after all, only a creature fo flesh. Now, she appears repulsive——a maggot, a slimy mass. He wants desperately to embarrass her.

"I'd like to rip your dress from your breasts."

There is an uncomfortable silence. Kristina turns her head away as though a gust of rancid air had been blown in her face. Her smile vanishes and a network of fine wrinkles appears on her forehead. Suddenly, the captain feels that it is he who is repulsive, standing there beside her. He feels a strong impulse to leave her in the center of her bright world and to hide himself in the dark shadows.

Kristina follows his movements with her eyes. For some reason she begins to feel great pity for the man. Why did she invite him? To recall the past? To rejoice in her new happiness? Obviously the rustling silk dress of the woman who now engages the captain in conversation is repulsive to him.

He answers mechanically, nodding at everything the woman says, agreeing quickly, deliberately. But his all-encompassing hatred only increases as he smiles. He loathes the bright electric lights, the happy laughter, the rustling silks. He wants to shout at the woman, to push her away.

The servants bring wine. Startled, the captain casts a slow, deliberate glance at the faces in the room and presses a trembling hand against his lips.

"What does it matter, after all," he concludes.

The toasts begin. "Let me be the first to congratulate you," someone cries in a merry voice.

The captain gags. Kristina's fiance glances automatically in his direction. A doll——just as she is, muses the captain. A strong dislike for the blond youth begins to well inside him. He raises the wine glass to his lips and can already feel the chills beginning to travel up and down his spine. He cannot endure even the aroma of wine.

"A handsome fellow," remarks the woman next to him, inclining her head in the direction of Kristina's fiance.

"Oh, very," mutters the captain. "Seems a shame that he should be devoured by maggots..." He smiles wickedly as the woman edges away.

"I drink to your health," resounds another voice.

"Yes, health is very important. One must be sure that the young man, especially, be healthy. There are all sorts of . . . you know . . . diseases."

A wine glass is set down suddenly. Someone pulls out a handkerchief. An older woman fixes her lorgnette in the captain's direction. Kristina's lips begin to tremble. Her eyes fill with tears.

"Phagh!"

"Is he drunk?"

Everyone is embarrassed and horrified.

* * *

The guests' eyes follow her hands as she plays *Autumn Elegy*. Yellow leaves and gray mists begin to fall in the room, piercing the hearts of the listeners, who sit holding cigareetes in their hands. Once again the wind rustles through the boughs, and the sadness of the moonlight envelops all. That soothing rustling——that black, cold, autumn world.

The captain observes the young man as he turns the music for Kristina, almost imperceptibly touching his shoulder to hers at the flip of every page. His entire body quivers as his head leans a trifle toward her. Happiness, desire, and entreaty are mingled in that delicate trembling. The sensitivity of youth. So many hidden desires.

The captain cannot contain himself any longer. Getting up and crushing out his cigarette, he walks to the table and gropes for the wine glass. But it slips from his trembling fingers and topples over. The guests turn to look at him. Kristina's young man smiles and looks away.

"Boor," that smile seems to say.

The captain approaches him and slaps his face. The mood that had been created by the music suddenly vanishes. Kristina leaps up and tries to restrain her fiance. The captain moves toward the door, pulling at his gloves as though he wanted to rip them to pieces.

"So you can see . . ." he mumbles in a dull voice, trying to smile.

For no reason at all he glances at his watch.

*   *   *

He rings for the servant. "Pour some wine and call her——the young laundress."

Through the smoke of his cigar he can see her enter. She is smiling.

"Well, Matilda," he shouts, beckoning her to come closer.

The girl laughs nervously.

"Why are you laughing?"

"It's so warm in here . . ."

"Take your clothes off, then," he retorts.

He sips the wine and stares at her, musing. He opens and closes his fists and relights his cigar. The girl continues to smile.

"Tell me, aren't you like the rest of them? A bad girl? Tell me."

The girl smiles.

"Well, never mind about that, Matilda. But what would people say if they saw you here alone with me?"

"I don't understand you, captain, sir."

He silently pours himself another glass of wine and presses his palms against his temples.

"I'm speaking . . . or maybe I mistook you . . . as though I could ever recognize what woman was, what love was. I knew nothing about woman, but I've already sinned with her. That's what I'm talking about." He starts to raise the glass to his lips but remembers something and sets it down again. He is beginning to feel dizzy.

"Drink," he tells the girl.

"Why aren't you drinking, captain?"

"That's none of your business!" he shouts harshly, again clutching his head. His face is contorted. His eyes are covered with a gray film. He chews his lips in silence.

Matilda begins to edge slowly away, looking furtively at the door, then at the writhing of the captain's grotesque, shrivelled fingers.

"You're afraid of me!" He smashes his fist against the table.

"You! What are you compared to other women? What are you next to that innocent, saintly . . . beside her you're dirt, you . . . ! He hurls the wine into her face and stamps his foot.

"Get out!" he screams.

He locks the door and stalks about the room, examining the furnishings, as though searching for something. Something indefinable annoys him: perhaps the whistling of the wind, perhaps some sad, remembered melody. He cannot understand where the sound is coming. He stops, listens and glances at his legs. He pulls off his shoes, strokes his kness and feels the soft leather.

Only my legs have remained straight and handsome, he muses to himself. Then his thoughts begin to wander again. He sees Kristina and her fair-haired husband. A baby girl is playing on her knees——a daughter with blonde hair and the blue eyes of her mother. Tiny . . . tiny hands.

The captain begins to gag. He unbuttons his jacket and resumes his nervous pacing about the room. He wants desperately to be able to run somewhere, to disappear, to forget. He wants, above all, to take some object in his hands and crush it.

He stands before the locked door, listening and waiting. There is the odor of violets and decaying leaves. And the wind.

Carefully he approaches the mirror and begins to examine his face. His hands fall to his sides in a hopeless gesture. His head drops. His lips part. His eyes begin to glaze. Flinching, as if from fear, he fumbles in his pocket and takes out a cigar, his watch and his wallet. Then he puts them back. Approaching the velvet-colored table, he unlocks the drawer in which his revolver is kept and removes the weapon.

He listens. There is no sound except for the ringing in his ears and his own labored breathing. Somewhere in the distance, he hears the hum of an approaching car. He waits patiently until it passes. Then he gropes for the light switch and all is darkness.

Translated by Nola M. Zobarskas

LIUDAS DOVYDENAS

Born in Trumpiskis, Lithuania, on January 1, 1906, LIUDAS DOVYDENAS made an early mark as a prolific writer and journalist. His experiences as an enforced "deputy" to the "People's Diet" during the Soviet occupation of Lithuania (1940) are recorded in *Mes valdysim pasauli* (We Shall Rule the World)*, 1971. After several years in Germany as a refugee, he arrived in the United States in 1949 and has resided since in Scranton, Pennsylvania. He received the State Literary Prize in 1936 for his novella *Broliai Domeikos* (The Domeika Brothers), 1936. His other prose works include *Cenzuros leista* (Passed by the Censorship), 1931; *Per Klausuciu ulytele* (Along the Klausuciai Lane), 1944; and *Naktys Karaliskese* (Nights in Karaliskes), 1955. Among his children's stories are *Kelione i pievas* (Journey to the Meadows), 1936; and *Buvo karta karalius* (Once There Was a King). Some of his recreations of Lithuanian folktales are assembled in the volume *Karaliai ir bulves* (Kings and Potatoes).

*This book was published in English under the title *We Will Conquer the World,* 1971.

Liudas Dovydenas

LIUDAS DOVYDENAS

(1906-   )

Petras

The old ones have said from time to time: a tale is easier to believe than life.

ONE NIGHT a calf with two heads was born. The farmer, who was named Petras, thought, "Anyone else would have had two calves; it is my bad luck to have a calf with two heads." Then he thought, "What will a calf do with two heads when it has only four legs and one tail?" The calf was nursing both heads, two teats at a time. "The cow will not have enough milk——even one head batters the udder," lamented Petras.

When evening came, Petras returned from the barn, lighting his way with a lantern. He saw, standing by the gate, an old man, bareheaded and gray-haired. Petras went into the house, grumbling, "It is not enough that I have a two-headed calf in the barn; there, by the gate, stands a man who will surely ask for a place to spend the night."

Petras had barely closed the door when he heard a knock. "Do you have a corner where I might sleep?" asked a voice at the door.

Petras replied, "I have no room. But there's no use breaking the door down."

The old man again rapped on the door and asked to be let in.

Petras had a wife who always agreed with him, but on this dark night she dared to say, "Perhaps we should not send him away from our door."

Petras softened as the thought came to him, "Maybe this stranger can give me some advice about my calf."

So the stranger climbed onto a bench, placing his arm under his head. Petras did not offer him food. It was enough for the old man to get warmth and a bench.

Petras could not sleep, "Here, in my house, sleeps a stranger," he thought, "while in the barn a two-headed calf is ruining my cow's udder." He roused the stranger and said, "You should know that there is a two-headed calf in my barn, and it is surely nursing with its two heads."

The old man rubbed his eyes and said, "Two heads are better than one."

Petras tried to explain to him what had been clear during the day and was even clearer now at night: "What good are two heads when there are only four legs and one tail?"

The old man merely turned over on his other side and said, "We will see tomorrow."

* * *

Toward morning, Petras fell into a deep sleep and did not hear the old man leave. He was annoyed because he had not fully discussed the calf with the stranger. When he got to the barn he was even more furious for the calf now had eight legs and two tails. Even if it were slaughtered, the legs and tails would be worth very little.

The next evening, at dusk, the old bareheaded man was walking by on the road again, and again he stopped at the gate as he had the night before. Petras was bothered because he wanted to know how the calf had acquired four more legs and another tail during the night.

"Maybe this evening you would let me sleep on the same bench again?" the old man asked pleadingly.

Awakening in the night again, Petras asked the stranger, "How do you explain it, old man? Last night, someone added four legs and a tail to my two-headed calf. Why couldn't he have made another calf? There are eight good legs, two heads and two tails."

"Be that as it may," said the stranger, turning over and beginning to snore. Petras wanted to continue the discussion, but there was nothing more he could pry from the sleeping man.

"Two bulls at a throw, not even the overseer could put it better," said his wife.

"And I should have asked for some hay. This great brute of a bull will eat up even my thatched roofs."

"You are quite right, the creature will eat up even the roofs."

For a long time Petras and his wife thought about the matter, wishing for more things than they could ever use. They should have asked for a milk cow because after St. Ann's Day their cow was going to go dry. They should have asked for a tub to salt the beef since there was going to be so much of it. And they should have asked for a pipe since the stem of Petras' old one was so worn down it singed his mustache.

There were so many things they had not asked for. Petras grew sad, and his wife grew sad with him. There were so many things they could have gotten when compared to the single bull.

Petras then cut a staff of ash-wood and began to carve marks in it for the things he would ask for when the tired, gray-haired old man appeared again in the evening. He made marks for two pairs of shoes, a bucket for sausages and two wooden spoons because one of theirs was worn out and the other was split and dribbled soup. And he did not forget a chimney because the old one smoked, stinging the eyes, and a healthy young cat because the old one was almost dead, sneezing in the ashes of the hearth.

With all these requests, Petras and his wife waited for the old man. They even made up a bed for him, tied the dog on a shorter chain, and put a glass of water at the bedside.

They ate almost half the beef waiting for the old man. Finally Petras said, "I will go out into the world. I really must find him."

His wife gave him two roast chickens, a loaf of bread, and a clay jar of water mixed with birch mead. "That is for the old man if he will hear and grant all the wishes we have marked on the ash-wood staff," she said.

So Petras traveled along main roads and side roads, over mountains and valleys, carrying the staff under his arm. He ate the two chickens, and drank the water mixed with birch mead, but still he did not find the old gray-headed man. When he had worn out five pairs of shoes, he turned toward home, disappointed and despairing of ever finding him.

In the morning, Petras was dumbstruck. Now, in the barn, two whole calves were nursing, one from one side, one from the other. He hurried to tell his wife what he had found in the barn, but halfway across the yard a thought came to him: "If someone can make two calves out of a single two-headed one, then he can certainly make a bull as well."

His wife agreed. "Certainly someone like that could make a bull very easily," she said.

A few days passed and one evening the hatless old man was at the gate again. Hesitating a bit, he walked up to Petras' house. Petras and his wife stared at the man. They began to suspect that it was he who had made two calves from one. Again, the old man asked to spend the night and he lay down on the bench, quite as if he were at home, using his arm for a pillow.

Petras was worried. He wanted to change the two calves into one bull; iif possible, into a very large bull. "Supposing someone could make two calves out of one two-head calf," he said. "He could certainly change the two calves into one big bull, don't you think, friend?"

The old man, already half-asleep, said, "Let's say he could," and he turned over to his other side.

Petras grumbled to his wife, "What can you expect from a man who tosses and turns in his sleep, as if he were in a frying pan?"

"Yes, yes, just as if he were in a frying pan," his wife hastened to agree.

*   *   *

When the little old man had left, the next morning, Petras heard a bellowing in the barn. He dashed out to see and stopped as if petrified. A black-and-white bull was moving on a tether. It did not take long for his wife to arrive as well, and all out of breath she stammered, "Buuullll, a buuullll!"

Petras was certain now that the changes were the old man's doing, and he began to blame himself. "If I weren't so stupid I would have asked for two bulls," he said. "It wouldn't have been any more work, two bulls at a throw."

As he came near home, Petras stopped by a spring in the forest to get a drink of water. There, under a birch tree, sat the old man sipping cold water from the palm of his hand. Petras did not waste any time; he told the old man how long he had been searching for him and how many miles he had walked on the roads and over the mountains and the valleys. And then, touching with his fingers the notches of his ash-wood staff, he began to count off all the things that he and his wife would like from the old man. At the end of the list, Petras added, "And also two roasted chickens, some water mixed with birch mead, and a loaf of bread."

The old man remained silent, now and then glancing at Petras, who added, "After all, I traveled a long time and it cost me a great effort."

Then the old man, as if waking from a dream, asked, "Petras, how would you like to have a mountain of flour?"

Petras scratched his head and answered the old man with a question of his own: "What did you say? A mountain of flour? A mountain of flour for me?"

The old man nodded his head and said, "Let's go."

How long it actually took, Petras could not say, but suddenly there he was——standing on a mountain of flour. He looked around; as far as the eye could see, flour, flour, nothing but flour. Petras scooped it up with both hands and started filling his pockets. He stuffed flour in his mouth; he fell down and began filling his shirt. Then he realized he was thrashing around in the flour with his muddy boots on, so he took them off. But there was no place to put them. Everywhere he looked he saw nothing but flour, flour and more flour. Then a thought came to him.

"How will I get around? I can't trample in this flour with my muddy boots," he complained to the old man. "I'll have to carry my wife on my shoulders, for I can't let her walk around barefoot, spoiling all this flour."

"On top of this heap of flour you will find a pair of boots with golden soles, as well as silk slippers for your wife," the old man said.

This made Petras happy. He wanted to know the exact size of his flour mountain.

"Seven-and-a-half miles in all directions," the old man said.

"And see that, disappearing in the clouds? That's a mountain of bread. Let's go."

Soon Petras touched it with his own hand and it really was a mountain of bread. "If you want it," the old man said, "you will have to run around it."

Petras did not have to be told twice. He started running as fast as he could around the mountain of bread. Soon, he came around on the other side, sweating and panting, and found the old man where he had left him.

"You see that reddish-colored mountain? That's a mountain of meat. If you reach the top, that mountain is yours, too."

Petras started up the mountain with a will, carrying a sack of bread; the fat warmed by the sun, made a poor foothold, but Petras was a determined man. He slipped, got up, slipped and got up again. It was the next morning before he waved from the top of the mountain to the old man far below. Before long he came down with a chunk of meat.

"Now, Petras," said the old man, "you have a mountain of flour, a mountain of meat, and a mountain of bread. Is there anything else you would like?"

"I would like to be able to eat for a long time without stopping," said Petras, "because there is so much food. The bread will soon dry out, the flour will be ruined by birds and animals, and the meat will be spoiled by the sun."

"You will eat forever, and forever be hungry," said the old man. So Petras fell upon the food. He ate tremendous quantities, stuffing himself with bread and not holding back on the meat.

"Now it would be good to have something to drink," he said.

The old man answered, "On the other side of the mountain of bread, you will find a lake of wine. If you can run around it, it is yours."

Petras began to run around the lake, taking a drink now and then and eating a chunk once in a while of bread from his bundle. His legs grew weak after a while and he began to stagger, but he continued to run. When he became quite dizzy, he fell down beside the lake and, cupping his hands, drank more wine. He drank until he found that he could not stand up. Out of breath, he continued on all fours.

Just then a rabbit ran by. Petras tried to stop him and said, "Run past that mountain of bread and you will see an old man. Tell him that I will soon be around the lake."

The rabbit just raised his gray tail and said he had to hurry home to his wife because a wolf was after him on that side of the lake.

Soon the wolf came by and Petras called out to him, "Over on the other side is a little old man," but the wolf answered quickly, "I must go after that rabbit," and disappeared in a flash.

Moving ahead a little on his hands and knees, Petras saw a Nightingale perched on a bush. He said, "Little bird, there behind the mountains of flour and bread sits a little old man. Please fly over and tell him that I have been delayed, but . . ."

The nightingale realized that a crawling man without wings like hers would not get far. She felt sorry for him so she flew over to the old, gray-headed man who was sitting beside the mountain of bread. She told him about the man who was inching along beside the lake.

By this time, Petras was fast losing what little remained of his strength. He tried to scoop up some wine but his hand would not reach his mouth. He raised his head with a great effort to look at the three mountains rising into the clouds. The mountains were really there, lit up and shining in the springtime sun.

Just then, the nightingale returned and said to Petras, "The old man is sitting there, smoking a worn-out pipe. His mustache is smoldering. But he will wait for you. He says you must not hurry."

"How can I not hurry?" asked Petras. "Next, the old man may give me a lake of milk if I can run around it." And so Petras gathering the last of his strength, pushed himself toward the wine, wanting just one last sip. He leaned over and drank, but he could not lift his head back out of the wine.

It was sunset, time for the nightingale to sing. She sang as usual, always the same and always a different song. She sang to the old man and to the wine.

The old man waited long into the night for Petras. Not seeing him, he finally picked up his stick and lit his worn-out pipe and walked down to the lake. He found Petras with his head in the wine. The nightingale was singing, and Petras was drowned.

The old man said to himself, "Man was given everything, but I forgot to teach him when he had *enough*. I forgot that one word."

In those times, God sometimes walked the earth. Often, he dressed in a shabby coat, was hatless and used his palm for a water-cup when he was thirsty.

Translated by Jonas Dovydenas

JURGIS GLIAUDA

JURGIS GLIAUDA, born in Tobolsk, Siberia, on July 4, 1906, returned to Lithuania, the native country of his parents, in 1922. He graduated from the Faculty of Law of the University of Kaunas in 1938, was displaced from Lithuania by the war, and emigrated to the United States in 1947. His novels include *Namai ant smelio* (House Upon the Sand), 1952; *Siksnosparniu sostas* (The Throne of Bats), 1960; and *Ikaro sonata* (The Sonata of Icarus), 1961, inspired by the life of Mikalojus K. Ciurlionis, the great Lithuanian painter and composer. Some of his novels, such as *Liepsnos ir apmaudo asociai* (Vessels of Flame and Despair), 1969, deal with the Soviet system and occupied Lithuania. He has also written documentary novels, stories and literary criticism. Two of his novels have appeared in English: *House Upon the Sand,* 1963; *The Sonata of Icarus,* 1968; and *Simas,* 1972, a reconstruction of the ill-fated defection attempt in 1970 by the Lithuanian sailor, Simas Kudirka.

Jurgis Gliauda

JURGIS GLIAUDA

(1906-   )

A Counterbalance

WHAT DID IT MATTER to any of them if someone called von Messkirch had lost his son? Frau Kirschner had related her troubles to me without so much as alluding to my misfortune. Like everyone else, she was wrapped up in her own affairs. I was like a sorrowing willow that would never lift its branches; I was like a crooked tree that would never grow straight. I had to lead my own life and heal my own wounds. I had hoped to find solace for my grief by mixing with people, but my plan had come to nothing. If I talked about my suffering, my words would go through their heads like a news headline, interesting today but forgotten tomorrow.

When I arrived home, I found Johann and Mollendruz in the glass veranda. They were playing chess. Both of them were smoking and the tobacco smoke rose in bluish clouds around them. The French military uniform of Mollendruz caught my eye.

"There's some news, Mr. Messkirch," said the Frenchman, raising his dark eyes towards me. "The town council wants to transfer me to other work. I should like to send in a request to be left here with you, but I don't think the town council will pay any attention to it."

"I won't part with you," I said. "I've heard about the trick they want to play on me. You're useful here and quite indispensable."

I went to my study, pulled out the lower drawer of my writing desk and began to search for a box of cigars that I had had for a long time. My hand came into contact with cold, polished metal. I took out my old revolver that I had forgotten about; I looked at it and put it back in the drawer. I found the box of cigars. Then I took some small glasses and a bottle of cognac, a rare possession in war time, and went back to join Johann and Mollendruz. We sat about enjoying ourselves like good friends. We filled our glasses a second time and a third.

"Your offensive is growing stronger, Mr. Mollendruz," said I. "We are withdrawing from France. It looks as if in a little while no town couluncil will be able to keep you here."

This was the msot delicate topic that could be mentioned in a conversation with a prisoner-of-war.

"The war will come to an end and we shall forget all these years of hardship, but good men will always be friends with one another," said Johann and his eyes smiled. "Happy memories will always be a bond between us. You will go away, Mr. Mollendruz, but long afterwards I'll be telling the young people on our estate that we once had a French prisoner-of-war working here and that he was a good man, called Mr. Mollendruz. I shall tell them just how you did every job and I shall say that you did everything better than they."

"You are very kind to a prisoner-of-war," replied Mollendruz, "I am convinced that we shall remain friends when these hardships are over. The recollection of the slaughter will fade, as it did after the first world war, and people will continue to be human beings. Everyone will live his own little life, pursuing his own goals, and he will be content. Even now in war time, isn't it often true that the personal and intimate things mean most to us, whereas the supposedly important events are distant?"

"I can't believe that you will have any pleasant memories of Germany," I said. "Internment camps and barbed wire are not agreeable things to remember. In your eyes Germany can only mean the place where your strength and talents were exploited. I don't suppose you will ever have a kind word for my country."

"You are mistaken, Mr. Messkirch," Mollendruz objected with some warmth. "I am talking about the Germans, not about their government. You must wait a little, but after the war I shall tell you something which will probably startle you, I think it will come as a surprise to you. But I don't want to divulge it until the war is over."

"I am very curious to know what the secret is," I replied. "And if the war should continue for a long time yet, what then? Curiosity will cripple me like the gout."

"I'm not worried about what Mr. Mollendruz intends to say," said Johann. "If he is going to say something about the Germans, he will give us a good report."

"I shall have something to tell you about the time I have spent as a prisoner-of-war and what it means in my life. I shall tell you about the suffering and the happiness it has brought me," said Mollendruz in a low voice.

"Herr Messkirch, isn't the cognac a little too strong?" asked Johann with a wink. "I can't believe my ears, Mr. Mollendruz is talking about the happiness he has enjoyed through being a prisoner-of-war. Either I've had too much to drink or my hearing is playing tricks on me."

"I can assure you," said Mollendruz in the same tone of quiet seriousness, "being a prisoner-of-war has brought me suffering and happiness. I could say a great deal about it, but I don't want to talk about it now."

"The only happiness a man can get from being a prisoner is the happiness of going home again," said I.

"Yes, it will be a moment that I shall remember all my life, like the moment when I last parted from my parents. Sometimes I imagine that I have walked the last few steps and am standing at the door of my parents' house. I knock on the door and in a moment it will open, and I shall see them and they will see me. My old parents! I shall rush to them and kiss my mother first. She will hold me close to her and weep for joy. My father will wait impatiently, until the two of us come to him and I embrace him. Of course we shan't say anything; we shan't need to. We shall simply look at one another and keep on looking greedily. Afterwards we shall begin to talk and words will flow from us like water from a broken dam. We shall keep jumping from one subject to another in broken sentences, trying to say everything and explain everything. My father will take me by the arm, feel my muscles and say, 'My son, my son!' as he used to do in my student days when I was very keen on sport. Just as in those days, my mother will try to draw his hand away and plead with him, anxiously saying, 'You're hurting him. Don't squeeze his arm!' I shall say that it doesn't hurt and I shall offer to let my mother feel my muscles, but she won't believe me and she'll go on pleading just the same, 'Don't squeeze his arm!' My father will be so pleased and proud and all the time he will keep repeating, 'My son, my son!' How I long to hear him now. I can almost see the whole scene.

"Are you an only son?" I asked, holding my breath and peering inquisitively into the Frenchman's meditative face.

"Yes, I am an only son. If the war had not spared me, my parents would be more stricken than you."

"Hedwiga is not a son. She is my daughter," I muttered, since he and reminded me of her indirectly. "A daughter is only a bird of passage, so to speak."

Mollendruz glanced at me with surprise. He looked as if he were trying to guess what I was thinking.

"Perhaps that is how it seems to you," he said. "The one you've lost is always more precious."

"Each is precious in his own way," said Johann. He was tapping the edge of the table pensively with his knuckles.

The alcohol had begun to dull our senses. Johann was growing drowsy and Mollendruz was growing sad. I was afraid that at any moment I might blurt out my theory of justice and what I thought about inflicting punishment with my own hands. I felt a strange desire to stare obstinately into Mollendruz's face, examine his muscular form and talk to him about his parents.

We stayed a little longer talking at the table. We discussed different things but all the time the words that Mollendruz's father had spoken rang like a bell in my mind: "My son, my son!" Sometimes I could only hear them very faintly; at other times they filled me with hatred; later they sounded idyllic and fascinating. They seemed to answer my most secret thoughts, telling me what I must do.

I went back to my room, but I could not sleep.

I kept my lamp burning all night under a dark shade. The old and heavy furniture kept gloomy watch around me. A solemn light played on the frame of my wife's portrait in the shadows. Just as in the first unforgettable nights after the loss of my son, I sat in a chair at the desk and gazed at Otto's photograph.

*   *   *

Once you have decided to kill a man, his life is in your hands. Like fate, you can shorten or prolong his life at will. If you allow him a few more days, you can watch him fail to make the most of them or you can admire how he puts them to good use. Like a gardener, you know the day and the hour when you will come to pluck the ripened fruit. Like a being from a higher plane of existence, you can look into your victim's unsuspecting eyes and despise him because he does not know. Your will is as powerful as the will of fate. For him you are fate.

Not everyone is destined to enjoy such knowledge. Few are those who can say that they have experienced the feelings of the superman.

Now that I had decided that Mollendruz was worthy to counterbalance the loss of my son, I knew the feelings brought with them a false echo. I knew that I must carry out an act of murder but I also knew that I was condemned in advance. The decision to commit murder is equivalent to the decision to commit suicide.

Every time I saw Mollendruz, I recognized in myself the supreme lord of his life and his death. The words, "My son, my son!" which his father had uttered with pride, and which Mollendruz himself had repeated to me, made the sentence of death irrevocable. Those words tortured me. I would pause in front of Otto's photograph and whisper the same words: "My son, my son!"

I found Johann shooting rabbits. A special light revolver was used for the purpose. As Johann took each animal by its strong fleshy ears and lifted it out of the wire hutch, its body hung helplessly and the hind legs twitched and tried to get a footing. Then he pressed the barrel of the revolver to the rabbit's head between the ears and squeezed the trigger. The shot made a feeble sound, like a sudden tearing of cloth. The animal thrust its hind legs violently forward and quivered for a moment in a death agony. Then its body stretched out heavily to its full length and grew stiff.

It was a necessary, though repulsive, task in running the estate. I used to hate it. But this time, when I saw Johann at work, I went up to him. He was busy with more than a dozen of the harmless creatures. He had already killed several of them and placed them carefully on the ground so that the blood would not stain the fur. I told him that I would like to try my hand at it, to see how well I could do it. He was surprised but he pulled a rabbit out of the hutch for me.

"This one's bad tempered and certainly ought to be done away with," he said. "None of the others can get along with him. He's quarrelsome."

The rabbit looked at us out of its glassy red eyes. Its nose, with restless pale whiskers, sniffed inquisitively at us from a distance. Johann was holding it by the ears without raising it from the ground. I hooked my finger round the trigger and counted: "One, two, three!" Johann jerked the poor rabbit's body smartly upwards. It began to thrash helplessly in terror, I placed the barrel of the revolver between the rabbit's ears and pulled the trigger. I watched again the brief agony of death; this time I was an actor, not a mere spectator. It proved to be very easy to take away life. It was only necessary to destroy a vital organ. I knew that this was true of all living creatures, and man was no exception.

The power of life and death lay in the finger with which I had pulled the trigger. The task of revenge had cost Krimhild untold labor and a wealth of satanic imagination. Now it was as easy as squeezing the trigger of a pistol. I was in unusually good spirits when I proceeded to the park and went to see what work was in progress on the estate. I had not made a tour of inspection for a long time. Now I gave everyone instructions, adding in some cases reproofs and reprimands. But they could all see that I was in good spirits. They answered me cheerfully and watched with deferential smiles as I took my leave.

My plan was maturing in my mind. I went back to my study and cuatiously opened the bottom drawer of the writing desk. As I pulled it, the drawer made a harsh noise that jarred on my nerves. I took out the revolver which I had found accidentally while rummaging for the box of cigars. It was an old Browning of light caliber. No one knew of its existence. I picked it up and balanced it reflectively in my hand. Then, with a gesture I had practiced long before, I took aim at the lamp, at the window and at the edge of the chair. My slow, methodical movements might have been controlled by an external power. I inspected the magazine and the cartridges.

Suddenly, my heart began to beat rapidly and painfully. I pressed it with my hand and felt its irregular and violent pulsation, as if a small frightened bird were struggling under my palm. I had to lie down and calm myself. I had no clear plan of action; in my mind there were only the germs of ideas. But a blind urge to perform some horrible act infected my blood, and my heart beat painfully in response.

In spite of my physical distress, I had a mounting feeling of stature and power. The sensation I had felt on shooting the rabbit lingered in my finger. Now I thought that I could kill Mollendruz on sight. The effect was so overwhelming that I could not bear to stay in the room. I went out and asked where Mollendruz was. Some said that he had gone in the direction of the woods and was making for the field that was still being cleared for pasture; others said that he was in the dairy. I thrust my hand into the pocket of my jacket, where the revolver was, and set out for the dairy. I walked with light, firm steps. I found several people at work. Mollendruz was wearing a blue apron over his khaki uniform. He had a screwdriver in his hand and was repairing a separator that had been dismantled. Hedwiga was in charge of another separator next to him. A jet of cream flowed from the spout. A farm boy was standing beside her and turning the handle. Hedwiga saw me.

When I saw her, I was as shocked as if I had been running at full speed in the dark and had collided with a wall.

"Father, you don't look well. You should go to bed," she said. In her eyes there was that gaze of maternal care and tenderness which makes even elderly men feel like little boys. Her glance had something in it that reminded me of my mother.

I went over to the farm boy and scolded him for turning the handle of the separator too fast. Then I told Hedwiga that she was mistaken; I insisted that I felt perfectly fit. I said that I intended to go and see how the work was progressing in the pasture. and that, as a land owner, my business was estate-managment, not lying in bed.

As I spoke, I watched Mollendruz and knew that I was no better than a thief scheming to rob him of his life. My resolution was unwavering; and my plan had fully matured. To me, Mollendruz was no longer a French prisoner-of-war but the scapegoat for my loss and the man equal in worth to my son. And beyond him was his father, who could still expect to utter the proud words, that I would never utter again: "My son, my son!"

Mollendruz asked me to help him with the separator. We worked together for about an hour, trying to repair the mechanism. We took the segments apart and put them together again in the hope of locating and correcting the defect. We talked while we worked, and Hedwiga joined in the conversation.

A new idea for my plan occurred to me. I would not take revenge by shooting the Frenchamn openly in the chest. I did not want to insure my own death with his. Vengeance must follow the pattern of Otto's death, and he had been killed by a bullet cowardly fired from ambush. I strolled about the estate until noon, all the while I kept my hand in the pocket of my jacket and clutched the handle of the revolver as though it were the hand of a friendly confederate.

In the afternoon I received official notification from the town council that it was taking Mollendruz under its direct supervision and he must leave my estate. Immediately, I telephoned the mayor and the commandant of the camp and persuaded them to let Mollendruz stay a few more days because I could not release him on such short notice. They probably regarded my insistence as the obstinacy and touchiness of old age, so they agreed to let the Frenchman remain with me for a few days longer.

The mayor disliked me as much as I disliked him. He did not like my pride, and I conjectured that the demand for Mollendruz was the method he had devised for demonstrating his power over my affairs. In normal circumstances I would never have asked him to postpone his request. If anything, I would have been amused at his intrigue. I would have brushed it aside like the buzzing of a gnat near my head. But this time I managed to overlook my dignity; I did not want to lose my Frenchman.

I felt as if I were trapped in an endless maze, where I wandered and bumped against the walls without finding any way out. I could not see how to carry out my plan. When I rose the next morning, my head ached and there were swellings under my eyes. My heart felt as if it had expanded unnaturally; it was like a foreign body lodged in my chest, where its beating hurt me and made me tremble. Hedwiga looked very anxious when she saw me. She brought me some brandy, urged me to go to bed and took my temperature. I promised to lie down shortly and went out into the park.

*   *   *

I knew by instinct, not by reasoning, what I was to do and how I was to do it. Everything was falling into place like a well planned game of chess. The auxiliary moves of the various pieces followed one upon the other until they approached the intended finale.

I found Mollendruz in the park and, avoiding his glance, I ordered him to set out at once for the pasture, where he was to hand over the duties of overseer to the best workman among the Russians and give him the proper instructions. Taken aback by my urgency, since I kept repeating the words "at once," Mollendruz said that he would start out for the pasture without delay.

Nothing worried me now. I thrust aside every thought of hesitation because I had only a very limited time in which to act. I could not invent any complicated schemes or involved plans; I dared not waste time on unanswerable questions. I was certain that the moves I was making on the chessboard were logical and sound. Besides, nothing could be more effective than a simple and direct course.

In the park I exchanged a word with a young widow who had come to live on the estate after the bombardment of the town. I complained of my weak health. After that, I saw Hedwiga and told her that I was going to lie down. I asked Johann to leave me undisturbed because I had spent a sleepless night and did not feel well.

From the moment I closed the door of my room behind me, I felt that I had shut the door to one side of my life and stood on the threshold of another. I was weighed down by the enormity of the climax that was drawing near. I was a superman, wielding power over another's life and death. I had crossed the boundaries of good and evil.

Methodically, I wound a scarf about my neck and put on my cap. At the door, I hesitated a moment for no reason, as if I were listening for something. In the index finger of my right hand I could still feel the pleasant sensation of pulling the trigger of the revolver with which I had killed the rabbit. Then, swiftly, like a thief, crawled out through the open window into a thicket of lilac bushes.

Here, the wilted leaves had not yet fallen because the lilacs were sheltered from the wind; and so I was hidden by a screen of rotting foliage. I hurried on between the bushes that grew close together; then I made my way down a slope, skirting the orchard, and came out by the stream. Here, I found a path that I had known since I was a boy. Following the stream, it led along the slope under a towering cliff in the direction of the pasture. I set off downstream, the heels of my shoes sinking into the soggy ground.

I was quite sure that I could overtake Mollendruz on the road at a place where it passed through dense bushes. If I did not overtake him, I would wait there until he came back. He always walked along this road by himself slowly without any Russians accompanying him. I was well aware of his habit of walking slowly alone, sometimes humming quietly or smoking.

The path along which I was hurrying came to an end at the far side of the pasture, where the cliff rose vertically above the valley and looked down on a bend in the stream. The road that Mollendruz was taking to the pasture was much longer, and I would certainly be the first to arrive.

I kept slipping on the damp and withered grass and I grew short of breath, but I tried not to cough or fall. The path led up and down along the steep bank of the stream; at times it dropped almost to the level of the water; then it climbed the granite masses near the top of the cliff before plunging downwards again. Close to the path there were green carpets of moss on both sides; but a little further off, tangled clumps of young spruces clung to the slope and sank their roots tenaciously into the crevices of the granite. In places, their crooked trunks rose in a curve from the roots as if they were glued to the massive wall of stone. I clambered upward, hanging on to branches that hissed like whips through the air when I let them go.

When I was near the top of the cliff, the stream below was hidden from me by the leafless bushes growing thickly on its banks. I could see a broad expanse of hills rippling like waves in the distance, and vast forests that looked like black splotches on the horizon. A thicket of young spruces and the slender trunks of hazel bushes that had shed their leaves separated me from the field which was being cleared for pasture.

The cool-smelling branches of the spruce trees afforded me cover. I crept stealthily along the edge of the cliff, stopping every so often to listen. Before long, I heard the voices of the Russians and knew that I was near the place where they were working. Keeping to my plan, I decided to make a detour through the trees in order to avoid the Russians and reach the road at the spot where I expected Mollendruz. I left the path and made my way through the spruces; I halted for a moment to recover my breath before crossing a narrow glade.

Now, all my movements were calm and precisely calculated. Like a hunter tracking down his quarry, I could devote all my energies to carrying out my plan. I still had no clear conception of the great moment I was preparing for, but I grew ever more insistently aware of the meaning and necessity of retaliation. I recognized that the choice for me was between killing Mollendruz and suicide; unless I killed him now, I could not go on living. His father must suffer that sense of loss which tormented me beyond endurance.

I saw Mollendruz sitting at the side of the glade. He was by the very edge of the cliff, a short distance from the hazel bushes. At first, I could not believe what I saw. I thought that my senses were deceiving me. I grew stiff and held my breath, like a wild animal lurking among the trees. My heart was beating so quickly that I felt a pain in my chest. I began to fear that I might suffer a heart attack before I could exact vengeance for Otto's death.

Mollendruz was sitting on a rock with his back to me. He was bent slightly forward and appeared to be reading a book. But on watching him more closely, I could see from the movement of his right elbow that he was writing.

Very slowly, I took the revolver from my pocket and released the safety catch. I held the weapon forward in one hand, rested it on my other outstretched arm and took aim by raising the muzzle. The distance between us was about twenty meters. I watched the foresight move gradually up Mollendruz's back and come to rest on the crown of his bowed head. I could scarcely restrain my longing to squeeze the trigger, but on estimating the distance I did not dare to risk a shot. The heavy beating of my heart made the pulse in my hand throb furiously, and the foresight of the revolver began to dance up and down.

Unexpectedly, the Russian workmen broke into song. They were close to us and their song rang out in strange and mournful notes like a lament. A dry twig snapped under my foot, I felt an icy shiver run through me, as if I were enveloped in a dank and chilly mist. Mollendruz was still leaning forward and writing on a piece of paper on his knees.

I put the revolver into the pocket of my coat. I bent down and seized a heavy stone that was lying at my feet. I was shaped like a prehistoric weapon. I lifted it easily and advanced, cautiously at first; then, with less attempt at concealment, I crossed the twenty meters that separated me from Mollendruz. When I had only a few steps to go, he stopped writing. He was on the point of turning towards the approaching footsteps, but I was already at his back. With all my strength, I brought the pointed end of the stone directly downward against the Frenchman's head and drove it into his skull. His shoulders and arms jerked upward, as if he were trying to beat his hands like wings. But there was no strength in his movement and he began to fall forward from the bent position in which he was sitting. I kicked him hard in the back. Losing its balance, his body slipped easily and swiftly over the edge of the cliff.

I did not hear the sound of his fall. There was a haze before my eyes and I could not bring myself to look down where he lay. I sprang back into the moist coolness of the spruce thicket and then, following my instinct and without thinking, I ran down along the terraced path like a wild goat fleeing from a hunter.

Translated by Raphael Sealey and Milton Stark

JURGIS JANKUS

JURGIS JANKUS was born in Biliunai, Lithuania, on December 27, 1906. After graduating from the University of Kaunas, he was a primary-school teacher for ten years and served as resident dramatist at the Youth Theater in Kaunas (1934-44). After six years as a refugee in Germany, he emigrated to the United States in 1950 and has resided since in Rochester, New York.

Making an auspicious debut in Lithuania with his novels *Egzaminai* (Exams), and *Be Krantu* (Without Shores), 1938, Jankus buttressed his literary reputation while in exile. His novella *Velnio bala* (The Devil's Bog) was translated into English, German, Italian, Flemish and Latvian, and was also made into a film. He has published two collections of stories: *Naktis ant moru* (Night on the Bier), 1948, and the novels *Paklyde pauksciai* (Lost Birds), 1952, and *Namas geroj gatvei* (House on a Good Street), 1954. His plays include *Peilio asmenimis* (On the Knife's Edge), 1967, which deals with the Anti-Soviet resistance in Lithuania. He has also written fairy tales and stories of adventure for young readers.

Photo by Vytautas Mazelis

Jurgis Jankus

JURGIS JANKUS

(1906–)

The China Bowl

IT WAS WHITE, ELEGANT and adorned at the brim with a wreath of tiny round notches.

"I could go on looking at it forever," Baniene would say with pride. "And to think of a design like that: a wreath full of notches like nails."

You see, it was no ordinary bowl, which one might pick up and bargain for at a country fair; it had been bought in Riga. Only once in her hard life had Baniene journeyed to town and, among other things, brought home with her this precious token.

But many days have passed since then: her children have grown up, and the First World War has swept past them like a torpid dream taking with it her husband. . . . Yes, a great deal has happened since those days, and it has been difficult to recall everything, but the bowl, the lovely white bowl, has remained.

And so, in time, it came to represent to Baniene a bowl into which all her experiences, both painful and pleasant, were stored. And since it had all happened so long ago, she could dwell on them without fear or anguish.

It usually stood in the furthest corner of the china cupboard and no one was allowed to put anything above or below it, and once, because of this, Baniene and her daughter-in-law had quarreled. Since then, Baniene's hands alone have had the right to touch it.

"Don't you go washing up that bowl," she had warned her daughter-in-law that very morning.

"If you were to break it, I don't know what I would do to you."

They were merely words, hard and full of roughness, but Baniene had a forgiving heart.

She was hastening now with the cows to the grazing ground, so that when she had them tied up, she would have time to run to the thicket and gather a few handfulls of nuts for her grandson. She wished that she could stay there longer, but her own son had been summoned to the local council that very morning and her daughter-in-law was busy raking the spring corn. Nevertheless, she must bring some nuts for Gintutis, the ceaseless prattler with his white, fluffy dandelion hair.

From time to time as she hurriedly recited her morning prayers, she would look up at the rising sun, and one could catch words like son, grandson, daughter-in-law, and God knows what about the old days, which long since glided away, cloudlike in the azure sky.

"Why, I see there's not much left of you, Marijona," she said to herself. . . . "In the old days, the housework would be done in no time at all, and you were always the first at the mushrooming. And now look at you, you run and you pant and the hazel thicket is still nowhere in sight."

But at the edge of the clearing she found that the bushes were already combed over, so there was nothing left but to wade into the dew.

"Lord, if they were to go and break it," she sighed to herself, and in her mind's eye stood the comely white bowl.

Yesterday, the schoolmaster had called to see them and they begged him to taste their honey. Her daughter-in-law thought that a deeper plate would do but old Baniene insisted on bringing out her china bowl, spooned it full of honey and placed it on the table.

And while the schoolmaster was eating he talked of many things, but to Baniene they were strange and uninteresting, and she kept glancing at the white wreath of notches above the clouded honey and looked as if she longed to ask him something. But the others were so quick with their questions.

At last, when everyone else fell silent, searching for new words, she summoned up enough courage to say,

"And has the schoolmaster been to Riga?"

To Riga? No, he had never been to Riga. And, he thought, if ever he did have occasion to go there, he was bound to get lost at once.

Oh, but she had been. And how wonderful it all was. And such wealth everywhere. And it was in Riga that she came to buy this very china bowl.

They listened to her in silence, and as she talked she found that she had such a lot to say to this young man who had never seen the town of Riga.

On her way home, as she waded through the wet grass, she recalled yesterday's talk and the words she had forgotten to say, but now, quite different words came to mind and her heart grieved that she had expressed herself so badly.

Gintutis was waiting for her on the threshold. A little while before, his mother had walked out to the fields and told him to sit at the window and wait for his grandmother. She would bring him a whole apronful of nuts.

"Grandma, have you brought me any nuts, Grandma?"

And when Baniene began to heap large clusters of yellow nuts from her pockets onto the table, Gintutis hurriedly pulled up a chair, clambered onto it, jumped up and down, clapping his hands and squealing.

A smile transfigured Baniene's face; she stroked her grandson's hair gently and looked at him with profound devotion. Then she seated Gintutis on the table and brought him a small hammer. At once, the child was absorbed in the serious business of cracking nuts. He was barely four and the task came none too easily to him. Sometimes the nut became hopelessly squashed or it shot from under his hammer like a bullet into the middle of the floor, and then the child cried:

"Grandma, Grandmama, reach me the nut, Grandmama!"

She never failed to find it, hobbling and looking for it around the beds and under the table. And suddenly he made a surprising discovery. When you hit the nut with the point of your hammer, it always zoomed away from you. And now the race began: earnest and full of zest. Gintutis, with his head thrown backward, laughed and shot the nuts as fast as he could, while his grandmother retrieved them faithfully from beneath the table and from the middle of the floor.

When, at last, all the nuts had found their way into Baniene's pocket, she came to the table, placed her toil-worn hand on his fair head, and said in a serious voice:

"That will do, Gintutis. You'll be the end of me yet! Be a good boy now, piglet is hungry. I'm going for some beetroot leaves, so you stay here, eat your nuts, and look out of the window."

And smiling, she went out to the kitchen garden.

Now the child watched her stooping and bending, with her skirts tucked up, among the thriving beds of beetroot. No, he did not like piglet. Let loose, she grunted her way towards him, as if about to hollow out his tummy with her pointed snout. He would rather his grandmother did not feed her at all.

After awhile, he went back to his nuts. He tried to break them carefully now, without squashing them and he almost succeeded.

But soon his attention was caught by a few nailheads which someone had driven in at the end of the table at some time or other; they stood out a little from the wood and gleamed with constant scrubbing. Gintutis hit at these nails once, twice, but to no effect; then suddenly, a passion for hammering seized him. The nails had long since disappeared into the boards, yet the child went on hammering. His face, when at last he raised it, was flushed and his eyes shone brightly.

"Oh," thought Gintutis, "if only there were more nails. Long nails and tiny nails like fir needles."

His grandmother, when she had gathered a sheaf of rustling beetroot leaves, sat down on the cottage doorstep to chop them up. Usually, Gintutis loved to sit near her, on an ancient stone sunk deep into the ground, and watch the beetroot leaves fall into an untidy pyramid.

He would gladly run to her now and sit at her feet if it were not for this strange object that he held in his hands, turning it this way and that and lightly fingering the round nail-like notches. His grandmother had forgotten it, in her haste, leaving it still unrinsed at the edge of the table. Gintutis lifted the bowl up once again, smiled and then giggled in a high, childish voice. Yes, he would drive all those nails in, so that it would be done before his grandmother discovered them. And that would be a far more difficult task for her, than picking up nuts from the floor. He listened in silence, smiling a clever traitor's smile. No, his grandmother was not coming back, for he could still hear the even, rhythmical sound of her knife. If only she had a huge heap of beetroot leaves and would go on chopping them until all the nails were hammered in.

And then he would say to her,

"See if you can find them, Grandmama!"

The child concentrated, then raised the little hammer above his head and brought it down on the nearest nail-notches.

Something quite undreamt of happened. There was a sharp breaking sound, several pieces of china shot into the air——and the lovely white bowl lay split in two on the table.

The child shuddered. He sensed that something terrible had happened, and sat there awestruck and motionless. Then suddenly he seized the two broken parts of the bowl and pressed them together with all his might.

Baniene's ears had caught the sharp, ringing sound, and she knew at once that Gintutis had broken something. Slowly, she laid aside a handful of beetroot leaves, brushed some away from the doorstep with the blade of her knife and, rising to her feet exclaimed,

"It must be the window!"

As soon as she opened the door, she saw everything at a glance. Pieces of broken china lay scattered on the table (it was strange how many of them she seemed to see), and Gintutis sat there white and trembling.

"Jezau, Marija!" she exclaimed in a frightening voice.

The child jumped. He saw his grandmother crossing the threshold and knew that he must get away. He scrambled to his feet and began to run but his shirt tripped him up——he missed the chair and with his arms held wide open, fell to the floor. He lay there motionless, as though embracing the earth.

Baniene was stunned and did not seem to understand what had happened. Her mind was still full of the broken pieces, yet she stood with her gaze fixed on her grandson.

Only a moment ago she was beside herself with anger, aching to punish Gintutis, to give him a good beating, but now, as she stood there looking at him, a thought more terrible than all others pierced her. Was the boy still alive? And, forgetting all else, she rushed over to him.

"Merciful God," she whispered humbly as she wiped the boy's mouth and tried to stop the blood from flowing. The child did not cry: he only trembled and sobbed silently . . . .

Then she seated herself on the bench and without a thought or a word, rocked her grandson for a long time; blindly aware that a hostile force had entered their lives to bereave them of this warm and gentle being.

And when the child began to breathe deeply, and started once or twice in his sleep, she put him carefully to bed, gathered up the fragments of the china bowl and knotting them in a piece of rag, buried them at the bottom of her dowry chest.

She felt that she had lost a great treasure, a part of her very life, her only pride, and words could not express her loss. Her heart trembled on remembering that something far more precious could so easily have been taken from them, but no one ever must know of it, and fetching a brush and a handful of ashes, she stopped to rub out the stains of blood from the damp, earthen floor.

Translated by Danguole Sealey

ANTANAS VAICIULAITIS

Born in Vilkaviskis on June 23, 1906, ANTANAS VAICIULAITIS studied literature at the universities of Kaunas, Grenoble and the Sorbonne. Having completed his studies, he was a teacher, magazine editor, diplomat and translator. During World War II, he emigrated to the United States, where he taught French in several colleges. For many years he was editor of the Lithuanian cultural magazine, "Aidai" (The Echoes). Currently, he resides in Bethesda, Md. and was on the staff of the Voice of America.

His numerous books include the collections of stories, *Vakaras sargo namely* (Evening in the Watchman's Cottage), 1932; *Vidudienis kaimo smukleje* (Noon at the Country Inn), 1933; *Pelkiu Takas* (The Path in the Swamp), 1939; and *Pasakojimai* (Tales), 1955. He also wrote a novel, *Valentina,* 1936, and has written travel books of high literary quality and literature textbooks. He is noted as a literary critic, and anthologist and a translator of French authors. His prose has been widely translated.

Antanas Vaiciulaitis

ANTANAS VAICIULAITIS
(1906-   )

Noon at a Country Inn

Dimmi un poco, hai tu nissun dinaro addosso?
LEONARDO DA VINCI

ON A WARM, SUNNY DAY like today and the one we enjoyed yesterday, a man was traveling on foot through the forest. He wore a pair of high, wide boots, velvet trousers, and a jacket of the same material. From time to time he stopped to wipe his face with a red handkerchief.

"Not a soul in sight for miles around!" he sighed dejectedly to himself. "I can already see myself having to fast for a whole year. But wasn't that a dog barking just now?" The traveler quickened his pace and soon arrived at a clearing, where he found a hamlet with an old, tile-roofed inn. The innkeeper, sprawled out in the sun, was lazily stroking his beard, blacker than tar, which flowed down to his waist.

"Please step inside, do!" he said, by way of greeting. "A good table awaits you, and a full jug, too, day or night. And then, it's cooler indoors."

In one corner of the room, which had a low ceiling and smoke-stained walls, lay a tame fox tied to a chain. A middle-aged friar sat beside the table, a book in his hand.

"Ah! A servant of God—this *is* a pleasure!" said the traveler. "Let me introduce myself. I am Severinas Sendriškis, from the city of Kaunas—though at one time I did reside abroad. I have a house in town, and a daughter. On my wife's side I'm related to His Excellency the Bishop of Zemaiciai—an image of wisdom, godliness, and every virtue. Whenever I happen to be in Varniai he graciously offers me his silver tobacco-box adorned with three rubies. . . . And he pats me on the shoulder, saying, 'My dear fellow! . . .'"

"Your merits astonish heaven," replied the friar. "In their light my faults become even more wretched. I'm on a pilgrimage to the Gate of Dawn at Vilnius, to atone for my sins. . . ."

"Gentlemen," the landlord interrupted them, "and when will you be wanting to eat?"

"I think we'd rather rest for a bit," said Severinas Sendriškis;

and he continued, turning to the friar: "You're on your way to the Gate of Dawn, did you say? I'm going there myself. Suppose we travel together.... What vows are taking you to Vilnius?"

"It's a selfish vow, my friend. Once I saw a little boy hanging by his shirt from the branch of a tree. The branch was beginning to break, and the child would certainly have fallen onto a large heap of stones below. As I hurried to save him, I made a vow then and there to visit our Lady of the Gate of Dawn, if I could catch him in time. As it turned out, I did save the rascal from dying; yet I could easily have turned to the protection of Saint Anthony. As patron of our order, he was quite available.... But I had always longed to make a pilgrimage to the Gate of Dawn, and could never find the opportunity. It was the very chance I'd hoped for. I explained the whole business to my superior, and he let me go."

"Your motives are as pure as yourself.... D'you know? I made a vow, too. This is how it happened. My daughter had been taken quite ill—she was even near death. Nothing seemed to do her the least good, neither doctors nor the finest medicines we could buy. Then I said to myself: 'I'll walk to Vilnius to pray to our Lady of the Gate of Dawn, if only my daughter gets well. I'll offer five pure silver candlesticks to Our Virgin Mother; I'll have masses said in all the churches; and for a whole half year, at the princely tomb of St. Casimir, I'll burn a wax taper as thick as the stick I'm carrying.' Almost at once my daughter began to recover, and now she's even walking a little, praise God. But where's the landlord now? You can see from my waistline, I'm no candidate for the religious life, what? Where are you hiding, landlord?"

"I'm here, gentlemen."

"We're both famished!"

"Well, then, what would you like to eat?"

"What can you offer us?"

"Everything's in the pantry, kind sirs; that is, except for swan's milk."

"Ah, let's see.... First bring us two bottles of wine."

"Wine? Hmm.... Did you say wine?"

"Yes, wine."

"As old as these log walls are, gentlemen, they've never yet clapped eyes on a bottle of wine."

"Well, do you have mead, then?"

"That I do—all you can drink."

"Would you have a pheasant in your pantry, by any chance?—No? Well, then let's settle for a suckling pig with fruit stuffing.—You don't have that? Very well. It'll have to be plain chicken. Two chickens do us quite well."

"Dear me, how can I explain?" began the innkeeper. "But only yesterday the hawk carried off my last chicken. And what a plump bird it was!"

"Quite so," remarked Sendriškis drily, pulling in his belt. "Only, that's no comfort to my stomach. But what's that I hear, if not a cock crowing?"

"It's a cock of the best breed, gentlemen, such as you never saw in your life," boasted the landlord, tugging at his beard.

"Why didn't you mention it to us before?"

"But sirs, you asked for chicken. How could I guess that you like cockerels?"

"Catch him! He'll do!"

"I'm not sure I can bring myself to part with him. He's been as good as a clock to me for the past ten years."

"I'll give you a whole sovereign for him. I tell you, man, I'm starving, and I won't be able to move from here till I've had a good, substantial meal."

"There's no help for it, then. . . . It's easy for you to say 'sovereign,' but another matter for me to be able to earn it."

Again the cockerel opened his beak and began to crow, either to record the changing weather or to lament his probable doom. His master, clasping his beard with his left hand and holding his right before him, crept stealthily toward the singer, who sat looking at him with mistrust. In reach of the bird, he made a wild clutch at him and fell down flat on the ground. The cockerel flew into the air and, with a shrill cackle, plunged into the kitchen garden. The innkeeper got up, clambered painfully over the fence, and began to dance about amidst the cabbage-heads, entangling himself more and more as he pursued the fowl. At last, safely established on the barn roof, the cockerel flapped his wings about him and scowled fiercely down at the landlord.

"What in heaven's name's the matter with you? Is a devil, or something else, lurking in you? D'you think it's the end of the world if I just want to put you in the oven? Believe me, I've done it many a time to the likes of you, and without half the fuss you're putting up. But no, whatever I do, you don't let me come near you."

"I'll go around to the other side and frighten him from there," suggested Sendriškis from the doorstep.

He picked up a stick, climbed a ladder, and began to wave his "weapon" about in the air. At first the bird couldn't decide what to do; then he beat his wings frantically and flew straight over the innkeeper's head to the ground; next, as fast as his legs could carry him, he scuttered off into the juniper bushes.

"Now we won't even see his tail-feathers," sighed the landlord. "He won't be back till evening, that's sure."

"But what about our meal?"

"Maybe you'd accept some ham, or a piece of wonderfully tasty sausage, seasoned with garlic? Or smoked bacon with black peppers?"

"Man!" cried Severinas. "You don't say a word, and you've got so much of God's bounty here! For heaven's sake, bring it all in, and now."

Bread, meat, bacon, and a comfortable, round jug of mead presently appeared on the table. As Sendriškis zestfully attacked the ham and sausage he did not forget the friar.

"I know that a servant of God must carry nothing on his journey, and that he must eat whatever is offered to him—like a cricket, I might say. Therefore, dear friar, I beg you not to refuse my invitation to this modest fare."

"May Our Dear Lord reward you a hundredfold for your kind heart!" said the friar.

For a time they ate in silence. Then, after Sendriškis had put away some mead and stilled his hunger pangs, he stared at his guest with astonishment.

"But my good man, you're eating meat! That means that you've broken your rule—and that interests me very much. When I was in Kalvarija I made a bet with my friend Fabijonas that some day, sooner or later, I'd find a friar who'd broken his rule. But I didn't expect to win this easily!"

"Please, dear sir, not so fast! You have certainly *not* won your bet, nor have I broken my rule. Our regulations state quite clearly that we may consume whatever we find along the way—meat, porridge, or plain water."

"Ah, that's a pity! And a disappointment. Now I'm afraid the Dominican will get to heaven the winner. . . . Damn, what a tough sausage this is! You could break your teeth on it, devil take it!"

"Why, you're swearing!" exclaimed the friar, hastily crossing himself.

"But surely, to speak of Satan is no sin— His name reminds us of hell and its everlasting fire and thus warns us away from the pleasures of sin."

"Please! Sir!—From the ugliness of sin, not pleasures of sin!"

"If you'll allow me—I'm no student of theology, but I do think people wouldn't fling themselves headlong into sin if it were ugly. I ask you, what man ever hopes to marry an ugly woman—and what woman would pursue a repulsive man? Everybody chases after things that are beautiful and pleasant. So surely we must say 'the pleasures of sin.' Otherwise, all sinners would be mere fools!"

"To your remarks about women," began the friar, "I decline to add one word. In my eyes, women are simply snares of the evil spirit, instruments that bring innocent men to their ruin—weather vanes, one might say, on the gables of the churches. . . ."

"I see you've got it in you to preach a fine sermon about women, and it wouldn't surprise me if women, seeing such a black picture of themselves, were to burst into tears. But, let me speak frankly, I wouldn't believe a word you might say."

"Why—?"

"Because, as a man of the cloth, you can't possibly know anything about women."

"Ah, but I can always view them from a theoretical standpoint."

"Oh? How could that help anyone? A woman is only interesting as herself. And in the flesh."

The whole time he was talking, Severinas ate on greedily. At last the timid friar could not restrain himself.

"If you're as concerned with your soul as with your body, then heaven's gates have been standing open for you a long time."

"But what in the world is wrong with loving our own body?"

"Everything! The body is the enemy."

"But didn't Our Lord Himself command us: 'Love thy enemy'?"

"Dear sir, you know that the body cannot save you!"

"And why not? Through love of the body, or of the soul, we can be saved."

"O Dear Lord, what heresy!" The friar stood up in his extreme agitation.

"My good friend, in the fulness of time our bodies will rise from the dead and ascend to heaven—if they deserve it. A man who loves his body will never wish to see it perish, but will so act that all he loves may find its way into the Garden of Paradise. . . . But what's that noise? D'you hear it?"

Thunder growled, deep in the woods, and they could see a black storm-cloud gathering in the sky.

As if carved in stone, the trees stood under the heat. The faint chirruping of a bird, and nothing else, could be heard.

Sendriškis stopped eating; the friar had already finished his meal. Then the wind came; it whistled through the gaps in the log walls and flattened the plants beneath the windows. The clouds swelled, heavy and swift, and the trees rustled and moaned. A few drops fell and then ceased. A muffled droning made its way indoors.

The two saw swallows, like black scraps of rags, flying before the wind. Then, all at once, as if someone had ripped the clouds apart, torrents of rain drenched the earth. Thunder followed on the heels of thunder, and lightning continuously slashed the sky. The woods seemed swaddled in muslin, and long fringes of water gurgled down from the ridges of the roof.

Then, as quickly as it had come, the storm blew past.

"Never in my life have I seen such a rain," said the landlord, opening the door.

"Ah," said Sendriškis, pointing to a tree stuck by lightning. "You can even smell the resin!"

The white disk of the sun floated out from the clouds, and the trees, flowers, and bushes stood forth clean and refreshed, as if newly created. The grass, glued before to the ground, righted itself; the puddles glittered; and brooks joyfully ran into the valley.

The air was so cool and refreshing that Severinas decided to have a nap before he set off again on his pilgrimage. When the friar came to waken him, the sun was almost touching the tree-tops of the forest.

"Thanks! I envy you your journey," said the landlord, as he pocketed the promised sovereign.

The moment the travelers had departed, the cockerel stepped out from the juniper bushes.

"Well, and what do we see here? You've had your feathers washed right and proper, that's for sure," remarked the innkeeper, as he leaned back to await new guests.

Making their way through a fragrant wood of linden-trees, Severinas Sendriškis and the friar came on a swollen brook. After the downpour, its waters had become a river, flowing over the field and bearing torn branhes, bushes, and twigs as it plunged on.

"Oh, what a misfortune!" cried Severinas. "I'll never be able to cross this swamp."

"But the water can't be so deep?" answered the friar. "It'll only come up to your knees."

"You may be right," said Severinas, "but I have a terrible rheumatism in my right leg. How can I cross that stream without getting my feet wet?"

"Don't worry! I'm tremendously strong. In the old days, single-handed, I could easily roll over an ox, I'll carry you across on my shoulders."

Almost at once Sendriškis found himself astride the shoulders of the friar, who walked straight into the water.

Then, in the exact center of the stream, the friar halted and spoke anxiously to his friend.

"Tell me, do you have money with you, by any chance?"

"Of course—and I'll give you as much as you want."

"Oh, in that case I *am* sorry, but I can't carry you farther. My rule strictly forbids me to carry money."

"But my dear friend, I'm the one with the money, not you."

"I know but I'm carrying you and your money, too. Certainly it isn't floating loose in the air—No, there's nothing else to do, you'll just have to come down. If I went on now, I'd be breaking my rule. And what opportunity that would be for you to win your bet with the Dominican! Please climb off, my friend—maybe God will spare you from rheumatism, this time."

"True, I can't lead you into sin now, can I? Thanks, anyway, for carrying me halfway across the river.—Ah, the water's quite warm! Maybe it won't hurt me after all. . . ."

Once on the far bank, Sendriškis waited a while for his leg to begin to ache.

"Hey, there's no pain!" he said cheerfully, after he had stood there for some minutes.

And then the sun began to set in earnest, and the two made their way along the sandy road, till they glimpsed from a hillock the belfries of Vilnius, gleaming far off in the valley. As the evening bells rang forth, both travelers bowed their heads and said the angelus, their eyes resting on the city of their forebears.

Translated by Danguolé Sealey

Photo by Vytautas Mazelis

Pulgis Andriusis

PULGIS ANDRIUSIS

Born in Gaidziai, Lithuania on March 18, 1907, PULGIS ANDRIUSIS travelled widely in Europe and North Africa, spent the years 1944-49 in refugee camps in Germany, and emigrated to Australia in 1949 where he died on December 19, 1973. He gained his popularity as a writer of humorous sketches and of a picaresque novel *Tipelis* (The Character), 1954. His literary stature was enhanced in exile by stories that were lyrically evocative of the Lithuanian landscape and character: *Sudiev, kvietkeli* (Farewell, Flower Mine), 1951; *Rojaus vartai* (The Gates of Paradise), 1954; *Anoj pusej ezero* (On the Other Side of the Lake), 1957; and *Purienos po vandeniu* (Marsh Marigolds Under Water), 1963. One of his best translations is the definitive Lithuanian version of Don Quixote, 1943.

PULGIS ANDRIUSIS

(1907-1973)

He Wasn't Allowed to See

UNCLE MYKOLA was already retired, if thus you could describe the bachelor farmer who, after long toilsome years, afflicted with asthma and stomach troubles, could now only shift his horse in the pasture or chop brushwood behind the house. Mykola would say to himself:
—Behold, now I'm almost eighty. Who knows if I'll ever see into the nineties?

On fine autumn days, strolling about the orchard, or offering a succulent apple to a random visitor, he would sigh:
—It's true. I'm like an over-ripe apple, myself. Just one drop more of the night dew, and there it lies, quite still on the ground!

As he chopped kindling in the back woodyard, separated from the outer world by a dark wall of nettles and mugworts, Mykola surely knew little of what was happening beyond. Sometimes a woman would trudge by, her yoke over her shoulders, carrying her laundry to the village pond. Or a neighbor's urchin would run past, chasing a gadfly.

Yet after a walk to Ozkaslaite to move his horse in the pasture and then back home, Mykola's sitting room would fill up to the ceiling with the latest news, so that you had to open the door, through which filtered broken fragments of the mild tales he told:
—By the gush of the spring! I think to myself . . .
—And then, behold, click! And it turned off . . .
—End of the world! I say to myself . . .

You could guess easily that Mykola had finished his long day's journey, and was recounting his adventures since early morning to a neighbor who has come to borrow his steelyard.
—Then I think I'll just sit down behind the hawthorn bushes at the edge of the loampit, to have a peaceful smoke on that boulder, you know the one I mean, the one that's hollowed out on top.
—I turn my head, and behold, above the birch grave of Skriaudakalnis stands a fairly tall cloud. Mykola, Mykola, old friend, you walk out to move your horse, and as soon as you pass the barn you walk straight under a rain-cloud, I think to myself!

—Look, the round cloud has stretched, and's now hanging a sleeve over Cecergis *sauna* bath by Devil's Footbridge, and has another sleeve pointing straight at my own collar. But what do I care? The barn and a good shelter are right here. And I think, well, now we'll see if thou'lst make rain, or if all thy efforts come to nothing!

—Near the little bath-house, right at Devil's Footbridge, a frog's croaking, oh, it's calling, trying to draw the cloud. Good thou canst croak on and burst! I think to myself. Not for thy sake do the clouds wander up in the sky, they can bring rain to good Catholics without thy help. Under the willows, hast some water covered with duckweed, just enough to wet thy belly, make the best of it. Thou hast no reason, none at all, to draw a cloud! It has its own ideas where to pour down a shower. Just think of my own barley field, gasping for water like Lenten fish—and not a drop falls.

—Well, my thoughts were running on like that, when the dark-edged cloud pauses just above the thornbushes by the loampits, casting a faint shadow across Devil's Footbridge, and here are my barleys, their beards gaping wide with thirst. All right, come on, I say. As for me, I've plenty of time to run to the barn for shelter. But we'll see—what willst thou do now, thyself?

—And while I was watching the cloud, up springs a whirlwind from Devil's Footbridge and hurls it to the other side of the barn. All at once the cloud swelled out like the sheepskin coat behind Tilindis' knees. And I was right not to rush back into the barn.

—My guess was right! How could such a skinny, shriveled cloud ever make rain? You could even move over it on your knees, squeezing and wringing it dry like wet trousers after a day casting the nets.

—And so I walk on through a narrow patch of meadow, and I think how we get teased and annoyed at every step. Then, all at once, my heel's bogged down, sunk into the earth. That's the end! I say. What's pulling me down?

—I turn around, and who do I see but a mole busily at work, lifting my own good meadow with his shoulders. Turn sour, will you? I think. Couldn't it move away, farther down, past Skriaudakalnis, into the fallow fields?—As if the soil wasn't just as good over there! And still the dirty beast raids my own meadow, my soul, not a poor patch of chickweed or thistles, but all clover and sorrel. When it's time for hay-mowing, those molehills can wrench the scythe out of your hands, and you have to go all the way home and hammer its edge straight against the front of the granary, because a whetstone wouldn't help when the edge has gone crooked as Cecergis' wooden plough.

—As I was thinking all this, the mole kept churning my dear clover, just as heartburn sometimes upsets your guts. And in your very presence, Mykola! And what can you do about it? With your heel you can trample in the molehill, that's sure. But who can promise you'll ever find your dear clover safe tomorrow? If the mole had any sense, you could ask him a straight question: Think, man, what do you imagine you're up to in these parts? Of course, you could pull him out of the earth by his ears, but alas, one of his brothers would finish what he left undone, and probably do still more harm—much more, to get even with you for wringing his neck. Still, you can't afford to stand a man with a cudgel by each molehill. Where would you find so many helpers, with such work to be finished: trips to the mill, welding your ploughshares, and hurrying to plough, again and again and again?

—So here I am, walking along the boundary ridge of Verstakis' barley field. Though a couple of days ago I didn't think much of his plants, they did find a good rooting—I was wrong when I thought they'd hardly crowd their beards up out of the mustard. Even my own barley can't be compared to Verstakis'—mine has managed to push down the mustard and couch weeds, but they've obviously been athirst with asthma, their beards spread out helter-skelter like Tartilas' whiskers, our bailiff of blessed memory, as he lay in state after his calamitous ailment.

—And I walk on down the ridge, thinking all this to myself, and behold! A flock of sparrows flies up from my feet, and in a while they settle at the edge of Darymas' meadow, all around the stone with the lightning-cleft hollow that holds water for two days after a downpour and gives drink to the ravens. And suddenly my hat bobs up on my head, it could easily have come down, because, God, how can anyone control matters in such an emergency?

—Here, Mykola, I tell myself, you labor and sow, you even try to pull the rain-cloud down with your own hands, and already the sparrows flock to your barley field with its unripe grains melting on the tip of your tongue, if you wanted to taste them!

—By gush of a spring! What brings such disorder into the world? If somebody's horse strays into your oat-field you lead it home and lock it in your stable to hold for ransom; or let a piebald pig get into your potato patch—you just smack it with a stick. At its first squeal, who should come running but Cecergis' wife with tears in her eyes!

—And I ask myself, all alone, who could be held responsible for the sparrows, if you injured one? It has no master to come running, that's sure, swearing with tears in his eyes never to let it happen again.

—A sparrow must live, too, that's clear, if God has breathed life into it and given it a crop. My faith, who minds a grain or two? But when it scatters more than it eats, that *is* something to make you sad.

—Before, I was about to throw a stone to the meadow's edge, but I was right to hold back. Because, you know, by the time you pick up a rock and move it into full swing, ready to throw, the sparrows are too far away and your target's lost. And anyway, they'd already flown into the tanner's wheatpatch.

—Well! I say to myself, I'll just sit down on the black boundary stone with the reminder of the plague years carved on its north side. It's a fact, I wanted to relax a little before I went into the fallow field near the gates. Because as I jumped over the ditch I felt a little "crack" in the hollows of my knees, and a pain went through me when I coughed. And that's no joke, you with your shoulders carrying the weight of eighty years!

—While I roll a cigarette with the tobacco from last year's crop, my eyes fall on Meldaikis' pea-patch. The peapod wonders if it should add one more pea—maybe it has enough. And while it was arguing with itself—click!—The sun finished the pod.—Enough! the sun said.

This is the way Mykola would talk when he was back home, after his great journey to shift his horse in the pasture just outside the fields. This trip usually took him the whole morning. For, slowed by his asthma and the fitful pains in his stomach, he had to stop often to rest on a stone or a stump by the lake, taking some soda powder or smoking some of his good yellow tobacco.

One year followed another, and his trips became less and less frequent. He was almost too weak even to chop the brushwood, and one day, as he was strolling in the orchard around the tobacco patch, he fell into the seedlings and had to be carried home, gasping for every breath.

—Now I'm like a perch tossed up onto the lake shore, my mouth agape for air. I'm afraid I won't breathe on into my nineties!

One spring, Mykola's condition improved. He planted some tobacco himself, pruned the apple-trees, and went to Bruzgakalnis Hill to cut a new supply of birch twigs for his *sauna* baths—he did enjoy using them, especially during the first three streams in the bath-house.

Just after Whitsuntide, when the fields were flowering in all their splendor and the primroses were in full blossom, Mykola felt safer in himself and walked out to Ozkaslaite near Lake Gilys.

And that was his last walk. They found him lying near a large stone, his tobacco scattered all around him.

When his nephew closed Mykola's dead eyes, the image of Lake Gilys still seemed to shine in the pupils.

—Well! I'm walking along the edge of the Degimai Bog, and the peewits hop from one stump to another and greet me: How are you? . . . How? I'm in good health, but for how long? I wonder. I'm glad you remember me, you crested ones, back after your winter of troubles. Ah, it hasn't been easy for me, either, wearing out my thigh-bones over the stove. Welcome! Welcome back to these parts!

—The breeze, warm as a human breath, blows lightly around the bend of my knees. I'd even loosened the belt on my sheepskin jacket. Let it shake the winter staleness out of my seams!

—And then I straddled my way over the plank bridge, farther down into the narrow meadow, filled to the brim with marsh marigolds. The frogs were croaking in unison, the brook purled, singing away the marks of winter straight into Lake Gilys. As I turned from the meadow toward the crab-apple tree I had a good mind to roll a cigarette, and I said to myself, when I get to the top of the hillock I'll sit down on that veined stone from where you can see all Lake Gilys, as flat as your palm.

—But as soon as I'd gotten halfway up the rise, by gush of a stream! A kind of darkness falls over my eyes. Just a moment ago everything seemed to be sunlight, and bright green carpets were laid over the fields. Now, all at once, everything looks drab, as if it were covered with smoked glass. And then I feel a stitch somewhere under my heart. It takes my breath away. Ah, I think to myself, this time it has you for sure, Mykola!

—I crawl toward the stone, my blue veins bursting; I didn't have a chance to roll that cigarette, I drop my tobacco-box, and my finecut yellow tobacco from last year scatters all over.

—And I fell so softly onto the stone, and Lake Gilys glittered a short moment through the alders, and my ears were full of the sweet warblings of the Ozkaslaite nightingales. Oh, God! The lake's getting bigger, the riverbank blurs and then it's gone, and at last all begins to fall in on me. I grope for the stone, I can't reach it. End of the world, I'm falling, falling into a pit, and still I reach for the stone, the songs of the nightingales deepen into rich organ music, the peewits are still calling me back to Degimai Bog, and the wild ducks soar up from the bulrush thickets, enshrouding me with their black wings.

—And now, again, I see such radiance! The marsh marigolds glitter everywhere, my heart is light, light, a greater music plays in it, louder and louder.

Thus may Mykola have spoken to the saints in heaven, after his long journey back to the eternal home, where he was brought before he was allowed to see into his nineties.

Translated by the Author with the editorial assistance of Clark Mills

Kazys Barenas

KAZYS BARENAS

KAZYS BARENAS was born in Stanioniai, Lithuania, on December 30, 1907. He studied literature at the University of Kaunas, worked as a journalist and free-lance writer, and emigrated to Great Britian in 1947. In London he was a long-year editor of the weekly *Europos lietuvis* (The European Lithuanian) and managed the Nida Book Club. He is the author of three collections of short stories: *Giedra visad grizta* (Fair Weather Always Returns), 1956; *Karaliska diena* (A Royal Day), 1957; and *Atsitiktiniai susitikimai* (Chance Encounters), 1958. His latest work, the episodic novel *Dividesimt viena Veronika* (Twenty-one Veronicas), represents the most mature achievement of his writing career.

KAZYS BARENAS

(1907-   )

The Queen Mother

VERONIKA GAZES at the photograph. For several years now, she has been constantly plagued by the thought that her mother is buried in a new cemetery. The worry never fails to come back: so that's how it is, a marsh, perhaps, and the wind rages and howls. Poverty had been her life, and after death they had to bury her in a swamp in some lonely field. Who has ever seen a poor person buried in a decent place! He always tags at the tail-end of the queue while still alive; he's tucked away in some goddamdest corner when he dies.

It was with a troubled heart that she heard her brothers' and her sister's idea that they should pool their resources and build a monument for mother. She yearned for a monument as grand as those that are built for queens, but she was made anxious by the thought that the remote corner of the cemetery where her mother lay buried would most probably look even more horrible with a monument. No path there, not even the faintest track; one had to wade through waist-deep grass. At least if she were walking there herself, she might not even feel that dismal eeriness so strongly. At least some crow might come cawing from some distance and dispel the oppressiveness of the surroundings. If only Veronika could set out to visit her mother's grave herself, even to such backwards overgrown with sedge. But when she visualizes that poor cemetery where mother lies buried, it is difficult for her to restrain her many anxieties. That's how the grave-site may look, but then it may be the exact opposite.

The photograph eases her difficulties and doubts. This is where the remains of Veronika's queen were laid to rest! A huge tree, a hundred or perhaps even two hundred years old, grows by the grave. As Veronika keeps staring at the photograph, it seems to her that the tree starts rustling—its leaves flicker, some patches lighter, some darker, and the lightness grows more somber again. She knows that all this flickering is only a trick her tired eyes are palying on her, but let them do it. She likes it. May it rustle for her, too, that huge tree, even if it is only in a photograph, because most likely she will never go back home again, she will never see and feel the live whisper of the leaves. And should she return and lean against that great tree, her thoughts but a couple of steps from the grave, would be the same as they are now: this is my sweet mother, *mamuliukas!* Fittingly, have they laid you to rest, my great queen mother . . . And while she was standing by the tree, swamped with memories, a bird on the branches might even sing a quiet song. What kind of bird? The names of those birds were alway getting mixed up in Veronika's mind, but she would like a soft, gentle melody. She finally decides on a thrush since it is a thrush's song she has been hearing every night next to her house. And why not? When, on some night she cannot fall asleep and keeps turning and tossing with her eyes open, into the morning, it is the thrush that always burst into his passionate tchyoo-tchyoo-lyoo-lyoo-tchyoo, lyoo-lyoo-tchyoo at dawn. And if mother's heart is exalted so will Veronika's be. That *mamuliukas* of hers, didn't she sometimes listen to a sparrow? Let there be a sparrow, too, let it chirp, a whole flock of them, a grand choir that never manages to harmonize its voices, as ong as *mamuliukas*-queen mother has a more pleasant sleep. She never liked solitude, that queen mother of Veronika.

  By now, Veronika was already smiling in her contentment. More than once, she had noticed royal traits in her mother. Just put her great straw hat on her head and see how well she carries herself. The hat is light. Not exactly a piece of fluff but light, nevertheless. With that hat on her head she would walk quite differently. She wouldn't look round but only straight ahead and would hold her head as straight as those Oriental women who balance pitchers of water on their heads. Or, if she were in the company of a man who was either learned or moved in the upper circles (but on whose favor her daily bread did not depend), she would dispense greetings as if she had just risen from a throne. Strangers could never tell that this was the same woman whose everyday routine was washing dishes in the house of the rich and who dressed her children in worn rags because new clothes were beyond her reach. A genuine queen of a lost realm! Veronika used to pin the queen's title on her mother, even in her presence, and would rejoice in its grandeur.

"A true queen," Veronika used to say, and that was her most powerful image. All queens in books were like that. But Veronika used to pronounce the title only when her mother alone could hear it. And sometimes, she would not even pronounce it, but merely think of it and smile. At home, you could not always say what came to your mind. She recalled her sister, Rozalija, the oldest of them all, whose fault it was that Veronika had to stop calling her mother a queen in everyone's presence. That last time, with everyone looking, Veronika admired her mother, dressed in her Sunday best, and said, "Our queen!" Rozalija retorted instantly, cackling like the ugliest duckling, "The queen of geese, her ass full of fleas!"

Veronika did not dare to jump Rozalija and to defend her mother's honor as well as her own right to express respect and her pride. Her heart seemed to drop from its proper place with these words of her sister. But just try to raise your hand against Rozalija! Not she would be sore afterwards, but you, and for days you would be touching gingerly all those black and blue spots where her fist had hit. You would go on touching them until you had licked them back to health, and for a long time afterwards you would know where the blue spot had been and you would keep feeling it as if it still hurt. Only when Veronika dies, only then will she take with her the most painful memories of her sister's fist from the days when she was so small that she could hardly rest her chin on the table top. In those days, she would say to herself, "Just wait, you bloody sister of mine, until I've grown to such a height that when I'm standing straight, it won't be my chin but the tips of my fingers, like my father's now, that will reach the table! Then we'll square our accounts for all the days past and you'll get it back for each and every bruise, for each punch, for every time you raised your hand against your little sister! All harm and pain will have to be made even. You'll come crawling and bawling to me, carrying ten such bags, and you'll kiss my hands, begging me to take them, to forgive and forget. Yes, that was the most painful injury, that red bag that her mother had made for Veronika's books during her first school year. Rozalija was already a chunky bulk and had taken two years to complete each of her grades. She knew her mother's strict orders to accompany her little sister to school and back home. After all, little Veronika might lose her way! And so Rozalija accompanied her. That particular morning, Veronika chattering gaily, toddled alongside her sister. From time to time she would stop to enjoy and admire her little book bag. Dear me, oh my, isn't it just out of this world! Mother had taken apart an old plush coat that she had brought from somewhere, found an unworn stretch with an even sheen, a snip here, a snip there, a little folding, a little sewing, and, surprise, little Veronika had something in which to pack her notebooks and readers. That evening, Veronika had gone to bed late and that was all the little bag's fault. Red plush was the last image she saw when she finally fell asleep. That's some bag for you! That morning they left together, and Rozalija kept silent. They went down the hill side by side. Then Rozalija stopped and seized Veronika's hand.

"Wait, don't turn!" she said, and Veronika stopped and looked at her. "Take your books out of the bag. Gimme the bag."

Veronika understood now.

"Not on my life!" Veronika replied and turned towards the road. "Mommy made it for me."

"You dare say no?"

Where can Veronika run away from Rozalija. Just look at her legs, how terribly long, compared to Veronika's short ones. One step for Rozalija, two or three for Veronika. She soon fell under her sister's blow. Falling, rising, she tried to hold onto her bag. Her eyes were flooded with tears. One and two, here and there, the blows kept raining, until Veronika became exhausted. Her sister packed her own books into the red bag, while Veronika's books lay scattered about.

"Get 'em and let's go! Faster!" Rozalija shouted.

The world was still there after that clash. The sun had jumped a few yards higher from behind the hill. Two large maple trees were rustling in the back, while near the third one, Veronika slowly gathered her copybooks. The sky was so pale blue. The world was carrying on as usual all about her, only Veronika could not see it through her tears anymore. Her own world had collapsed, although to this very day she still carries with her an image of the hill with the sun, the trees and the road, and whenever she sees that special bright red, she always remembers her school bag.

If that's how things were, could she then have jumped Rozalija in order to defend her mother against these disrespectful words? And so she did not. But words that would be certain to offend her sister seemed to enter her mind by themselves. At first, she repeated those words to herself softly: "Rosie, Rosie . . ." But the words increased her own pain. As long as they had not reached her sister's ears, they would be nibbling at Veronika herself. Let them pour out and strike her sister; then she would feel it, that bloody sister of hers. Veronika's lips were now beginning to move. She murmured words that nobody could hear. A little louder! Everybody will hear them now.

"Rosie, Rosie, fat and nosey," she mumbled. "Rosie, Rosie, fat and nosey! Rosie, Rosie . . ." And now each and everyone could hear her. Rozalija dashed toward her from the window, her heels making a dull noise.

"I'll show you!"

The fists were in readiness. Veronika clutched her head and screamed:

"Ma-ma! Ma-ma! Rozalija's going mad!"

Mother jumped to her feet and Rozalija managed to unload only one or two blows.

"Quiet, girls!" their mother scolded, and Veronika slipped out through the door. Her sister would most likely return to the window, where she was flipping through postcards with pictures of movie stars. She was admiring Ramon Novarro when Veronika blurted out the ditty about Rosie. Veronika was consumed by an overwhelming desire to retrieve the postcard with Ramon Novarro on it from her sister. Had she not saved the money when she bought her grammar in a used book store? A used textbook always went for half price. That time, she got the book for even less than half-price because the cover was torn off. And on top of that, she found a picture there of Ramon Novarro, which her sister begged her to give her. "What do you need it for, you're only starting your collection," her sister was saying. "You've only got one, and look at mine, what a pile! You can start collecting when you reach my age." Rozalija went on. "Besides, you're much too young to get involved with movie stars. Give it to me!" Veronika believed her then, and now just look at that Rozalija! She was repaying with her fists for Ramon Novarro.

Veronika slips out through the door, although she knows that her mother would not allow any fighting. When she says, quiet, then everything must stop, peace, sabbath. She slips out, because she feels that there is much injustice. Why couldn't she pummel Rozalija for insulting Mother? Is it because Rozalija is older and bigger? Why didn't Mother bawl Rozalija out, when she started oinking about those fleas? Mother could have said more severely, "Well, well, Rozalija! What d'you think you're doing?"

Rozalija would have shut her mouth in the middle of the sentence. She wold have gone back to her movie stars. It seems that Mother is also afraid of Rozalija. But who the heck is this Rozalija? A hog, a porky! Ogling at Ramon Novarro will not save her. But if even Mother is afraid of Rozalija then it's the end, all's finished, chewed up and swallowed. As for Mother being afraid, Veronika believes it. Only look at mother's hands with those prominent veins. And then take a look at Rozalija's hands. Disgustingly healthy, slightly puffy, like buns. Healthy and painful.

That is why Veronika takes a walk across the railway tracks. She will stand under the maple tree for a while, listening to the rustling and the chirping of the birds in the branches. She will climb the hill—how green, green all around. Veronika feels better. Green, green all the way up, and downhill daisies blossom all over. Veronika slips to the ground—here's a tiny bug, tsip, tsip, tsip on its tippy toes, so quick, so terribly quick. Tsip, tsip he runs through a tiny clearing in the grass. Veronika plucks a blade of grass and blocks the scurrying bug's path. "Stop, no transit! Stop!" she repeats the command, but then immediately reverses herself. Let it run. She will gather instead a huge armful of daisies for her mother. She'll take it home. Here, your majesty, please take it! Even mother is afraid of Rozalija, the armful of daisies shall be a sign and a pledge: I'm with you, your obedient and loyal subject! Let me enter your castle, the single-windowed one, and we shall defend ourselves together against the terrible foes until the last drop of blood. And if we fail, if the enemy's blows are too painful, then we shall make a big fire and perish in it, like the legendary Prince Margis in Pilenai with his garrison. Sure, the entire garrison consists of Veronika, but what can you do when there is no money to hire soldiers? As for the draft, only the state can proclaim it. And so Veronika's queen has only a single loyal soldier.

The daisies are piling up, a whole armful, but Veronika is not hurrying to get back home. Let Mother go out, look around for her and call her: *"Veruuut, Veruuuut,* come home." Now, she is still too far away from home. But once she gets to the maple tree by the railway track, she will be able to hear her. Mother will even be able to see her standing there. And that is exactly what happens. Mother comes out, looks around, *"Veruuut,* go home! Go home, child!" she repeats when Veronika crosses the railway track.

"What's that you're bringing now?" her mother asks. "Flowers? How beautiful, how very beautiful!" She smiles and now Veronika is seized with doubt as to whether her mother is really happy about it. That is what she always says, as she marvels and smiles. She always puts the flowers in fresh water and keeps them there until the blossoms begin to fall or dry out. Even during the winter, Mother welcomes with the same smile the gray dry twigs which Veronika gathers on the hill. But once she heard her mother complaining to the neighbor: "She keeps bringing those twigs without end."

With that doubt, Veronika's castles disintegrate. Margis is no more and Pilenai turns into a one-window cottage. The potato soup is already on the table. Veronika sits down in her place and takes a slice of bread. She is lucky that Rozalija left her flowers unnoticed. Should that happen, bread would lose its taste, or Veronika would start watering it with bitter tears.

When she is finished eating, mother gives her a large, red apple.

"Here, enjoy."

It seems to Veronika that she has never held such an apple in her hand, the queen and prince Margis were again with her. Such are the rewards for the loyal. How could fail to do your best for those who never forget you! Long live the Queen Mother! She sinks her teeth into the apple. After the first bite, she pulls herself together. Rozalija would also like some, of course, everybody would. She takes a knife and cuts up the apple. Here, take it, this piece is for you. She is surprised when Valentinas refuses his piece.

"Eat it yourself," he says, and Veronika remembers her brother's gesture to this very day. She also remembers that she was sorry to have given a piece to Rozalija. Did her sister ever share a bite with anyone? But even today, Veronika is ready to give everything away to the Queen Mother.

It was now, when Veronika was living in England, that she promoted her queen to the rank of Queen Mother. Kings and queens had fascinated her since childhood. Their clothes were always so embellished, and the queen's dresses with their long trains trailing and the pages carrying them. And those castles with their innumerable windows . . . True, the windows were merely open holes, but so numerous, enough for all and even some to spare. Let Rozalija sit by one window, and Veronika, should she get angry with her sister, could go ten windows away from her, and she would still have the light. What good was the lone window of their cottage, always closed, and even doubled in the winter to keep the cold away!

The long trains of royal dresses have vanished in the mists of time for Veronika. Trivia, nothing else. But standing next to the machine in the factory, she thinks how nice it would be to dress up, to take a ride in a car, or to ride a dappled stallion like the Queen of England. Now, she must jump when the foreman lifts his finger. And if she were a queen, she would walk with her head raised high, like her mother on these festive occasions, and slightly raise her gloved hand to acknowledge the gawkers standing on the sidewalks waiting for her to pass. She would raise her head and give them a smile. Here is a queen for you.

If she were a queen, what, then, should everybody call her mother? Just as they do it in England, of course. And the Queen Mother would sometimes accompany her in her car for the sole purpose of giving her the opportunity to listen to the applause and the admiring voices. Mother could also go to more receptions that demanded solemnity, the proper gestures and grandiose words from plebian lips. On Monday and Wednesday nights they would both watch "Peyton Place" on television. Veronika is sure that mother would like that program replete with bourgeois tragedies and mysteries. On Sundays, Veronika would most likely read her own poems to the Queen Mother, three copybooks of which were already in the drawer. On one of these occasions, she might even read one of the first ones that once upon a time had strained her relations with Rozalija. She had written it and she read it to the whole family:

> The butterfly is flying high.
> I see the cloud so far away.
> The cloud is rising. Butterfly, please
> Hurry to fly across the seas.

Valentinas was in a good mood that time: "Well done, *Verute*, bravo!"

Even her father had some words of praise. Mother did not say a single word, but embraced her and gave her a silent kiss. But Rozalija turned the poem into a joke: "Butterfly, butterfly, my-oh-my. Buttercloud, butterfly, beddy-bye!"

Nobody had reprimanded Rozalija at that time, or told her to put aside that poor joke for a rainy day. But nobody had agreed with Rozalija, either. And so her joke died an instant death that very night, without penetrating more deeply into Veronika's heart. As for the poems themselves, not a single one of them ever left the copybooks to be seen by others. Was it not because of Rozalija's joke that Veronika remained too bashful ever to send one of them out for publication? They would laugh, she thought, and her friends would think of "butterfly my-oh-my" when they read it. Thus, she still does not know today what her writing is worth.

In school, Veronika had a thick, hardbound copybook into which she would copy poems from books. At first, she wrote on the lines only, but halfway through the copybook she compressed her writing to accommodate more poems. She became short of space anyway, and then she began copying poems on loose sheets of paper. Those poems were Veronika's treasure until she started with her own attempts. She never had enough money to buy a second copybook.

Those poems by Lithuanian authors transcribed in her copybook were her primeval wellspring of inspiration. She saw the butterfly on the hill and the little cloud in the skies. And if the rains should come, how much longer could the butterfly flutter its wings? The seas she simply borrowed from the thick copybook.

If she were the queen, then she might be bold enough to take her copybooks out of the drawer and put them on the little table by her bed. Here, the proofs of the queen's talent! But even then, she probably would not dare to print her writings. What if the critics were to say that her verse resounded with mediocrity? What then? Kings and queens have no choice: either the flame of talent or lost thrones!

If she were a queen, where, then, was the Duke of Edinburgh? Kostas would not be quite right for those ducal duties. Will he ever walk so straight and ducal as Philip of Britain? The factory heat nad finished him off. There was nothing left for him. He could work around the clock and still would return home as slow and indifferent about everything as every day. What could stir him, refresh him, return him to life? The bottle, perhaps. And he does not care a fig about dukes. Anybody with a human spark is duke enough for Kostas. Consequently, the Duke of Edinburgh's position would remain unfilled.

She would probably make her brother Valentinas the Duke of Kent, and Julius, the Duke of Bedford. They would have to follow Veronika's orders and pay a weekly visit to Windsor Castle where, at an agreed hour, they would present themselves to the queen mother and kiss her hand. Yes, yes, both of them. If Valentinas was still busy with his drawing, he would have to bring his new painting to show to the audience. Valentinas is no goody-goody. There is a lot of the devil in him, but Veronika forgives him much. When he gets into one of his fits, he lets words fly, and some of them quite dirty, against his father or mother, brother or sister. And he will scream to the point of tears and run out of the house if victory is not conceded to him. Valentinas can make the whole house resound when the hour of anger is upon him, so that a stranger passing by might think that in that cottage a grown man cannot control his pain over the dying of his closest loved one. But let a little cloud of kindness waft over Valentinas and he will not only take off and give away his last and best shirt, but he will even sell his soul and use the money he gets for it to buy a gift or to entertain you. Veronika feels lenient toward him not because of his character swinging between these extremes, but because he likes to draw. He takes a big sheet of cardboard and a postcard with a picture of a horse and just given an hour's time, with a stroke here and a stroke there, before your eyes and exactly the same as on the postcard, but ten times bigger, is a picture of a horse. Veronika still remembers his winter scene with a cottage and a brook with large trees beside its banks. Once, a real painter turned up on the other side of the railroad track, by Veronika's favorite maple tree, and started sketching. And at dusk, their mother saw him coming home with Valentinas.

"Show me, show me," said the painter. "Show them all." And when Valentinas got together all the pieces of cardboard with his drawings, the guest started imploring mother, "Let that boy go to art school. He'll become a great painter. Imagine, doing such work without any schooling!"

Mother smiled and started excusing herself. If Valentinas ever became a doctor or an engineer, that would be something easy to grasp; he would have money and a plush life. And what good would come out of his messing around with paint? . . . And most important, of course, how could she let him study art when he had only two hands and those two were already being worked to the bone. Valentinas is a grown man now, and he no longer stares meekly at mother's hands when he gets hungry. He demands a filled larder and a proper service, but now he brings money home. When he gets paid, he buys a chunk of bologna sausage and a bottle of brandy, proudly puts them on the table and makes mother sit next to him. Valentinas prefers that his father be absent on such occasions.

"There'll be more left for us," he tells mother. He swallows a long gulp and pours the same amount into her glass. She berates him for following in his father's footsteps. Valentinas' brandy frightens her. But after a few gulps her eldest one becomes so sensitive and infinitely kind and covers his mother's hands with kisses. Mother's health, his wealth, cheers! Mother also gets into the spirit of festivity, because she does not see such sausage every day. The liquid is too bitter for her and so Valentinas empties her glass, too. How can he be expected to throw out God's gift, or to store it until the brandy has lost its kick? He cannot do it, because he has paid good money for all that. Mother agrees that one could not do such a thing. Apparently her apprehension about Valentinas' following in his father's footsteps is beginning to fade. As her fear wanes and she relaxes, she even starts belching. Yes, marvelous sausage. The drink is bitter, but the sausage is good and filling.

If Veronika happens to be studying, she starts intoning the magic prayer in her mind: "Let Valentinas get drunk fast, let him fall asleep! Let Valentinas . . ." If his eyes get hazy, there is good reason to hope that he will be falling asleep at any moment. For if he stays awake, he will inevitably start a quarrel with mother, because there is always guilt between the two of them, they have wronged each other and the wrongs remain unrighted, and all disagreements become inflated again when the words of Valentinas grow louder and louder.

If Veronika were a queen and resided in Windsor Castle with her mother, she would not allow any drinking bouts. Even if Valentinas were to bring a bottle in his pocket, as in those times past, he would not settle at the table with his mother and the two of them would not nibble bologna so that her little brother could forget the bitterness of the brandy. Mother would be old and quarreling with Valentinas would be quite improper for her. All is past and forgotten; the Queen Mother cannot stoop to a washerwoman's petty habits. If Valentinas wants to drink, let him take his pleasures in his own castle. And if a drunken bellow will arise from there, the shame will be Valentinas', Duke of Bedford, alone. Should he go on persisting in his drunken rages, some indignant courtier will tell the newspapers one day how he had steered the dead-drunk duke to bed. Then, of course, a drop of shame would touch Queen Veronika as well. See, what your brother has done to you! Meanwhile, several paintings of her brother are hanging in Windsor . . .

Moved by her boundless forgiveness towards her eldest brother, Veronika would most certainly give orders to remove several old royal paintings from the castle walls and hang Valentinas' drawings in their place. If Valentinas has still preserved that piece of cardboard with the huge horse, which he had copied from a postcard, she would have it exhibited in the great hall, where hundreds of thousands of visitors would walk past it. Abundant silks, sparkling silver, gilded ornaments, and here, ladies and gentlemen, Valentinas' horse! Alas, Veronika has doubts if that horse has survived. She suspects that Valentinas has cut that piece of cardboard into little pieces to stuff into his worn shoes, too big for his feet. He might have cut it up when, a strapping lad already, he began fancying himself as a pigeon keeper. He went after any odd piece of lumber and started hammering his dovecotes together. As if through smoke, Veronika remembers how happy he had been to acquire a couple of bluish pigeons and how, that same evening, he exploded when he found out that his mother had burnt all the spare pieces of wood. Was it then that he cut up the cardboard to use it for his dovecote? She does not remember having seen that horse in recent years.

Her little brother Julius might create quite a few problems for her. You put him in a ducal castle and what if he starts acting like a Bolshevik! Even if she shunted him off to remote Kent, farther away from men's eyes, not even Veronika herself could guarantee that he would not resume his old habits and start hanging red flags in the trees and provoke the police. But maybe Julius has grown fat spiritually? His photograph shows nothing but a fat, thick face—all that is left of the old Julius is a little area around the eyes. When Veronika received that photograph, she kept jesting about her little brother for a long time:

"Bourgeois! What's left of him? A bourgeois!"

A nasty laughter was seizing her. He sits there, ensconced as the head of some department, and grows ever new layers of lard. A life of comfort. He has probably forgotten his own youth and the great concerns that he experienced himself and imposed on others. Veronika remembers as clearly as if it happened today how Julius disappeared. No Julius at night, no Julius in the morning. Where has the devil taken him? In the morning, Mother ran from one neighbor's door to another: "Has anybody seen my Julius?" At home she kept breaking into tears, her son's name on her lips. She did not even go to work. People may come and tell her that Julius lies dead by some bush. How, then, can she go to work, and what kind of work would she do? Her dead son was in her eyes when she saw policemen approaching her cottage. She ran outside.

"You found Julius?" she asked.

"And where is that Julius of yours?" The policeman tossed the question back to her.

"We don't know where he is. We're looking for him."

"When you find him, tell us."

Mother immediately realized that the policemen's world was quite different. They were also speaking about Julius, but they could be quite happy to see his corpse. Before long, she learned that two of Julius' friends were already behind bars.

"We'll soon grab that smart cookie, too," the policeman gloated after telling her, inadvertently perhaps, about the arrest of Julius's friends. "We've got two, we'll get the third smartass too."

During the house search, the policemen found and took with them the photograph showing Julius sitting with Ignas Keberda and Petras Samilys, all friendly, arms linked.

"All three birds together!" exclaimed the policeman to his companion after inspecting the photograph. Mother understood, then, how Julius was involved and who the two others behind bars were. She also pieced together the deed they had done. When she had gone out to milk the cow, she glimpsed a red flag on the tall maple tree on the other side of the railroad track, at the intersection.

As the morning wore on, and Julius was still missing, Mother's fears grew. Julius was a budding revolutionary. When the policemen, seated at the table, were fingering Julius' meager belongings, mother could not stand still any longer. It was getting late and that rascal had not yet had a bite to eat.

"*Verute,* dear child, go, run, Mother had urged while covering a slice of bread with lard and pouring some on it. The policemen had already crossed the railroad track and disappeared. Veronika understood where she should run. In the west, where the railroad track made a sharp turn, there was that little clearing surrounded by birch trees and bushes. That is where she had to run to, the place where Julius liked to lie around on holidays. "Run, run, but keep your eyes open, so that nobody sees you."

And so she ran away. Julius was keeping a watch through the brush for anybody suspicious coming in his direction. When Veronika thinks about it now, she realizes that only a formidable fool would have chosen this clearing as a hideout. Let a single policeman come that way and where would you run then? Beyond the bushes, there was nothing but open fields. It could not have happened otherwise. Two policemen came in the afternoon and caught Julius trying to slink away from the brush to the field. "Hands up!" and they took him away. Until Julius came home from prison, Veronika blamed herself for the arrest. She probably did not keep a proper watch when she carried the lard sandwich to him. Was a policeman standing by the roadside and watching where she ran? Mother was convinced of it, and also blamed Veronika. But Julius knew better and he washed Veronika's guilt away.

"No, it was young Keberda who squealed on me!" he explained everything. "I turned to the brush and managed to run away, but they were caught. Ignas told them who the third fellow was."

"But they must have seen little Veronika when she took you something to eat." Mother still seemed unconvinced.

"Keberda betrayed everything! That's why Petras and I had to sit in the clink, while he was set free."

Young Keberda vanished from sight, of course, and several years later, even Julius was not sure if it was him he saw in another town, parading in a snugly fitting policeman's uniform.

Mother's grumbling met Julius upon his return from prison. Look at the jail-bird coming home! What shame, one does not even dare to meet people's eyes. In her entire clan, neither on her nor on the father's side, anybody had ever sat behind bars, and that is why her eyes are burning with shame.

"What shame?" Julius disagreed.

"Honor, not shame." Father sided with Julius. "One person, at least, in our whole family will be a true human being."

"Be that as it may, from this day on, there'll be no proclamations brought here!" mother protested noisily, remembering the past. Julius used to bring them regularly and would read them with his father. Father also felt that he belonged to the left. Everyone at home knew it by heart that once upon a time in Riga he had marched with the revolutionaries to a forest to celebrate May First and hear the orations. These were Father's most precious recollections.

And Julius exasperated Mother on that same day by bringing

some old proclamations from the shed.

"They're smart, but I'm also nobody's fool." He was boasting about the policemen's failure to find them under the ridge of the roof, where he had hidden them.

"You didn't tell your friends about the papers, so they didn't find them." Mother was explaining it to herself. "When they find them, you won't come home again."

Julius did not believe it. How many times had he brought them home, read, hidden and distributed them, and nobody even batted an eyelash. Yes, nobody batted an eyelash either when the police grabbed Julius right by the hand as he was posting an appeal on a telephone pole. That time he left the prison as a great man and was met at the gate with flowers and speeches, but Veronika did not see him again. He changed cities and offices and then vanished in Russia's limitless spaces for the entire period of the war. During those years, Veronika would deliberately listen to Moscow Radio, hoping to hear something about Julius. No, apparently he was too lowly to have his name mentioned on the radio. Or perhaps he was wading through the forests with Bolshevik partisans and could not be mentioned anywhere. She followed all newspaper reports about skirmishes with Bolshevik partisans, searching for her brother's name. She was most deeply affected by the hanging of the three seized in Kaunas' Oak Park. Who knows, maybe they were not operating under their own names, and perhaps Julius was among them!

Valentinas brought her a letter with the news that Julius was alive and was now living comfortably in Lithuania and that he had a wife called Varvara and two boys and a girl. She seemed strange to her, that Varvara. They probably spoke Russian at home and that was part of the strangeness. *Cheba-pacheba,* smack on the ass! No, that's how one imitates the Poles. And how does Julius converse with Varvara? *Potomu chto bez vody, i ni syudy i ni tudy.*

Veronika is now waiting for the speedy appearance of Julius' memoirs. It is already several years since Valentinas had written them that Julius had a co-author. At first she did not understand what the word meant. She managed to piece its meaning together from dictionaries and had a good laugh. Just imagine, Julius will become something of a celebrity—with injuries and struggles and rewards. The book will be his, and so will be the honor and joy, while Veronika is tickled only by the fact that one of her family members has written a book. Will he remember his childhood, and Veronika? No, he probably will not dare to remember her, since she does live abroad.

She has not received a single letter from Julius. And was it not she who took him food while he was in prison? And he was still acting like some renegade when he returned home. He did not give a hoot about Valentinas' pigeons. He could not stand his parents' quarrels, and so he constantly disappeared from home in the evenings. In the daytime, he worked, of course—he splintered stones, dug ditches, drained rivers. He was a Jack-of-all-trades. Through his friends, he had even found his father a good job at road construction, but father just could not keep up with it—he collapsed after several days, seized with perennial illnesses.

Now, he must be living quite comfortably, that Julius. Is not he one of the reliable and loyal citizens, brimful with good deeds? Veronika was therefore astonished when, by way of Valentinas, she received a request from Julius.

"J. would like to get some of those nice nylons like you had sent me."

"It's not nylons he deserves from me, but a sound thrashing," she fumed at first. And she became even more enraged when, again by way of Valentinas, Julius asked not only for all kinds of feminine trifles for his Varvara, but also for a nylon winter coat. Now that beats everything! All everybody knows is how to be a leech! Just imagine, a commissar, and he wants to exploit a worker, Veronika. She had already drafted part of the reply in her mind: "Tell that commissar of yours . . ." But then her anger began to cool, and she remembered the shoes Julius had bought her; and during that religious festival long ago, wasn't it Julius who had showered her with gifts by the church: candles, long and short, and bagels? These memories made her heart soften. She was left with a suspicion that perhaps Valentinas had gotten the idea to ask her for all kinds of things, even for a nylon winter coat, in the name of Julius. And so she wrote, after sending out the winter coat:

thing. Veronika is unable to allow her to enter her heart as one of her very own, try as she may. Valentinas' Terese is closer to her. And perhaps she is closer because she sometimes writes a letter for Valentinas. Varvara, meanwhile, remains a mere name, although in the photograph one can see her face drowning in the winter coat.

Rozalija would also give her a lot of trouble in Windsor. Just make her a duchess and she will start walking with her nose high in the air, and neither Mother nor Veronika would be able to get a word in edgewise. Duchess Rozalija will be feeling tall way behind her height. But if you demote her, she will never leave your side and will go on complaining that she is being slighted. Veronika wants to forget the old hurts but the deepest among them keeps emerging from the past against her will. Yes, she would forgive the old sins of her sister, let it be, those times long past, most dating from childhood. But the later years are also not free of bitter experiences. As long as Rozalija just kept staring at Ramon Novarro on the postcard and kept raining blows on Veronika, she was still a child. But when Rozalija began sprouting tits, you never saw her without a boyfriend.

"Watch out, Rozalija," mother kept reminding her, and Veronika still could not understand what her elder sister had to watch out for? To see that the boys did not split her head open, or that they did not beat her black and blue as she was doing to Veronika?

"Don't worry," Rozalija would retort. And when Veronika glanced at her mother, she got the impression that her queen was content with her daughter's success. Mother radiated an even greater contentment, her whole face was radiant, when Rozalija met a student, a doctor's son. They met, they clicked, because everybody fancied Rozalija's looks, one-two, and Rozalija got married. They occupied the attic of the cottage where Valentinas with his pigeons had reigned before. Valentinas was screaming and raging that wedding day, and fighting with his brother-in-law for that kingdom!

"The attic's mine, and you can go to the devil, you and your bag of a wife, and my eyes better don't see you and my ears don't hear you, or else!" Valentinas was roaring in full view of the

"My brother dear, should I catch you pretending, and asking for a second winter coat for your Teresa, then you would become as much a brother to me as a lump of clay. Then I'll get angry with you for all ages eternal, for all your life, and even after my death I'll remember that you swindled Veronika."

That letter aroused Valentinas' wrath. How can Veronika throw such ugly suspicions on him? You still don't believe me? Alright—here is a photograph! Although it is midsummer, Varvara sits wrapped in her winter coat, next to Julius and her children. Let Veronika take a close look at the winter coat, especially the collar. Teresa's collar is different. Veronika is convinced already. She is only surprised that whatever Valentinas asks for himself he also asks for Julius. Remembering the family's habits, it would be much more natural if Valentinas would write as follows: Don't give anything to them, they have plenty of everything! Apparently, Julius is helping Valentinas out and that is why Valentinas has been interceding for him with Veronika.

All suspicions would be dispersed if she made Julius the Duke of Kent. Then his Varvara would have to come here in all her furs, and then it would come out if Valentinas had committed any fraud. But what would Julius do here? He probably would not have enough strength any more to climb to the top of the maple tree, to raise his flag; he would have to ask his children for help. And his children in the photograph look like rich spoiled brats, used to having baked pigeons fly into their mouths. It seems that Julius has become a stranger to her. He has not written a single letter and all that just because he became a chosen one, for whom there is no way to reestablish a direct link with a refugee sister. Veronika does not want to accuse him. Let him live in peace. Let him live and work and accomplish something decent.

Even Varvara does not bother her any longer. So many Lithuanians now bleat in broken English, at home and among the people, with their English, Irish, or Italian wives. Yes, it is a strange situation to her. Having weighed everything, she is not sure anymore if she would still want to see Julius as a duke in her fantasies, just to have him idle around and think out all kinds of rubbish. Let him sit in Lithuania with his Varvara and his children and do his work. That Varvara is probably spoiling the whole guests, in spite of all the mother's and father's quieting. In her heart, Veronika was on her brother's side. Fancy that, one more mouth, Rosie brought him and all's rosy, and you go away, they'll take your place!

On her return in the evening, Veronika could not find her blanket. Her dear sister had taken it away. Mother had given it to her! They have to start from scratch, she said, they have nothing. Veronika then probably felt not less angry than Valentinas, when he was defending his attic from the newlyweds and transferring his pigeons to a windowless pigpen. He could get his sleep outside, if necessary, he said, with his head propped against the wall, but the pigeons needed light. If there was no sun, at least there must be light. And what would Veronika cover herself with for the night? Mother brought all kinds of rags: Here, that's for you, child. Let Rozalija and her sweetheart lie under the rags! Mother already knew that he son-in-law was not a doctor's, but a shoemaker's son. Yes, she was able to clear that much up and her respect for the braggart evaporated. Yet, she still gave him the blanket, as if he were a decent fellow. Veronika's anger was so overwhelming that she was ready to scream with rage like Valentinas, if only she had not been afraid that her voice would draw the neighbors' attention to their cottage.

And what did she ever get from Rozalija in her life? Her sister just walked away and put all thought of her parents and her home aside. Mother suggested to her that she baptize her son Valentinas, so that family names would go on with the new ties of blood. But Rozalija took into her head that her son should have a high-class name. Her son, just listen, shall be Richard-the-Lionhearted! Veronika soon found out that he was growing up stone-hearted and not lion-hearted. And to think that Rozalija had blurted to her mother that she was ashamed to visit the cottage in daylight and to bring her Ricardas with her. And so she sneaks up at dusk only and leaves loaded down with things! If Veronika happened to be away, Rozalija goes through her things. When you see everything in disarray, then you know that Rozalija was here and took something with her. Even if you could catch up with her, you won't be able to retrieve your possessions, unless you were bold enough to knock her down and to take back your things by force.

No, Veronika had neither enough courage nor strength to be able to roll on the ground with her sister.

Veronika experienced with a special painfulness, the true cold-heartedness of Rozalija and her Ricardas when her mother became ill. No work, no bread.

"Run over to Rozalija," mother says, looking at her pale youngest child. "She'll give you a bite. Maybe even a sliver of meat."

Veronika finds it very difficult to beg for a bite. What joy would it be if mother had enough, if she would eat and feed her, too. She would be content with a tiny bit of good, if only she did not have to go to her sister's.

"And what will you eat?" Veronika asks.

"I don't feel well, I don't want anything. Go, you go." She strokes Veronika's hair softly. How can Veronika refuse now, after that caress? It is not the first time that Veronika has gone there, and that brother-in-law always demands that she do some work for the meal—take Ricardas outside for some fresh air so that he can sleep more sweetly. And Veronika herself still a mere wisp! Lugging Ricardas around deadens her arms.

"Mama, mama," she complains, upon her return, and Mother strokes her hair again, mollified her, and voices the hope that never again will they face such shortages at home. Veronika insists that she would be content with some dry bread and a drop of milk. "Mother, dear, if you only earned enough for bread. I hate so much to be dependent on Rozalija's and her husband's favors." Mother knows already that Rozalija will feed her, if she gets paid one-half litas. Veronika does not want to work for her food, then let her bring money. There is no more way in which Rozalija could exchange food for work, because Ricardas-the-lionhearted does not have to be lugged around any longer. He has grown heavier and Veronika simply could not carry him in her arms for one half-hour. One-half litas buys quite a few things, after all.

"No half-litas—no food," said her sister, and Veronika rushed out so as not to cry in Rozalija's presence. Mother would have repaid those fifty cents, and that was what she had taught Veronika to say. Perhaps Rozalija needed money badly, because her husband gave her a set amount with which to buy food. After this experience though, Veronika would never sit at her sister's table again, not even if she was offered a pile of money. She will chew on some linden leaves, or gather some sorrel, or even go to sleep on an empty stomach, rather than take a single bite from her sister. After her wedding Rozalija had been able tp put aside enough from her food money to purchase a deluxe album jammed with movie stars. They also kept a dog, but that beast was the husband's property, with Rozalija acting only as its feeder. Ah, that dog, that wolf! It was the beast's fault that Veronika never went to say good-bye to her sister before going abroad. She was still going to school when one evening her mother sent her to see Rozalija.

"Go and tell her that I'm sick," her mother said, and Veronika hurried out. "Let her come, this may be my last day. She'd better come today because I may not last through the night."

Veronika literally flew to her sister, but at the gate she was met by the dog. It barked at her fiercely and Veronika did not dare go by it, lest the devil leap at her. She stood by the gate and peered through the windows. Ricardas was the first to stick his head out of the window, to be soon followed by her sister. They watched her and laughed.

"Come, come," Rozalija yelled, coming to the doorway.

"The dog . . ." Veronika could barely manage to speak. "Mother is very sick . . . She wants you to come."

Only then did Rozalija grab the dog. "Come inside," she said.

Ever since that time Veronika refused to look at her sister's house even from a distance. What hurt her the most was the attitude of Ricardas-the-stone-hearted. She could not hear his words through all the barking, but she could read from his lips that he was setting the dog on her.

What could be their place in the royal house?

When Veronika, before her final departure, said good-bye, her mother asked her several times, "Pay at least a brief visit to Rozalija."

At first, Veronika disguised her revulsion at the idea of the visit in a cocoon of words. Her mother would remind her again, and she would suddenly change the subject. When Kostas urged her to hurry up, she finally replied to another of her mother's reminders. "No more time."

"You'll leave now and you may never see eacn other again in

your life," her mother admonished.

"Mama, the time's up," Veronika replied in the same tone. Then she left. Yes, she wanted to say farewell. She had taken leave from everybody, and Rozalija was the only one left. But that dog!

As was to be expected, Rozalija expressed her dissatisfaction in her first letter already: "How could you dare to leave without saying good-bye to me, the only one thus neglected in the entire clan? Am I not your sister? And Veronika answered: "Yes, you are my sister, but do you still remember that beastly dog of yours? It died? Your husband took it away when he left? If that dog is no longer at your home, if I ever get back I may then step over your threshold. I know that immediately after the war you lived in the cottage at my Queen Mother's, so we could meet there, say our hellos and good-byes and wave to each other by the railroad without any haste.

Veronika would want to stand at her mother's grave awhile. There lies the Queen Mother who has never sat in Windsor and who never sat reception hours for her children. Death came to her in that single-windowed cottage, and her festive hat has probably been thrown away, or, it may have mouldered away by itself, destroyed by the years. But just dare to go back and stand there! The sparseness of that cottage, has it not always haunted and tormented Veronika as the embodiment of all kinds of misery? But just go home again, and everything will come to life again and Mother's image will shrink in size in accordance with the surroundings. Everybody will possibly want to settle accounts and the screams will again start echoing far and wide. In their letters now, they are exchanging accusations about the cow that Mother had bought with the money she had received from Veronika. Where is that cow? Who sold it and pocketed the money? According to Rozalija, it was Mother who sold it, and Valentinas was the one who took the money. In Valentinas' version, Rozalija sold the cow and gave the money to Ricardas who squandered it. And what if commissar Julius ever wrote a letter— who would turn out guilty about the cow then?

After reading her fill of letters from her relatives Veronika decided not to write to them any more. And so far after awhile, they started asking, one and all: "Why don't you write anymore?

Aren't you a sister to us? Their inquiries did not come too soon. At first the children wrote sweet letters, one after another. Why didn't I respond? Veronika replied. According to the birth records, I'm your sister, of course, but from your letters I can see that for you my mother had disappeared behind the back of a cow. Cow, cow, always the cow! After so many years that decrepit cow would not be able to chew a blade of grass, and they still try to raise her from the dead . . . Resurrect my mother and see her off to me and I will place her on a royal throne. And if you need cows, all right, just say it. Which one of you has the right to keep a cow? Just say it—and you'll have it.

As for her mother, with the grave and the tombstone already marking the place, she will not see her anymore. The Queen Mother is but a dream, but Veronika likes it. There is something to live for. *Mamuliukas* is Queen Mother for Veronika all the same, one who has gone to rest under a centenary tree and who keeps calling to her in memories and reveries.

Translated by Zemkalnis

Nele Mazalaite

NELE MAZALAITE

NELE MAZALAITE was born in Darbenai, Lithuania, on August 20, 1907. She gained popularity as a writer in Lithuania before her refugee years in Germany (1944-49) and emigration to the United States (1949). She now resides in New York. Her favorite genres are the story, the literary legend and the novel. Some of the titles in her prolific output are *Miestas, kurio nera* (The City Which Does Not Exist), 1939; *Gintariniai vertai* (The Amber Gate), 1952; *Pjuties Metas* (Harvest Time), 1956; and *Miestelis, kuris buvo mano* (The Town Which Was Mine), 1966. Several of her stories have been widely translated.

NELE MAZALAITE

(1907-)

The Thorn

AN HOUR AFTER MIDNIGHT, someone knocked at the window of the presbytery. The glass rang like a warning bell and woke the priest abruptly. He slept lightly, and with interruptions, yet he had to force himself to get up (his bones ached and were heavy, as if time were turning them to stone.)

The glass was still ringing in his ears. Whoever stood outside the window was either impatient or afraid, but the priest went calmly to meet him. People breaking into the house nowadays generally came through the door; besides, he had long since ceased to have any fear.

He unlatched the window carefully. He recognized the man.

"Why have you come at such an hour, Kazimieras? Has your wife been taken ill?"

"Worse than that, Father, much worse than that!" The man stood and spoke through the grating of the confessional; it joined and separated them at once. What he had to say was indeed a confession, thought the priest as he listened to him.

Kazimieras Sauklys was an old carpenter and builder who used to make altars. Now he spent his days fashioning rakes and besoms, and—God forgive him for the sin!—late at night he sometimes dared to go to the little woods, which had once been his, to gather raw material for his carpentry. This evening, as he was looking for birch branches to make brooms, he heard something; no bird was singing and no tree was sighing. It was a young man crouching in the grass, deep in the juniper bushes, where not even a rabbit runs to hide himself for fear of tearing his skin. He was lying in pain and trying to stifle his groans. A patch of warm blood shone like a light in the darkness. When he heard steps approaching, his hand reached for his gun (the priest sensed how the timid and peace-loving old carpenter was almost boasting of the wounded man's courage) but there was no strength left in his arm.

As soon as the old man had come closer to him, the young freedom-fighter knew that he was not an enemy. For there was joy in the old carpenter's voice, and even a dying man had not mistaken him for a traitor. The young freedom-fighter had smiled to himself—you could see it in the darkness—and said that God was merciful, for in the last hour of his life, He had allowed him to see a man of his own people, a Lithuanian. The priest saw Kazimieras Sauklys wipe his eyes as he went on talking hurriedly. He had told the young man that he would take him into his own house, but the young man protested. No, he had said to him, and his voice was very stern, as if he were used to giving orders and being obeyed. There had been times, it was true, when he had had no choice but to expose other people to danger, but he had always been in a position to defend them. Whereas now, as anyone could see, he was unable to move, much less to walk. At the point of death he would not and could not bring anyone, no matter how friendly, into danger. It made him happy, he told Kazimieras, just to hear such words and he thanked him, for there was nothing that he needed. Nothing, that is, for it would be a miracle if his last wish were to be fulfilled: to see a priest.

Kazimieras Sauklys worked on the collective farm. He had been deprived of his meagre plot of land, his children, the work he had loved, and his health. But now he had carried a tall young man on his shoulders all the way home from the woods. He had carried him in such a way that neither his head nor his feet touched the ground, although he was astonishingly tall. There was nothing the freedom-fighter could do about it, for he was almost unconscious at the time. But when they reached the edge of the village where Kazimieras Sauklys lived, the young man began to regain his strength and said that under no circumstances should he be carried into the house. Wasn't there a barn or stable somewhere? He even laughed and said that God himself had once deigned to lie in a stable. Kazimieras did what was asked of him. He carried the wounded man into a shed and laid him on a bench. The shed had served as a workshop at one time, and he still used it for making rakes and brooms. When the wounded man opened his eyes, Kazimieras explained to the priest, they were like the eyes of a martyr.

Again, he murmured, "a priest," and his voice reminded the old man of his own son's voice.

Kazimieras Sauklys called his aged wife and hurried out. It seemed to him now, as he expalined apologetically through the window, that he had run all the way to the presbytery. But, in fact, it must have taken him a long time to walk those three miles.

"Let us go," said the priest. "We had better hurry. Forgive me for not asking you in to rest, Kazimieras."

"Later," replied Kazimieras. "I'll rest later." As he told his story, he had rested his body against the wall. But it seemed to him that he had scarcely time to breathe before the priest appeared at his side. They walked in silence through the sacristy into the church, which was lit only by sanctuary lamps so that no unwelcome eyes would be drawn to the place where God was waiting.

Without a word, the two old men began their journey. As they walked side by side, it seemed to the priest that a Third one was talking to them from the cobbled stones of the market place and the clouds at the borders of the night where dawn was breaking slowly, as if a man with a lantern was climbing the other side of the hill. He talked to them all the time, as they crossed the meadow and woods where birds awoke suddenly, their chirping sounding like the pipes of an organ or the strings of a violin, or very small whistles. The flowers that they could smell, but not see, talked from their hiding places in the shelter of the leaves. The two men, in their silence communicated in Christ's language. The old carpenter begged that his steps might not prove to have been too slow, and the aged priest prayed that God might allow him to reach the wounded man in time.

It seemed to the priest that his whole life had been a preparation for this journey. His strength and health were failing. He had retired long before the first Bolshevik occupation, but since he was the only priest left in the presbytery, he was called again, like a newly ordained curate, to bring the power of the Keys. He was to bless and to comfort, to bury and to baptize the faithful. His own people could come to him—secretly, it is true—but they all knew where and when to find him. "For the sake of this wounded man, who has no strength to come to You himself, Lord; for the sake of this young man who has offered his life for this land and its people of his own free will, like the saints, overlook my ninety years and strengthen my steps and the beating of my heart. Let me find him still alive."

He did.

Now, the priest saw another wonder of the night. The old woman had done no less than her husband, who had carried the stranger into their shed. She had lifted the heavy, injured body, had spread her finest sheets underneath him and had brought him a pillow covered with a white linen pillow-case. She had bandaged his wounds as best she could and when she had finished, she had prepared a Communion table on an old tree trunk on which Kazimieras used to trim billets of wood. She had placed a small cross on it and had brought some holy water in an earthenware bowl and a wooden aspergill such as one might expect to see in a carpenter's house. A candle was burning, its light half-hidden behind a tall earthen jug so as not to attract attention. Even when the two old men approached the shed, all they could see was a stream of pale moonlight between the two doorposts, like a river between two dark hills. Kazimieras' wife was sitting at the side of the stranger, wiping his forehead. The priest knew that her presence comforted him as he waited. As soon as she saw them, she rose from her place, knelt down before God and then withdrew from the shed with her husband. They sat down on the grass outside, waiting to be called when the time came.

The priest heard the man's confession.

He bent his lips close to the lips of the freedom fighter and the lips parted to raise the curtain from the man's soul.

Suddenly, there was a sound like the breaking of glass or crockery. Two aged voices shouted and then fell silent on the other side of the door. Five men crowded into the shed, pushing the old couple in front of them.

Four of the men were in uniform but the fifth appeared to be a man from the neighborhood, as indeed he was. He began talking at once.

"So we've caught a whole nest of criminals! Move out of my way, priest, and don't put on an act, you bandit. Get up!"

The priest merely turned his head. He had not risen when the men came in and had only looked up from the wounded man's face. He spoke quite calmly, "I should say that you were born here, from the way you speak. Have pity and let me finish my holy task."

"Get out of my way!" the newcomer shouted. He evidently wanted to make his importance felt in front of the others. "Out of my way, I said! Don't obstruct us in the discharge of our duty! Giving shelter to a bandit! You know that nothing could be more antisocial." He went over to the priest and raised his arm to push him aside but the priest stretched out his hand to ward him off.

"Wait," said the priest, "aren't you the son of Vincas Jurginis?"

The man jumped as if he had been struck. He glanced at the Russians and his face was suffused with guilt as he heard his father's name.

"Happily, your parents have been spared this misery—to see their son as a traitor. Your father was a volunteer soldier. He pledged his life for our country. You know that; you remember it perfectly well. It's not a thing to forget easily, once you've heard it. But perhaps you don't know now much it meant to your father that you were born the very year we won our independence. I baptized you. Was it ill done?" The priest looked sadly at the man who had once been a Lithuanian. Then his gaze returned to the freedom fighter who lay still with his eyes closed. "Hasn't it alwasy been so, from the time of our Blessed Lord, that where is loyalty, Judas is only one step behind? Are you Judas? Let me finish hearing his confession."

The man began to laugh loudly. Then he spoke to the soldiers in Russian and they laughed too.

"All right, all right, get on with it. We'll be your witnesses. What are you waiting for? Speak!"

The priest looked at him again. How could any man behave like that? Was he still a man?

His father had fought for his country against the Bolsheviks, but now he had come here with the Russians. The man turned red in the face and began to shout, "Why don't you go on with the confession? Why are you silent, bandit?" He pushed the priest aside, bent over the wounded man and began to tear at him with his fingers. "Well, go on talking then. Go on talking, bandit. Tell us where your accomplices are!"

Suddenly the priest became agile and strong as a young man. He put himself in front of the wounded man and shielded him from the tearing fingers. Then he turned around and looked the traitor straight in the eyes.

"When our Savior was betrayed by His disciple, and condemned to death by unjust men, He was given into the hands of alien soldiers and their cruel servants. They crowned Him with a wreath of thorns and pressed it hard on His head to injure Him. They humiliated Him; they spat in His face and hit Him with the palms of their hands. Among them was a man who was a great coward who wanted to appear very brave before his friends. He waited until Jesus grew very tired and His head drooped with such weariness that He could scarcely open His eyes, which were covered with blood. And only then did the coward dare to come up to Him and strike Him with his hand. But it happened that as the coward raised his fist, Our Lord let his head hang down and a thorn pricked him very lightly, so that his skin was scarcely torn, but the wound never healed. And when the time came for him to die, he died a bad man and a coward, but the thorn was still in his hand."

"Arrest them!" the man who had been born a Lithuanian commanded his Russian comrades. They obeyed him at once, although they were his masters. When they seized the freedom fighter, he opened his eyes, looked at the two old people and said to the priest,

"I have one more sin to confess. I forced these good people with my gun, to give me shelter and I made them bring a priest. They are innocent."

"Did you hear that?" said the priest quietly. "Did you hear his confession? Let the old people go."

The four Russians and the son of a Lithuanian volunteer soldier then drove out Kazimieras Sauklys and his wife, and the priest who had given absolution. Only the body of the freedom fighter, who had died, remained.

And from that time on, as he left with the others to the lorry and drove away, after daybreak and during the night that followed, the man who had been born in the neighborhood never stopped looking at his right hand. When he touched his hand, he felt something cut into his flesh. It might have been the broken blade of a knife, but it felt more like the wound of a sickle. No one can predict the hour of his death, but he knew that even then he would still feel the stab of the thorn. He and many others.

Translated by Danguole Sealey

JUOZAS KRALIKAUSKAS

Born in Kareivonys, Lithuania, on October 9, 1910, JUOZAS KRALIKAUSKAS worked as both teacher and principal in various Lithuanian schools, an activity he continued in the schools of Lithuanian refugee camps in Germany (1945-47). His first collection of short stories, *Septyni kalavijai* (Seven Swords), 1937, was published in Lithuania but the bulk of his literary output was created in Canada, where he settled in 1947. Two of his novels, *Urviniai zmones* (Cave Men), 1954, and *Sviesa lange* (Light in the Window) 1960, describe the problems of Lithuanian immigrants in Canada. His most ambitious undertaking has been a series of four historical novels from the time of the Lithuanian King Mindaugas: *Titnago ugnis* (The Flame of Flint), 1962; *Mindaugo nuzudymas* (The Murder of Mindaugas), 1964; *Vaisvilkas*, 1971; and *Tautvilas*, 1973.

Juozas Kralikauskas

JUOZAS KRALIKAUSKAS

(1910 –   )

Seven Swords

I

"SEE THERE, OUR JERONIMAS PLOUGHING. Let's go and watch."

"No time for that, Vytukas. They'll be bringing the cattle home soon."

"Just a teeny bit, Mommy."

"Go alone."

"It's no fun alone."

"Well, then, harness yourself to the shafts, you won't be alone, and all will be well."

"Oh, Mommy, how can you. Shafts and shafts. I'm going away and I won't come back."

"Get along. I won't be sorry—not much."

"And who'd bring you wood chips? Who'd feed the chickens, who'd bring water for Rudis to lap, ah? Eh, Mommy, you'd miss me, you'd be sorry anyway."

"Oh, you little sweet stork of mine. Can't you see the sun is already sinking? Who'll cook supper for you,—Jeronimas?"

Rudkis, his pug nose high in the air, is chasing the crows and yelping.

Vytukas stretches out in the furrow.

"Whoa! Where to, nag! Keep to the furrow!" Jeronimas urges his horse up the field.

"Got you-you!" Vytukas jumps to his feet suddenly and then crawls on all fours to confront the ploughman.

The mare stops in astonishment. And Jeronimas shouts, "I'm scared, oy, how I'm scared! . . ."

Vytukas cackles joyfully as he straightens himself out atop the black furrows.

"If you do, then let me plough some."

The large shadow of the mare falls on the ploughland. The curve in her back permits the rider to sit more comfortably. The head is in front, so that the ears, eyes, snout, and halter could have something to hang on. The mare needs the snout so she could neigh and eat the grass. Her lower lip is large, hangs loose, and moves.

"You're still puny. You'd better wait, I'll be finished soon and you can ride her home." Jeronimas lights a cigarette.

"But why is her lip so big? And it moves!"

"That's how God created her."

"And why is the foal's lip pretty, and doesn't move?"

Jeronimas does not answer. He looks westward, where the sun will sink into dark clouds. It will be raining tonight. Smoke is rising slowly from the chimney. Mother is cooking. It is a good feeling, but mixed with some kind of sadness, to see the smoke rise thus, so slowly. Mother is at work there . . . in the cottage with white shutters . . .

And Vytukas, who has been waiting for the answer and has grown a little angry, says, "Just you go on smoking, and your lip will get that large, and it'll tremble. That's what'll happen to you."

Dumplings are cooking on a tripod in the stove. Mother waits by the fire. A tear ripens and trickles down her dewily shining eyes because of her dream last night.

It seemed that Jeronimas was already married to Aniute . . . and now he's building a new cottage for himself . . . While she is digging potatoes on the Lyginiai hill . . . People are driving to the *kermis,* past the Ciurkonys swamp . . . suddenly the cuckoo in the wild apple tree calls out! Cuckoo-oo and again, cuckoo-oo on a dry branch . . . Dear God—a cuckoo during potato-digging season! . . . And then a long black arm pops out of the ground and seizes Vytukas! . . . "Mommy!" her little son cried out and sank into the earth! . . .

Holy Jesus, she rushes to dig away the earth but her hands are like wood! She cries, she screams on top of the hill but people just drive past the swamp of Ciurkonys and neither hear nor see her. Only their wheels rumble-grumble . . . She's off toward the road, but her foot slips on the slope . . . she grasps at a clump of grass . . . but it tears away! She falls—falls—and . . .

She woke up trembling and soaked with sweat. Oh, Lord, dear Lord! Thunder and lightning were raging outside. She quickly felt around. Vytukas, warm and curled, was snoring gently at her side. What a relief, oh Lord, that it was only a dream!

She got out ot bed and checked to see if the flue was closed. Then she pulled out a willow twig from under the ceiling, crossed herself and placed it on the window.

At dawn, Agota by the well explained the dream to her. To build a house, to dig potatoes, a cuckoo out of season—all these mean a funeral. The cuckoo's song will take away one member of the family and will segregate him into a house of six planks.

The village, all in wood, is clearly visible from the churchyard. And the greenish lake, rimmed with white birch trunks.

By the churchyard, a blind beggar, "Ho-o-ly-y A-an-tho-o-ny!" The crown of his head is bald and yellow. He sits as he chants and holds a cap between his legs.

"Mommy, Why did you give the meat away to Kocka?"

"It must be done, child."

"And why must it be done?"

"So that he will pray for your father's soul."

"And what happens when Kocka prays?"

"The souls have it easier in the other world."

"And what's that there, Mother?" Vytukas points to a barrel organ player, cranking away at his sad music. A guinea pig peeks at him from the top of the barrel organ. "Kind of a cat?"

"No, not a cat."

"What, then?"

"Some little animal—to fool the people."

"But what kind?"

"Persistent, aren't you? There are quite a lot of animals around. D'you expect me to know them all?"

II

It is fall already. With mornings spent mushroom gathering and the sadness of seeing cranes flying away.

The sky is gloomy. Clouds over the saw-like forest line.

Aniute is doing the laundry. Stooped over, she is beating the wash with a beetle.

Vytukas sneaks up to her from behind and pushes her into the water.

"Just wait, lover!" She chases him.

He falls down and defends himself by kicking and swinging his little fists.

Aniute picks him up and cradles him. How much he resembles Jeronimas. She kisses him and lets him go.

Angry, Vvtukas sticks out his tongue at her.

"Here, let's shake, peace, all right?"

"Don't want to."

"Why not?"

"You're no good, slobbering all over me like that."

"When you come to visit me, I'll give you buttered bread."

"You're kidding."

"I'll butter it real thick. Didn't I before yesterday?"

He observes her. He has come to the conclusion that she is not lying. All right, they make peace and go back to the brook together.

Aniute returns to her laundering.

His pants rolled up, he wades and sings:

> *My horse is mighty and bold*
> *He's thirty-three winters old.*
> *Long his neck, his body squat.*
> *Stone-blind like a bat.*
> *Sees nobody-y-y*
> *And fears nobody-y-y . . .*

Winter.

The morning sun splinters away in the snow, giving a roseate glitter to the hills.

In the fields where oats rustled, and bright clover, and hairgrass, seven full moons ago—so much blinding light. So many silvery coins. Vytukas' eyes grow dull.

Jeronimas brought him a pocket knife yesterday. A knife with an ivory handle. Agota, who had come to borrow a sieve, said that nobody in the whole parish owned such a knife. She must know, if she says it aloud. She may not know as much as the teacher, but she still knows quite a lot. Last summer she recited a charm over the red blotch on his leg: the skin inflammation went down immediately. Would the teacher know how to recite such a charm?

He finds an ice patch and slides over it. Nice, pretty ice, nice sliding. Mommy had told him not to dally on the frozen puddles, not to be late for school.

That day, on the way back from school, the children were raising a rumpus.

"You mean that fish has no voice?"

"Of course not."

"And what about the minnow, doesn't it squeak when you catch it?"

"Badger cap—badger head, twenty cents alive or dead."

"Cut it out, stupid, stop throwing!"

"You afraid? Snow never killed nobody."

"And you, cripple, give back my pen. You shouldn't have gambled. You lost—now give."

Anupras snatches the badger cap from the lame boy's head: "Amen with that, skin the cat!" he yells and flips the cap along the ice.

The cap glides quite a distance over the glassy surface and then comes to rest near the hole in the middle of the pond, the spot rarely freezes solidly.

The wind singes the cripple's unevenly shorn head. He cries at a loss what to do. He could go back and complain to the teacher but the school is far away.

The children become serious.

"Well, Anupras, you're gonna get it. He'll tell the teacher."

"Go hang yourself!"

Nevertheless, Anupras plods to retrieve the cap. But halfway is as far as he can get. The ice bursts with a thud. Anupras stops short. A couple more steps and there is another cracking sound.

"It's creepy! Some dumb woman drowned herself here the year before last. Someone else drowned, they say, several years ago..." Anupras comes back.

"You got yourself into a nice pickle."

"I'll just go home; my father will bring a pole."

"But won't your father take care of you, first?"

"Boy, he's gonna give you one good licking!"

"There's your amen with that!"

"And if the wind should rise the cap will plop into the water."

"And you'll have to buy a new one."

"So much for the badger cap—badger head."

That father of his! Mother keeps crying, she cannot bear to watch him abuse the child. The black and blue marks last for a long time afterward.

"A fellow who's tasted the strap is worth ten who were never beaten." That is how Father usually answers the mother's reproaches.

"No doubt, the same thing is to happen now. The cripple's mother will run, crying, to Anupras' father. Or she may first dash to the teacher, who'll call in the father or even drop in on him, himself."

"Hey, Vytas, you're light; the ice will hold you. Three pens if you can get the cap." The biggest boy in the group is tempting the smallest one.

"Don't go, don't listen to him!" A piece of advice comes from the group.

"Six pens, and it's a deal."

"Six pens?! You're kidding! Four?"

"No deal."

"Ah, well five, then."

"Give it, then."

Vytukas parts from the cluster of boys and walks onto the ice alone. He toddles more and more slowly. He stops. He taps the ice with his right clog. Now he slinks along, his steps not larger than a span. Again he stops, again he taps the ice with his clog, checking the thickness of the ice. Now he inches along, his feet almost together . . .

The badger cap is almost within his reach . . . One foot slightly forward . . . Then the other . . . He'll reach it now.

Suddenly—the treacherous ice gapes horribly!

"Aaa-yy!" Vytukas screams in a voice no more his own . . .

III

The entire parish inside the night's maw. Deaf blindness all around.

One-third of men's lives is spent thus. Under blankets, eyes shut. They very much resemble the dead.

It is probably past midnight already. This is the time most deaf to everything, difficult and dangerous for the sick. Between midnight and the cock's crow.

A little lamp glimmers at the foot of the bed.

Vytukas, utterly enfeebled, stops wheezing. And his eyes are fastened at a single spot—that corner only.

His eyes are growing larger and his pupils are expanding. Does he see something horrible? Is somebody waiting for him in that corner? Has that somebody appeared only now?

"It's done . . . " Agota whispers.

"The candle, quick!" The neighbor woman's voice is filled with dread and mystery.

"Light it on the lamp."

"Hurry!"

Vytukas's eyes, corroded by terror, are fixed on the women's faces as if they were ghosts or witches. But then he meets his mother's eyes and stops as one who has found shelter, his tension subsides a little.

His little eyes are fixed on his mother's eyes. As though he were seeking some kind of help. And as if he were asking: What was going to happen now, mother, what will happen? And he startles, perhaps because he has never seen such an expression in his mother's eyes before.

He shudders again, opens his mouth and his head falls back . . .

Vytukas makes one more faint effort to survive . . . to save himself . . . And suddenly!

Suddenly, everything sinks into a horrible silence.

Only the gentle flicker of the wax candle. In the tingling silence only the blossoming of the candle, like the fern blossom he knew from fairy tales.

Huge shadows of kneeling neighboring women appear on the walls. The windows melt into the endless gloom and darkness.

And the mother still turned to stone. Finally she lifts her trembling hand. She will close the eyes now empty of sight.

But as soon as she touches his face, she kneels and screams in God knows whose voice . . .

Tears erupt and the wringing of hands, as if she has gone utterly mad. Then come howls punctuated by what sounds like the mournful song of the cuckoo.

"Mother, mother!" Jeronimas embraces her, trying to console her.

The women also try to be helpful, but they also speak and move through tears. Mothers, too. Their voices resemble cranes at night, the last ones in late fall.

Day refuses to break.

In the yard, Rudkis howls as never before.

The wind makes the shutters squeak. Eerily like blind puppies . . .

And still no daybreak.

At last, the darkness began turning gray . . .

A wretched day was dawning slowly in the frost-covered windows.

With icicles hanging under the roof.

Frost flowers wove themselves in the window pane. Among them the wind twisted the smoke of the Geniai chimney.

Day of the wake, burial tomorrow.

Day of wrath. Vytukas' last in mother's cottage with the white shutters. They would see him off tomorrow. They would chant him away and then leave him there.

Day without sun. Even impossible to tell the hour. Evening may be close, and then the last night.

Vytukas is stretched on a plank covered with white linen

cloth. A holy picture in his fingers folded over his chest. So serious is Vytukas now—like a prince. In handsome clothes, as if he was going to receive his first communion. He seems to be merely asleep. It cannot be true, no, that he will never walk or speak again.

His words come back and pierce his mother, the words now laden with so much meaning. She remembers his laughter. She sees him on the way back from school, turning into the yard. She hears him open the outside door and his steps in the anteroom.

But it is no more a dream. It won't evaporate, you won't wake up, things will never again be as they used to. Otherwise, why would the people be gathering here? Why would they be chanting from their old hymnals, with such drawn-out voices? Could he feign silence for such a long, long time? Why would the teacher have come here with all his students? And for what reason would they have left behind that wreath of spruce branches adorned with a whitish ribbon with black letters that say: "Vytukas, we shall come to you, too!"

The mother's eyes are closing and she feels somewhat relieved. Oh, to be able to fall asleep and not wake up again! Vytukas, I'll come to you, too. Green . . . red circles . . . We'll be together again . . . Oh, to sleep, and not to waken ever again . . .

The cemetery is waiting.
Everyone's last place, unavoidable as the night.
"The Angel of the Lord is revealed . . ."
The first handsful of earth pattering on the small coffin.
The mother moaned as she fainted.
". . . now and in the hour of our death . . ."
". . . right from the heart everyone . . ."
In the pine fo-orest o-o-oy-yyy—
". . . Vytukas, dearest mine! From what country will I see you coming back? Through which window? My son, my sweet, poor son! Where will the day dawn for you, where will the sun rise?" Her eyes red and swollen; the third day without food; her voice hoarse and utterly different.

Agota looks at the tiny grave, already girded with the wreath of spruce branches. A white ribbon with dark lettering: "Vytukas, we shall come to you, too!" Vytukas' mother remembers the dream that Agota explained once. There by the well whose sweep is gallowlike. Didn't I tell? And she almost feels satisfied that what she had foretold, lo and behold had come true.

V

On the narrow shelf—three copybooks and "The Road to Light."

Christ's Mother looks down from inside the frame on the wall.

With seven swords piercing her heart, and a dead son on her knees.

Through the windows, children can be seen on their way to school. They went and they returned during Lent, and after Easter, and when the snow was melting away . . .

Spring came back again, and the birds returned. But not for Vytukas any more—only for his schoomates, and not for her but for other mothers.

And lo! The Sunday of the church festival is dawning again. Fiery daybreak. Homecoming Jeronimas opens the threshing-barn door. The Geniai family dog barks but then quiets down when Rudkis lends him no support. Aren't those dog roses blossoming on the windowpane? As if the frost had woven them! And isn't this the hay harvest dawn?

Vytukas across the river. But the ice splits and breaks! A black floe stirs . . . and the whole river!

Mommy, help! Mo-o-m-m-m-y! . . .

She wakes up soaked with sweat . . .

Quickly, her hands feel around at her side . . . Vytukas mine, my sweet, poor son!

Then the rosary until sunrise. Without moving her eyes from the seven swords piercing the Mother's heart.

To the church festival, through winding paths by the meadows and past the fields of rye. Sun, clover, cornflowers, caraway, hair grass.

Bees and swallows.

A greenish lake. White trunks of birches . . .

After the sermon, the priest announces the banns of Jeronimas and Aniute.

By the churchyard, the same old Kocka.

"Pray for Vytukas . . ."

She remembers.

"Mother why did you give it to Kocka?"

"It must be done, child."

"And why must it be done?"

The barrel-organ player cranks his tunes again. From the barrel organ, again the eyes . . .

Translated by Jeronimas Zemkalnis

Photo by Vytautas Mazelis

Antanas Skema

ANTANAS SKEMA

ANTANAS SKEMA was born in Lodz, Poland, on November 29, 1911, and returned with his parents to Lithuania in 1921. He was an actor with the Lithuanian State Theater in Kaunas (1936-40) and acted as well as directed in the Vilnius State Theater (1940-44). In the displaced persons camps in Germany and since 1949 in the United States, he was actively associated with efforts to maintain a Lithuanian stage in the diaspora.

He published collections of short stories, *Nuodeguliai ir kibirkstys* (Charred Stumps and Sparks), 1947, and *Sventoji Inga* (Saint Inga), 1952; a collection of poems in prose, *Celesta* (Celeste), 1960; and a novel, *Balta Drobule* (The White Shroud), 1958. His plays contributed importantly to the creation of a modern Lithuanian theater abroad: *Pabudimas* (The Awakening), 1965; *Zvakide* (The Candlestick), 1957; *Kaledu vaizdelis* (The Christmas Sketch), 1961; and others. Two of the planned three volumes of Skema's complete works have been published (1967, 1970), and several of his stories have been translated into English.

ANTANAS SKEMA

(1911-1961)

In the Hospital

SISTER ROSE, in nun's black habit, holds out a long pan.

"Spit, Wolfgang!"

Wolfgang is three years old and frail. His thin legs quiver, and he cannot sleep at night. He yearns for bread. Wolfgang often dreams of bread. Huge chunks of it whirl up and disappear right at his nose. At first, he grasps the air with his withered hands, and when he finally awakens, he raises himself a bit, holds on to the side of his bed and whines monotonously. "Bread, bread, bread..." About fifty times. Until he is tired and falls asleep.

Wolfgang cannot eat. His throat is full of sores. Milk is poured in through a small rubber hose inserted in his navel. But this food is not enough, and he cannot forget that wonderful sensation—chewing. Especially, when full, rich bites are churning between his teeth. That is why he wanders around the room all day, whimpering and searching.

Sometimes he succeeds in stealing a bite. There are sixteen children in the room, and Sister Rose is always busy. Wolfgang is driven by a single desire and this has made him shrewd. His little brain works intensely in a single direction.

"Ch-ew-ing!"

He is as thin as a concentration camp prisoner. Two limp bags hang in place of his buttocks. He still has beautiful dark eyes, thick eyelashes, and fuzz on his sunken cheeks—perhaps the result of malnutrition. His lips are pursed forward and form a round letter O, from which the tip of a bluish tongue hangs out.

His brain and the lower part of his face work in only one direction—chewing. Wolfgang wanders through the room and swallows whatever he finds: soup in a plate (no one leaves more than a spoonful here), a trampled leftover on the floor, and—his highest dream—bread. Whenever he sees a piece (the children sometimes overlook it), he stops for a moment and tries to calm himself. A convalescing boy is hitting his neighbor over the head with a spoon for stealing his soup. Convalescing children are voracious, and the hospital food is poor. Wolfgang stands still, he does not even blink. His pupils are expanding and the letter O is becoming even rounder. There is a large piece of bread near the bully's elbow. Wolfgang holds his breath. He turns his head toward the window as though he does not care, as though he is looking at the yellowing chestnuts outside. And he walks slowly, hesitatingly past the excited bully, and at the right moment turns around and attacks. He snatches that miraculous piece, stuffs it into his mouth, swallowing greedily while kneeling on the floor like a Buddha worshipper. It is all right that the bully is hitting him on the head with a spoon, it is all right that Sister Rose is running towards him. It is perfectly all right. He is chewing the most wondrous miracle in the world: synthetic German bread.

But his ecstasy is short-lived. The chewed-up delicacy does not reach his intestines; it chokes in his throat. Wolfgang's swollen face is plum purple. He caws, crowlike, his eyes bulging from sheer effort, and the chewed-up pieces come out into Sister Rose's waiting pan.

"Spit, Wolfgang!"

Oh, how he hates those words, spoken so pleasantly, and that awful enamel pan.

A thought keeps coming to his head: In this world, there are two obsolete things: Sister Rose and the white pan. They must be removed from this light shiny room. It is too bad that Sister Rose is tall and strong. She can hold him up with one hand. Whenever he beats her soft breast with his tiny fists, weakness quickly overcomes him and Sister Rose just laughs, the rest of the children joining her with their delighted squeals. Sister Rose cannot be removed but the pan is small and it can be thrown out the window when no one is looking.

This is a feasible plan for Wolfgang. Swabian autumns are peaceful and warm, and the Germans habitually keep their windows open. The children's throat disease room is on the fourth floor, and on the other side looms the top of a golden chestnut tree.

Wolfgang carries out his bold action when the convalescing children are greedily eating their lunch, a watery noodle soup, and Sister Rose is feeding those who cannot feed themselves. He picks up the disgusting pan from a low table and stealthily inches toward the window. He is following everyone with his eyes and is ready to fake a vomit at any moment. But the children are chattering away and only Sister Rose's round behind can be seen as she bends over to feed a half-year patient with the baby bottle.

Wolfgang crawls up on a chair, flings the enamel pan out of the window and, his waxen face sticking out, watches it fall. The pan whirls downward and clatters woefully when it reaches the asphalt. Wolfgang opens his mouth contentedly, his tongue hanging out over his lower lip. Now he begins picking at the window sill. Sister Rose, naturally understands everything and turns around. But Wolfgang is already defending himself.

"I wanted to spit, but it fell. Over there. There's no more pan. No more."

When Sister Rose approaches the window, Wolfgang is uneasy. He sees the pan, lying in the street undamaged. Wolfgang pleads:

"Close the window. Close it!"

Sister Rose glances downward, then strokes his fine hair. The battle is lost and Wolfgang weeps hopelessly and forgets his crime. He begs as though it were night, "Bread, bread, bread . . ."

Next to Wolfgang lies Rita, a Lithuanian girl, whom her parents nicknamed Smilga when she was very small. She is slender and fragile, with bright blue eyes. Smilga is six and cannot walk around because two days ago her tonsils were removed improperly. The nurses had whispered among themselves and decided that the new surgeon had hurried too much. The little one was bleeding profusely.

Actually, the doctor had been distracted and nervous during the operation, because Surgeon Mahle had lost his wife that day. Frau Entrautel Mahle did not finish her morning cup of coffee. Her once slender and elegant hands, now rough with chipped nails, were trembling. Frau Entrautel finally blurted out: "I'm leaving."

Surgeon Mahle did not understand his wife. He finished stuffing his pipe and examined the cigarette lighter. The flint was not working properly.

"I'm leaving," she repeated, enunciating the words clearly and dryly.

"What?" he finally asked and glanced at her after the lighter had suddenly produced a flame. He noticed for the first time her wild eyes and restless hands. Her hands were aimlessly turning around a half-filled cup of coffee. Mahle was somewhat surprised but his surprise soon increased so that he forgot his precious morning smoke. Frau Mahle stood up abruptly and announced in an expressive and rather melodramatic voice:

"I'm leaving this house. I'm leaving you."

Everything became clear. This Reiber had a car. This Reiber ran a shady business and in the mornings was able to offer a woman real coffee, the kind Mahle once used to drink. Mahle's name had been Gomper and he had lived well under the Nazis. Now he hid behind another name—one that nobody recognized. The times of good coffee had evaporated forever. His pay was meager and Frau Entrautel was no longer pampered by two maids. Her fine white hands had cracked and blackened and the red nail polish she wore was no longer flattering.

Mr. Reiber caressed her hands before enveloping her whole body in his embrace. He promised to bring back the past. A new Opel was waiting on the street, and on the other side of the city— a warm room and blessed comfort. The love act lasted only a few minutes, but its discomfort was only slightly more unpleasant than the hot and cold water. Frau Entrautel belonged to a class of women who were dubious of love's pleasures and she stated so pathetically. "I'm leaving this house, I'm leaving you!"

This morning surgeon Mahle, like small Wolfgang, had lost a battle. True, he slapped his wife across her face and broke a naive china statuette (a girl and a boy, in eighteenth century garb, embracing, with the inscription: *"Als ich Wiederkam"*), but the clinic awaited him and he was already fifteen minutes late. Fifteen minutes was no small matter in today's world, and surgeon Mahle, pale, his coat unbuttoned, ran down the stairs and into the street.

In the clinic, he quickly removed pimply Fritz's adenoids and, defeated, called for the next patient.

Sister Rose brought in Smilga who gave him a friendly smile.

Her long face waited for a friendly word. Her parents had taught her to look at life with bright eyes. Anything unpleasant was only temporary. If you hurt your foot, sing for a while and the pain will disappear as though it never existed. And crying does not help. Whenever pain became very bad, Daddy would skip around the room in a funny way, making believe he was a ballerina. Then the tears filling her eyes would be quickly dried by her smile and ringing laughter. And, actually, Smilga knew only nice people. Her parents protected her from the others. Sometimes the school liked to push little girls around but after all, they were not grown-ups.

Surgeon Mahle gripped Smilga's throat tightly.

"It hurts, it hurts!" Smilga screamed sharply. This gentleman (she called all grown-up men "gentlemen") was not nice. He did not ask her name, did not stroke her hair like other nice men, but instead grabbed her with his big hands.

"It hurts, it hurts!" she repeated.

"Who is she?" Mahle muttered. And when he heard Sister Rose's "A foreigner—a Lithuanian," he gave Smilga his first careful look. Well, there was fear in her eyes—nothing unusual. They all cry at first and then they forget about it. Mahle stuck the shiny, sharp needle into her trembling throat.

Screaming and tenseness transformed Smilga's face into a wrinkled, red mask. Her thin screeches, now resembling the yelps of a beaten dog, pierced his ear drums.

Then Herr Mahle remembered his wife.

Yes, yes . . . after the slap on her face . . . very similar, very similar, very similar, very similar.

Running down the stairs, Herr Mahle heard the screams. A surgeon's hands are strong, Frau Entrautel would be bruised by black and blue marks for a long time. But her heart was probably thumping with joy. No one will notice her temporarily marked face. The new Opel will take Entrautel to the other side of the city, and self-satisfied Reiber will pompously steer the wheel.

Then surgeon Mahle operated. He was wet with perspiration and operated badly. Even Sister Rose's pale nose was covered with beads of sweat. In all her years of experience she had never seen a surgeon's face so distorted.

"Doctor, she'll choke on her blood," Sister Rose warned discreetly.

*   *   *

The next day Smilga's parents came to visit her. The little girl lay waiting, pale and calm. But childish innocence had drowned in the blue wells of her eyes. Oh, what a bright and happy world! No, it was no longer happy. There are many windows in the room, in the white, shiny room, but the light is like ice, the world frozen and immobile. Her throat is oppressed by a glass rock until it is no longer bearable, and then the sour blood wells up. Sister Rose runs over, a black witch from a fairy tale, and stabs her in the leg this time. And the black nun's habit, like a magician's cape, covers the clean, icy world, and the hot pain is torturing her, and nobody is concerned about it. The convalescing children are singing in German, and Wolfgang pleads: "bread, bread, bread . . ."

The girl's parents are standing next to her bed, like remorseful sinners.

"You don't know, you don't know what they did to me," Smilga accuses softly, and the accusation prompts her mother to speak.

"You'll get well and we'll come home. Look what your father has brought you."

Her father pulls a children's book clumsily out of his pocket.

"Look, what big letters! You can read them yourself."

Smilga tries to read. She looks at the book but the letters are spinning; The capital "B" merges with the "I" and the green-colored blacksmith, his hammer raised, is falling down.

"Read it to me," Smilga orders her mother, and her mother quickly wipes her tear-stained glasses. The bags under her eyes are droopy and sad. She starts to read standing up, although there is a chair next to her. Her emaciated father, whose face resembles that of an old parrot's, moves closer. Each word grates, like a knife scraping a pan.

" . . . Johnny and Simon went to the blacksmith's shop. There, the blacksmith was hammering: tin-tan-tin, tin-tan-tin. Johnny and Simon want to hammer. The blacksmith says: Do you know how to hammer? No, we don't know how to hammer, Simon answers."

Sister Rose whispers in the father's ear,

"That's enough for the first time. She's weak. Come again tomorrow."

The father looks at his daughter and sees two purple spots suddenly appear on each sunken cheek. He pulls the mother's sleeve.

"Let's go." Mother understands. Smilga's eyes widen. Her bloodless lips quiver.

"We'll come again tomorrow; we can't stay any longer, today. You'll get well faster if you're left alone. If we don't leave right now, we can't come back tomorrow. You rest quietly. Lie still and when you're hungry . . . Did you eat anything today?"

The bags under mother's eyes are quivering, like her daughter's lips. Smilga is silent. She knows that as soon as her parents leave, the glass rock will weigh down on her again. She is silent when her mother showers her with tiny kisses and when her father touches her cheek as though it were a cross.

"Gruss Gott!"

"Gruss Gott!"

Her parents leave.

From a corner of the room Wolfgang is greedily spying the chocolate bar on the girl's pillow. He does not know what kind of food it is. But probably, it's chewable. Grown-ups leave nothing but food here. Wolfgang is standing up and trying to calm himself while waiting.

Now the evening sun peeks in through the window. Its searching rays slide, find the object and the children and flood them with a thick, syrupy light.

Sister Rose raises her eyes to the ceiling and announces grandly: "Do you see, children, the beauty of God's world. Look how the sun is setting. It blesses all of us. It is the eyes of Almighty God and the bearer of His everlasting light. Let's go out on the balcony. There, we'll sing the evening hymn."

Sister Rose puts her arms around the convalescing children and leads them out in a procession. Wolfgang is left with the dozing children. He manages to hide behind the closet. He stares lustfully at the chocolate bar lying right next to him on Smilga's pillow.

And Smilga is trying to remember what her mother was reading.

Simon and Johnny . . . in the blacksmith's shop—the blacksmith. Tin-tan, the blacksmith hammers, tin-tan, tin-tan.

Tin-tan rings in her ears. Tin-tan, a pleasant tickle in her throat. Tin-tan, her heart-beats. How fast! It has never beaten this way before.

My father was a blacksmith.

Tik, taku, tik, taku, he was a blacksmith . . .

Her last memory is born. She once learned this poem. She wrinkles her brow. What is the next line?

He was a blacksmith . . . blacksmith . . .

The room is expanding and the light, shiny walls are falling in. Smilga leans on the side of her bed on her hands, rises up and then falls back. The thick blood collects in her throat and then spills out. It resembles the rays of the setting sun. Then Smilga turns over and is still.

Wolfgang walks over to Smilga's bed. Quietly, cautiously he stretches out his hand and in a flash grabs the chocolate. Trr . . . the wax paper crinkles. Wolfgang chews. For the first time, as much as he wants. He chews quickly, choking on the bar, his eyes closed in bliss. He chews until his face turns a deep purple. His lids are open and his eyes are bulging from his stubborn effort, but the chewed-up pieces fall on the floor next to Smilga's bed.

On the balcony, Sister Rose and the children are singing the evening hymn.

Translated by Skema

Stepas Zobarskas

STEPAS ZOBARSKAS

STEPAS ZOBARSKAS was born in Lithuania on January 17, 1911. Educated in Lithuania, France and Germany, he made his reputation as a magazine editor and as a writer of short stories and books. Two of his works, *The Children of Pasture* and *The Refugee*, received literary awards from the Lithuanian Red Cross. For two years he also served as the Lithuanian representative to the League of Societies of the Red Cross in Paris.

Mr. Zobarskas emigrated to the United States in 1947, where he worked variously as a manual laborer, a counselor for orphan refugee children, and as a bank clerk. He is the founder and president of Manyland Books, Inc., a publishing house primarily dedicated to presenting in translation the works of the leading authors of those countries whose literatures are little known to the English speaking world.

He has published two collections of short stories in English, *The Maker of Gods* and *Young Love and Other Infidelities*. He has also compiled and edited three volumes dealing with Lithuanian literature, *Lithuanian Folk Tales, Selected Lithuanian Short Stories* and *Lithuanian Quartet*. Some of his own short stories have been translated into Estonian, Latvian, Italian, German, Flemish, and French. A German translation of one of his books, *Das Lied Der Sansen*, was published in Tubingen.

STEPAS ZOBARSKAS

(1911   )

Elena

KLEMENTAS APPROACHED me late one afternoon, as I sat on a park bench, watching the falling leaves and listening to the happy laughter of young people, who strolled along the paths or reclined concealed from view behind the green walls of shrubbery. He was tall and so thin as to seem gaunt. His lips were remarkably thick and red, and his nose appeared somewhat swollen, as though he were suffering from a cold. His brown eyes peered sharply through the black rims of his glasses, and his hair fluttered flag-like in the gusts of wind that blew through the park, so that he was forced to push it behind his ears every few minutes. He had written beautiful poetry once, but now had turned alcoholic and behaved as though he were a near-derelict.

"How about having a drink with me, Petras?" he asked by way of greeting.

"Do you have any money?" I asked in return.

"Hell, no. If I had the money I wouldn't be walking in this park —not while the bars were open. Otherwise, it isn't really such a bad place." I said nothing.

Klementas drew a crumpled cigarette from his jacket pocket and proceeded to puff on it until the glowing tip nearly scorched his lips. Only then did he spit it out.

"I'm sure you're not as broke as I am right now," he resumed. "Come on, lend me enough for a bottle of gin—and I'll even treat you to a few drinks from it. As for the money—you'll get it back as soon as the publisher sends me an advance for next book."

"So you've another book ready?"

"Nearly ready. All I have to do is polish it up a bit before submitting it to the publisher."

I listened to Klementas in silence.

"You don't believe me, do you, Petras? Well, I did write another book, and I assure you it will be my best."

"If you say that you have a new book, then you have a new

book. Who am I to doubt you? But I don't have very much money, just the same. Barely enough to pay a second-rate whore, as a matter of fact.

Klementas regarded me with mock surprise.

"My dear man, would you defile your body with a fallen woman's flesh? Would you risk catching syphillis, or worse yet, mortally injuring your immortal soul?"

I laughed.

"The lady I have in mind is probably healthier than any of your so-called respectable matrons," I said.

"Don't bet on it!" said Klementas, licking his lips and swallowing with difficulty. He seemed to be concentrating on something. Mystified, I watched his huge Adam's apple bob up and down above his shirt collar. I waited for him to pronounce some other moral sentiment, but since he still seemed to be lost in thought, I took the opportunity to slip away.

"If you'll forgive me, I must leave now. The lady of my dreams awaits."

I stood up and began to walk somewhat hurriedly towards the park gate.

"Wait!" Klementas shouted suddenly, running after me. "Wait, if it's flesh you're after, I have a much better idea—a thousand times better than yours."

"Like what?" I asked, without slackening my pace.

"My sister-in-law. My wife's sister."

"I didn't know your wife had a sister."

"Of course she has. The girl's been living with us for almost a year, now."

"Well, what about her?"

"I'm sure she's man-crazy, even though she appears rather shy and innocent. Given a chance, she would fall head over heels for you. I pointed you out to her in a theater last winter, and even now she blushes like some high school girl whenever I mention your name."

"She might be a fine woman," I said. "I'll be glad to meet her some time, my plans for tonight are made already."

"All right, so you must have a woman. You're a bachelor, and it's not so easy for you as it is for a married man like myself. If I want to make love I simply embrace my wife. You, of course, have no wife waiting for you at home, so you must shop around. Now here is my plan. First of all, we buy a bottle of gin."

"I can't buy gin," I protested. "I don't have enough money for both gin and the girl."

"Let me finish. We'll buy a bottle, we'll have a few drinks to pass the time. Late at night we can go to my place."

"Why at night?"

"Why not? Night is the best part of man's life. Beautiful thoughts emerge only at night; the most moving poems are created at night. So we'll go to my house. My wife will be asleep—and the sister, too. They go to bed yearly. You'll tiptoe towards her bed, raise the blanket and crawl in beside her. And then— she's yours: a woman as pure as spring water."

"Just like that?"

"Yes, just like that."

"And what if she wakes up and begins to scream?"

"Silly man. Why should she scream?"

"Won't she be frightened to find a stranger in her bed?"

"No," Klementas assured me. "And let me tell you why. But before I do, you must swear that you'll never tell anyone else what I'm about to say."

I promised.

"I've done it several times with her myself when my wife was visiting her family. And do you want to know something else? She pretended to be asleep and just let me do it. Afterwards, she acted as though nothing had ever happened between us."

The idea began to fascinate me. It was something new and adverturous, and since I really had no intention of engaging a whore (I had made up the story just to get rid of him), I decided to find out more about this sister-in-law.

"What does she look like?"

"She's tall. She has blue eyes. She looks very much like my wife."

"Your wife is a beautiful woman," I remarked.

"Well, as I said, my wife and her sister are very much alike."

I was hooked. Without further word, I steered Klementas to the nearest tavern, ordered martinis for both of us, and continued to re-order until it was time to buy the bottle of gin and start toward Klementas' place. By now, the sky was filled with stars, and Klementas began to mutter poetic praise to the eternal galaxy, to the moon, and to mother earth which, he insisted, was the mos beautiful thing ever created by God's hands, and no woman could ever rival such beauty.

I thought about his sister-in-law sleeping alone between the warm white sheets.

The windows of Klementas' house were dark. He stopped at the threshold for a moment, inhaled deep draughts of cool night air and unlocked the front door. We entered with the stealth of two thieves and tiptoed into the room where a woman lay sleeping.

"Don't utter a word," cautioned Klementas. "Remain silent, no matter what she does. Let her think it's I embracing her."

As he spoke, the woman stirred.

"Is it you, Klemka?" The voice was sleepy. "Drunk again."

"Shush," said Klementas. "Go back to sleep."

He motioned for me to remain, and began to grope his way towards the door. I thrust the bottle of gin into his hands.

Left alone in the darkness, I listened to the woman's breathing, until the regular wheezing assured me that she had gone back to sleep. My heart pounded heavily as I approached her. I could smell the mysterious feminine scent so exceedingly pleasant. I stood beside the bed for a moment, shivering as the blood began to race through my body, then I slipped in beside her. I tried to pull her closer to me, but, sleepily, she twisted away from my hands.

"I'm tired," she moaned. "Why don't you leave me alone?"

Despite the roughness of her voice I felt that she was beginning to yield. Whether she did so out of desire, or because she had lost interest in fighting me off, I didn't know—or care. Whatever it was, she heaved a deep sigh as I rolled her on her back and pressed myself against her body. I kissed her. Her lips were hot and dry. Her fingers played over my ears, and my neck, and began to stroke my hair. Suddenly her hand stopped as though frozen in mid-air. In a second she was out of my arms, on her feet and putting on the light.

"What the hell you're doing here?" she gasped and began to back away towards the door.

I was stunned. There, shaking, was Klementas' own wife, Elena.

"It's a terrible mistake," I mumbled. "A terrible mistake."

She kept on backing away.

"I'll explain it all," I mumbled. "A terrible mistake."

"I'll explain it all," I continued wondering how I would go about it, but Elena had already run out of the house and into the yard, screaming:

"Klementas! Klementas!"

I ran after her, trying to grab hold of her and to plead to her, "Stop screaming. You'll arouse the neighbors. Stop and listen to me.

It's a terrible mistake. I'll tell you all about it."

Breathless, she finaly stopped—and stood staring at her husband who was sleeping slumped over a table under a chestnut tree. The half empty bottle of gin stood at his elbow.

"I knew he was here," she gasped. "I heard his voice."

"Now please listen to me."

Elena raised her eyes for a split second, looked at me, then lowered them again. She clutched the collar of her night gown, as though trying to wrap it tightly around herself.

Haitingly, I told her about our scheme to seduce her sister. "I would have married her after this," I added somewhat irrelevantly. My mouth was dry.

Elena just stood there, biting her lips. Suddenly she shoved her sleeping husband to the ground and shouted:

"You despicable beast! You degenerate! You're worse than a mad dog!"

She circled around the prostrate form, spitting, kicking, beating him with her fists. I have never seen anyone as enraged as she was. A thin trickle of blood was beginning to seep out of his nose and mouth.

"Stop it! Stop it!" I shouted, pushing her away.

"I'll kill him! I'll finish him this time!"

"Are you out of your mind? Stop it."

"I want to kill the beast!"

"And spend the rest of your life in jail?"

"I don't care what happens to me. I don't give a damn."

"Elena!"

I seized her arms and held them in my grip, and even though she tried to kick and bite me, I managed to keep her from lashing out at Klementas once again.

"You're hurting me," she finally said. The fight seemed to have gone out of her.

I released her arms. There were a few drops of blood on her face, and I wiped them off with my handkerchief. As I did so, Elena lowered her head and started to cry bitterly.

"It's all my fault," I whispered. "I guess I was as drunk as he was."

When her cry subsided, I asked her if we should bring Klementas into the house.

Elena nodded.

Several times I tried to set my long-haired, bloody-nosed and beaten-up friend on his feet, but he slumped back to the ground. Finally, I seized him by the armpits and dragged him into a small room adjoining the kitchen. I left him on a cot and washed my hands in the kitchen sink.

"I guess he'll be all right," I muttered.

Elena stood in the doorway, saying nothing.

I reached for her hand and kissed it.

"I pray you never mention this idiotic plot to your sister."

Elena followed me to the door in silence. Just as I was walking out, she whispered in a trembling voice:

"I have no sister. It was all in his imagination."

*   *   *

Three or four weeks had passed since that night, when—suddenly Elena appeared at my door. It was drizzling, and she was wearing a white raincoat and a little umbrella over her head. A golden autumn leaf fallen from some tree clung to her shoulder, and looked like a ray of sunshine on that drab day.

"I'll only stay a few minutes," she said, her voice clear, calm and formal—the voice of a rent collector. She left her umbrella in the anteroom, unbuttoned her coat and sat down on the sofa.

"Would you care for a drink?" I asked her.

"No, thanks."

"I have some fresh hot coffee on the stove. Will you have it black of with milk?"

"I'll take it black."

Ill at ease, I could hardly keep our conversation alive. I poured out two cups of coffee, as well as two vials of benedictine. If I remembered correctly, she had seemed to enjoy its taste when I gave it to her and her husband several years ago.

Elena crossed her legs and pulled down the hem of her green wool dress carefully below her knees. She drank the coffee in silence. When I handed her the vial with the liguor she murmured, "Really, I shouldn't," but took a sip and put the vial back on the tray. There was a trace of sadness and desolation in her appearance.

"Klementas and I have parted," she said in a low voice. "My lawyer says there is more than enough evidence against him for a quick divorce. Mental cruelty and incompatibility or something."

My upper lip trembled. The news was not entirely unexpected, yet it irritated me.

"You shouldn't have rushed things," I said. "I'm more responsible for what happened that night than he. Some kind of madness must have overcome me."

"That night's farce was only the drop that made the bucket overflow. I haven't even mentioned it to my lawyer. I was too ashamed."

"Then why are you separating?"

"I simply can't bear the sight of him in my house any longer."

"What will you do now, all alone?"

"The same thing I've been doing for years. I'll keep on working."

"And what about him?"

A spark of anger flickered in her eyes.

"He's not only an incurable alcoholic; he's also a wicked man. He can live and die as he pleases."

Nervously, she picked up the vial and finished the liquor in one gulp. Then she washed it down with coffee. She stared at my hand as I began to pour another drink, but said nothing. She picked up a cigarette, lighted it and inhaled the smoke deep into her lungs. Leaning back against the sofa, she continued:

"About that incident. The more I think of it the more ridiculous it seems. You know, you nearly fooled me, until I began to stroke your head. Your hair is cut short, not long and falling over the ears."

Saying this, she laughed, and her laugh seemed to break the tension.

"I'm glad you've forgiven me," I exclaimed warmly. "We can talk things over, calmly and reasonably."

I sat beside her and placed my arm around her shoulders. Elena carefully disengaged herself from my arm and reached for the vial of benedictine. I could read her thoughts: Don't touch me. You're a snake, repulsive and dangerous. But I was not dangerous. And I resented being compared to a snake. How could I prove it?

"You're still angry with me, aren't you?" I was surprised at the pleading tone of my voice.

Elena heaved a deep sigh. Her voice, when she replied, was remote and impersonal.

"I'm not sure that I've ever been angry with you. I was frightened for a moment—until I realized that it was you. Then plain amazement replaced any fears I had. And then came shock. I guess I was more concerned about my reputation than anything else."

I leaned closer to her and whispered into her ear: "You have the most beautiful eyes in the whole world."

Elena shook her head.

"No, not this! Why can't you be decent and tell the truth?"

"But it is the truth, Elena. I swear on my heart." And I added aloud: "Years ago Klementas wrote a poem about your eyes. I know. I read it many times. It has been included in his prize-winning collection."

Elena licked her lips. Her face blanched.

"Why did he have to change so drastically?"

She bowed her head and burst into tears. I stared for a moment at her shaking shoulders, at her trembling lips, then I moved closer toward her, cupped her chin and pressed her face against mine.

Outside, the rain had begun to descend in torrents. A bolt of lightning flashed across the sky and a loud blast of thunder shook the walls and windows. Elena leaned towards me, as if searching for a shelter. I embraced her with both arms.

"Thunder's always frightened me, ever since I was a little girl," she whispered. "It still frightens me."

"I, too, was frightened of thunder when I was young."

I felt her tremble every time the thunder sounded, and each time I pressed her more tightly against my chest. Her face felt very warm. We were both panting as though we were trying to scale some difficult mountain peak.

When we finally separated, we stared at the darkness, now and then illuminated by the lightning, and held hands. For a long time we did not speak, for what was there to say?

"My God!" exclaimed Elena. "And I thought I'd be here only ten or fifteen minutes—just long enough to straighten things out. Now look what I've done!"

As soon as the sky cleared up, Elena prepared to leave. I draped the raincoat over her shoulders and placed her umbrella into her hands. Then I offered her my key.

"Come anytime you like," I said. "I'll be waiting for you."

Elena smiled.

"Suppose I came unexpectedly and find you with some other girl?"

"You may not believe it, but I have no other girl."

"Well, anyway, if I ever come again I'll come when you are at home. What would I do in your apartment alone?"

At the door, she stopped for a moment, fished an envelope from her hand bag and thrust it into my pocket.

Inside the envelope I found a note wrapped around a few dollar bills. "I am returning the money you paid for Klementas' gin that night. He was still my husband then, and I feel obliged to pay at least some of his debts."

* * *

Days and weeks and months passed by, but Elena never came to me again. Then one afternoon in the Spring, I spotted Klementas' picture in *The Literary News.* The caption underneath was brief. "A well-known poet of the late Fifties was found this morning floating in the river, apparently the victim of foul play."

So he had killed himself, the thought flashed across my mind. He had lost the strength to live, but he still had enough guts to destroy himself.

Immediately I dialed Elena's number, but the phone was disconnected. I went to see her at her house, but the door was locked, and no one answered the bell when I rang. The I checked with the newspaper again. It had announced that Klementas was to be buried the following day, and I decided to go to the church in hopes of seeing Elena.

Klementas' casket lay on a catafalque among candles and flowers. It was sealed, and I could not see his face. Maybe it was better that way.

I watched Elena from a distance. She was dressed in black. Her face was pale and thin. When the pall bearers picked up the casket on their shoulders and started moving out of the church, I fell into the line of mourners and accompanied them to the cemetery.

I listened while the priest uttered a few prayers and watched the casket disappear into the waiting embrace of the earth.. "Mother earth is the most beautiful thing created by God's hands," I remembered Klemantas' words." No woman could ever rival such beauty."

As soon as the ceremonies were over, I approached Elena and expressed the usual condolences. She raised her eyes, which seemed blue, dry and cold, stared at me for a moment, then bowed her head and muttered impersonally, "Thank you."

"Is there anything I can do for you?"

"Not a thing. Thank you."

Another man was approaching her to express his sympathy, and I moved aside. After him came a woman. Then another man. Soon

Elena was flanked by the mourners. In vain did I wait for her to look up at me again.

After standing about aimlessly for a while, I left the cemetery and rode back to the city. I did not feel like going home. I wanted to see Elena first. I knew she needed some comfort and encouragement. I could not forget the whiteness of her face and coldness of her eyes.

What would she do when it was all over, when all the mourners had gone back to their nests? Would she return to her house and lock herself in among the walls filled with haunting memories?

I went twice to her home, but the door was still locked. None of the neighbors had seen the widow coming back.

I wandered to the park and strolled along the same paths that Klementas used to frequent. Elena was not there. I rode back to the cemetery but that city of the dead was completely deserted. On my way home, I stopped at a tavern for a drink.

I was startled to see a woman dressed in black sitting alone in a remote corner, her head hidden between her hands.

"She's been sitting and drinking there for quite a while," remarked the bartender in a low voice, when he noticed the curosity in my eyes. "Some sailor wanted to join her, but she told him to go to hell."

I looked at the woman again. Yes, it was Elena in her widow's weeds. I walked straight toward her table and placed my hand over her shoulder.

"For heaven's sake, what are you doing here?"

She pushed my hand away.

"Elena, don't you recognize me?"

She raised her head and blinked her eyes. She was drunk.

"Of course I recognize you. Sit down. I'll buy you a drink."

"Stop that nonsense! Let's get the hell out of here!"

"Where will you take me? To show me a grave?"

"No, darling. I'll show you life."

Gently, I helped Elena to stand up on her feet and led her out into the fresh, cool air.

"I'm awfully sorry," she said as I seated her in a taxi. "I guess I had too much today. I'm still a novice in the art of drinking."

When we pulled up at my front door, Elena wanted to climb out of the taxi herself, but slipped and fell on her knee."

"Damn it," she muttered. "I cut a hole in my stocking."

I carried her up the stairs and seated her on a chair. One of her knees was bleeding. I removed her shoes and stockings. She trembled as I cleared the wound and applied an antiseptic. Tomorrow we'll see the doctor, I thought.

Suddenly she stood up and staggered to the bathroom. I heard her groan and curse and vomit, and then the splash of water running into the basin. I went to the kitchen to make her some coffee.

At long last she walked out of the bathroom, a towel tied around her waist, her hands covering her breasts.

"I was too late," she said. "I got it all over my clothes."

I found some clean pajamas and threw them at her.

"Get dressed before you catch pneumonia."

The pajamas were too large, and Elena had to roll up the sleeves and trouser legs. She refused to eat anything, but she drank the hot coffee eagerly.

"Now be a good girl and go to bed," I said. "You've had more than enough for one day."

She obeyed me. She walked over to my bed and slid between the sheets, covering herself up to the chin.

"Could you hold my hand until I fall asleep?" she pleaded. "I'm scared to be alone tonight."

"Yes, of course."

I turned off the light and sat on the edge of the bed in silence. Elena pressed my hand against her face. She mumbled something about being guilty of Klementas' death. "Did he die because of me? Or was his destiny already written in the stars before I even met him?"

Instead of answering her questions, I asked her, in return, "Did you get your divorce?"

"All the papers were signed but the decree hadn't become final."

Then she began to talk about the sailor in the tavern who had wanted to take her to his ship. 'Baby,' he had cried, 'you're the one I've been looking for!' Why is it that the very minute a man sees a woman he likes he wants to possess her even though she's a complete stranger?"

"There are two things in this world that every man feels entitled to," I said. "Somebody else's money and a beautiful woman."

Elena released my hand and turned her face away from me.

When I was sure she was asleep, I tiptoed to my study and stretched out on the sofa. She'd better get used to being alone, I thought, before she begins to suspect that the whole world has turned against her.

When I woke up the next morning, I discovered that Elena was already up and setting the table for breakfast. The room smelled of fresh coffee and ham and eggs. Her dress and slip were flopped on the line in the backyard. She must have washed them early in the morning.

"You, too, must have been exhausted," she said. "You slept like a perfect baby boy." Her voice was calm, and her cheeks had regained their natural color.

"How is your wound?"

"Nothing serious. Only a scratch." To show me how well she was, Elena turned around like a professional dancer, and for the first time I noticed how well-built and athletic she was.

When breakfast was finished, Elena washed the dishes and cleaned off the table. Then she took her dress and slip from the line, and disappeared in the bedroom. In a few minutes she emerged dressed in her own clothes. I noticed that she was limping slightly.

"I must go home now," she said.

"Be brave." I patted her on the shoulder. "Whenever you feel like crying your heart out, come to me."

* * *

At least once a week, mostly on Sundays, I took Elena to the movies. Sometimes we had dinner in a restaurant afterwards, at other times we simply walked in the park holding hands. Neither of us said very much.

She stopped mentioning Klementas by name. She sent all his books and manuscripts to his parents, and she donated his clothes to a charitable organization. Their wedding portrait had long ago disappeared from her dressing table. They had no children, and there was nothing to keep Klementas' memory alive.

"I'm beginning to feel free, as free as a lark," Elena exclaimed one evening, as we sat in my apartment, watching an African documentary on television.

"Sooner or later someone will clip your wings," I teased. "You're too precious to be lost forever in the sky."

A herd of majestic elephants rumpled across the green plains. A graceful leopard emerged out of the thickness of the forest and began to stalk a young gazelle. The gazelle was so beautiful and so desperately frightened. Its thin legs shot into the air as it fled for its life. Elena closed her eyes and buried her face in my breast. She could not watch so graceful an animal being slaughtered.

"Is it still alive? Is it still running? Is the leopard about to sink sharp teeth into its neck?"

I watched the chase intensely, almost as excited as Elena. And then . . . a miracle!

"The gazelle escaped!" I shouted. "It's free!"

When she saw the leopard looking angry and foolish and the gazelle rejoining the flock, Elena leaned over me with outstretched arms and kissed me. Her whole body vibrated with joy.

When the program was over, I turned off the television set and poured some benedictine into her vial and mine. We sipped in silence. After that sudden outburst of joy she had become sad again. It was that sadness that made her beauty so attractive.

"How long can we go on like this?" she asked looking straight into my eyes.

"What do you mean?"

"Well, I don't know how to put it. I don't want to offend you, but I must begin to think of myself."

"Open your heart. I won't be offended."

"Frankly, I don't like the way you're treating me. You've almost made a mistress of me. True, you came to help me at a time when I needed help. You've partly restored my self-confidence. I enjoy being with you. But what about the future?"

I remained silent.

"I've had enough struggles in my life. The greater part of my marriage was a total loss. I'm a normal woman, you know. I want to be more than an instrument for man's carnal satisfaction. To put it bluntly: I want a husband, not a lover."

"Is there anyone in particular you'd like to marry? Anyone I know?"

Elena tightened her lips and slapped my face. She tried to jump on her feet, but I pulled her back. She became enraged. She fought me, she kicked me in the shins. Her face was scarlet. It took quite a while before she settled down, exhausted and panting.

"Larks are beautiful singers," I teased. "I didn't know they were such ferocious fighters, too."

Elena stirred again but I held her tightly in my arms. She showed her teeth and tried to bite my lips.

"I'll crush your nose if you do it," I warned her.

"I'm not afraid of you," she said, giving up the fight at last.

Would she really walk out on me and look for another man? I asked myself. A beautiful widow attracts more men than a single girl. What would I do if I lost her forever? Would I miss her simplicity, her warmth, her softness, even her rage? Could I find this in any other woman?

Elena stood up, pulled back her hair, and walked towards the window. She stood there smoking a cigarette while I watched her profile, thinking of how, of all the women I had known, she was the only one I had genuinely admired. I thought I loved her, too. But could I make her happy?

She left the window, ground out her cigarette, put the butt in the ashtray, and looked at me:

"Will you walk me home, or shall I go alone?"

"I'll walk you home."

*   *   *

The following month we were married. There was no wedding party, no celebration, not even a honeymoon. We moved her belongings into my place and put her house up for sale.

A constant stream of warmth and softness now filled my rooms. Elena's presence was evident everywhere: in a vase of flowers, in crisp new window curtains, in a neatly-made bed.

"I look at you and hardly believe my eyes," she whispered one morning, leaning over my chest. "You and I, both united in the same destiny. And then again . . . sometimes I feel so sad . . . it's almost impossible to hold back the tears."

"Why? Am I not what you had expected me to be?"

"No, not because of you."

Elena closed her eyes. We lay silent for a long time. Then she spoke again:

"Why didn't we meet years ago? I would have been yours—the first and the only one. Death would not have overshadowed our lives, then."

"Don't you think that all this was decreed long before we ever saw each other?" I tried to find something just to soothe her, to ease her pain.

"Do you honestly believe in predestination?"

"I don't know what to believe. Whenever I think of that stupid night. . . . Who knows, had it not been for the macabre joke of a sick poet, would you and I be together this morning? Maybe destiny did select him as our go-between, to help us find each other at last."

We ate breakfast. Or, to be more precise, I ate alone, while Elena sipped black coffee. It was a lazy murky Saturday morning. Since neither of us had to go work, we decided to go back to the bedroom.

"It's been a long time since I read a good book," she said. "A few more years like this and I'll become absolutely illiterate."

"Let me read you something beautiful," I offered.

Elena settled herself on the bed, her head resting against a pillow, her right hip slightly raised, while I was searching among the volumes of poetry. Suddenly my fingers touched the anthology of Klementas' writings.

For a moment I stood still, frozen. I shot a glance at my wife. She lay with her eyes closed, waiting. Should I read it? Why not? I took the book, turned the pages until I came to one particular poem —a poem dedicated to the woman with the most beautiful eyes in the world.

Holding the book in my left hand, I placed the right one on her knee and began to read in a slow, clear, dramatic voice. For a moment I thought she did not recognize the poem because she remained motionless while I read the first two stanzas. But when I began to recite the third, the one in which the poet addressed the woman directly, imploring her not to shut her eyes to him, not to walk out on him, because, by leaving, she would walk away with his very life, Elena jumped up, seized the book from my hand and hurled it against the wall. Then she fell on her stomach, covered her face with both hands and began to wail.

For a moment I stared at her, waiting, but when her sobbing persisted, I leaned over her and began to stroke her head.

"Don't touch me!" Elena shrugged her shoulders and pulled away.

Without thinking, I slapped her.

At long last her sobbing subsided. She sat up, dried her tears, and lighted a cigarette.

"Why did you read it?" she asked quietly.

I did not know what to answer.

A long silence followed. I lay beside her, my hands clasped behind my head, and stared at the ceiling. Elena heaved a deep sigh and said in a whisper:

"Petras, why have you caused me so much pain . . . and such an abundance of joy?"

"Because I love your eyes, I suppose."

MARIUS KATILISKIS

MARIUS KATILISKIS was born on September 15, 1915, in Gruzdziai, Lithuania. He had acquired his litarary reputation long before his first collection of stories, *Prasilenkimo valanda* (The Hour of Passing By), 1948, was published in Germany where he was displaced by the war. He later emigrated to the United States and now lives in Lemont, Illinois.

    Katiliskis' works include two collections of stories, *Uzuoveja* (The Shelter), 1952, and *Sventadienis uz miesto* (Sunday in the Country); 1963; and the novels *Miskais ateina ruduo* (Autumn Comes Through the Forests), 1957, and *Isejusiems negrizti (*A Journey of No Return), 1958. A long excerpt from the latter was published in English in "Lithuanian Quartet," 1962 under the title, "On Whose Side is God?"

Marius Katiliskis

MARIUS KATILISKIS

(1915-   )

Midsummer

THE OLD MAN VETRA stood guard over his cherry orchard while Vale, his adopted daughter, sat on the threshold singing. Vetra's wife was saying her prayers, seemingly unable to come to an end. Her voice drifted out through the open window of the bedroom; it was coarse and it wavered, fading away gradually into the night. And whenever she drew a deep sigh and fell silent, the clatter of her rosary against the floor woke her up again and she began anew, "Holy, holy . . ." in an unsteady voice that rasped like the dried-up wheel of a windmill.

"Why isn't she asleep? What's the matter with the woman? Mumbling away at those prayers as if she hasn't recited them enough in her lifetime . . ." Vetra grumbled at his wife as he took down his rusty gun from the wooden hook.

It was a fine summer night and a young moon had risen in the sky, implanting itself firmly, like a brass horn, in the topmost branches of the cherrytree. The trees sagged under their heavy burden of fruit.

Vale was still singing. She sang better and more beautifully now, without even trying to drown out the sound of the prayers, so that her song did not interfere with anyone. She knew that there was no need, in one's youth to trouble much with prayers, and as she sang her voice was full of longing and a dark unquiet, as though she alone were young in the whole world, with her heart yearning and waiting for something. When she began to sing more joyfully, and her voice flowed like a freshet from a spring, it was as though she alone had been created for happiness—as though only for her the summer had promised its rich and unfathomable treasure.

Vetra still remembered how quiet and dull it had been at his house before their adopted daughter came to live with them. But as soon as she began to grow up and sing her songs, it seemed to him that even the brown moss on the roof grew greener, and that the glass eyes of the cottage shone brighter.

Yes, and peace, too, had quickly disappeared from his yard, now that Vale was almost grown up. The old man could no longer keep the gates in good order, for the man and the lads of the village would lean too heavily against them, constantly thrusting them out of joint. And as for the grass . . . Why, it looked no better than the grass in the churchyard, that was trampled by the horses of the entire parish.

It was Saturday evening, and the young people were strolling along the village street, laughing and shouting to each other in loud voices. The white, hot dust on the road absorbed their footprints, while the air they disturbed in passing breathed the summer heat. At the end of the village, near the school, someone started to sing a song; a group of young men stood talking outside the gate and the red points of their cigarettes glowed in the summer dusk.

No one had known the way to his yard when there was no Vale about. Of what use had he himself been, then, to anyone? His neighbors would have waited till his death, and then gathered to see him to the graveyard . . .

Humph, thought the old man to himself, the far, red-faced girls from the farms are quite angry with me. I suppose they're jealous. But what can I do about that?

Why, it often happened nowadays that as soon as he took his woven baskets and other wares to market, a young chap whom he had neither seen nor heard before would come up and invite him, if you please, to have a drink at the inn!

Only the other day, Pranciskus, a fine looking boy, a good farmer, sober-minded, and by no means a ruffian, had seemed particularly interested in his wares.

"You see . . ." he began hesitantly, "I can't seem to find anywhere what I am looking for."

"And what is that you're after, young man?"

"Well, I'll tell you—I'm looking for a sieve. We do have quite a good one at home, made by my grandfather, God rest his soul, but it's very old-fashioned now, and so if you could make me a new one, Uncle, I won't begrudge you payment. I need a light one, for sowing linseed and clover."

"Don't you worry, I'll make a fine one for you out of the

root fibers of a fir tree. It will be just what you want."

"Thank you, Uncle, I won't forget you when we again brew beer. You'll get the first half-barrel of it, I promise you."

Vetra felt very pleased with himself and he kept coughing into his palm as he tried to hide his pleasure. But after all how could it have been otherwise?

In the meantime the young moon had waded deeper and deeper into the dense orchard that lay shrouded from the ground upward by the mists of the night and the endless, monotonous croaking of the frogs. Everywhere, countless voices could be heard on this July night that was steeped in the scent of hay and the fragrant scents of fruit. Out of the tall rosebushes and thick growth of the asparagus, shadows seemed to crawl and whisper to each other, and it was as if the entire summer night lay submerged under the dark forms and moving shapes of things.

Vale was sitting on the bench under a luxuriant tree. She had laid her head on her knees and was clasping them with both hands. The thick stream of her black hair covered her sunburnt legs. From time to time, she would raise her head to gaze at the distant tree-tops and the pale void of the sky, aglitter with countless stars. When she turned and spoke, her words were a continuation of the sad and the happy songs that she sang on midsummer evenings and nights.

"Come closer, let me stroke your hair . . ."

The old man strained to hear what they were saying; for he wanted to know if it was the same young man who had promised him a barrel of beer that day in the marketplace, but the sound of branches being torn in the heart of the orchard defeated his intentions.

"I'm afraid he may hurt one of the children with that gun of his. He's been nursing it in his hands the whole evening," the young man said to her as he bent down and allowed her to stroke his hair.

"And why, may I ask, did you have to bring a whole gang of urchins to my uncle's orchard? As if there weren't enough cherries in the village."

"Well, I'll tell you straight. I wanted to be alone with you a while . . ."

"No need to worry then, dearest. I poured the gun powder

out of his rifle and filled it with tow!" And the girl laughed in the darkness.

Those cherries! thought Vetra to himself as he tried to catch his breath at the bottom of the orchard. Did anyone ever run short of them in this village? Why, when the trees were in blossom the whole village looked like a ship afloat in undulating snowdrifts. Or wreathed in waves of deep red as the fruit ripened in midsummer. Then, there was no way to drive back the thrushes and starlings. They came in clouds, not just in single flights or flocks. And the damage they caused! It broke your heart to see it. You'd spend the whole day trying to defend your orchard from the birds. It wearied you so that you wished you could drop down under a tree at the end of it—and never rise again. How could a man get his rest, I ask you, when there was no end of those little ruffians from the village, ready to plague you at all hours of the night? No, it was never as bad as that in the old days.

If only he could catch one of them, he would be sure to teach him a thing or two. He would shut him up in the pigsty with the sow, and call all the neighbors at daybreak to show them who it was that would not allow people to live in peace. But no matter how careful he was, or how hard he tried, they always sensed when he was coming, the rascals. Before you knew where you were, they would be moving toward you, or calling like owls from the other side of the garden.

The young moon had already set, yet the sky did not grow any darker. One could easily make out the broad backs of the horses through the thin veil of mist that had spread itself over everything—the meadows and the fields and wherever the eye turned. A faint light was still aglow in the north, while the sky was tinged with green and lulled by endless croakings of the frogs.

They've had enough of each other's company for tonight, Vetra decided, as he made his way back into the yard alongside the fence. He could hear Vale's voice clearly, now as a subdued laugh, now as a whisper; and when the young man replied to her, his voice sounded like a low rumble.

"When will you sleep, Pranciskus, if you're not going home yet? It'll soon be time to get up and go to church, and you won't get as much as an hour's rest."

But the lad merely stirred on the bench and said nothing. Only his teeth shone in the twilight under the thick foliage of the tree.

"You, too, go indoors, girl—it's past midnight, you know."

They must have been paying attention to what he said because suddenly everything grew still and silent about him. Only a cricket chirped in the grass near the house, and drops of water fell in a steady trickle on a flat stone near the curb of the well. The village rascals must have tumbled into their beds by now and were no doubt snoring with open mouths. Vetra was ready for bed himself, now that he came to think of it; his feet ached and his eyes smarted after the long summer's day. But he decided to sit down under the cherry tree for a moment and finish his pipe.

Wreaths of smoke dispersed into the air and a feeling of contentment stole over Vetra, as he rested after a hard day's work. Suddenly, he heard his wife say to him, during a respite between her endless prayers:

"You'd better watch the cherries and not the wench. If she's taken it into her head to go courting, your keeping an eye on her won't help a bit."

Wasn't she just silly to talk like that, thought Vetra to himself. That was neither here nor there. Cherries, after all, were only cherries. There would be no lack of them, year after year. Whereas, a fine lass like Vale grew up once in a lifetime.

After looking at the wreath of smoke rising before him, it was as if he himself had risen and disappeared with it, high above the trees. His eyes began to feel heavy, as if someone had stuck them together with the sap of the cherry bark, and he was afraid that sleep might overpower him, worn out as he was.

Perhaps he did fall asleep unaware, for his pipe had grown cold and was damp with the chill of the night.

The breaking of the day could not be held back any longer, as dawn rose powerfully on the horizon, whitening the sky. The wood lark sang his morning song, and hens began to stir on their perches.

Vetra shook himself and started to walk towards the house. He had stayed out too long into the night. He stopped suddenly, as if someone had tugged him by the skirt of his coat. Across the footpath, where the grass was wet with dew, the old man could see twin tracks stretching straight across the clover meadow. He followed them as they went downhill past the orchard where the grass was already mown and haystacks hid under a delicate gauze of mist.

On the ground, close to the nearest haystack, lay their adopted child Vale and Pranciskus. They were holding one another's hands and lying so close to each other that not a drop of water could have fallen between them. Vale's thick, dark hair was spread out on the strewn hay and glistened with minute drops of dew which the rising sun caught and set alight, while her eyebrows, with their soft wings, reminded one of a swallow halted in its flight. Her breast rose and fell lightly, and together with it rose the man's large, dark hand. They were smiling; they slept the deep sleep of early morning.

The old man's pipe shook in his mouth and his few scant teeth were scarcely able to hold it in place. He fingered the gun in his hands and was uncertain what to do with it. Should he fire at once, into the air, of course, to give them a proper fright, or should he wait a while? He did not notice when his anger began to change into wonder. He had seen much in his life, but never had he come across anything like this. He began to draw back slowly and carefully so the rustling of the grass would not wake the happy pair. Yet, for a short while before he hurried away, for a fraction of a minute, only, he remained rigidly stiff, as if in a trance, unable to take his eyes from the couple. His eyes closed of themselves before that unspeakably white patch of skin, which had never been exposed to the sun and which shone now through the unbuttoned blouse and was shielded by the possessive hand of Pranciskus.

Suddenly, he felt very unsure of himself. He must hurry home and wake his wife. It was all too much for him. He could scarcely believe what had happened.

But as soon as he opened the passage door, he recovered himself and began to order everyone about, like a rooster in a hen coop.

"Wake up, you sleepyhead! You've been lying there the

whole night long and don't know what's going on in the world."

"Holy Virgin, what's happened to us now?" exclaimed his wife as she felt around for her skirts.

"You'll run there at break-neck speed when I tell you, woman. Be quick, if you want to go to heaven when you die."

"Jesus and Mary, is it a fire or something? Or have the bees taken to swarming?" muttered the old woman with her toothless mouth.

"Ah, it's not a fire, so don't you worry, but didn't I tell you that our Pranciskus is a cut above the other chaps, and a better farmer, too, than most?"

Vetra wasted no time. He went to the wall, took down a smoke-blackened picture of St. Joseph with a rod in his hand, picked up the old woman's rosary from the floor and strode out of the room with resolute steps. His wife could scarcely keep up with him. She looked so small and dark-skinned, and wrinkled as a boot.

The young couple had not stirred an inch from their old position. A strong scent of hay permeated the field, and birds were singing loudly to the rising sun.

Vetra lunged forward with his gun, which he had carried about with him since the evening before, and nudged the young man's foot with it. Pranciskus sat up like a flame out of a straw roof and stared at him with his eyes wide open.

"Don't move!" bade the old man, in as strong a voice as he could muster.

"Mother, hold up the picture of St. Joseph properly and lay the rosary across his hands."

When this was accomplished—and it was all done so quickly, too quickly for such a solemn occasion—the old woman opened her mouth as if to say something but Vetra turned toward her at once with his gun.

"Now, don't you begin any of your sermons. This is no church and you are not a priest. What we have done, we have done."

Vale remained sitting there with her hands over her face as if nothing had happened. She looked through the shield of her fingers at her benefactors, at the orchard and at the haystacks standing in rows in the field. Then she placed her arms on Prancis-

kus' neck and said to him as she stroked his hair:
"Why are you trembling, Pranciskus? Didn't I tell you? There's no powder in Uncle's gun."

Translated by Danguole Sealey

ALOYZAS BARONAS

ALOYZAS BARONAS was born in Birzai, Lithuania, on December 12, 1917. He studied literature and philosophy at the universities of Kaunas and Frankfurt, Germany, until his emigration to the United States in 1949. At present he is editor of the Lithuanian daily, *Draugas* in Chicago, Among his numerous novels are *Uzgeses sniegas* (The Extinguished Snow, 1953; *Vienisi medziai* (Lonely Trees), 1960; *Trecioji moteris* (The Third Woman), 1966 (English translation in 1968); and *Abraomas ir sunus* (Abraham and Son), 1973. His stories are collected in *Zvaigzdes ir vejai* (Stars and Winds), 1951, and other volumes. He has also written poems, humorous sketches and biographies. His novel with autobiographical overtones, *Footbridges and Abysses,* was published in English translation in 1965.

Aloyzas Baronas

ALOYZAS BARONAS

(1917-   )

The Brink of Madness

NOW TAKE JULIUS BAKUTIS—he never elbowed his way to the front. Even in Lithuania, where he was in the quartermaster's warehouses, he was a calm man and accepted salary increases without a qualm. He wasn't miserly, but at the same time he didn't squander his money. From his savings he was able to build himself a modest home, where he lived with his wife. And, as the old saying goes, he never bothered anyone and no one was any trouble to him. During the summer months, he either mowed the lawn and pruned the dry branches from his cherry and apple trees, or he just sat on the front porch and stared out at silent sunsets that colored the quietly running streams.

Then, in spring and autumn, he worked in his garden; and in the evening, he read books. He enjoyed reading so much that he might be called a poet-farmer, though he had never written a poem.

Bakutis was of medium height, and balding; he would gaze out through half-closed eyes with a quizzical squint, as though the sun were constantly blinding him. His wife was just as calm as he. If there had not been chaos in Europe, these people would have lived out their lives like millions of others, as peacefully as grass fades and ripened fruit thuds to the ground at occasional puffs of the breeze in autumn. But the war drove them from their home, and Bakutis recalled with real sorrow how the fruit trees had murmured quietly in the summer and created melancholy and solitude in the winter and spring. Then, at other times when he was away from home, he thought he could hear the patter of rain on the tin roof. On stormy nights he was fearful, too, that strange winds might shake the cherries or unripened apples from his trees. But time passed and he overcame these preoccupations.

When Bakutis arrived in America, he was almost sixty years old. Often, he wondered why he, at his age and without any interest in politics, should ever have thought of leaving his homeland. But his nostalgia and doubts disappeared when he read in the newspapers of Communism and the life there. What made Bakutis shudder was not the thought of being deported to Siberia or being crammed into the tiny confines of a communal farm, but the many lies the Bolsheviks told. Bakutis hated fraud and he trembled at the thought that he might be forced to lie and even to respect lying. He hated lying and that would have been the bitterest remedy for his homesickness. He had lost much, but he was free. And that thought was like refreshing water on his time-weary bones. Here, he need not honor what he hated. At first, he did not know what to say to those who asked him how he liked it in this country, because everything seemed upside-down. And when they referred to people as transplanted, he understood them in the literal sense, because he thought of his orchard and it seemed to him that his trees would not grow here if they were transplanted. Nevertheless, he managed to live. He got used to it, and he survived. Man must be more sturdy than a tree. He clings as moss does on a rock, and lives.

Those first days were sadly shameful for Bakutis, especially when he rented a small apartment and the kindly neighbors gave him their old furniture and dishes. "This is for your new start in life," though he had lost everything with no hope of ever regaining the accumulation of previous years: they could never be restored or exchanged. He was angered by a poverty that he had never merited or brought about. And as the neighbors handed him their gifts, Bakutis did not rejoice, even though he knew that he needed all those things and that sooner or later he would have had to purchase them. Gifts lower a man, even though they are sincerely given. Bakutis swallowed his embarrassment like a bitter pill and each day he worked harder in this land of plenty, since he knew there was a chance to regain what he had lost. He did not buy new furniture, and he wore the same old clothes, saving money to buy a new home with a garden and an orchard, for he reasoned that he would again have, at least in part, some of the life he had once known.

Bakutis found a job in an enamel factory, where he worked

with older men. His own job was not too hard, nor was it too clean. No one hurried too much. This suited Bakutis perfectly, even though he had already acquired a certain nervous tension which he had not felt before. He worked in an orderly, scrupulous manner—perhaps too scrupulously—as though he were in the quartermaster's warehouse.

""I'll die here," he would say to his friends. "I'll never go anywhere else. I like it here. Besides, who will hire an old man like me."

The days passed quietly, one after another, as though they were waiting for some earth-shaking event. Time ticked on, and the tiring shrieks of sirens jangled the nerves. Each week the aging laborer punched a new time card and on Fridays he received his checks. This was a customary happy event. On Sunday, the thought that there would be more of the same on Monday, caused a deadening pain in his chest. On Tuesdays, the pain began to decrease and he felt better.

"I'll work here until I am pensioned," he murmured constantly when his wife reminded him that others were earning more elsewhere.

The old saying: "A bird in the hand is worth more than two in the bush" had real meaning for him because he could almost feel the bird in his hand. He knew that by changing jobs constantly he would be in real danger of losing that bird. He worked, he saved and gradually, he won out, saving enough to buy himself a little home. Here, he could live in retirement, or if an opportunity to return to his homeland should present itself he would not be empty-handed.

True, his home was small and built of wood, but somehow it all reminded him of the days in his homeland. The yard behind the house was large and it contained wildly growing lilac bushes and an old apple tree. Bakutis trimmed the lilac bushes and carefully pruned the branches of the tree. He was still occasionally homesick because he always felt that in the low-hanging fog, Lithuania was not far away. His home was a peaceful place in any event. He planned to claim his pension in a few years, and he thought it would be nice to be able to work in his garden planting berries, bushes and apple trees.

He moved the old furniture into his new home. Some of it was still quite good, but other pieces were badly worn. For this reason, Bakutis decided to destroy an old sofa he had received seven years before from an old bachelor who had died some years before he gave it away, and it had long since outlived its usefulness. Thus, Bakutis was determined to go out and buy a new one. He bartered for it a long time and tried it out a few times before he handed over the money. Without wasting any time, he dragged the old sofa out to the backyard and began hacking it to pieces. He pulled out the cushions and quickly chopped at the wooden armrests of the frame. As he did so, a bundle of dusty, yellowing newspapers, tied together with a rope, fell to the ground. He kicked the bundle and then bent over, picked it up and untied the rope.

It was a chilly but clear September day. A brisk wind stirred in the apple tree and rattled a loose board in the fence. Nevertheless, Bakutis began to perspire. Inside the bundle of newspapers were green bills. They were dusty and faded but the green of the dollar bills shone through quite clearly. He narrowed his half-closed eyes to slits, because he could see ten-and hundred dollar bills. There were not just a few; he could not say how many there were. He thought he must be dreaming. It was as though he heard the murmur of the swaying apple tree or the clatter of the loose board in the fence in the stillness of the night. But it was not a dream. The wind was cold and tugged at his loose coattails, and there before him was the old hacked-up sofa, which reminded him of a butchered animal carcass. How often he had dreamed of having money and a home, only to awake and find neither. Now, he had not only the home but an uncounted bundle of money as well. His forehead broke out in sweat and his fingers became numb. He had that strange, sickening feeling which could precede a heart attack.

Then suddenly, he felt like a thief. He was filled with fear and ran quickly into the house. His wife, who was in the parlor gathering up the dead leaves of the potted ferns, wondered why he had come in with such haste.

"Mother, look what I found!" he exclaimed, dropping the bundle on the table as if it were on fire. Among the pages of the newspapers the green of the money gleamed, a little the worse for the ravages of time, but nevertheless real money, in a huge amount.

His wife's handful of fern leaves dropped to the floor as she began to tremble. She could not say a word.

She turned an astonished glance toward Bakutis, who said, "Look, I found it in the old sofa. What do you think of that?"

He placed the money on the table as if he had stolen it. And then, as though he had really stolen it, he walked over to the door and turned the key. And, as he returned, he remembered the story about the sale of souls to the devil. He recalled an English play he had seen on his neighbor's television set about a devil who had purchased a man's soul for a bag of money and had sealed the bargain in blood. Bakutis had not sold his soul, but there he was in front of the money, which he could neither pick up nor push aside. Finally, he moved the money. The paper sent up a cloud of dust. One would think that Bakutis could smell burning sulphur. Yet the money belonged to no one; it had been destined to be lost, and that was the intriguing and awesome truth.

They began to count the money. With trembling hands, they separated it into piles of hundreds and tens. Altogether, they counted six and a half thousand dollars.

"Well, if we hid this money, and then just took a little at a time," the old man began, "we could use it for emergencies. We could even finish paying for the house sooner."

"Whoever had it before certainly didn't seem to need it," agreed Mrs. Bakutis at first, and then, as though she feared the words she uttered, she added, "But why do we need it? Money that belongs to others only brings bad luck."

Bakutis argued the point, "Oh, I wouldn't say that! Don't some people win lotteries and others inherit money?"

The green piles of money gleamed with an enticing sheen and with a promise of countless possibilities.

"Oh, that is a different matter," his wife argued against her wish.

The money was precious. It represented happiness—a return of all they had lost during the war and exile.

He dreamt aloud: "Ah, we could travel in Europe. Why, we could even go to California for the winter!"

Then he fell silent for a few moments. He considered all the possibilities and the uncertain origin of the money. It was either a gift and good luck, or bad luck and a sign of doom. Beyond the window it was a September day. The wind in the orchard stirred the apple tree, which was like a symbol of all the happiness he had enjoyed in his homeland. In the distance, he heard the roar of a motor. Overhead, a lone plane was lugubriously forging ahead through the autumn clouds. A siren wailed. The fire department, an emergency patrol, or even the police. A shiver ran down Mrs. Bakutis's spine. And as the siren wailed again, she had visions of robberies, murders and hold-ups. Some teen-agers had once murdered an old pensioner for sixty cents. The thought shocked her and suddenly she cried: "No, I don't want it. Throw it out or even burn it! It might be bloody. Someone may have murdered for it and then hidden it. It might be someone's life savings. No, we don't need it. Throw it away."

"How can that be?" Bakutis asked quietly.

Even though the woman's words seemed real, he could not completely understand their meaning. He knew the value of money. To throw money away or to burn it, was just as great a crime as to throw a man out of the house. This was hard-earned money, and jobs are not so easy to come by. To throw it away would be a sin, like throwing out bread or some holy object. "No, it cannot be thrown out. We must give it to the Church, or an orphanage."

Both thought for a moment. It seemed as if the money and the apple tree rustled quietly together. It was, in fact, difficult to distinguish between the gentle rustle of the green leaves of the apple tree and the green leaves on the table. The one reminded him of the past, of autumn and a certain, unending melancholy; while the other stood for a life that one sometimes experiences and sometimes attempts to improve each day. He felt something like the contact of two opposite electric currents, and this shocked his soul.

Their hands trembled.

"If someone called for this money, we could never get it back from the Church or the orphanage," the old man said as though he hated to think of giving the money away after their few minutes of joy and concern.

In the distance, the long dying wail of the siren sounded again, filling Mrs. Bakutis with fear.

"Take it to the police. Let them do what they want with it. Tell them where you found it, and that will be the end of the matter."

Again, the currents shocked Bakutis. The green scraps of paper uttered thousands of promises. Travel and rest. A paid-up mortgage. Suddenly, all his unsolvable problems were resolved.

"Let's keep part of it," Bakutis said, as though he were trying to find a compromise in the agreement between himself and his wife.

"No, no, take it out of here now, at once!" cried Mrs. Bakutis. She went into the pantry and found a grocery bag and jammed the money into the bag with the newspapers. Then her hands stopped trembling and her voice regained its natural tone.

Bakutis lifted the bag. A strange flame smoldered in his eyes. His cheeks reddened as though they were chapped from a cold February wind. Again, he placed the bag on the table, put on his coat and then stood as if waiting for something to happen.

"Take it out of here and you'll feel better," his wife commanded.

Without a word, he picked up the bag. It seemed to him as though he had refused to bargain with the devil and that peace had returned after a sleepless night.

As he walked through the backyard, he noticed the hacked-up sofa. All his desire for the money seemed to have vanished. His great concern now was how the police would take his explanation. On his way to the police station he began to think of what English words he should use; he thought of common, everyday words and tried to form sentences that would explain this unusual case. He decided that no one would claim the money and that it would then become his—part of it, at least. His hope thus led him to believe that he might obtain something for himself.

That September Saturday was a little on the cold side, although traces of the past summer were everywhere. Autumn flowers were blooming beside some of the homes. Some of the wilted leaves looked a little ragged. The police station was only about seven blocks away, and the old man walked.

Here and there, neighbors were raking leaves. An occasional auto streaked down the pleasant tree-lined streets, and a few pedestrians passed by, their coat-tails waving in the wind. But no one dreamed that this old man with a paper bag under his arm was lugging a home, an auto, furniture and a collection of other unusual items.

Before he entered the police station the old man was filled with a certain dread, but then his fear, which reminded him of the time he had stolen peas from a neighbor's garden, and of the time he had asked for his first job in America, suddenly vanished as he walked down the corridor that led into the squad room. Here, everyone was on the move and quite preoccupied. Some were paying fines; others were registering lost or stolen goods. There seemed to be any number of reasons why people crossed the unfamiliar doorstep of the police station. There were no sawed-off shotguns or iron bars there. It was a place as ordinary as anywhere else.

At the information window he could see a uniformed officer listening to the baseball results over the radio. Bakutis went up to the window and said in an ordinary tone, " I found some money." The officer raised his head and gave him a quizzical look. Just then, his favorite team was at bat and this old man annoyed him. Automatically, he reached for his record book and asked, "Name?"

Bakutis slowly pronounced his name and, from the officer's writing, he could see that the first letter was written incorrectly. But he said nothing. He immediately stated his address.

"How much did you find?" the officer asked.

Just then, another officer approached the desk and they discussed the baseball results. They cast an occasional glance at Bakutis, as though they expected him to agree with them, but he only smiled sheepishly. He could not understand a thing they were saying, and he didn't care. After a few moments the officer asked, "How much did you find?"

"Six and a half thousand."

"How much?" said the officer with a start and a wild-eyed stare. Bakutis did not look him in the eye but lowered his gaze and mumbled the figure a second time.

The officer kept staring at Bakutis, who pronounced the figures incorrectly and seemed quite eccentric as he did so.

"Do you speak Polish?" asked the officer in bad Polish, with every good intention of helping Bakutis, who said nothing more but hurriedly pushed the bag under the grill.

Quickly, the officer looked in the bag and pulled out some of the newspapers and took a deep breath. This officer had once had a gunfight with a group of bandits. Bullets had whizzed over his head and lodged in the back seat of his car. One time, he had chased a bank robber who threw a bag of money out of the car. All this had been in the line of duty. There had been other such events in his life, and he had never been afraid. But this bag of money shocked him. Rarely did anyone ever come in with money; usually, they came to report sums that were lost. The officer's heart began to pound, his eyes sparkled and he yearned to take a handful of the money. His hand trembled. He needed help. He telephoned his superior officer. Bakutis stood there and smiled. He was almost at peace with himself. The thrill of finding the money had already worn off, and his sense of balance had returned. It was as though he had swum the deep waters and could now feel solid ground under his feet.

The officer took the money out and threw the bag on the floor. For a moment he had forgotten about Bakutis. Suddenly, he faced him and, conscious of his unnatural tone of voice, said, "Wait here."

Bakutis grinned broadly. He would have waited without being told. Seeing the grin on Bakutis' face, the officer felt silly and uncomfortable, as if he wanted to say, "You fool, you bring in a bag of money and then just grin about it."

A yound police lieutenant walked in. He invited Bakutis into his office and the officer followed with the money and waited awhile, as though he were expecting something to happen. The lieutenant waved him out and his contact with the money was ended. For him it was like simple surgery, such as the removal of a splinter from a finger—painful but necessary.

Bakutis described all that had happened, and the lieutenant noted everything down. Later, he called in two other officers who carefully counted the money. Then he placed it in a fireproof safe, together with his notes. Bakutis wanted to finish with the whole business as soon as possible. He had freed himself from the money and temptation. Gone were the thousands of burning, fearfully tempting desires. Everything was finished.

"Can I go now?" asked Bakutis as he moved towards the door.

"Wait," said the lieutenant. He picked up the phone, spoke to someone, and then walked towards the door. He motioned to Bakutis: "I'll take you home."

As they reached the street, two officers were seated in the car, quietly talking. Bakutis got in and again repeated his home address.

When they reached his home, he saw a crowd of curious people watching the policeman in his backyard. The police lieutenant called Mrs. Bakutis from the house and they photographed the couple beside the sofa. There it stood, its insides sticking out and the stuffing scattered about by the wind.

In ten minutes the affair was over and the lieutenant said that the money would be turned over to the court, which would decide to whom it belonged.

It was now evening. The wind had subsided and the sun drew its reddish disk behind a cloud. The air was heavy with the smell of burning leaves. The apple tree trembled ever so slightly as the setting sun painted its leaves an odd shade of red. Bakutis piled the remains of the sofa on the trash heap, and when he went into the house and sat down to his supper, he felt both sad and relieved.

"Eat your supper," his wife told him and, almost reading his thoughts, she added, "The money wasn't ours—it wouldn't have brought us any happiness."

"Quite true. Now, we can sleep peacefully. Otherwise, we would have been afraid, as though we had stolen it," Bakutis said as he ladled the cabbage soup. Its aroma and warmth quieted his nerves, which were beginning to act up like the tiny insects one feels as one lies on new-mown hay.

That night Bakutis dreamed of his old orchard, which he visited in a plane, of a California beach he remembered from a picture on a calendar he had picked up at his bank, of a wild dash from the police station, and of a battle with the devil. In the morning he got up without having rested much, but he was calm. His wife did not say a word, They did not refer to the money again but on their way to church, Bakutis did remark, "Now, we walk calmly to church; otherwise we would have felt like thieves. If no one calls for the money, it will be ours. Then it will be a different matter entirely."

"There is no reason to talk about it," Mrs. Bakutis replied.

They tried to forget the matter, to get it out of their blood, and to quiet their nerves. They tried to pretend that it had never happened, but still their thoughts returned to the event.

As the priest preached from the altar about the frailty and ignorance of man, Bakutis thought about how many years he had sat on that same sofa and never dreamed that he was sitting on money. When the collection was being taken up, he thought of how much more he could have donated if he had kept it. He could have had a Mass said for whomever had hidden the money, and that would have had eternal value.

Usually Bakutis felt depressed on Sundays because he thought about going to work the next day. But this week he was anxious. Bakutis wanted the time to fly by, so that he could get into his ordinary routine and so that his every-day worries could cover over the recent event.

On Monday Bakutis went to work as usual and worked a full day. It was no different from other Mondays. With that day over, the week was started and the rest did not seem too difficult. Bakutis felt wonderful as he returned from work. The day, warm and sunny seemed like summer. He walked briskly and began to hum a song, almost too loudly, thinking: "What's the name of that tune?"

Tuesday was the same, and when Wednesday morning rolled around, he had forgotten the whole matter. On Monday, the garbage collectors had carted away the remains of the sofa, and it seemed to him that they had also carted away his disquiet, sadness and continual worries.

Two Lithuanians worked in the factory laboratory. They were in charge of mixing the enamels. Bakutis usually greeted them, but he had never tried to establish a close friendship. And they did not try to be especially friendly. One of them, Liudzius, was a chemistry graduate, while the other, Kamcaitis, was an agriculturist from the same district in Bakutis' homeland. They started work half an hour later than he did each day, and on their way through the factory they would stop to chat with Bakutis. But on Wednesday, Bakutis had not yet started his work and they approached him with curious grins. Liudzius, the younger of the two, had with him a copy of the community newspaper that was published on Wednesdays, Fridays and Saturdays.

"Congratulations to the most honest man in the world!" Liudzius said, and it seemed that he really meant it.

"Brother, the papers are writing about you and it looks as if Diogenes does not need to hunt for an honest man with his candle," added Kamcaitis.

"Look," Liudzius said, spreading out the newspaper.

Bakutis blushed. Sure enough, there he stood with his wife beside the hacked-up sofa, somewhat uncomfortable from the wind, and shying away from being photographed. He and his wife seemed odd and almost ludicrous beside the broken frame of the sofa. The springs poked out through the stuffing in perfect circles, while the two ole people looked as though they were ready to walk out of the picture. Above their heads were the huge numerals: $6,500.00. Not one cent of the money was missing.

"See how beautifully you advertise our country," said Kamcaitis. "This is a very good story about you."

"You'll get the money, if no one calls for it. Buy yourself a copy of the paper," Liudzius said as the two walked away and left Bakutis gaping at them.

From that minute on the dark aspect of the problem appeared. The devil went to work because Bakutis had refused the money. And he worked with devastating effect. On the surface, he worked with consistency and decorum, but his efforts were actually merciless and destructive. He bored in deeper and tighter, as a screw is twisted into an oak frame. Thus, when Liudzius and Kamcaitis walked away, a younger worker closed in and, tapping his head with his finger, shouted, "So you found it and turned it in!" Then he pointed to the newspaper, "This is you, you crazy guy. Whoever hides money has no use for it."

"He'll get the money back. The court will award it to him," said another, as a crowd gathered, talking loudly and arguing. Then the foreman came along and sent everyone back to work. When he had sent the men to their places, he said to Bakutis, "Don't be disappointed. If no one claims it, you'll get the money. Be happy—you're a lucky guy."

Nevertheless, this lucky guy had trembling hands. He did not want publicity for his country; he wanted to remain invisible.

Actually, he did not want to be bothered until he received his pension. He had not sought publicity for himself, nor the money, not even a court order. He reproached himself for having allowed the photograph. If he had only known, he would have run away or driven the reporters away with a stick. "This is a free country," he kept repeating to himself. He was angry at everyone and thought he would have done better if he had thrown the money into a trash can.

Just before lunch time, one of his fellow employees said, "Since Julius is now a rich man, he can buy the coffee."

Bakutis did not say a word. He went out and bought seven containers of coffee for the group, paying seventy cents for them. He was exasperated. That was hard-earned money and he would have to work almost half an hour to pay for the coffee.

On his way home, he bought the newspaper. The storekeeper tried to make him talk about everything that had happened but Bakutis did not allow him to pursue the conversation. He hurried home as though he were being pursued, as if it were raining, or as though some misfortune had occurred at home.

In the house, he and his wife read the article with the help of a dictionary. There was nothing more to the story than what he already knew, except there were some kind words about his honesty.

"What are you so sad about? They wrote it and now it's forgotten," his wife commented. But he knew that it was not forgotten. People still talked about it.

"They'll forget about it, once they . . ." he consoled himself as he stared out the window into the dusk. In the backyard his apple tree swayed ever so gently, and in its branches and leaves he could almost see the laughing eyes of Satan. Bakutis trembled.

"Put something on; maybe you can even light the stove. It's a chilly night," his wife advised.

Bakutis remained silent. He gazed out the window and could see the laughing glances of Satan until his wife turned on the light and drew the drapes together.

That night, Bakutis slept fitfully. He was turning over the pages of the newspaper; he was arguing with the police officer; and he was worried about whether he would be able to explain things correctly, because the dream was in English. When he awoke later he got up and drank some water. Then he went over to the window and looked out into the street. Solitary lights were burning. Off in the distance, an airliner buzzed by like some flying star. Through the edge of a cloud he could see the new moon. And again, Bakutis saw the devil, the same one he had seen on TV exchanging money for a soul. The devil grinned and winked, Bakutis drew the drapes tight.

Towards morning he fell asleep. He went off to work with some foreboding, as though unforeseen difficulties awaited him. He felt like some men as they go to the trenches. At work, the men reminded him that he would soon be a rich man, that he would be able to buy a home and a cat and that now he should at least be able to buy the coffee.

The days slipped by. Little by little the whole affair began to be forgotten and Bakutis began to feel better. Six months went by. The autumn was dry and winter was cole and wet and chilled one to the bone. Again, Bakutis became famous. The court declared its decision: When no one claims the money, it goes to the State according to law. Since no one had claimed the money, it was certain that Bakutis would not receive it. Again, the newspapers ran stories and included Bakutis' picture. And now the devil went to work again. At the shop, the matter had been almost forgotten. Now, however, the hostility and scorn began to reappear.

"Millionaire!" cried one red-headed employee, pointing to Bakutis. "He gives the Government six thousand dollars."

"You've got a screw loose," said another with a wave of his hand.

Then all the others turned against Bakutis, as though the court decision were his fault. If some especially difficult job turned up, everyone would say, "Let Julius do it. He is a millionaire. He doesn't have to work. He had the money, but he likes to work. He gave it to the State."

"A real millionaire," said another as he placed his finger to his head with a laugh.

Bakutis could not sleep nights. Going home from the factory was like leaving a prison, being freed from the electric chair or escaping from a field of execution. A few hours at home and he felt relieved; but during the night and towards early morning, he was seized by a severe depression. He left for work each morning as though he were going to his own hanging.

"I wonder if I'll last the year and a half until my pension," he would say to his wife when she asked whether he could not quit his job and look for another somewhere else. Bakutis often wondered if the employees would ever forget the whole business, but it seemed that they were just getting started.

Sometimes, when he could not sleep, he would look out into the street. Snowflakes would spin and fall around the street lights. Mournful, cold stars would flash through gaps in the clouds. They scarcely seemed to tremble. At other times, there was a chilling fog, and frost clung to the branches of the apple tree. All this made him happy. Bakutis knew that many things could pass away, but this yard, apple tree and home were his. He would enjoy this solitude. But when the hatred began to swell up in him, he tried to pray. He asked the Lord for help and strength, and that everyone be made to forget about his honesty. This prayer sometimes turned to anger, and in his mind he would shout, "God, do you try me, because I was too honest?" At other times he would calm down and then his prayer became almost pharisaical, crying that it was good that he was not a thief even though the factory cursed him because of his honesty and seemed to hate the just.

Bakutis withered. Sometimes, it seemed to him that his heart had begun to beat faster, then, at other times, it slowed down because of his rage and worry. In the factory, he was persecuted with the name of millionaire and he saw that the workers considered him a fool, and that there would be no end to it. Bakutis shriveled up. His wife forced him to go to the doctor.

"Your heart is weak. Don't drink any whisky or coffee. Don't smoke," the doctor told him. Bakutis did not do any of those things. "Avoid fats and don't let yourself worry," continued the doctor.

Bakutis was thin and he didn't worry. The fact was, he was driven crazy. His was not a worry, it was an obsession.

The snow was beautiful. The apple tree was the center of a romantic picture; the snow was fluffy, the heavens were gray and cold and the clouds were drifting high. The evening air was so dry, it would certainly turn cold. Bakutis shoveled the snow and took his time about it. He dug slowly, taking deep breaths of air. He remembered reading about that in the newspaper. When he finished shoveling he felt a little tired and when he returned to the house, he lay down on the sofa, panting heavily.

"Are you tired?" his wife said with a worried look.

"Just a little, but it is nothing," he replied. He actually looked fine—his cheeks were tanned and healthy.

"Don't go to work any more. We'll be able to manage for a year and a half until your pension."

Bakutis said nothing because he was thinking of the five thousand dollars he would lose if he stopped working. That meant, too, that he would lose the interest on that amount. And now he was asked to stop working because he had not kept the money he had found! No, he would suffer through it, even if it killed him. But then, on second thought, no one was trying to kill him. All he needed was a little more will power—and let the others go hang.

In the morning, Bakutis felt that his left arm was a little numb, and there was a slight pain in the back of his neck. Oh, that must be from the snow shoveling. And at work, he had been lifting sheets of tine.

In a joking tone, a fellow employee had said, "Millionaire, you must count those sheets like dollar bills!"

"A crazy fool likes work," a young worker yelled at him in Russian. His pronunciation was bad, but Bakutis understood him. He did not say anything, but with lowered eyes he kept piling up the sheets of tin.

"Don't talk in Russian, say it in English," another said, berating his friend. When the phrase was translated, everyone had a good laugh.

Bakutis kept piling the sheets of tin without raising his head. Bakutis, slave away; Bakutis, don't give up. Not much longer to go, now. Just a year and a half. Still, Bakutis did not raise his eyes. He kept staring at the sheets of tin and suddenly they began to spin around. Everything whirled—the tin, the dollar, the grinning devil of the TV, the police officer, Bakutis' wife and the apple tree. Bakutis strained, thinking: "Why are they so white? Is it because of the snow or the blossoms?" Then it dawned on him and his mouth gaped.

They carried Bakutis out, gave him oxygen and injections, but after a few days he died.

"Yes, our countryman gave away thousands and worked until he keeled over," remarked a fellow employee to Liudzius and Kamcaitis.

"And he could have lived without working," added another.

The shop whistle shrieked. Inside, it sounded stifled, but outdoors, its scream was loud and angry. Everyone dragged himself off to work.

"There is nothing you can do about it," mumbled Liudzius as he shrugged his shoulders. As they approached the laboratory, Kamcaitis remarked, "Yes, it's as I said before, he was crazy. But who can tell how all this will be recorded in the eternal books?" And, as he took off his coat, he added: "The cunning and the cheats are one step apart, and so are honest men and fools."

"That's quite true," agreed Liudzius. as he picked up his test tube. He continued, "Yes, quite true. Who can say where the brink of honesty, goodness or madness begins or ends?"

Translated by P. P. Cinikas

Julius Kaupas

JULIUS KAUPAS

Born on March 6, 1920, JULIUS KAUPAS spent the first 24 years of his life in his native city of Kaunas. He received the degree of doctor of medicine from the University of Tubingen, Germany, in 1946 and went on to study philosophy and literature at the University of Freiburg, 1947-49. Emigrating to the United States, he specialized in psychiatry. He died in Chicago on March 9, 1964. His collection of fantasy-colored short stories, *Daktaras Kripstukas pragare* (Doctor Kripstukas in Hell), 1948, placed him in the front ranks of Lithuanian writers. Additional stories as well as a number of literary and psychological essays were published in Lithuanian periodicals.

JULIUS KAUPAS

(1920-1964)

The Organ of Kurkliškės

ABOVE THE STEEPLE ROOF, silvered by the moon, the droning of an organ hovered in the humid August night over the village of Kurkliškės.

"What could that be?" wondered the shoemaker Kupstinis' wife as she shuffled to the window and looked out at the church.

"What's it to us?" grumbled the shoemaker in his sleep, drawing the blanket up over his ears. "Haven't you ever heard an organ before? Why don't you come back to bed?"

"Look, Juozas! Isn't that Sexton Vaišnys walking toward the church?" she cried, and then shook her husband by the shoulder. "Get up, you lazy thing! You should go help the man. God only knows what's happening. If something went wrong, your conscience wouldn't let you rest," she insisted, knowing quite well that it was only her curiosity that had pulled her out of bed.

"What the devil can happen?" muttered the shoemaker as he fumbled at the buttons of his shirt. "Who cares, anyway? It's none of our business."

Kupstinis' last grumblings faded away in the dark church square. "Wait, Vaišnys!" he shouted, as he walked with a heavy tread under the wide branches of a linden.

The sexton stopped. "Oh, it's you, Juozas," he murmured, and sighed with relief. "What do you think it can be?"

The shoemaker looked into the sexton's lean, freckled face, then shrugged and turned his eyes up to the ripe moon. He shrugged again and scuffed his feet. For a moment the moonlight turned the pebbles to jewels and played about his shoes. The two men cautiously circled the church, crunching chestnut shells and cigarette stubs in the churchyard. They halted under the big chestnut tree near the vestry door.

"Look, they climbed in through the vestry window," observed Vaišnys. "But who ever would do such a thing?"

He took out a key, unlocked the door, slowly reached into the vestry, and turned on the light. He stared into the calm stillness. Nothing had been disturbed.

"Everything seems in order," the sexton breathed with relief. He dipped his fingers into the holy water, made the sign of the cross, and entered the church.

"It's a good thing there's the two of us," the sexton encouraged his reluctant companion, as they paused near the blackened confessional. "Well . . . let's go on up."

Quietly they climbed the choir stairs and stopped.

On the organ bench sat a man of about forty, relaxed, a pair of gold-rimmed spectacles lying near him, his eyes lifted to the ceiling. He was balding and unshaven. His shoes were muddy, and his clothes, although of good quality, were wrinkled. His left trouser was torn. A suitcase stood nearby.

"I've never seen him before," whispered the sexton.

Then, into the peaceful silence, soared the trembling chords of the restless organ.

They moved closer and studied the man. He turned his head, cast a surprised look at them, then again raised his eyes to the ceiling and began to play.

Puzzled, the sexton pushed aside a pile of sheet music.

"Who are you?" he asked hesitantly.

When the stranger made no reply, Vaišnys shook his shoulder. The organ rose to its full, aching volume.

"Enough! That's enough!" he blurted out. "Who ever heard of breaking into a church in the middle of the night!"

The man pushed the sexton's hand away. "I am an organist," he declared, "and no one may forbid me to play when I must. Don't touch me."

"A real maniac," mutered Vaišnys, and he gazed at the shoemaker, who quickly seized the man by the elbow. "The sexton's right. This is no time to be playing the organ. Come on, we must go."

Vaišnys grabbed the stranger by the other arm, and after a short struggle, they pulled him off the bench.

"Your suitcase?" asked Kupstinis.

"I don't know," he replied blankly. "—Might be."

The shoemaker picked up the suitcase. "Where are you from?"

The man stood for a moment, squinting a little, as if to find something just out of his sight. Then he shrugged his shoulders and tried to climb back onto the organ bench.

"Easy, Mister, easy," said the shoemaker soothingly. "That's enough. Now, who are you, anyway?"

"An organist!" he said crisply.

The two villagers looked at one another.

Together, the three men went back don the dark staircase, passed through the vestry, and stopped on the threshold. The moon sat on a linden branch. An owl cried softly in the belfry.

"Well, what shall we do with him?" wondered the sexton aloud.

"He's no criminal. Let's let him go. Why should we poke our fingers into it—Just as long as he doesn't come back."

The dull beat of many footsteps filled the night silence. "What's up Sexton?" asked Kaladé, the town joker. "Is it the end of the world or something?"

Without answering, the sexton turned to the stranger, who had raised his right hand and fixed his eyes on the steeple cross. Tears streamed down his cheeks. "Don't you see, there's nothing more beautiful than the organ," he said in a solemn voice. "Many forsaken souls serve the life of the spirit, while all the time God's children are searching for a path to their Father . . . Do you know what the organ is? It relieves us of our misery. It lifts our hearts toward God. What do you want from me, you slaves of the earth? I can see you don't understand the ways of Providence. Let me go!" And he lunged back toward the church. But the villagers held him fast. "Let me go! Or God's curse will fall on you!"

Finally the sexton spoke. "I think there's something wrong with him. We can't let him go like this."

"Let's take him to the police," suggested Kaladé. "He must be drunk. And now he's trying to fight, too. Come on, it's none of our business."

The sexton nodded. "Yeah. Let's go."

He and the shoemaker walked the stranger between them. Kaladé, the postal clerk, took the suitcase and set it down when they reached the police station.

"Maybe we'd better keep an eye on this fellow," said Kupstinis to the sexton. "Why don't you go wake up Kazlekas?"

The sexton nodded and hustled off. The shoemaker sat down on the stone step and filled his pipe. The light from the tavern window across the street gilded the cobblestones.

The stranger leaned against a wall that was covered with shreds of advertisements. "What town is this?" he asked slowly.

"What a question!" smiled the surprised shoemaker. "Kurkliškés, Mister, Kurkliškés."

Kurkliškés . . ." repeated the stranger, gazing up and down the street. The moonlight flashed on his spectacle lenses.

Vaišnys tried faithfully to tell everything he had seen and heard, as Kupstinis nodded from time to time. Kazlekas turned to the stranger, who sat quietly, his eyes fixed on the wall opposite.

"So it was you making all that racket. What's your name?"

Moments later, the man replied. "I—I don't know."

"What do you mean, you don't know!" cried Kazlekas, pulling out a handkerchief. "You don't look drunk.'

"He says he's an organist," remarked Kupstinis.

"An organist!" bellowed Kazlekas. "Give me your papers."

The man searched through his pockets.

"It seems I don't have any."

"We have no choice, citizen," said the police chief, rising from his chair. "We'll have to search you."

The stranger stood up and held his arms in the air. In his pockets Kazlekas found a handkerchief, a ring of keys, a billfold and a handful of coins. "But where are your papers?"

"I don't know. I guess I don't have them with me."

"Unlock your suitcase."

The man fitted the key and opened the lid. Inside were socks, a tube of toothpaste, a prayer book, three clean shirts, a bundle of sheet-music, a pair of handsome brown shoes, a book of poetry, and a blue suit. A photograph dropped from the book and fell into the wastebasket. Kazlekas pulled it out and studied it. He mopped his brow and glanced at the stranger.

"Aha! Now we have a lead!" He held out the snapshot to the man. "Do you know these people?"

The stranger took the photo from Kazlekas and studied it intently. "Yes, that's me, there."

"We can see that. But who is that woman, and the girl?"

"There? I couldn't say. Maybe—no, wait, I think I've seen that girl, somewhere . . ."

"Blast it!" roared Kazlekas. He snatched the photo from the hands of the trembling man, flipped it over, and jabbed it with a sweaty finger. "Do you see that inscription? 'Nikodemas, Julija and Onute, Kaunas, 1937.' This photo was taken only last year, and you say you can't remember who was with you! Do you expect us to believe that? And whose handwriting is this?"

"Mine," the man admitted. "Yes, mine . . . Nikodemas. I remember, now. My name is Nikodemas . . . Nikodemas."

"See, we've got you! Why do you try to get out of it by lying?" Kazlekas drew himself up to his full height. His head brushed the bulb hanging on a cord.

Sweat ran down the stranger's face. His eyes turned to the flypaper dangling from the ceiling.

Kupstinis, who had carefully followed everything, slowly took his pipe out of his mouth. "Who knows, maybe he really has forgotten everything. All kinds of things can happen. I wouldn't be surprised if . . ."

"Forgot!" laughed the police chief scornfully. "Come on, now. He's a criminal. That's why he doesn't remember."

"Might be," said the shoemaker, his words slow. "But who ever heard of a criminal playing a church organ?"

Kazlekas, reddening, glanced at the shoemaker and slapped the photo down on the table. He looked at the clock. It was three o'clock.

"It'll soon be dawn," he remarked. "We'll have to keep this fellow behind bars until we can clear the matter up. I'll have to call somebody to go on duty."

He made a phone call and began pacing the office.

"Kurkliškés!" the stranger suddenly exclaimed. "Kurkliškés! Now I remember. Long, so long ago . . . Yes!"

"What? What is it?" asked the shoemaker quickly.

"A long time ago, maybe thirty years back, I remember coming here to a fair. With Uncle Anupras. He bought me candy. It was a very big day in my childhood. Now I see it all clearly. Later my uncle took me to the church. Stained glass windows, flowers, candles, and a kind, gray-haired organist. He said to me: 'Come, Nikodemas! If you like, I'll teach you how to play the organ.' Of course, I didn't do very well. But it was fun just to push down the keys. My uncle laughed. Then the organist said: 'No, let me try.' When he began to play, I couldn't believe my ears. No one will ever be able to play like the old organist of Kurkliškés. Later I studied the organ for years and years, but it's impossible—no one can ever come near him."

Kazlekas leaned on the desk, pushed aside a pile of clothes, and scratched his neck. "So who are you, then? Really an organist?"

"Oh, no. I had to give that up. There wasn't an opportunity. Yes, I remember now . . . I'm a bookkeeper."

"A bookkeeper? From where?"

The stranger looked down at his shoes, grimed with mud and grass. "Kaunas. Somewhere in Kaunas."

The door burst open and policeman Gairys, straightening his rumpled uniform, rushed in.

"So, here you are. Good!" Kazlekas jumped up. "You'll have to watch this fellow tonight. Vaišnys and Kupstinis caught him a while ago, playing the organ in church. He's probably some crackpot, but he might be a criminal. Put his stuff back in his suitcase."

Gairys unlocked the barred door of the narrow cell. "Get in there."

Nikodemas shuffled in and sat down on the wooden bed.

The chief nodded and tramped outdoors with the villagers. A cool breeze stirred the peeling posters on the station wall. Kazlekas buttoned the collar of his uniform. "Well, who do you think he is? Isn't he probably blowing fog in our eyes?"

"I can't understand how he could forget where he lives," said the postal clerk.

Vaisnys took a deep breath and looked off at the steeple. "But, boy, how he could play! . . . He d sure have made a good organist."

"Maybe," the shoemaker replied, "but that's over my head. From his shoes, I'd say he walked all the way from Kaunas."

The next morning, as Kazlekas strolled into the police station, he thought how he really might have hooked a big one this time. The names Kurkliškés and Kazlekas would be in all the papers. He might even win honor and fame for such an achievement!

Kazlekas slipped into his chair, crossed his legs and opened his collar. "Well, how'd it go, Gairys?"

"Not bad, sir," he managed out of his wide-eyed doze. "No trouble from the prisoner, but in his sleep he was arguing with someone and shouting that he couldn't stand it any more."

"Hmm. I wonder what we we've got here."

"He asked for the clothes in his suitcase. He said he wanted to change. So I gave them to him. I thought it'd be all right."

"Sure, why not? Tell him I'd like to see him."

"Yes, sir!"

The stranger entered timidly. He rubbed his eyes, ran his hand through his hair, and then, as he saw Kazlekas, he froze. Pale as he was, he made a much better impression in his fresh clothes.

"Well, how'd you sleep?" asked Kazlekas. "Have a chair."

"All right, thanks."

"Now, why don't you explain yourself? Why'd you have to come here and raise all that racket?"

The man took off his glasses and cleaned them with a handkerchief. "I must admit, it's pretty hard to remember. I'm not sure what happened. I remember playing the organ in church. Then some men brought me here. You asked me questions, but I can't remember what they were about. Everything's foggy . . . like a dream. Yesterday, with your help, I remembered a few things . . . but not my name. I just can't quite remember it. You know how it is, to forget things sometimes."

"Forget, yes! But not, my dear sir, your own name. You remembered that. It'll go much easier with you if you confess at once. We'll find out everything about you, anyway."

"I wish I could! You see, I haven't anything to hide. It's just that . . ."

"Well, out with it, come on."

"May I look at that snapshot again?"

"Certainly." Kazlekas dug into the papers in his drawer and fished out the photo. "Here."

"Thanks." He turned it over a few times, then adjusted his glasses and brought the photo up close to his nose.

"Why, that's my family!" he said finally, with surprise. "Here's my wife, and that's my daughter on her knees, and that's me. I even remember my friend taking the picture."

"That's a different story," said the police chief, pleased with their progress. "And you say you live in Kaunas."

"Yes, that's right. On Poppy Street, in a red house—third from the corner."

"Good, good. Now think hard and tell me why you left Kaunas. For a vacation? Or did you steal some money?" Kazlekas noticed the man's frightened face and fell silent.

"Wait. Let me think. On August third I was still in Kaunas. You see, that's my birthday. What day is today?"

"Today?" Kazlekas said, astonished. "August the eighth."

"The eighth!" The man looked stunned. He struck his forehead with the palm of his hand. "Where've I been all this time? Five days! My family, my job!"

"Take it easy, Mister, take it easy. We want to learn everything, too. There's no reason to get so upset."

"But, tell me, Sir," said the stranger as he swung his head slowly, "what's happened to me? I can't be drunk. I'm a family man. I have the best wife God could give a man, and a daughter. How long, how long have I been here?" he cried suddenly, seizing Kazlekas by the front of his uniform. "This is Kurkliskes, isn't it? I haven't been here since . . . my childhood!"

Kazlekas cleared his throat, turned to Gairys, and covered his mouth with his hand. "Put this guy back in the cooler. He's gone out of his head again."

Then, turning back to the stranger, he said, "Since we're still in the dark about everything, we'll have to hold you here for a while. I'll phone Kaunas. The Central Office there should certainly know if anyone's missing." And he went to the phone and made his call.

"We have a suspicious character here. About forty, a little bald, wears glasses. First name Nikodemas. We picked him up last night for making a disturbance. Otherwise, he seems all right. He says he's a bookkeeper from Kaunas, but he doesn't want to give his last name or else just doesn't remember it. The wife's name's Julija. Somewhere on Poppy Street. Are you looking for such a person? . . . How's that? All right, check and call us back. We'll wait."

Kazlekas sat down at his desk, opened a newspaper and started munching an apple. Soon the telephone rang. He reached over his desk and picked up the receiver.

"Hello! Yes, the Chief here. Oh, Kaunas? Any news? Good. Fine! Yes, we're still holding him. What? Imagine that! Wait, let me jot that down. Nikodemas Rasutis. Disappeared five days ago from the 'Maistas Company.' No embezzlements or anything? You say everything's in order? How 'bout that, an honest citizen! His wife—what? Could you please speak a little louder? You say she's coming in on the six o'clock bus? So, do you think we can let him go? No problems, huh? Good. What? Ha! That's a hot one! To tell the truth, we didn't know what to do either. You should see this guy. No, he's all right, I guess. Caused a little disturbance in the church, playing the organ in the middle of the night. Otherwise, a nice fellow. Pretty queer case, though. What? How well did he play? How should I know? But the sexton said he could really play. Hey, if you need an organist up there, why don't you take him on? I think it might help him out. But he told Gairys that Kurkliskes was the place to play the organ. Huh? What do you mean, I'm crazy? Listen just say hello to the Chief for me and tell him we've got the situation in hand. Six o'clock, right. So long."

The bus was late. Coated with dust and wreathed in a smell of gasoline, it rolled into the village. Chickens scattered about the street.
A dog barked at the left rear wheel.
Gairys, assigned to meet the visitor from Kaunas, threw down his cigarette and rose from the bench.
Among the few travelers, he recognized her at once. Probably in her late thirties, she was tall, proudly statured, and heavily made up. She raised the veil of her hat and, pulling a light glove onto her hand, surveyed the village. When she saw the policeman she approached him without hesitation and smiled.
"You're probably waiting for me. Kindly take me to the police station. I have come to pick up my husband."
The fragrance of strong perfume enveloped her.
"Oh . . . Oh, yes. It's not far. Here, just down this street."
She walked with small steps, silent, ignoring the villagers' eyes that followed her. Gairys was embarrassed, because he couldn't keep in step with her, and didn't dare start a conversation. He felt it was not proper for him, a common policeman, to address such an elegant lady from Kaunas. When they finally got to the station he breathed more easily.
Gairys opened the door and stood to one side. The lady nodded and quickly stepped indoors. When Kazlekas saw her, he grinned broadly and made a polite gesture with his hand, as if he intended to say something. But she spoke first.
"I'm glad to meet you, Mr. Kazlekas. I've heard about you in Kaunas. My name is Mrs. Rasutiené. I believe my husband is in your care. I do hope he didn't cause too much trouble. He *has* upset me so! He disappeared without a word to anyone, without giving us a thought, as if we wouldn't even care that he was gone."
"Yes, Madam, he's here. We had to put him in a cell temporarily until we could find out who he was," Kazlekas said apologically, unlocking the cell door. Nikodemas Rasutis stood in the doorway, pale and motionless, his gaze fixed on his wife. Yet he made no gesture of recognition. His eyes were half-closed. He adjusted his glasses and opened his mouth slightly as if to speak, but said nothing.
"Well, Nikodemas, have you traveled enough?" asked the woman coldly.

The voice broke his stare. His lips trembled, and his face came to life.

"Julija! It's you! What's happened?"

He looked about him in the room. Suddenly he ran to his wife and kissed her warmly on the cheek. This she permitted, then she stepped back and gestured with her white gloves.

"How in the world did you get here, Nikodemas? And why didn't you let us know? It's been almost a week since you left, and not a word from you. You must have known we would worry."

"I swear, Julija, in the name of God, I don't know. All day I've been trying to remember who I am, how I got here, and why. It feels as if someone had taken those days out of my life. My conscience tormented me during the hours I was trying to remember. The last thing I remember is Saturday. I know I packed my suitcase, planning to go somewhere, but where, I still don't know. I remember leaving the house, tying my shoelace on the doorstep of a store and then . . . then, nothing. Something . . . something must have overpowered me. I realize now that I was wrong, that I've only myself to blame. Thank you so much for coming!"

Kazlekas, in amazement, snorted. He balked at the idea of a man confessing when he obviously didn't remember a single thing that had happened. Kazlekas stared at the proud woman who received this admission. She stood in the middle of the room, her calm glance fixed on her husband as if it were his own conscience.

"Do you feel all right?" Kazlekas asked the bookkeeper sympathetically, dropping his hand on the man's shoulder.

"Oh, yes," he smiled. "I'm all right now. I can remember everything quite clearly. Thanks for your help!"

"Gairys, escort the gentleman out into the hall and wait there. I have a few matters to clear up with the lady. It won't take long, Mr. Rasutis. You know—formalities."

"I have a few questions," began Kazlekas, taking up his pen. "We're not exactly sure ourselves what really happened. Your husband woke up the whole village last night, playing the church organ. When we asked who he was, he said he couldn't remember. But he didn't look drunk."

The woman adjusted an ornate earring. "My husband never drinks, Mr. Kazlekas. They say it's not good to drink, but sometimes it's convenient. For instance, whenever we entertain, almost everyone takes a drink. But not my husband. If he drinks just one glass, he becomes ill—nauseated. He says he's against drinking, by principle. As you may guess, this can make social occasions—quite difficult."

Kazlekas coughed into his fist. "Is that so. Well, then, why did he come here? Maybe you could help us on that point."

"I rather doubt it. Last Saturday, around five o'clock, my daughter and I went out to visit some friends. For some reason, Nikodemas was restless and irritable. When we got back, about eight o'clock, he was gone."

"Are there any places he likes to go to in Kaunas?"

"No. Evenings, he usually sits in his room and reads. He almost never goes to the movies, or any kind of entertainment. Sometimes he does go to church. So it seemed strange that he had left. I didn't really think much about it, though. Later I noticed some of his clothes and a suitcase were gone . . . Then I began to worry. I called some of my friends, but they hadn't seen him. I waited a while and then I phoned the police. Today was the first I heard anything about him—thanks to you, Mr. Kazlekas!" She smiled pleasantly.

"I'm glad I could be of service. Please excuse my question, but did your husband have any serious reason for wanting to leave the city so suddenly? Trouble with the police or anything of that sort?"

"Who, Nikodemas?" she exclaimed, laughing loudly. "Don't be silly, Mr. Kazlekas! He wouldn't dare do anything risky. Why, even when his colleagues invite him to a restaurant, he refuses. Not that that's bad, but why should he be so different? He doesn't even like to play cards. He is the most reliable employee of the 'Maistas Company,' and he works harder than anyone else. Yet he receives the lowest salary. And how many times have I urged him to ask for a raise—! But no. On his last birthday, as he was cutting the cake, I told him: 'Nikodemas, you're close to fifty. It's time to become reasonable. Instead of chasing the wind, you ought to think of your social position.' But talking to him is like talking to a wall. Just listen to this. Nikodemas says that when his boss thinks it's time to raise his salary, he will. He says, 'Why should I push myself on him?' Ha! I was so upset, I went to visit my friends. Everybody thinks he's a very good man, but I've lived with him for twelve years and I know how difficult he is. He's like a child that has to be shoved into everything. Without me, he would have been lost long ago. Why, instead of concerning himself with the welfare of his family, he even reads poetry! When he could be out meeting influential people, where is he? With the organist of the Carmelite Church. What a man! I admit, he's obedient and kind, but what of it? He lacks manliness. I don't know anything about this trip of his. This is the first time he ever took one without my permission. When we get back to Kaunas, I'm going to take him to a doctor."

"I see, Mrs. Rasutiené. And thank you." Kazlekas entered their names, their address, and other routine data in his record book, and then called back Rasutis.

"Excuse us for the uncomfortable accommodations, but, you see, in the circumstances . . ." he said, laughing heartily as he wished them a good trip. "I hope you'll understand and forgive us."

Rasutis shook his hand and assured him he had slept well.

Kazlekas and Gairys stood in the station doorway watching the couple walk away. "Well, Gairys, that's it, I guess. A pity he can't drink."

"God, that's true!" replied Gairys.

The two men strolled down the quiet street. At Kupstinis' fence they waved goodnight, and each headed his own way toward home.

Adapted by Peter Sears

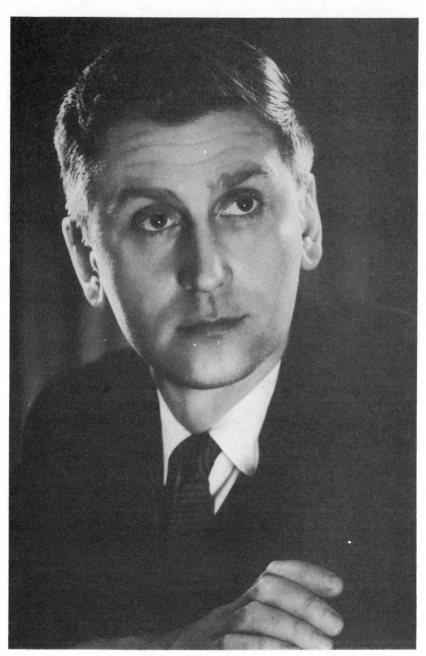
Algirdas Landsbergis

ALGIRDAS LANDSBERGIS

Born on June 23, 1924, in Kybartai, Lithuania, ALGIRDAS LANDSBERGIS studied in the universities of Kaunas and Mainz as well as in Brooklyn College and Columbia University. After writing his first novel, *Kelione* (The Journey), 1954, and a collection of short stories *Ilgoji naktis* (The Long Night), 1956, he concentrated on playwriting. Among his plays are *Meiles mokykla* (The School for Love), 1965, *Penki stulpai turgaus aiksteje* (Five Posts in a Market Place, 1966, and *Vejas gluosniuose / Gluosniai vejuje* (Wind in the Willows / Willows in the Wind), 1973.

Of the English-language versions of his plays, *Five Posts in a Market Place*, 1968, was produced professionally in the United States and Canada, while *The Last Picnic* is slated for publication by Manyland Books in 1977. He has coedited anthologies for Lithuanian poetry and folk songs in English, *The Green Oak*, 1962, and *The Green Linden*, 1964.

ALGIRDAS LANDSBERGIS

(1924-)

The Heavens Are Full Again

ADELE STEPPED INTO THE SECOND FLOOR veranda and, as always gave her first look to the sky turning muddy gray above Queens, her everyday sky crisscrossed with television antennas, an embroidery in somber linen cloth. *Oigi grazus, grazus tolimasis dangus* (Oh, how lovely, lovely the faraway heaven), a line of Lithuanian verse she had heard far away and long ago sang out briefly in her memory.

A muffled roar interrupted her contemplation of the sky. She saw a moving van heave its house-size bulk into the narrow space across the street and flash its noisy inscription at her: "Horizons Unlimited—Movers of America." New neighbors, she thought. Italians. Or, rather, Sicilians. Who else would move into the second of three brick houses inhabited by all those Sicilians and, as her distant cousin's son, the art student, once said, evoking Sicily with their painted bricks, arches and little balconies?

Laughter came back to Adele's ears from the butcher shop where she had waited in line patiently one-half hour ago. Three women were cackling in front of her, Sicilians, she immediately decided from their speech. The dandruffed back facing Adele belonged to the grandmother in a black dress she must have inherited from her mother. Her dirty gray hair had been pushed into absentminded curls, her neck was a pile of wrinkles, and one of her black stockings was sagging around her thick ankle. The daughter and the grandmother, one in a black raincoat, the other in purple, had been showing off their beehive wigs, quite unashamed of their artificiality. The fronts of the three women were reflected in the glass of the meat counter: faces, necks, stomachs embossed on Italian sausages and plucked chickens. Adele's ears tingled with the shrillness and the speed of their talk and laughter. It had taken her twenty years to master, even halfway, the English language, still strange to her in so many ways, and now these women were surrounding her with a second wall of alien sound.

Adele shook her head to dispel the oppressive images from the butcher shop and fixed her attention on two giant Blacks carrying trunks from the van and up the steps into the middle brick house. The huge patches of sweat in their green uniforms appeared to her as exhibitive as the laughter of those women. A couple appeared in the doorway. The new tenants? How young, was her first thought, safely, this side of thirty. She critically scrutinized his short blond beard (and caught herself comparing it with her husband's thinning hair), her bare midriff, the knot of the kerchief at her back (no brassiere?), the tight shorts. The bearded man embraced the young woman's waist with an owner's gesture, while she evaded him slowly and affectionately. A boy—six or seven, their son?—was pounding a rubber ball on the sidewalk. Then the ball rolled into the street, the boy chased it, and the young woman's yell (as frightened and angry at the same time as only a mother could produce) penetrated through the walls of Adele's veranda: "Petruk!!!"

They were Lithuanians! With that realization, the picture in Adele's eyes changed completely, as if someone had flicked a TV knob. No doubt, they had come to America as children, grew up here and became part of that alien mass surrounding her. What a hideous plastic chair, hospital-white, death-white; she'd never allow such a monstrosity in her home. The young woman's hair cannot be that thick, that lustrous—she's wearing one of those wigs. Their brief embrace, which Adele had observed with indifference only a moment before, now appeared brazen to her. Why was she flaunting her nakedness in front of those sweating Blacks? Why don't the two stop cackling, as those Sicilian women at the butcher shop? Cackling in English, no doubt, having come to America as children, having learned English easily, led by the hand to cozy schools, without ever having tasted Adele's sorrows and trials.

She did not stop to sort out the emotions flooding her now—in recent years she had been taking less and less time to weigh and to check them—because she suddenly saw her daughter, Danguole, turn the corner from the avenue into their side street. The view through the veranda window seemed to expand and grow brighter,

Adele's tense lips relaxed in a smile. Slender, flaxen-haired, slightly stooped ("straighten up, Adele, straighten up," her mother used to keep telling her, as she now was repeating to her daughter), in her modest parochial school uniform, Danguole, now outlined against the word PRESCRIPTIONS inscribed on the painted-over corner drugstore window, seemed to be safe from the alien roar, the sweat, bare waists, shrill words; safe, as though Adele's glance was enveloping and protecting her.

Was she safe, though? Surrounded by so many dangers outside the range of her mother's eyes? As Danguole drew nearer, Adele reluctantly observed how quickly her daughter was maturing. How many greasy youths, and even men, already followed her with their eyes when she walked by them. Several days ago she had spotted Danguole in a distant, long conversation with a black-haired and very dark-skinned youth from a neighboring street, no doubt from one of those Sicilian families. Their relaxed motions—undulating shoulders, head tossed back, bried touches of hands—clearly showed her that they liked each other. The day will come, Adele thought, when the slender body of her Danguole will belong to some strange young man who will embrace her with the proprietary gesture of that bearded Lithuanian across the street.

Danguole was beside the moving van when the boy's ball bounced toward her on the sidewalk. She nimbly scooped it up and tossed it back to the boy who ran over to her chattering. Danguole responded and pointed at her house. Adele stepped back automatically, but the first, unexpectedly early, link between her and the newcomers had been established.

Danguole's quick steps soon clattered on the stairs and Adele walked inside to meet her in the kitchen, always her daughter's first stop after school. She tossed her books, tied together with a leather strap, on the kitchen table, brushed Adele's cheek with her lips and, still out of breath from chasing the ball and running up the stairs, burst out in her slightly accented Lithuanian: "Mommy, Mommy, the family, across the street, they're Lithuanian, his name is Petrukas..."

"I know."

"Isn't it nice! You and Daddy can visit them. Right now?!"

"Not so fast, Danguole."

"Oh, Mother," Danguole sighed in her usual exasperation with Adele's strange proprieties. "And why not?"

Adele gave her a patient smile and sighed in return. How little do these children know.

"Because these things are not done that fast. Especially between strangers."

Now it was time to remind Danguole of her place and of her lack of experience in general. "Danguole, on the subject of chasing balls for little boys, it's not quite proper for young ladies. And to throw the ball in such a—masculine—way . . ."

Danguole opened her mouth to tell her mother that she totally but totally, disagreed with her, yet she managed to remain silent. Now, more than at any other time, she must refrain from antagonizing her mother. Everything was different now, because the day before yesterday, Tony had asked her to be his girl at the high school prom. Yes, the same Tony whom the older girls in the neighborhood, those with falsies and elevated shoes and jobs, compared with Johnny Mathis and would have refused him nothing, but nothing. Of course, proms were not the same things now as during those weird fifties, when she was born, centuries ago. but Danguole still could not help seeing herself in a chiffon dress, her shoulders naked, dancing first in today's, and then in the old-fashioned style with her head on his shoulder, in some nice Village place or even Uptown, and then leaning on the railing of the Staten Island ferry, or some other romantic spot. With such great things about to happen, her relationship with her mother must be the best possible, because it was going to be very difficult, as it was, to get her to agree. She could imagine her mother's answers: You're much too young, Danguole. If only he was Lithuanian, then, maybe.

"Well, am I not right?" Her mother's voice interrupted Danguole's wandering thoughts.

She forced a dutiful smile. "Yes, Mother." Then Danguole pecked her cheek again and danced out of the room.

Adele stood for a while in the kitchen, trying to understand her daughter. This sudden submissiveness, where did it come from? Why that self-satisfied smile? And why the unexpected second kiss? She found herself on the way to the veranda again, without any special purpose. We probably won't be moving anywhere any more, she thought. This small house, this veranda, whatever her eyes could encompass through the window, all that was her last arena of action, her magnetic field, yes, her battlefield. She raised her eyes. Yes, and that precisely outlined plot of sky, crowded with television antennas, different from the more spacious Lithuanian skies above antennaless roofs, part of her longing and of the strangeness surrounding her.

2.

The Sunday sky two days later was appropriately clear and festive. Before turning into her side street from the main avenue, Adele inhaled deeply as was her custom each Sunday on the way home from church. She knew that eyes would appear in the neighbors' windows—mostly dark, Sicilian eyes—for the Sunday review. Her fingers in the white gloves took a tighter grip of her black patent leather handbag harboring the prayerbook that she had brought all the way from Lithuania. Her hand-made Banlon dress, in sky blue with modest flowers, nothing loud about it, fit her still girlish waist snugly. The sky, her outfit, the rhythm of her steps—everything blended in perfect harmony. Since her earliest childhood memories, ever since her farthermost Lithuanian sky, she was passionately enamored of Sundays, of their dignity and order. The ribbon of Sundays stretched back into her youth and childhood, one of the few threads and ribbons of her life not torn asunder by exile.

"Oh, how very lovely the faraway vault of heaven," she whispered unconsciously and smiled at her husband. Her face clouded immediately. His eyes wandering aimlessly, he was traipsing a half step behind her, although she had been constantly chiding him for this recent bad habit of his. (Man and wife must walk side-by-side, especially on Sunday!) She noticed the open button right above his belt buckle, and his protruding belly, which he sometimes, in very poor taste, called his Rheingold cattlemound. Couldn't he be satisfied with one bottle of beer per night, or even exercise, like other men? His armpits must be sweaty now, she thought suddenly, and the image of the black moving men flashed again, the dark blotches on green unifroms disfiguring her bright Sunday poster.

Carefully, from the corners of her eyes, Adele surveyed the yard of their new neighbors on the other side of the street. The young woman was sunbathing on a beach chair. One of those who hire maids to do their housework, Adele decided. Could she have managed to return from the early Mass, as Danguole had, and to change? The young woman gave Adele a big wave, but she pretended not to have seen it. She slowed her stride and the husband fell in step with her. In full view of the newcomer, they would enter their home in complete order.

"Good morning!" The shrillness of the young woman's voice reminded Adele of the Sicilian family at the butcher and seemed to offend modesty as much as her bathing suit at arm's reach from the sidewalk.

"Good morning!" Adele's husband roared back. "Beautiful!" he added, waving at her.

Did he mean the weather or the young woman? Adele pretending that she saw her for the first time, waved in her most reserved manner and chilled her husband with a disapproving look. As he was unlocking the door, she said: "Shouting on Sunday. What next?"

He shrugged his shoulders. Adele hurried up the stairs in front of him, giving him further indication of her displeasure. A trail of blaring radio music led her to the kitchen where she found Danguole with a glass of milk in her hand and the fashion section of the Sunday paper spread out on the table. Adele turned off the radio and braced herself for the inevitable protest. But, to her astonishment, Danguole spoke in a very different vein.

"Mother, you know what, the neighbors want me to babysit for them."

"We're still capable, thank God, of taking care of you."

"But, Mother, didn't you say—you, yourself!—that I must start learning how money is made?!"

No matter how Adele might try to avoid the newcomers' family, the link between them was inevitably tightening. New trials were awaiting her now in her distrubed domain, in her theatre of war. Such matters of import had to be negotiated in proper surroundings. Adele decided that her husband, especially after the morning's experience, would have to stay outside, for a while at least.

"Let's go to my workroom."

Adele was proud of her little room into which she had crowded her Singer sewing machine (a brand she had respected even in her pre-American days), an ironing board and countless pins and needles, but nevertheless managed to keep it clean and uncluttered. Once destined for their little son, who died in his third week, the room still seemed to retain the hush and sombreness of that event long ago.

Adele's eyes caressed in passing the small flower pots in the window. "When did they ask you?"

"This morning, on the way home from church."

"They went to the same Mass?"

"No, they don't go to church."

"How do you know?"

"She told me: 'No, we don't go to church!'"

There was a flicker of triumph in Adele's eyes. But, of course! She was always good at making an instant evaluation of people! Her new neighbors might speak Lithuanian, but they nevertheless belonged to that all-enveloping strangeness surrounding Adele. Now she felt superior to them, their youth, fancy furniture and chic clothes notwithstanding.

"And the boy?"

"Petrukas? He doesn't know anything!"

"Is that so? Well, well."

"He walked me to the door this morning and he asked me, "What's a church?"

Why was her mother smiling so strangely? Why the hesitation?

"Danguole, you may babysit. Once a week."

"Gee, thanks, Mother!"

"But under one condition—that you teach Petrukas religion!"

"Who, me?"

"Explain to him about God. But only in Lithuanian!"

"What? I haven't got time!"

"While you're there."

"But how? I don't know how!"

"Just think about it. You'll change his life. Some day, a very special day, he'll start going to church. And it will be thanks to you."

Danguole was about to go on resisting but she thought of the high school prom and again felt Tony's lips on hers, just as they were two days ago. She felt herself blush. Now, she had to agree with mother about everything. "If you wish, Mother."

Adele stroked her shoulder, confirming their agreement. Her eyes, past the flaxen strands of her daughter's hair, found a Lithuanian calendar on the wall, with a picture of a spacious sky above piles of sheaves.

3.

"But where is God?"

"In heaven."

Petrukas grabbed Danguole by the hand and dragged her over to the window. "Where, where?" he asked impatiently pointing to the dark sky with the lone pulsating red light of a plane.

"In heaven, you just can't see it."

"Why not?"

"God isn't human."

"What's human?"

"Me, your parents—people. Maybe even you."

"Is God like a plane? A balloon?"

"Petrukas, you're too much! You're stupid!"

"No, I'm smart. Mommy says so."

Patience, Danguole admonished herself. Patience. She took Petrukas by the hand. "Come, let's try again from the beginning." They sank into the white sofa. Danguole admired the white rugs, white soft chairs, and white globe lamps, the likes of which she had seen only in magazines. Their sitting room was so strange and at the same time so appealing, a total contrast to her parents' old-fashioned living room that seemed to have been transferred intact from the show room of the furniture store a block down the avenue. She opened the school catechism she had brought along.

"Will you read me a fairy tale?" Petrukas asked.

"No, the truth. About God."

She glanced at the inscription in the corner of the title page: Danguole Sauka, Religious Award. She had not expected the ink to have turned so pale—that's how long ago she had first opened the catechism.

"First question: Who created the world? Answer: God created the world."

"What's cree-ate-id?"

"Made."

"Why don't they say it?"

Danguole's religious lesson was turning out to be much more complicated than she had expected. Her own questions, unforseen, began pushing Petrukas' questions aside. How much did she, herself, still believe, what did she believe? Many girls in school were saying they didn't believe at all. The old nuns seemed to be shrinking; and sometimes, she thought she saw their black habits gliding by on their own, empty inside. The girls who usually snatched the best grades were saying that they believed in the "principle of cosmic unity," or some such thing.

"Is God bigger than man?" Petrukas asked again.

"Much, much bigger."

"Can he lift a house?"

"Just like you pick up a ball."

"With one hand?"

"Petrukas, he's got no hands!"

Danguole was receiving Holy Communion, but she would no more be able to draw such a clear and simple picture of God as she did for Petrukas. She thought of the prayer book her mother had brought from Lithuania. Her God, too, was a different one. And now, Petrukas' God was turning out to be unlike hers and unlike Mother's.

"What's that?" Petrukas stuck his finger at a little red star pasted next to the catechism's question.

"A little star."

"Why here?"

"I answered my questions correctly—not like you!—and they pasted a little star on my book. When I get a right answer from you, I'll give you one. Right on your forehead!" She poked Petrukas' forehead.

His grin immediately gave way to deep seriousness. "A little star. Like in heaven?"

"Just like in heaven."

"God's in heaven."

"Yes, in heaven. See here?"

As she pointed to the first picture in the catechism, we've come back, she thought, ring-around-the-rosy, to his first question and my very first answer, and she sighed in disappointment. Petrukas, though, had eyes for the picture and nothing else. There was a circle in the center, and in the middle of that circle sat God Himself, with hair longer than his mother's, and beard much longer than his father's. His arms were raised high and His wide robe rippled like a pond. God was surrounded by a ring of lambs; a rose of clouds circled Him; a halo of small curly heads, all singing, rested above His divine mane. Two smaller circles floated above the large circle and another two hung below, crowded with chanting angels above and caroling people below. And now the circles left the page and expanded, circles in a pond, a lake, across the rug, through the walls, outside, heavenward.

"Petrukas, where are you going?"

"Brush my teeth."

Danguole shrugged her shoulders. He's bored. So much for my first lesson. Petrukas was on his way to the bathroom upstairs.

"Why the upstairs bathroom?"

"I like it better upstairs."

Danguole began pacing the room to gather her thoughts, and, as at home, she ended up in the kitchen. She admired the huge and gleaming refrigerator, much larger than theirs, on the side of which a festive plane was streaking through a PAN AM calendar's copper-colored sky.

Instead of brushing his teeth, Petrukas hurried into the upstairs porch. More sky could be seen from here than from the living room below. His eyes agleam with amazement he marvelled at the clouds drifting and joining to outline a forest of hair and a gigantic beard, rolling to form undulating robes. The heavens were not empty! Multitudes upon multitudes swarmed in the sky, the catechism page was spreading across the sky, bales of heavenly cloth unrolled themselves and cascaded down like jubilant waterfalls, whirlwinds swirled themselves into the shapes of lambs and of chanting curly heads. How full, how full of God were the heavens!

4.

The following night Petrukas' parents stayed at home. They were in their usual places: father wrapped up in a newspaper on the sofa; mother bent over a letter at her little writing desk; Petrukas in front of the television set.

"What a sky!"

Petrukas shivered as if his mother had read his thoughts. She opened the curtain wide and exclaimed in a voice she used only for moments of special enchantment. "Ah, what an unusual sky!"

Father raised his head from the newspaper and mumbled affirmatively.

"Come to the window, lazybones," mother pretended to scold father. "Petrukas!"

All three now, huddling close as one, with Petrukas in the middle, observed the evening sky.

"That color, a copper pot." Mother's enthusiasm was undiminished.

Why did she speak of pots when it was God who lived in heaven? God, lambs, curly heads caroling. "Not a pot, God," Petrukas said loudly.

His parents' heads quickly turned to each other.

"God..." his mother repeated in disbelief.

How quickly they forgot the copper-pot sky. They slowly returned to their places—three, no more one. Father pushed aside the newspaper with a plane streaking across its first page, and Petrukas picked it up.

"God can make a plane in ten minutes," he announced triumphantly.

"Can he?" father asked. "We two must have a talk about it."

But instead of talking with Petrukas, they turned up the televison louder for him and began whispering together, using many words that were incomprehensible to him and that were mingled with the words from the television pictures.

"You explain it to him."

"Out of the question; it's definitely the father's role."

"Why should it be?"

"Because he's going to identify with you, that's why."

"Anyway, what's the big tragedy?"

"To absorb a dogmatic image of God in early childhood, to lock all doors, to shut all windows? I'm surprised. I'm really surprised!"

The tradition of her atheist family would sometimes erupt in her with religious militancy, all flags flying. He was used to it and would give in to her without much ado, because for him both religion and atheism were matters of profound indifference. All he could think of in such moments was how desirable she looked, her cheeks flushed, her eyes sparkling, and how much he would like to get her into bed immediately.

"We've got our babysitter to thank for that," she proceeded with her attack, utterly unaware of the bedroom train of his thought. "Didn't I tell you that her mother was avoiding us? That's religion for you!"

"She may just be shy."

"A shy zealot?! My foot! Uneducated, and therefore dogmatic and suspicious. We're going to get a new babysitter!"

"No, no, I don't want a new babysitter, I don't!" Petrukas exclaimed.

His parents turned to him with guilty smiles.

"Petrukas has good ears," his father said, smiling.

"I'm gonna marry her. We'll be mommy and daddy."

Father and mother sat down on the sofa and encircled him in their embrace; three were one again. "We'll see, Petrukas, we'll see," his mother said, kissing his cheek. "But now you and Daddy will talk about God."

She got up and walked to the book shelf.

"So you say God can make a plane in ten minutes?" Father was still searching for words.

"Yes! When God was a baby, he knew how much is twenty and twenty!"

"O.K. Now listen to me. The TV picture, where does it come from?"

"The TV box," Petrukas poked at the TV set.

"No, Petrukas. From TV stations, across the skies, come the signals—little pieces of faces, trees, furniture. The TV antenna catches them, the innards of the set put them together, and then—bingo! A picture!

Petrukas was politely silent. He knew that what flew and waved across the heavens were not pieces of color or chips of furniture, but God's beard, hair and robes.

"And now, we'll read some very interesting stories," father said, taking a book from mother's hands.

When big people want to talk about God, they always grab books, Petrukas thought.

"You see, Petrukas, if people didn't know about TV, about the electrons, as we know, now, they would think that some kind of gods are sending the TV pictures. When they heard thunder, when they saw lightning in the sky, they asked themselves: Who? From where? And so man created . . ."

"That means made," Petrukas chimed in.

"Yes, very good. Where was I? Yes, and so man created gods, stories about gods. Well, in this book we've got stories from the whole world, stories about gods and how they created the world."

Father took a deep breath and glanced at mother. She nodded to him slightly, confirming his tactics.

"We'll start with the Eskimos," father resumed his lecture. "The first is an Eskimo story. It's very cold where Eskimos live. Cold and white, snow all over the place. See the picture? Snow drifts everywhere."

Petrukas' eyes were turning toward the window. Snow drifts, like snowy mountains in the sky. Father's voice began to recede, giving way to Danguole's words about God. The picture in the book was nowhere near the splendor of the catechism. God's beard flooded through the window, enveloping Petrukas. His robes waved like a victorious army of flags, lambs were licking Petrukas' face until he dozed off, long before his father finished the story about the Eskimos.

5.

Danguole hesitated briefly in front of her mother's workroom. Behind that door the fatal moment was waiting for her—the question to her mother could not be postponed any longer because Tony had to have her answer tonight. She tried to guess her mother's mood from the rhythm of the sewing machine. The machine answered with an even buzz, without nervous interruptions. Mother could only say yes, Danguole encouraged herself. In all her life she had never heard so much praise from her mother as during the last week, since the day she had started instructing Petrukas about God. Now or never she whispered and crossed herself (an old parochial school pre-exams habit).

As the door slowly opened, the buzz of the sewing machine died down and Danguole's mother unfocused her eyes from the piece of blue material to which she had given her customary fierce concentration.

"Well, Danguole, how's your little star pupil?"

"Big star pain, you mean. I can't get a moment's peace—questions about God, questions about heaven . . ."

Mother rose and took Danguole's hand. The warmth of the sewing machine still adhered to her palms and Danguole felt the recent indentation in her thumb.

"You should be proud, Danguole, very proud. Just look at the other girls of your age. Prancing around like some hussies, getting involved with boys before their time, while you, d'you realize what you have accomplished?"

Now or never, do or die! "Mother . . ."

"Yes, my missionary?"

"Mother, I've been invited to a prom. I want to go. I really want to!"

Danguole's request intruded quite unexpectedly into Adele's orderly world, a sudden cloud casting a shadow on last week's bright victories. She sensed a danger, faceless still, but a tangible danger nevertheless. Instinctively, she tried to prolong the conversation, until she could marshal her forces and establish her positions on the battlefiedl.

" 'Prom,' what does that mean in Lithuanian?"

"When they graduate from high school, you know, like taking your date to a good restaurant for dinner, dancing."

"Those teenagers with naked shoulders, painted faces?"

"Can I go, Mother? Please?"

"But you're too young."

"Oh, Mother, younger girls than me are going. Lithuanian, too!"

"Who's the boy? Do I know him?"

"It's Tony. He lives on the next block."

The swarthy, black-haired boy who had held Danguole's hand! Panic began to flood Adele. His hands ruffling her daughter's flaxen hair, pressing her still too narrow shoulders.

He's a very nice boy," Danguole jumped into the silence.

Adele's lips were sealed. The wave of foreignness that pretended to recede last week, rolled up and broke against her. She was standing in the butcher's again; the three Sicilian women in front of her were chattering louder and louder, trying to outshout each other; their wigs turned into exotic birds' nests and transformed them into giantesses. Three Sicilians; daughter, mother, grandmother; time's flow and time's end all recorded in their trip; three Sicilians, one death. How noisy they are in the face of death. How nude their voices, without a shred of cloth covering their fleshiness. Their silhouettes engraved themselves on the glass of the butcher's display case; purple-veined Italian sausages, still moist like recently torn out organs of some bizarre beasts, were crowding themselves into their silhouettes; guillotined chickens embraced each other's creeping flesh inside their silhouettes. These were the Sicilians gutted here, their entrails spilling out. This is how her unique solitude would be sliced open, too, in her own hour of death, in the strangeness of the butcher's shop, in the foreign land, while the three Sicilians would go on shrilling, disregarding her lonely death. Tony would join them, Tony winding Danguole's hair around his greasy fingers, Tony, Tony, a piece of that flooding, oozing foreignness, Tony embracing her daughter's slender, still maturing body amidst sausages, chickens, livers . . .

"No!!!" Adele exclaimed, and was instantly frightened by her own voice.

Fear, stupefaction, disillusionment, anger flashed in Danguole's face. Her lips began to tremble. Adele felt a sudden painful compassion for her. She reached for her daughter's hand, but Danguole drew it back.

"Why not?"

"Danguole..."

Perhaps, I shouldn't forbid her, Adele thought. They're young. The young rule the world. All she needed was to say "yes" and Danguole's arms would be around her. But she could not say yes immediately; she must make one more appeal.

"He's Sicilian..."

"No, Mother, he's Puerto Rican! Any objection?"

The word took Adele completely unawares. She had been wrestling with all those Sicilian phantoms and now a new uncharted foreign world opened before her. Puerto Rican! It seemed to her that she was trying to reach her daughter, stretching her arms after her in vain, past the Sicilians; in vain past the mounds of purple meat; in vain past the familiar and toward the unfamiliar foreignness, while her daughter was zooming further and further into the distance.

"No," was all she could whisper.

"Why not?!" Danguole screamed in frustration.

How could Adele explain all that she felt? "Puerto Rican..." she started.

Danguole's face changed almost unrecognizably. Such a face Adele had never seen before, this expression of a strange, hunted, wounded animal. How?!

"Because you're a bigot!" Danguole spat out the English word, because she did not know the Lithuanian equivalent, and ink-and-paper word in her social studies class, but a bursting sewer pipe in her mother's tidy room. She ran out, fiercely slamming the door, thundering down the stairs. In the deep silence Adele heard a piece of plaster fall and felt a solitary tear forming in the foreignness of her face.

For what seemed an endless moment Danguole stood in front of her house and watched the leaves whirled by the wind. Windy day, she said, and giggled mirthlessly without knowing why. Yes, the flowers were shivering and bending in their beds, flowers were cowering in their window boxes, the shadow of a tree trembled across their house, as if some giant hand, a god's or a demon's were covering it with a hesitating brush.

"Danguole, Danguole!"

It was Petrukas bounding out of the door across the street. She hurried toward the avenue, pretending not to hear him. She could not face him now. He was a living reminder of her mother's strange plans and her own shattered hopes.

He dashed across the street, oblivious of automobiles, caught up with her and greedily seized her hand as had been his custom the whole week. His touch made her feel nauseous.

"I'm in a hurry."

"I'll go with you."

"No!"

"Let's talk about God."

Danguole stopped. Her rising fury now found a solid target on which to vent itself: the product of her mother's whimsy, her mother's creation. She pressed his hand, fastened her eyes on him, and exclaimed: "There is no God! You hear! No God!"

His hand separated from hers as a puppy would from a hostile mother. He stared at her in shock and disbelief. Danguole swung around and hurried on. At the corner she quickly turned. He stood there as she had left him.

Petrukas' eyes followed her back disappearing beyond the corner drugstore. There's no God. Danguole was here; now there's no Danguole. Did he disappear behind some corner? Behind which corner? No God. His head hanging low, he crossed the street and stopped indecisively at his door.

He glanced at Danguole's veranda. Her mother was standing there and pierced him with such burning eyes that he felt them on his body like two live coals. He shivered and raised his eyes to the sky. "There's no God," he said automatically.

How empty the sky was, as though someone had swept away all the long hair, waving robes and frisking lambs. Why had he seen them all earlier, but could not see them now? His father was right. And his mother. Their book was more powerful than Danguole's.

As Danguole's book began to fade from Petrukas' mind, his father's words about television came back to him. The pictures come through the skies and the TV antenna catches them. Pictures through the skies? But then—the heaven wasn't empty! Stunned by his discovery, he let mouth fall wide open. The skies, the heavens weren't empty! Television pictures sing and dance in heaven, they fly across the skies. There, Popeye comes waddling, followed by Big Bird craning his long neck; and after him, Mr. Kangaroo and Mr. Greenjeans prancing with banjos in their hands. New, magnificent gods were crowding the skies, they spoke and sang in English, only Danguole's god spoke Lithuanian, but he's nowhere, girls with straight long hair, Coca Cola bottles in their hands were flooding the skies, the snow-white Man from Glad flew just above their heads, the Man Who Ate the Whole Thing sat on his bed in a cloud, they were all searching for their antennas and then crawling through them into their TV sets, jostling each other in heaven's noisy marketplace, in the chock-full heaven, godless heaven, faraway heaven.

Translated by the Author

Icchokas Meras

ICCHOKAS MERAS

ICCHOKAS MERAS was born on October 8, 1934, in Kelme, Lithuania, and lost his parents during the Nazi anti-Semitic campaign in 1941. He graduated from the Polytechnic Institute as a radio-engineer in 1958 but devoted himself mainly to writing. His avant-garde novels, *Lygiosios trunka akimirka* (The Draw Lasts Only a Moment), 1963, and *Ant ko laikosi pasaulis* (The Foundation of the World), 1968, were widely translated. The dominant theme in them, as in the collections of stories, *Zeme visad gyva* (The Earth Is Always Alive), 1963, and *Geltonas lopas* (The Yellow Patch), 1960, is the holocaust of World War II. Following Meras' emigration to Israel in 1972, his name disappeared from publications in Lithuania. He is now associated with the Diaspora Research Institute at Tel-Aviv University.

ICCHOKAS MERAS

(1934–   )

The Old Woman With a Green Pail

SLOWLY, AS ALWAYS, she walked over to the sink and placed her little pail in it, and then she turned on the faucet, and the water started running. It ran in a thin jet while the old woman stood patiently and waited till the pail was full. She could stand here and wait because nobody rushed her and she liked listening to the even pouring of the water. Time she had in abundance, and, here in the kitchenette, it was easier for her to protect herself from the heat. From time to time she would touch the cool jet of water with her dry, bony fingers and then put her fingers to her face, her neck, and her flat chest, and breathing would become easier, as if the heat had stepped back for a little while.

So the water bubbled in the little pail, the old woman stood, waited, moistened her face and pondered, because she liked to ponder.

This woman, Sara, lived on the second floor. Quite comfortably––for an older person. And the house was the same as all the houses, where the new immigrants settled, neither better nor worse.

A roof over my head, and thanks to God, Sara thought. Did a Jew always have a roof overhead?

The house stood at the edge of the town––a town just like all little towns that rise out of wastelands or desert sands and shelter those who arrive, like all those little towns that have nothing townlike about them, only a name and some house, uniform like matchboxes.

Thanks to God; The Jew has seen stranger things than that, Sara thought.

So the house was like other houses, the town like other towns, and Sara, herself––a human being like other human beings. Doing neither good nor evil to others, the woman went on living and that is all.

She lived through the winter shivering from the cold, wrapped in some older warm garment or a threadbare woolen blanket, and now, in summer, she cowered from the heat and, with her eyes half-closed, gasped for air intermittently, craning her neck so that her face and open thin lips could catch the pleasant draft, crossing from the room window to the kitchenette opening, while she went through the entire March and through the beginning of April almost without any sleep, chasing cats that made love to each other in shrill stinging baby voices.

The spring nights were still cold although Sara had managed to grow warm in her iron bed under two blankets and two old overcoats, but she could not resist the urge to get up. And not only because she wasn't able to close her eyes. As soon as that undescribable nuptial scream of the cats would rise, she felt a knife across her heart, because it seemed to her, although she knew that it was the little animals screaming and nothing else, it still seemed to her that a man was being knifed in some dark nook; or little children were being whipped, or their tiny heads were being smashed against the walls, or women were being raped, or gods know what terrible things were going on somewhere near. And on hearing their screams, Sara would feel uneasy being there all alone, and would grieve for something, and would rise from the warm bed, get into one, second and third garment, would pull the curtain aside, open the window and, looking around in the dark, shout, "Scat, scat, you fiends! Scat!"

The little creatures would quiet down for a while, but then Sara would feel even more uneasy. Her heart would have a twinge, and she would blush in darkness, suddenly ashamed, since it was kind of improper to scatter that nocturnal wedding, because the little creatures were making love to each other. They were living beings after all.

Sara would lie down again, after closing the window, again she warmed her bed, closed her eyes and made an effort to think of her past, to remember her long life, to promenade the old paths, the even and the bumpy ones, so that she could forget herself and would not hear the rising caterwauling of the little creatures, and then at dawn she would doze off.

So she lived, and it was the same, it seemed whether she lived or as if she had never lived.

Sara almost turned off the faucet, to make the jet even **thinner**, so that she would not have to move from here that quickly, because it was truly pleasant to listen to the purling of the water, to the bubbling of the thin stream, while her moistened fingers refreshed the body, and the path of the bracing draft went through her.

And Sara took pleasure in the pail getting fuller, although water cost money, and quite a penny at that.

Sara saved each penny, even the tiniest one, which was worth nothing. When she bought fruit or a couple of berries, she picked the smaller and the less than fresh ones. If she needed anything, she looked for a used, secondhand item. She heated water as rarely as possible, turned on the light only when darkness was complete, and only the night bulb at that, which she could transfer from the room to the kitchen, or from the kitchen to the room whenever needed. Only on the ceiling there hung a larger lamp so that if some guest should drop in, he would not be frightened by the darkness. But no guest had ever visited her yet, and so she had not turned on the ceiling lamp.

Nor would she ever shed a drop of water needlessly. Only for tea——whatever she would drink, only for soup——whatever she would eat, only to wash the dishes, only to wash herself——as much as she needed it, each drop accounted for.

And as for the little pail, in which the water was rising now, she never filled it to the very brim, only three fingers below it so the water would not splatter when she carried it through the room.

But the old woman never skimped on water in that pail of hers. She filled it several times during the day.

And after she had filled that green pail and had carried it cautiously across the room, she would toss it through the open window, and the earth would instantly soak up that water.

Because Sara did not busy herself with anything, she did nothing and did not want to do anything——what can an infirm old person do? She had a single job to do——to water the sapling under her window, because she wanted that thin gray stalk to spread and become a tree some day.

So that it may become a tree some day, so that it would provide greeness and shade.

For there was nothing green around, nothing but sand. And farther away, where no houses stood yet, there was nothing—— only sand and naked dunes.

There was a faucet downstairs too, by the house. And that water was free of charge. But old Sara, although she was human like all people, had one trouble, her very own trouble (thanks to God, not everyone is a Jew, Sara thought). Her legs had grown weak and thin, and were now crooked like bows, just like a little child's as it happens sometimes. And although the old woman did not live high up, she just was not able to climb the stairs up and down several times a day and to water the sapling. She would leave her home sometimes, she had to go out, you can't sit cooped up forever, one must eat, and shopping's got to be done, and when you get there, you have to pay, you can't sit behind closed doors all the time, if you live alone. Ask the others——would you really? Everybody is up to the neck in his own affairs. A body's got to work, and to make money, and to take a rest. So, can you ask them? Everybody was up to his neck in his own troubles.

That's a Jewish heat, oy, Jewish, Sara thought. If the Lord gives something to a Jew, He doesn't spare it, if it's trouble——it's truly large size, and if it's a heat——it's enormous.

And that tree, Sara thought, will grow despite all that, and how will it grow. And when it will have grown stronger and taller, then it may start suckling the moisture——with its deeper roots and with the branches it will have grown with the help of the dew absorbed at dawn.

The difficulty of walking up and down is not a very big deal. Neither is it much trouble to toss down several pails full of water through the window. And what if it costs a few pennies—— could she begrudge some water for a tree?

The litle pail was almost full now, three fingers to the brim—— just right, as every time. Sara tightened the faucet to prevent dripping. God forbid, here's the last trickle, crooked like the old woman's legs, falling into the pail, and the last drops trickled from the closed faucet. Now Sara could take her pail and slowly carry it toward the open window, the young tree was probably waiting impatiently for the refreshing water, but the old woman hesitated and did not move from the spot.

Sara was hesitating because she was afraid to stumble again on the man who lived on the first floor. The man——that's what Sara called him since she knew neither his first nor last name, nor his occupation, nor how he made ends meet. As if on purpose, he would creep out into the yard just when Sara emptied her pail and he would always manage to get right under the water.

Some evil spirit, God forgive me, Sara thought.

But time went on, the sapling was waiting and the old woman, both her hands on the handle, lifted the pail from the sink and inched to the window slowly, slowly——to make sure that her legs didn't get entangled and the water didn't splash.

Sara was mincing along, green pail in her hand, and thinking: Will the man crawl out today, too, at the wrong time, or won't he? That's what Sara thought, but not as much in fear, as always, of drenching the man, as in anger——in serious anger.

When she had accidentally drenched that man for the first time, she cowered by the open window and wanted to run away in shame, but she stayed put, she wanted to lower her eyes, but didn't. She stared at that man, neither able to help him in any way, nor knowing how to apologize, waiting for him to turn around and scream in rage (there was ample reason for it), perhaps to curse with real vigor (who could say that it would not be deserved).

It might have been better that way, Sara realized only now.

But it was quite the contrary, she felt as if a load had been lifted from her heart, a smile even appeared on her thin lips, when she failed to hear a single word, neither a shout nor a curse.

The man did not even raise his head, clumsily wiped his soaked shirt with one hand and then with the other, and, without even a glance upward, he entered the house. He went in and did not appear again.

And so the old woman had forgotten this event, and watered the sapling as before, until she again poured a whole pailful on the man's head. It seemed to her that she had done enough looking around before emptying the pail, and chose the best time, but there he was again!

Now she was interested in what the man would say. And whatever he might have said would have been deserved, and Sara would have accepted every word, even the angriest one.

But this time, too, the old woman heard neither a word nor a sound. The man merely shook himself and, without lifting either his eyes or his head, entered the house and did not show himself again.

This happened a third time and fourth time.

Then Sara started getting angry and took even greater precuations while watering the sapling and her anger kept growing, because she had to be on guard and, tilting the pail with trembling hands, she sometimes missed the sapling. But there was further reason for her anger, since she had poured the water on that Jew's head four times already but he kept silent, he did not utter a single word, as if this was how it should be, as if he had to be mocked this way, abused at will, while remaining silent, that Jew.

Maybe that's why all the troubles are landing on our heads, Sara thought, perhaps that's why everybody who wants to push us around simply does ahead and does it.

Now she looked around several times, took a careful look down and was just about to tilt her little pail when she noticed the man coming out right under her window.

Was it anger or fear, or the desire to mock that made her hands tilt the green pail, without even aiming at the tree, point-blank at that man?

Sara waited an instant, but when this time, too, not a single word came from him, she flung the empty pail to the ground, grabbed her cane which she needed to go anywhere, hurried to the door and, without even closing it, rumbled down the stairs as fast as she could so as not to be late.

And she got there in time.

She met the man from the first floor eye to eye and looked him up and down. Soaking wet and still silent, his shirt clinging to his body, his white mouse-like gray hair, his wrinkles under the eyes and along his cheeks.

"Man!" Sara exclaimed, threatening him with a cane as if with a finger. "Why are you silent? Why can't you defend yourself by word at least. Shame, shame on you, old, gray Jew . . ."

Thus, old Sara said what she wanted and fell silent.

She fell silent and thrust her eyes like daggers at the old man's.

And Sara was struck with fear because the man kept silent

even now.

So they faced each other silently for a long time, and then the old man raised his arms slightly, nimbly moving his fingers, wanting to explain something and unable to, and therefore ashamed. Finding no other solution, he opened his mouth and emitted a faint bellow.

And that inhuman sound made Sara's flesh creep, because she heard again the cats screaming in humanlike voices at night, and she heard a man bellowing like an animal.

And old Sara understood, she understood everything immediately, although she did not want to understand.

Since that encounter, old Sara kept watering the sapling from the window, and the man from the first floor obstructed her no longer.

As before, Sara wanted the thin gray stalk to rise, spread and become a tree some day.

And the old woman still wanted to hear the man speak out.

And in the evening she would descend, although climbing down the stairs was difficult, very difficult, just as climbing upstairs, with two canes for support, and she would knock with the cane at the man's door, because each night she taught him how to speak.

And it did not take long, not long, until that man started speaking. Only not everybody can understand his speech.

Translated by Jeronimas Zemkalnis

VYTAUTE ZILINSKAITE

VYTAUTE ZILINSKAITE was born in Kaunas, Lithuania, on December 13, 1930. She received a degree in journalism from the University of Kaunas and worked on the editorial staffs of humor and youth periodicals. Starting with poetry and documentary prose, she later excelled in humorous and satirical sketches. Collections of these include, *Angelas virs miesto* (Angel Above a City), 1967; *Romantikos institutas* (The Institute of Romanticism), 1968; *Humoreskos* (Humoresques), 1971; and *Paradoksai* (Paradoxes), 1973. She also writes for children, and some of her books have been translated into Russian and other East-European languages.

Vytaute Zilinskaite

VYTAUTE ZILINSKAITE

(1930–)

TWO STORIES

The Most Unusual Story

THE DIRECTORS OF A LARGE TOWN had thought up an original plan to instill a breath of fresh air into the hitherto moldy, cumbersome format of an annual program.

It was a cold and rainy afternoon. (The way it usually is when you plan a large, public outdoor function.) Half the people who lived in the town, flowed over to Brassband Hill, covering themselves with umbrellas and newspapers.

The director stood on the slope of the hill. Satisfied with the large crowd which had gathered, he thundered through the microphone: "Beloved Citizens! We have asked you here to take part in a very different competition which, by virtue of its originality, should bring fame to our town. We would like you to describe a true experience which you have had while living here. Some event which was so bizarre, it approached fantasy. And to the person who will tell the most unusual story, we will award a fine prize!"

The crowd roared and waved. People began to whisper and think, rubbing their foreheads. Reporters rushed home to get their notebooks. Students predicted speech-defying messages. The fishermen and the hunters smiled knowingly at one another.

From the crowd, a housewife appeared. She came up to the microphone and laughingly began her tale: "My neighbor boiled a dishrag instead of a chicken!" She rambled on with such trivia, giggling endlessly as she held onto the microphone.

"Enough!" said the head official impatiently. "Someone else!"

Another citizen stepped forward from the crowd.

"I bought a loaf of bread and found a toothbrush in it. So I ate the bread and brushed my teeth."

No one even smiled.

"Enough, enough!" grumbled the official. "Once more, I will explain. Tell a real fact that is so amazing that when anyone hears it they will holler out, 'It can't be! It can't be!'"

So all the townspeople pondered a little longer, trying desperately to remember something which would astound the crowd.

Another citizen came to the microphone. "I saw this with my own eyes. In the morning they put a roof on the building. In the afternoon, a pigeon sat on it and went right through!"

Then another came. "Once, during a torrential rainstorm, I saw the street-cleaning machine going through the town pouring out water in order to wash the streets."

Throughout his talk, different people nodded their heads and said, "It was that way. It was."

And so up to the microphone other people came and went. One said that three families tried to put their keys into one keyhole because all three families had requisitions for the same home. He went on to say that yesterday an asphalted street had broken open for the seventh time so that tomorrow it could break open for the eighth time, but how? How?

The storyteller flowed on and on like a stream until he was exhausted, and no one said, "It can't be!"

Then, at the very last, hopeless moment, an old, old woman hobbled up to the microphone. Quietly, in a voice shaking from age, she began to speak:

"I'm a very ordinary, plain old lady. I knit and weave clothes for my grandchildren. And I did not come up here to tell you an unusual story. But I just wanted to tell you, standing here in front of this wonderful apparatus," and she jokingly touched the microphone, "that this would be a good time to use it to express my thanks to certain people. I live," she went on, "in a small room. One time, I felt some plaster falling down from the ceiling. I went to the housing authority. Immediately, they took me in and asked me to sit down. So I sat down. I asked them to repair the ceiling. They said that the next day at eleven o'clock, the workmen would come and make all the necessary repairs. The next day at the eleventh hour, on the minute it was eleven, truly they came. And the workmen repaired everything. Thank you to the housing authority. This is all I have to say." And the old lady moved quickly away.

The entire hill was very silent. Thousands were stunned. Even the officials were numb. The reporters couldn't write a thing because their fingers were frozen from shock.

Finally, the crowd revived. "What did she think she was talking about? Where did you hear of such a thing? Impossible! It can't be!"

Then the head official came to his senses. "The next morning? On the eleventh hour? On the exact minute of the eleventh hour? For a very plain and ordinary old woman?" He kept mumbling to himself, "knitting stockings..."

And everyone in unison proclaimed that this had to be the most unusual story in town.

Orchestral trumpets blared triumphantly. The people grabbed the astonished old grandmother and placed her on a pedestal. And on top of her kerchiefed head, they clapped a wreath of oak leaves.

The head offical addressed her. "And now our beloved grandmother, we will present you with your prize. Tell us what kind of gift you would like to have. Whatever your heart desires: a Volga refrigerator, a television with all the accessories. Don't hesitate. In our great Town we have everything."

The old lady thought for a while and then said, "I'm really a very plain and ordinary old woman. How much do I really need? I knit and darn clothes for my grandchildren. So, what I would really need..."

At the bottom of the hill, everyone was silent.

"... is a thimble. A plain, ordinary thimble so that when I sew the needle will not prick my finger."

The head official heaved a long sigh. "Truly, you are a wise and unpretentious woman." Overcome with emotion, he touched the oak leaf wreath on her head. "We will fulfill your need immediately."

A messenger left for the department store.

After awhile, he returned without bringing the thimble.

"I couldn't find one," he said.

Then about twenty messengers left for other nearby stores and purchasing areas. The crowd waited patiently.

But they also returned without success.

"This is very strange!" the high official shouted.

Then he waited, almost as though he were hoping that a thimble might fall from the sky. A drop of rain fell. The crowd began to disperse. The head official said sadly:

"I regret to inform you, grandmother, that in our great Town . . ."

The Carousel

THE OPERATOR OF THE CAROUSEL appeared to be completely bored. Not one child could be seen in the park. Even the wooden horses, with their half-open mouths, looked as though they were stifling yawns. It was catching, and I, too, yawned.

"Where are the children?" I asked, out of curiosity.

"Oh, they have been swung enough," replied the operator of the carousel. "Would you care for a ride?"

"I'm too old for that."

It would be embarrassing to be caught taking a turn on the carousel, but I allowed myself to be talked into getting on a horse. As I sat down, the operator started the motor.

"I have to fulfill my quota," he admitted, and with a flourish, he sat on an elephant beside me.

Slowly, the carousel began to turn.

"Do you find this boring?" I asked holding desperately onto the wooden saddle.

"Why now madam," he replied in a hurt tone, "is it possible to be bored while working in a worthwhile area of public service?"

"Worthwhile?" I felt that I must have misunderstood.

"Why, yes. This is an area, a section of public service. There is no such thing as an unrewarding profession in the service of the public," he explained as he urged his elephant on, "Every area of work requires maximum efficiency," he went on, pressing his heels into the elephant's sides, "and undivided attention."

Each time it went around, the carousel moved faster and faster like empty mill stones. My head began to whirl.

"It is important never to stay in the same place," the operator insisted. "That is why we keep moving forward and only forward. Isn't that right?" he asked with a furtive glance.

The wild speed had forced my mouth open and my head seemed to be filled with rushing air.

"Only forward! There can be no deviation from a straight course!" His shouts came effortlessly through the rushing air as he sat astride his elephant like some Maharajah. "How fantastic! Such spirit! Do you know what? We will pledge to increase our four revolutions to six in the same length of time!"

I turned green as a strong wave of seasickness swept over me. Weakly, I began to slide down from my horse.

"Deserter! No mercy!" Angrily, he struck me across my back.

Frantically, I clung to my horse's mane.

"You are improving! You have purpose! Soon, you will even be heroic!"

Suddenly, the automatic safety brakes of the carousel caught and it began to slow down.

"Did I give you enough turns?" the operator asked.

"Oh, yes, yes!" I replied. All I felt was an intense fear that I would never again unwind.

In a thundering voice, he boomed through the park, "Five turns in the space of a half-turn! Without any deviation from course!"

Translated by Dorothy Bowen

ROMUALDAS LANKAUSKAS

ROMUALDAS LANKAUSKAS was born in Klaipeda on April 3, 1932. He studied Russian language and literature at the University of Vilnius (1950-53) and worked on the editorial staffs of several Lithuanian periodicals. His collections of short stories include *Klajojantis smelis* (Wandering Sands), 1960; *Trecias seselis* (The Third Shadow), 1964; *Pilka sviesa* (Gray Light), 1968; and *Dziazo vezimas* (The Jazz Wagon), 1971. His selected stories were published in Russian under the title *Oseniye kraski zemli* (Autumnal Colors of the Earth), 1963. His two novels, *Vidury didelio lauko* (In the Middle of a Vast Field), 1962, translated into Russian and Polish, and *Tiltas i jura* (A Bridge to the Sea) aroused considerable controversy. He also wrote film scripts and plays, and translated several of the novels of Ernest Hemingway.

Romualdas Lankauskas

ROMUALDAS LANKAUSKAS

(1932–   )

The Striped Trolley Bus

I

SHE TURNED BACK from the cupboard and said,
"We're out of bread; I'll run to the store."
"All right," he nodded.
She slipped into the blue raincoat and went out. There was a sound of the slammed door. The steps on the stairs receded, their echo fainter until it vanished altogether.

The newspaper rustled in the wrinkled hands; the old man read slowly, his dry bluish lips moving slightly as if he was chewing word after word. Each time he read a newspaper, he searched in it for something new and unknown. The black rows of letters were always filled with mystery, repelete with all kinds of heart-stirring adventures. He would become so absorbed that he felt physically transported to some distant continent. He was always shaken by the laconic but in its essence horrible item about an airplane crash ("all the passengers were killed") and he would think: "Only yesterday they enjoyed the spring, and today, they are no more. Man's life is full of terrible accidents."

He read on, adjusting his slipping glasses, until a sudden grief pierced him: A woman's scream echoed in the street below, terrible, brief, and filled with horror.

He shuddered; the newspaper slipped from his hands and rustled to the kitchen floor. The scream died instantly and was not repeated again, but the silence that ensued was even more ghastly. He quickly got up from his chair, ran over to the window and looked down from the fourth floor. A yellow-striped trolley bus stood in the middle of the wet street——in front of the trolley bus, under its wheels, she sprawled. He clearly saw her feet, the worn shoes and the silver of a blue raincoat. A crowd was rapidly gathering about the trolley bus. People were yelling and jostling, but he could still see the blue raincoat.

He was startled by the dizziness flooding his head and instinctively clutched the window frame so as not to collapse. Agitation, terror, pain, they all vanished. Groping, as if in darkness, he reached the door and started down the staircase. It seemed to him that the stairs were interminable, that he kept descending endlessly into the dark bowels of the earth.

A cool sensation of raindrops on his face made him realize that he had reached the street. The yellow-striped trolley bus stood in front, the backs of onlookers were moving about. Many backs. He tried to push his way through them, but the backs were very many, and they all barred his way. Then a hoarse scream escaped his numbed throat:

"Let me through! Let me through! I'm her husband!"

The backs suddenly parted. He squeezed himself through. But the blue raincoat was no longer under the wheels of the trolley bus. She lay on the sidewalk, immobile, peaceful, and some man with a hat was kneeling next to her and checking her pulse. The man with the hat got up, glanced at the crowd, shrugged his shoulders imperceptibly and cast his eyes downward. Next to him stood a girl in a red sweater. Her face was unusually white, her cheeks and lips were twitching convulsively, as if she was trying in vain to say something. The old man realized that the girl was the driver of the trolley bus. He set upon her and clutched her sweater with his fingers; the buttons scattered from the sweater. His fingers were tearing at the sweater with a terrible force and several men had a hard time in prying them open.

"Murderess..." he said softly, but everybody heard it.

The girl broke into tears.

Afterwards——the wailing of an ambulance siren. The people moved aside. The flickering of white coats, a faint odor of drugs. The old man saw her arms hanging helplessly when they placed her on the stretcher and lifted it into the car.

The siren again, and the ambulance wailed away down the street. The people began to scatter in all directions, but he kept standing in the same spot, unable to move; his feet seemed to be glued to the asphalt. He still seemed to see the blue raincoat under the wheels of the trolley bus, but there was nothing there anymore, not even the blood stains, and then he saw again the driver's blanched face and turned away, afraid to gaze at it any longer.

"Why am I standing here?" He lifted his heavy feet off the asphalt and slowly crossed the street, feeling that he had become even older. It was raining harder and the old man heard the passing women open their umbrellas.

II

He opened bottles of brandy with his trembling thin fingers. The people were conversing about something in his room, but for him all the voices seemed distant, as if they came from behind the wall. He did not try to distinguish what they were speaking about and only intermittently a few distinct phrases reached his ears: "... she was a splendid woman," "He loved her dearly——look how much money he spent on the funeral meal!"

When they all dispersed after the funeral meal, the rooms turned very quiet and unusually empty. It was already dark outside; cars and motorcycles kept scurrying up and down the street; trolley buses howled by every several minutes. The air was filled with an irksome, irritating roar. Each time the old man heard the howl of an approaching trolley bus, he startled unawares and cowered. The lightning of electric sparkles would flash, the roar would recede, only to be heard soon again. It was an ugly sound.

He closed the windows tightly, but the echo of the howling still forced itself into the room. Even after midnight the trolley buses did not stop their droning. It seemed as if some frenzied beasts were chasing each other.

He pulled the blanket over his head, stuffed his fingers into his ears and lay without moving. Cars, trolley buses! Their noise and ceaseless roar annoyed him, but now he began simply hating them——it was all the yellow striped trolley bus's fault. How flat and disgusting was its snout! Yes, each trolley bus, each car has its own physiognomy, its typical features. He had noticed it more than once on the street. Some snouts are indifferent, squashed flat, others seem to be rapacious and insolent. And inside, always crowds of jostling people, especially on hot summer days, and that endless importing by the conductress: "Keep moving to the front! Tighter! Tighter! Get your tickets. Pass the change!" Or the poster above the window: "Beware of flu. Flu is a serious and infectious illness."

How had he managed to avoid catching the flu so far? How could he bear to ride the trolley buses at all? At night as he looked at the lighted windows of the trolley buses, the people inside looked like marionettes arranged by a stage director. Finished! Enough! He wouldn't be seen inside one of them as long as he lived.

It was only towards morning that he was able to catch a little sleep. When he got up, he sat down at the table and wrote a long resentful letter to the trolley bus company demanding payment for the funeral expenses and all the other damages. "A new blue raincoat was torn up, four rubles were spent for telegrams...."

III

Several weeks later, he received a negative answer: the trolley bus company refused to pay the bills he had enclosed. "So we've come to that," he thought almost jubilantly. "In that case, I'm going to slap a lawsuit on you. I won't leave you in peace for the rest of my life."

The case came on trial, and he won it. But the victory did not bring him much satisfaction; he started submitting new claims and requesting additional remuneration. One complaint followed another. Soon the whole city was talking that there was some fellow who wanted to make profit from his wife's funeral. Neighbors and acquaintances began to look at him with undisguised contempt and disgust. Friends turned their backs on him.

The howling of the passing trolley buses kept issuing from the street; they circled the city from early morning until late into the night. "Like giant striped dogs, attached to a chain," he would think, his fury rising. Sometimes a trolley bus would disengage from the overhead line, and the driver, with a throng gaping, would hurriedly clamber on the top. That sight always filled the old man with malicious joy. Soon the car would screech on, striking sparks from the copper wire, glistening in the sun. There was something imperturbable, inescapable in their ceaseless motion. A cruel invisible force inhered in them. He avoided looking at the street through the window, because every time he did so he thought he saw a blue raincoat and feet in worn shoes there below.

One day, when the old man was sitting in his room with a newspaper in his hands, the bell rang. He put the newspaper on the table and went to open the door.

A young woman in a red sweater stood in the corridor. He recognized her instantly. It was the same girl who drove the striped yellow trolley bus that day. She lowered her eyes unable to endure his stare; her pale face suddenly blushed.

"What do you want?" he asked her, furious.

The girl's lips trembled.

"I don't drive trolley buses any more," she said softly. "I'm selling newspapers now."

"What do you want?" he reiterated, raising his voice.

"I don't know . . . I just wanted to tell you . . ."

She choked and was silent.

"Go to hell!" he shouted and slammed the door.

It was silent outside the door for a little while; then he heard her steps receding. The girl was slowly descending. When the echo of her steps died away, he went back to the room and collapsed on the chair. Never before had he felt so lonely and utterly crushed. The ceiling pressed down against his head and shoulders. He felt that several thousand, no, a million tons were bearing down on him, and that he would not be able to withstand that weight, and suddenly jumping up from the chair, he ran out of the door and dashed into the street, as though trying to overtake someone.

1962   *Translated by J. Zemkalnis*

Kazys Almenas

KAZYS ALMENAS

KAZYS ALMENAS, born in Gruzdziai, Lithuania, on April 11, 1935, combines the vocations of a writer and a physicist. Now a resident of Maryland, he received his doctorate in physics at the University of Warsaw, Poland, in 1967. He published the collections of stories, *Begiai* (The Railroad Track), 1965, and *Gvyenimas tai keke vysniu* (Life is a Cluster of Cherries), 1967. His main interest lies in historical fiction, as exemplified by the two-volume novel, *Upe i rytus, upe i siaure* (River to the East, River to the North), 1964, set in the immediate post-Napoleonic era, and *Sienapjute* (Hay-harvest), 1970.

KAZYS ALMENAS

(1935-   )

The Yellow Buick

I REMEMBER HIM WELL. Too well, it sometimes seems to me.
The bushy blond hair. The impossibly wide smile. The sparse row of teeth. And his laughter: forced and always too loud.
Those overly dramatic gestures.
And, of course, that imagination of his. Poor Vladzhio...
My great friend Vladzhio.

I met him right at the beginning of my first term in college, during the very first ROTC session. My neighbor to the right was called Biro. He looked at me with a somewhat superior glance.
"You said your name was..."
I repeated my name.
"Oh yes (a wide smile). Mine's Biro. Friends call me Mike. We'll be friends, OK?"
He had an unmistakeable Slavic accent.
"Sure. It looks like we'll have to march together, anyway."
"Hell, these guys here know nothing about marching! Nothing!" he laughed. His laugh was so different from his speaking voice; it seemed as if someone else and not he were laughing. It was much too loud.
"I've known marching for a long time!"
"Yeah? When did you learn?"
"Oh, a long time ago. It's nothing—I have all kinds of experience." He shrugged, took out a pack of cigarettes and offered me one. As a rule, I didn't smoke, but in this case, I took one.
"You have to know the ins and outs, right? You got any more lectures?"
"No, this is my last one."
"Well, let's go and have a drink at the Union, then!" To seal the invitation, he slapped me soundly on the back.

I wasn't used to such a direct approach. Here in college, it seemed that everyone was sort of stuck up, and that all the joking and talking went on in groups to which I didn't belong. But Mike acted as though he didn't notice my reserve at all. He probably didn't.

"Oh, gee . . . nobody's in here," he said, after glancing around the Student Union cafeteria. He sounded disappointed.

"Who's supposed to . . ."

He smiled and blew some smoke out of the left corner of his mouth without bothering to take out the cigarette.

"No girls. I know a lot of girls here. But . . ." he gestured apologetically. Indeed the cafeteria was almost empty.

"Yes, that's too bad," I said, though to tell the truth, I wouldn't have known what to do if the place had been jammed with females. That first year, the girls all seemed to be very mature and I could never find the right thing to say to them.

So we sat. Mike seemed to take up all of the opposite side of the booth, and certainly all of the conversation. He laughed from time to time, always managing to sound too loud. He blew smoke at the ceiling, insisted that I smoke, too, and ordered two cokes.

It turned out that he came here from Slovakia. But now, he was an American citizen. Yes, he had his citizenship papers—he emphasized that fact. Yes . . . his father had a farm in Slovakia. A large farm—more than four hundred acres—with twenty, maybe more, farmhands. Not bad, ha?

Oh, but that damned war! What he lived through in that war! My God, nobody here could even begin to appreciate it.

"But you, well, you do understand, don't you?"

I nodded my head significantly, though to me the war was but a hazy childhood recollection. Mike was my age but at that time I didn't dare question his obviously superior capacity for suffering.

Yes, the damned war which these Americans don't understand . . . But now, that is over and he is an American himself. And that makes everything just fine again.

You just have to go to school and everything will be within reach—everything! And school's not hard. For instance, marching. He knew all there was to know about marching, from way back!

He's studying medicine. That's the only thing to be in. Want to know why?

He became serious, leaned on the table and looked directly at me. "You can help people. You're needed. Oh, yes, a doctor has a very important, very responsible job. He can do an awful lot of good. And you can earn plenty of money."

He gave me another one of his wide smiles and leaned back. "It's a fact! Who do you think have the biggest cars around here? Doctors, that's who! Yes, medicine—that's the only thing to study here."

He paid for my coke. I tried to protest, but he wouldn't hear of it.

"I invited you here and I'm paying. I have the money." He pulled out five dollars to prove this and winked at the girl by the cash register.

"I had a car but it broke down," he continued as we were going out.

To me, at that time, a car was a necessary but unattainable dream. "Really?"

"Yes. Know what kind?"

"No, a Ford?"

"Ha, a Ford!" he sniffed. "I had a Buick—a brand new one. You should have seen it! But I'll get another one. A Buick is a very good car."

We parted the best of friends. "We'll have to meet tomorrow," he said. We'll go to his house, yes? And watch TV. Oh, he has a huge TV set . . . OK?

I shrugged. Why not, after all? Why not . . .

He lived near the University in a frame house with creaky stairs. His mother met us. She was stout, with the flabbiness characteristic of a farm woman living in the city. The sleeves of her dress were very tight around her plump arms.

"Hya," Mike said loudly. "This is my friend, Mama." He spoke slowly, breaking up his words into syllables.

The woman smiled and nodded. "I learn speak English," she explained.

"Yes, Mama goes to language classes." Mike patted her shoulder. "She speaks very well already. Isn't that right, Mama?"

"Vladzhio wants all be Americans . . . learn speak English . . . Oh, so much!" She shrugged her shoulders but smiled as she did it.

"We're in America now, Mama . . ."

"Vladzhio?" I asked. "Not Mike?"

"Vladislav Biro. My Vladzhio, always . . ." she said glancing fondly at him. "Good name, Vladzhio. Holy name. Why Mike?"

"Ah, Mama doesn't understand that now, we're really Americans . . ." he interjected, somewhat at a loss.

"Americans . . . Oh, so much . . ." she said turning to me. "He is good boy, my Vladzhio."

"Oh, Mama! Let's go look at the TV. We have a big one—come."

A curtain hung in the doorway separating the two rooms. The room we walked into was cozy and unpretentious. Holy pictures hung on the walls and flowerpots jammed the windowsills. The sideboard and several small tables were covered with lace doilies and cluttered with faded photographs. In one corner there was a large velveteen couch covered with embroidered scatter pillows. A man rose from the midst of these.

"Hello, Father." Vladzhio turned toward me and made a face: "He doesn't speak any English at all."

Slowly his father came over to us. He was a hefty man, though shorter than Vladzhio, with red cheeks and tiny eyes that were almost hidden by bushy eyebrows. He looked a bit stooped.

Vladzhio said something in Slovak. The old man looked at me, then again at Vladzhio, blinking rapidly. Finally, a slow grin spread across his face.

"A Litvak!"

"Yes, Lithuanian."

He gave me his hard, rough hand.

"Sidiom," he said, nodding toward the sofa. *"Pazhalstva, sidiom."*

"Dad likes TV very much," Vladzhio explained.

The set was really big and was reverently placed right in front of the sofa. At the moment, a gang of bandits was galloping across the screen, shooting at random.

"—A, *charasho?*" asked the father and he nodded toward the screen. He grinned with self-satisfaction and showed a set of teeth much better than Vladzhio's

We sat there till suppertime. Mama proved to be an excellent cook and, despite my protestations that I wasn't very hungry, I really stuffed myself. Mama was constantly bringing in this from the kitchen or urging us to eat more of that, so that she hardly had time to eat anything herself.

This proved to be the final step in my initiation into Vladzhio's friendship. He was quite dramatic about it.

"My home is your home!" he said. "Now, we're truly friends, right?"

I agreed, though at the moment I couldn't think of any appropriate gesture with which to reciprocate and seal this new relationship. To tell the truth, I was quite pleased to have him for a friend. I didn't really fit in with the Americans and didn't know any Lithuanians. And some sort of friends are, after all, necessary. Vladzhio filled this void completely and enthusiastically. We spent almost all our free time together playing table tennis, swimming, or going to the movies. Vladzhio was always thinking up something to do and if I was reluctant to participate he badgered me into it. If my excuse was being broke, which was quite often true, he treated and wouldn't even hear about accepting repayment.

"That's what friends are for," he would say. "To share! Isn't that right?"

And, of course, we marched together during the ROTC drills, and when the weather became too cold for marching, we sat together during the ROTC instruction sessions. Vladzhio loved the course and the uniform. My own enthusiasm for things military had always been negligible but his gusto was catching and so for awhile, I also tried to be a "model cadet."

Vladzhio was sure he was one of the most exemplary cadets who ever attended the university, and he used to give me all sorts of friendly advice on how to affect the proper military manner. I remember how we used to swagger about after class in our blue uniforms, smoking, puffing up our chests and glancing about to see if anyone noticed how impressive we were. At such times Vladzhio used to laugh and talk even louder than usual. And he would yell "Hya, baby!" at passing girls. This last bit of audacity never failed to impress me.

My great friend, Vladzhio . . . I got used to his boisterous behavior and his tendency to brag, and even if I noticed certain discrepancies in his stories, I never paid them much attention. To be honest, this friendship was profitable to me and I could afford to give in some instances.

There was only one thing that puzzled me from the start. As far as I could see. Vladzhio never studied. On the other hand, as the first semester wore on, it became ever more apparent to me that one had to study here. It was a sad observation, but a true one. Consequently, it used to bother me when he came around with all sorts of new suggestions just when I had finished making solemn promises to myself that all frivolity was out and that life hereinafter would be devoted to studying.

"Good God!" I used to say. "What about you? Don't you ever have to study?"

Vladzhio immediately became serious. "Oh I have A's in all my subjects. Why should I study?"

That sounded somewhat unconvincing, especially since there was an unwritten rule that one should complain about being on the verge of flunking out no matter how good one's grades were.

Seeing that I was unconvinced, Vladzhio used to say something like, "Maybe not in Economics. I only got an 89 on that last test. Really messed up on that one!"

Hell, messed up! My own grades were in the low seventies, so I had no choice but to change the subject.

Though Vladzhio wasn't the only one who had such a high opinion of himself, Mama agreed with him completely. I recall vividly the desk in his room. The books were always arranged in a neat row, according to size, and the pencils were laying in a neat pile, their freshly sharpened points aligned in one direction. On a nearby shelf covered with an embroidered cloth, there was a vase and flowers. A picture of the Madonna hung on the wall. Mama smiled proudly as she showed me all this. It was obvious that she was the one who maintained this meticulous order.

"My Vladzhio learn here," she said, straightening a doily.

"He learn good." She lowered her voice respectfully. "He be doctor. Doctor, my Vladzhio." She looked at me as if to catch the surprise on my face. I nodded agreement.

"He be good doctor, my Vladzhio . . ." she finished almost in a whisper.

Time flew by. I remember how, for the longest while, it seemed that the semester had just begun and that tomorrow or, at the latest, next week would be the time for really serious study. Then, quite unexpectedly, there was an onslaught of exams and before I could get organized, or was even fully aware of what was going on, it was all over. The first semester had joined the ranks of history and, from my point of view, it should have been grouped there along with the times of pestilence, war and other comparable tragedies. I made grandiose plans for the next semester. It was to be a time for scholarship, sacrifice and forebearance. All my energy was to be sacrificed on the altar of knowledge. Amen.

I was true to my vow for a full week. And even later, though that planned rigid discipline crumbled, I was studying harder than ever before. This became a hindrance to my friendship with Vladzhio since time was the one commodity he always seemed to have plenty of.

"So you'll be cramming again?" he used to ask, wrinkling up his nose. "How much time do you need to learn a simple subject like Econ?"

This hit my ego pretty hard but there really wasn't anything I could answer.

But perhaps the one most important reason for the cooling of our friendship was his success in the ROTC. I couldn't even begin to match him in this area. I finally stopped trying and, like a "good loser," adopted a sarcastic attitude toward all that "solider playing." But Vladzhio practically lived for his uniform. He was the real star in that class. His shoes always shone like a well-polished mirror and the crease on his trousers looked sharp enough to cut bread. In class, he was always answering and always asking questions. Most of his questions weren't exactly profound but he asked them in a military manner and this, it seemed, was a more important aspect in this particular course. He used to raise his hand stiff and straight, and when the captain nodded toward him, he used to jump up and stand at attention.

"Captain, Sir, I would like to ask . . . Thank you, Captain, Sir!"

His shout was clear even if it had an accent. In general, our class wasn't exactly an enthusiastic one, so naturally Vladzhio became the captain's favorite. He received a promotion and the privilege to wear two stripes. In addition, he was accepted into the Military Club and this gave him one more stripe.

"To those that have, it shall be given," it says in the Good Book, and from that time on, I didn't care very much about walking around in uniform with Vladzhio. Those three stripes shone on his straight shoulders, and mine felt uncomfortably bare. Besides, he made a number of new friends at the Military Club whose chests were just as puffed out as his and who had just as many stripes as he.

So our friendship lost ground somewhat that second semester, but as far as Vladzhio was concerned, it was just as vigorous as ever. We used to slap each other very heartily on the back when we met. And Vladzhio would introduce me to his new friends and we'd drop in for a meal at his house.

At the end of that first year, as friends should, we got properly drunk together. We discussed the past, told all the dirty jokes we could remember and made grandiose plans for the future. We parted at dawn and I promised him I'd write. Friends must write each other!

Those good intentions remained with me all summer. But summers pass all too quickly, leaving little or no time for writing letters.

I returned to school with a good tan and a noble resolve to study.

Vladzhio came over the very first day. He burst noisily into my room, wearing a great big smile. "How are you, you so-and-so! Boy, you look good! Tell me all about it, man!"

I really had a lot to tell and was ready to do so but Vladzhio wouldn't give me a chance to open my mouth.

"Boy, you should hear what I did!" He could hardly contain

himself. "Guess what I have? Just guess!" He didn't even wait for me to give an ignorant shrug. "Want me to show you? Come on, come on—you'll see for yourself!"

He yelled over his shoulder as we hurried down the stairs, "I bought a car!"

"No kidding!" I yelled back. "What kind?"

"Brother what a car!"

We dashed out the door and right by the dorm, by the red line which meant "No Parking" there was a Buick. A brand new Buick! The sun glistened on its shiny new chrome and Vladzhio patted its mirrorlike top.

I was truly flabbergasted. A car in itself, any car, was just a dream. A *new* one would never have entered my mind.

"No ... Not this one! Really?"

His smile became even wider. "Well, what do you think? Do you like it? You should see it go! Oh, brother!" He made a sudden gesture with his hand—"Whoosh! You can hardly see it pass!"

I was speechless.

"I can go a hundred miles, believe it or not, a *hundred!*"

Only now did I notice a girl in the front seat. She was sitting on the edge of the huge, shiny seat. Her dress went well with the upholstery and, on the whole, the girl went well with the car. She reminded me of the girls one sees in car advertising posters. Just as slender, with a tight smile on her meticulously made-up lips.

"This is Lois," Vladzhio said, opening the door. "Lois, this is that friend of mine I've been telling you about. My very good friend."

Lois' smile didn't change. I must have stared at her because she suddenly lowered her eyes. But she quickly regained her composure. She had a somewhat narrow nose in a narrow face, but was very stylish—almost too stylish. Her hair was as beautifully groomed as any girl's on a magazine cover, and her dress seemed to be uncomfortably tight for a warm day. She shook hands with me very gently, very stylishly.

"How do you do? Very glad to meet you."

"Of course, you should be glad!" Vladzhio put his arm around her. "This is my girl. Not bad, ha?" he said, laughing. "Well come on. I'll give you a ride!" Vladzhio was getting impatient.

"Oh boy, how it goes! Zoom! Everyone out of my way!"

The front seat was big enough for all three of us. Lois sat straight up, with her hands folded in her lap. Vladzhio shifted gears very gently.

"The police were after me, yesterday. You should have seen it, through half the town! But how can those Fords catch a Buick?" He turned a smooth, practiced corner and we started down the road. The speedometer was climbing slowly but steadily, and the car was moving as smoothly as silk. You could hardly tell that you were actually riding.

"When school starts, we'll really live it up, right?" He winked at me. "This year will be different, you'll see. You'll find yourself a girl. OK?" He patted Lois' thigh and let go with a loud and meaningful laugh.

I finally got a chance to ask something. "Where did you get the money?"

His eyes gleamed. "Know-how, Brother! You just have to know how. Live right—that's what I say. Hey, look, we're doing eighty!"

The needle was quivering near the eighty mark. We hadn't passed the city limits yet and I looked back to see whether anyone was after us.

"Do you believe that I can go a hundred?" he asked.

"Oh yes, I don't doubt it," I replied.

"Of course! With a beauty like this? Where have you ever seen anything like this? You should see the neighbors stare!"

We rode around for a long while and Vladzhio showed me everything about the car: how it turned, stopped, how the brakes worked, the radio, how he could press a button and a spray washed the windshield. I was genuinely impressed and tried not to let my jealousy show. Lois sat quietly, occasionally smiling at Vladzhio's constant chatter. She, too, impressed me. She was quite young but nevertheless very poised. There seemed to be a certain mystery behind her silence and her thin smile.

Such was the beginning of our second year, and so it continued for a while. Vladzhio, the car and Lois became an inseparable trio. We used to meet at the Union, and after a cup of coffee it became a must to get into the car and circle around a few blocks. I used to see him with a carful of his uniformed friends and with Lois—as always, smiling; as always, wearing a tight dress.

Her illusion of mystery, unfortunately, didn't last long. She only had to open her mouth a few times to change that air of serene maturity into one of naive childishness. By the second year of college, my expectations with regard to the reasoning power of girls had taken a steep nosedive. But even then, Lois was something else again: a queer mixture of child mentality, fantasy and fashion. She didn't go to college and I doubt if she had ever finished high school. But Vladzhio liked her. He could show her off, and she complemented the Buick.

Despite this new-found status, Vladzhio remained my friend. This is just about the way he put it himself. "We're still friends, right?"

"Of course," I agreed. "What else?"

We used to play ping-pong in the dorm—he used to come to see me in my room. My roommate didn't appreciate these noisy visits at all and glared at us from his bunk. He used to talk about his Buick, tell me what went on at the Military Club, how smoothly things were going for him and, of course, he always talked about women. How did I like Lois?, he would ask. And then he would listen intently to my answer.

"Oh, Lois is fine . . . a fine girl," I would reply.

"If you only knew how much Lois loves me!"

"Really?"

"Oh, boy!" His laugh was forced, as always. "I can't get her to leave me alone. Especially at night. Some woman!" He winked at me and then grinned with an all-knowing grin.

"Is that right?" I tried to appear as nonchalant as possible. "That's not so bad."

To tell the truth, I didn't really believe him. He was a good talker, I knew, with a good imagination.

Up until that time, I remember Vladzhio very clearly—my great friend, Vladzhio: his silly laugh and his oversized imagination. I remember his pride behind the wheel of the Buick, the noisy games of table tennis and the tight little smile on Lois' face.

These memories are real—a part of my first two years in college. Some day, they'll be part of the memories of my youth. The good times will seem to have been better, the more boring ones will fade and Vladzhio will always remain there with that broad smile on his face.

What happened later seems to belong to another time. It has nothing whatever to do with college, with my life there, or with Vladzhio. It doesn't fit into my memories and it never will. Even then, at that time, I felt like a spectator watching some unreal drama in which the actors weren't suited for their parts.

Two months of the new semester had gone by. Vladzhio came into my room after having first knocked on the door. That, in itself, surprised me since Vladzhio never bothered to knock before. His manner was very strange and he hardly laughed at all. He just sat on the edge of the bed and was intently cleaning his fingernails with his pocket knife. It was obvious he had come to see me for a specific purpose.

"What would you say if I told you I wanted to get married?" he asked in a deliberately casual tone.

"Well, get married, of course," I answered, going along with his joke.

"I mean, really get married . . ."

"What!"

"Get married," he repeated.

"Are you completely nuts?"

For a short while, we were both quiet. I was waiting for Vladzhio to burst into laughter—to fall back on the bed in a laughing fit.

He licked his lips. "Why not?"

"Lois?"

His smile was forced. "We . . . we love each other . . ."

It was hard for him to say it. The words were trite, heard in dozens of movies, and now they sounded sillier than they did on the screen.

I nodded, still unsure if I shouldn't laugh instead.

Vladzhio stood up and crossed the room to the window. "You

wait till you fall in love . . ." He turned toward me as if he had wanted to say something else but changed his mind. "You'll see. And besides, Lois wants to get married."

He really wasn't joking. "Yes," I said without conviction, "Lois is a good girl."

Vladzhio smiled. "And how! You couldn't find another one like her anywhere. Really!" He tried to resume his usual manner of speaking. "And she really loves me. Oh, brother! Yesterday, for instance . . ."

My thoughts were in a turmoil. World War III would have been less of a surprise. We were both nineteen, and I had never even thought of marriage. I knew that some Americans married that young but, in my opinion, that was just another example of their typically immature behavior.

"Yes, I'll get married," Vladzhio continued, sounding as if he were trying to convince himself. "My friend Steve's married. You know Steve. He's only a sergeant in my company and he's been married for quite some time now—something like two months. If he can get married, why can't I? I have a better car than he has, I have money . . . and we love each other," he added slowly. But his words sounded as hollow as before.

I didn't really believe it until the very day of the wedding. To tell the truth, I didn't quite believe it even afterward. The ceremony itself seemed unreal.

There weren't many guests, but everything went according to established traditions. Vladzhio looked like a waiter from a plush restaurant in his white dinner jacket with a red flower tucked in his lapel. His smile seemed a bit sickly. I remember trying to look at his knees to see whether they were trembling.

His uniformed friends were there, of course, with all sorts of stripes and ribbons on their coats. And Lois was the center of it all—very pale and unbelievably tiny-waisted. Her white gown billowed out below and above, while the middle was pinched into nothingness. She shyly clutched her white lily bouquet and smiled in answer to the stream of congratulations, repeating: "Oh, thank you . . ." over and over again with a theatrical inflection.

I was late and missed the ceremony itself. I met the newlyweds as they were coming out of the church. But I was a full participant in the important festivities that followed.

Of course, the picture-taking came first. We all lined up and smiled until our cheeks ached. The bright lights made our eyes water, and the photographer danced around his big black box doing his best to make us smile more.

Later, we rode the streets with all horns blowing and finally ended up in a cold, rented hall, ready to start the proceedings. Everyone ate a piece of that white, cloyingly sweet wedding cake. Vladzhio, of course, cut and Lois put the fragile slices on plates. We had some wine and Vladzhio's colleagues made a poor attempt at singing. Before long, there was nothing to do and we all sat around waiting to see if we'd get anything more to drink. But since no drinks came, we scattered some more rice about and someone tied a bunch of old shoes and tin cans to Vladzhio's Buick. Then, horn blaring and cans rattling, Vladzhio and his bride drove off. Lois turned around and waved, and the photographer used his blindingly flashing camera to capture the moment for posterity.

I remember thinking that all he had to do now was carry Lois over the threshold, and everything would have been done according to the book. I have no doubt that he did exactly that.

Vladzhio came back a week later with his Buick and his slim, stylish wife. They both came in to see me, ignoring the fact that it was against the rules for girls to be in the dorms.

"But she's my wife, now!" Vladzhio explained with a laugh. "A *wife,* not a girl," he said, patting her shoulder.

I looked them both over critically. It seemed that people should change somehow, after they got married, but Vladzhio looked the same as always. He was, as usual, very verbose and now he really had a lot to talk about. They had an apartment—only a few blocks north of here. I must come and see them—definitely.

"My home is your home," he repeated.

I felt like asking whether this applied to his wife as well. But Vladzhio wouldn't understand that sort of joke.

When I went to visit them, I couldn't get rid of the feeling that this was all a game, even then. The apartment was small but nice, with a rug in the living room. The kitchen was clean and filled with gleaming cabinets. There was a large television set in the living room, which came equipped with remote control. Vladzhio showed me how he could change the channels by simply pressing some buttons while sitting in his chair. Lois served some cookies and coffee in tiny cups, and we watched TV. She sat on Vladzhio's lap and he nuzzled her neck. I felt awkward and out of place but didn't know how to leave gracefully. We had more coffee and Vladzhio constantly used commercial time to change the channels by pressing his remote control buttons.

I never went there again.

"Who knows?" philosophized my roommate, "maybe it's catching. Pretty soon, you'll be wanting a yellow Buick yourself, and a wife to go with it."

"If I ever bought a Buick, it sure as hell wouldn't be yellow!" I retorted. "And you can forget about the wife."

But Vladzhio used to come over to see me. He would bring along armloads of books and assured us that he studied them all. He became more serious and somewhat thinner and we laughed at this. That's what one should expect from a bridegroom after all.

"You should see how hard I'm studying," Vladzhio said. "Things are different now. I have responsibilities. I'm going to be a doctor, you know, and now I have to earn a living for my family." By then, I was quite used to the pattern of his conversation and merely nodded my head.

Perhaps I'm imagining it. Looking back, it's easy to see all sorts of things now. But it seems that even then I had noticed a marked change in Vladzio. His famous grin seemed to stretch and then break off like a drawn-out string. He also seemed to have lost a lot of his noisy boisterousness and what was left was much more false, much more put on. I had the feeling that he used to come for something else besides the usual talk. It was as though he wanted to ask something or even—which is, after all, much more difficult—to say something important. Our conversations used to run down after awhile and we would sit together, not knowing what to do, until Vladzhio started telling some silly joke or other, or until he left.

But, of course, I could be imagining this now, very easily.

o'clock in the afternoon. I was called to the dorm office to answer the phone. I remember going down the stairs and trying to guess who the hell would be bothering me right before the finals. It turned out to be Lois. She spoke hesitantly and had to repeat herself.

"Mike is dead . . . I don't know. He was killed . . . yes . . . no . . . I don't know . . . in the car . . . on the road . . . I have to go to the police station . . . I don't want to. Oh, I don't want to! . . . Please . . . I don't want to . . ."

I don't remember whose voice shook more, hers or mine. "That's all right," I told her. "I'll go." There was a click and I was left holding the receiver.

Got killed? . . . What sort of joke is this? Are you all crazy? My God! She's really crazy! I tried dialing her number but I'd forgotten it. Then, with shaking hands, I aimlessly riffled through the phonebook until I noticed that the clicking of the typewriter had stopped, and the office girl was staring at me. I gathered my wits and slowly dialed the police station.

"Biro," I said. "Did a Biro get killed?"

"Who? This is the police."

"I'd like some information . . . about an accident. About Biro . . . Mike Biro."

"Just a moment." The voice at the other end was calm. "We'll check it out."

I heard the rustle of paper and someone sneezing.

"V. Biro?" asked the voice. "B-i-r-o? Yes, we have papers like that. Can you come to identify him? Are you a relative?"

"No. Are you sure it's Biro?"

"That's what the papers say. We have his driver's license. Where can we reach his relatives? We called his wife but she didn't say a word."

"Yes," I said. "I'll be right over."

The big red-faced sergeant sitting behind the desk gave me an impatient glance. "Oh yes," he nodded. "Oh yes, we have him here. We've been waiting for some time now for someone to come."

He led the way, whistling softly through his teeth, his steps keeping time to the tune. We went down a narrow passageway with no windows. The white light came from recessed fluorescents in the ceiling. When we reached a heavily bolted metal door, he stopped and buttoned his collar.

"It's cold in there. It's OK in the summer but unpleasant in the winter." He paused and thought awhile, "Have you seen corpses before?"

I nodded.

"He's not your brother?"

"My friend."

"Yes, it's sad . . . Really sad. We get all kinds of them here." He pulled at the bolt and the heavily insulated door opened with a metallic rustle. The cold air hit us like a gust of chilly wind. The room was small and on one side there was a row of what looked like metal file cabinets with huge square doors. The sergeant opened door number five. It contained a wheeled hospital stretcher. I saw a corner of a white sheet. It felt as if my heart were beating high up in my throat, and I was afraid.

The sergeant pulled at the cart. It slid out silently and easily on its rubber wheels. I could see a pair of shoes. One was sticking straight up, the other was at a slight angle. One of the corpse's arms was lying across its chest.

"He won't be very pretty," warned the sergeant as he pulled the sheet off the upper part of the body.

I waited, my nerves taut, and tried to form some image, some picture, beforehand, so I wouldn't flinch too obviously.

No, he wasn't pretty, but it certainly was Vladzhio: the familiar bush of blond hair and there, on the right, where, strangely, there wasn't any blood at all, his blond crewcut looked as if it had just been combed. There was no forehead on the left side. It was caved in, like some nutshell, down to the earline. That side of the face was just a black mass of blood, and a blood-red jawbone stuck out from the middle. The left eye must have been crushed and forced down. The right eye was open.

"Do you know him?"

I nodded, without speaking. I wanted to ask him to pull the sheet over that head for I was very close to vomiting.

"It's too bad . . . too bad . . ." he muttered as he carefully replaced the sheet. "But he died quickly." He pushed the cart and it slid quietly back into its cabinet. Then the door slammed shut. The accident was sudden. Vladzhio never knew what hit him.

Currents of warm air surrounded us outside and I became even more nauseated. Vladzhio had died quickly. Really quickly . . .

As we walked back, the sergeant said nothing.

"He has a wife," I said, for some reason.

"Too bad . . . Too bad."

I had to sign some papers. I gave them Vladzhio's parents' address. They would notify them, and the body would have to be claimed within three days.

"How do you guys manage to do these things?" the sergeant asked after he had finished the reports. "How do you do it? A bright, clear day . . . an even, dry road . . . and to hit a *bridge!*"

I just wanted to leave, to get out of there as quickly as possible. "I don't know," I said. "A bridge?"

"A new, wide, perfectly good bridge. On that stretch of Route 66 that they just fixed up—just thirteen miles out of town. How do you guys manage to do it?"

I finally managed to get away. For awhile I was afraid I'd start throwing up right there in the station. I stood at the bottom of the outside steps and tried to keep down the rising feeling of nausea. The sun was shining through the clouds, shining westward, where Route 66 ran. Somewhere it was whining on Vladzhio's bridge. Along the sidewalk, piles of dirty snow were slowly melting.

Lois was sitting on the corner of the couch, her slender hands folded in her lap. She looked like a doll in a doll's house. She was staring straight at me, her small, narrow face expressionless. But she said nothing.

On my way over to see her, I tried to imagine how she would act: maybe she'd cry, hunched up on the couch, or dash around the apartment aimlessly. I counted on having to calm her down . . . tried to think of what I'd say and even put a few calming sentences together.

But she just sat there, thin and pale—but no more so than usual—wearing a tight, navy blue dress. She bit her lower lip. "Is the car smashed?"

It was an unexpected question. I hadn't even thought about the car. But there was no doubt at all about it being wrecked.

"Yes, it's smashed. Smashed completely."

Her lips trembled. "Smashed? OK—now they can have it back! Since they want it so bad, now they can have it . . . stupid jerks . . ." She stopped talking briefly and stared at the floor. "Jerks . . . always after their lousy hundred ten bucks a month." She looked at me and shook her head. "Poor Mike . . . he got the car last summer and they're still after more money. Twice, he paid them a whole hundred and ten dollars, and then the following month, they were after him again! Poor Mike . . . they said they'd take the car away from him. Would you believe that?" She stopped talking again and stared at her hands. "OK, they can have it now!" She finished what she had had to say and sat there silently, her throat working and a slight tremor shaking her thin shoulders.

I crossed the carpeted floor to the place where the fancy TV set should have been. It wasn't there. In that silent room, both of us noticed at the same time the void that was so apparently there.

Lois straightened her back and tried to smile. "Oh, that!" Her voice sounded quite normal now. "We didn't want it any more. We had taken it on trial, anyway, but didn't like it and returned it. Actually, it was much too small for us. They have bigger ones now, so Mike told them they could have it back."

I nodded. Some of the tension had left her face, and she looked away.

"What'll they do now?" She was afraid again." . . . with Mike? . . . I won't have to . . . oh, I don't want to!"

"No, his parents will take care of it."

"But, I'll have to . . ." She caught her breath briefly. "I'll have to go to the funeral? They'll bury him, won't they? Oh, I'd rather not! Poor Mike . . . oh, poor, poor Mike . . ."

She turned toward me like a small, frightened child. "He was so educated! And such a good student. He was always going to the library at night, leaving me by myself. He used to stay there all evening, but I didn't complain. He had so much studying to do. Doctors need to know such an awful lot!" She nodded her head, trying to drive this fact home, "Such a lot! And they can help people so much. That's why Mike wanted to be a doctor. His mother always said I was too uneducated for him, but I never did know how to study," she shrugged. "Never. But Mike knew. Poor, poor Mike . . ."

She settled back on the couch again and I sensed that this time she had really finished; she had nothing else to say. I felt horribly helpless. There was nothing more to say, no way to comfort her—no words, no gestures, nothing. It had always been difficult for me to talk with Lois. Now it seemed impossible. As I got up to leave, she extended her fragile little hand and smiled.

Walking down the stairs, I remember thinking what a brave girl she seemed to be able to smile in such circumstances. Outside, it dawned on me that this was Lois's usual "goodbye": the same tight little smile, the same nerveless little gesture.

The funeral was not part of the play. It stands out from that chaotic jumble of events: clear, irrevocable and final. That day, I truly buried Vladzhio. It was cold, and I had lost my gloves. The grave plunged downward, near my feet, and there, at the bottom, was the end of all that ever began. The frozen piles of earth around the pit looked out of place amidst the snow-covered cemetery. They lowered the casket, pulled up the ropes and left it there, black and lonely in the icy earth.

Vladzhio's mother started weeping loudly as the casket was being lowered. Her voice tore out of her as if it had overflown some great dam. It wailed, rose in pitch and then broke, and her body shook. She had difficulty catching her breath between the racking sobs.

Vladzhio's father stood beside her, hunched over, wearing a threadbare, obviously refugee-camp vintage coat, one arm tightly gripping his wife's shoulders. Tears were slowly rolling down his frostbitten cheeks.

My fingers were freezing, and there was a cold feeling of emptiness inside me. The priest's words echoed in my ears: meaningless, incomprehensible words, like the sound of rain hitting a slack tent surface. Only one word many any sense, and it put everything else into perspective: amen.

"Amen, amen, amen . . ." reverberated in my brain. I wanted to cry, to scream like Vladzhio's mother; to spew out that feeling of emptiness, that inner cold, those memories: that one open eye and the other that wasn't even there . . . And I knew that now, everything was truly finished.

"Finished, finished . . ." I repeated to myself. That knowledge beat against my eardrums with every step I took. Finished. And I knew then what the word meant.

"Come spring, and you'll disintegrate, Vladzhio. Your one and only eye will rot." My thoughts revolved about this one idea. And there was something which I realized very clearly, without even having to think about it. For the first time in my life, I knew that I, too, would die some day. And I was afraid of death. I had to grab on to something, some other word or idea, and force this hollow drumming out of my brain.

"Why?" I asked myself, and the question seemed to have meaning. "Why, this way? Why did that bridge have to get in your way on a straight, smooth road, Vladzhio? Why, on a sunny, winter day, Vladzhio?"

After leaving the cemetery, I turned to walk down to the bus stop. I had no desire to ride back to town with Lois. Suddenly, wheels braked on softly, crunching snow and a car pulled up beside me. It was our captain, the one Vladzhio had admired so much. I recalled seeing him at the funeral, standing a bit farther away from the grave, his military cap under his arm. I got in and thanked him.

The captain was silent and thoughtful, looking straight ahead. "It's a shame," he repeated several times, as if to himself. "It sure is a shame. You were a friend of his, weren't you?"

"Yes, we were old friends."

"And he was married?"

"Over two months . . ."

"Too bad. And only two weeks ago, he almost cried when he said his good-byes."

"He said good-bye to you?"

The captain gave me a questioning look. "Yes, two weeks ago . . . when we had to let him go."

I didn't understand at all what he was talking about. The

captain fell silent.

"Why?" I finally managed. "Why did you let him go?"

"If you're suspended by the University, we have to let you go. We're just part of the University here, though we certainly would have liked to keep Biro. He did a lot to boost the morale of the whole platoon. But what could we do if he couldn't pass any of his other subjects?" He looked at me. "Maybe you know why he did so poorly in school? Last year, the ROTC was the only course he passed. He dropped or failed all of his other subjects."

I was hearing words, but not understanding any of them. Vladzhio had flunked out? It made no sense at all.

The captain went on, after awhile. "This year, we had to ask for special consideration for him. They took him back on probation. But what can you do . . . he didn't do any better . . . and he was such a model cadet! It's a shame . . . double shame, now!"

The captain drove me right to my dorm. I was so upset and confused that I almost forgot to thank him for the ride. I watched him drive away, and slowly repeated the words I had just heard: Vladzhio flunked out . . . thrown out of the University! "Lies!" I said to myself. "It *can't* be. The bastard's lying, and poor, dead Vladzhio can't defend himself."

But then I caught myself. "Is he *really* lying? It doesn't make any sense . . . but why? *Why?*

The "Why" took on a different meaning, now and something began to dawn on my consciousness. I sensed something, without really understanding what, and I was afraid to face a new and unexpected truth. Now, there seemed to be an answer to the "Why?" I sensed it, and knew that I had only to get rid of my fear and uncertainty and the matter would finally be settled.

I ran up the stairs and asked my roommate to let me use his car. Without asking too many questions, he threw me the key and I located his beat-up Chevrolet at the end of the street. The cold metal stuck to my skin as I tore open the door. I sat there stiffly for awhile and watched my breath form a hazy white curtain on the windshield. I was tense, almost groggy, and still strangely afraid, and my teeth chattered, partly because of the cold.

I whispered to myself, "What reason could the captain have for lying? Hell, Vladzhio, he *wasn't* lying! No matter how much you smile, Vladzhio, he *wasn't* lying. The lie is yours—only yours. And, oh God, how many lies there were!"

I felt something rising in my throat and pressed my forehead against the cold glass. Then the tears came. I hadn't cried for a long, long time, and I tried to hold them back but it was no use. The intensity of my feeling had risen, and when it seemed that I'd burst, the tears came. I sobbed, and it sounded strange—like someone else, not me, crying in that cold car with frosted windows. With a stiff hand, I tried to wipe the tears, but they kept coming. Everything was wavering and dancing in front of my eyes, like an unfocused movie. Then slowly, things began to take shape again.

"My God, Vladzhio, what did you do, then? What did you do when they finally kicked you out? Mama's doctor, what did you do?"

I could feel the torment that must have overwhelmed Vladzhio for a year and a half. "For one entire year and a half, it kept closing in on you, Vladzhio, and you kept inventing new lies. But the truth finally caught up with you. And then there wasn't any place to run. God, they even wanted to take the Buick from you! The shiny, yellow Buick! And the blond TV set . . . the uniform with its stripes . . . and the doctor that Mama believed in . . . What then, was left?"

I suddenly, and very clearly, realized what I had to to. I started the car and the cold engine sputtered and then choked awhile before it actually started. Not like the Buick, brother! Not like the Buick at all! That car could really run. It could do a hundred easy. You could get away from anything.

I turned into University Street. It was early afternoon; the traffic wasn't bad and I happened to hit all green lights going through the shopping centers. Soon, I was on Route 66. The town ended suddenly at this point, and the road led into a huge bend. I stepped on the gas and the car lunged forward. The engine labored, caught again and then assumed a strange whining sound. The cracked right window rattled and the steering wheel vibrated in my hands.

"Not like the Buick, brother!" The Buick was quiet; it loved roads like this. "Did you hear your own heartbeat, Vladzhio, when you were making this turn?"

The car left the curve and headed downhill. Here, the road followed the ups and downs of the rolling hills. Red, snow-covered barns were scattered here and there along the road. The wind whistled amidst gusts of powdered snow and the tires whine as the car plodded ahead.

"Run, Vladzhio, run! Floor it, man! down to the very bottom. The Buick is sure to do a hundred. Run!"

The car made another downhill dive, leaving a nauseous feeling in my stomach, and the momentum carried it up to the top of the next hill. The engine whined, pushing it on.

"You're not smiling, Vladzhio. God, you used to smile so much! But did your *eyes* smile? Did *they* ever really smile—or was it just your *lips?*"

The car hugged another curve, jumped a small hill and then, all of a sudden, the road straightened out and headed into the horizon. It looked like a railroad track: shiny black and losing itself somewhere up ahead. The wheels of the car were humming smoothly now.

And then I saw the bridge: far ahead, like a child's toy placed right on that smooth road leading into the horizon. Slowly, it grew longer; and then, straddling the road, it expanded and rose up over the horizon.

I understood then that there was no place for us to run. "No place, friend Vladzhio, no place at all!"

The bridge was swallowing the road even faster now. Freshly painted columns held up a mass of riveted steel. Just a bit to the right now . . . I gritted my teeth and had to use all my strength to keep the car moving straight ahead. The bridge beams merged into a continuous blur; the whiny sound changed to a smooth rattle; and then, I was over. I stopped the car, then drove it to the side, and tried to think. But there wasn't anything to think about. So I turned it around and started back—slowly, this time.

Translated by the Author

Juozas Aputis

JUOZAS APUTIS

JUOZAS APUTIS, born in 1936 at Balciai, Lithuania, graduated from the faculty of history and philology at Vilnius University and worked as a journalist. His collections of stories include *Zydi biciu duona* (The Bread of Bees is in Flower), 1963; *Rugsejo pauksciai* (The Birds of September), and *Horizonte bega sernai* (Wild Boars Against the Horizon), 1970, which established him as one of the major prose writers of Lithuania.

JUOZAS APUTIS

(1936-   )

Wild Boars Against the Horizon

Rue, green rue,
Let me go home,
Rue, green rue.

THAT EVENING, HE FELT himself oddly alienated. And perhaps everything around him was strange, because Petras Gvildys had never felt so sharply about his surroundings. Staggering slightly, he climbed the hill on which a white lookout tower had been built from poles last year, but you did not need it—from the hill, one could see far and wide, and the sun was setting anyway, waiting for no one in its pitiless haste to drown the woods, and the peat bog, where Gvildys left the tractor in darkness and then to submerge the Satrija mountain looming in the distance and the fields with clover in bloom. As he looked beyond the horizon, Gvildys felt in his heart a sadness that does not come frequently in life, a sadness that makes you feel like the world's clock, not of the winding kind, but one on which everything depends. You radiate lights and colors, you water animals and let men drink in rivers, you build nests for birds and protect their bare nestlings, you regulate things most intellectual, and if you weren't around, each and all would fall on their knees, both things living, and dead, and, ah: Lord, o Lord!—then you perceive that one day you will be no more. Thus comes the great pain and longing because you realize that you are a god who knows that he must die.

Gvildys sat down on a large lichen-covered stone, his head was growing dizzy, he did not want to go home yet; the man still wanted to be a lord for a while, to go back to his childhood. Our childhood pursues us every hour of our longing and sadness. We run to it as toward a well. Water is never absent there because only in childhood are we true gods and only in childhood can we dig wells to satisfy the thirst. Then one day we begin to understand that we are rolling a stone up the hill and that we will never get it there. But we refuse, we refuse to let it go.

The man looked around. One could see very far away. The sun flooded the fields with light, and tractors were crawling across the faraway hills against the horizon, they resembled wild boars that once upon a time, after the war, Gvildys recalled, would come from the forest and clamber on the potato piles. The bottle he had emptied made his head swim. It was already difficult to distinguish anything there. The man got up and walked down the hill. He had to go home, you can't stay on a hill forever; you have to get down and return. He opened the door softly and cautiously crossed the anteroom in order not to give himself away, he tried to chase his blues away, to cheer up. Two children ran out of the kitchen, grasped his hand and started to tug him. Gvildys did not say good evening but merely put his heavy hand on his wife's shoulders. A vague premonition flashed through his hot and dizzy head. His wife said nothing but kept rattling the dishes, upbraided the children, pushed a chair; her incomprehensible wrath kept rising and growing. Suddenly, she snatched a broom from the corner and began to stalk her husband. Her eyes were terrible, Gvildys had never seen such before. He tried to laugh but had no more time—sharp stalks stabbed his face, the man felt a horrible pain, while his wife let out an unusual scream. Clutching his face with his hands, the man still managed to see her. His wife stood there as if crazed, her arms hanging, her hair disheveled. Trembling, she whispered,

"That's for your drinking, that's for your bottle, for not caring about your home, for not caring about anything here . . ."

She most probably did not hear her own words, she was not able to comprehend with any certainty why she had done it. Nor would she ever be able to comprehend. She was a woman, she had raised children, more than once she had stared through the narrow window of the cottage when the children screamed or pestered her almost to death, she had stared through that window many times, strange sounds lured her away from home, where almost nothing mattered for her any more—neither the forest, nor the meadows, nor the animals, and—what a terrible thing to say—not even the children. She would remember her mother, who was young once also, and had raised her children in her young days, she used to tell something similar to her daughter, and yet of what would her mother get hold in her hour of hopelessness, of what?

His face in his hands, he sat down at the table, Racking pain scraped his eyes. The children were clustered in the corner, dirty and frightened and their mother did not move, either. Gvildys got up, groped for the towel on the wall, tied it about his face, wrapping his left eye with it. He could still see a little with his right eye. Then crouching, staggering, he left the cottage, stumbled on the bicycle in the barn and pedalled away.

Progress was difficult, the sun had set already, darkness fell swiftly but Gvildys knew each path and he pedalled quickly through the field of clover.

In the dispensary he was told that he had no chance whatsoever of saving his left eye, and that there was doubt about the right eye as well, if the nerve was injured. Would he be able to travel immediately to Siauliai or Kaunas, there are more doctors there. He would have to hurry or it would be too late soon. If he did not have money now, the doctor could lend him some and his wife could repay it in a day, or two.

Gvildys stood in the dispensary, peering at the tiny bulb through his swollen right eye, and decided not to hurry. There would be time to get there tomorrow; nothing would run away. They did a better job of bandaging his face in the dispensary but his left eye was completely gone, only a terrible fire was burning there, and his swollen right eye did not see too well, either.

Without saying good-bye, Gvildys walked his bicycle toward the beerhouse, where one could get a stronger drink. There was no shortage of people inside, they all took note of Gvildys, they pounced on him with questions. Some tried to poke fun at him, others lamented, for such happenings were not that frequent in their village. Gvildys did not respond to their questions. Perhaps, if he had not climbed the hill this evening, if not for that painful longing, he might have tried to console himself with his neighbors and tell his story, but now everything was not that simple. Gvildys found an unoccupied worn table in a corner and sat down. If he had ever seen the painter's earless self-portrait, he would certainly have thought how woefully alike they were, now.

The people did not settle down, they kept bothering him with questions, but Gvildys refused to open his mouth. When a girl in a white smock approached him, he quietly asked her for a bottle and some bread and then he continued staring through his white bandage over the people's heads.

He emptied one tumbler and rested his chin on his hand. He looked awful. In one corner, a voice was heard saying that it might not be a bad idea to call a militiaman—can't you see that Gvildys has gone crazy—but someone else spat out a curse and ridiculed the jittery fellow.

When he had downed a second tumbler, his wife's father came over to his table. He was old and already thin as a lath with shaggy gray hair, and knotty hands. The old man sat down with his back to the other people and that alone made Gvildsy feel better. He asked the girl for a second tumbler and filled it for his father-in-law.

A good hour passed, the drunks dispersed, only a few were left in the beerhouse now, but the two men still sat there and drank in silence.

"How as it, tell. For what?" the old man finally spoke out, fiercely scratching his shaggy jaw.

Gvildys emptied another tumbler.

"I don't know, Father. That's the whole point . . . I don't know. Yesterday, I took home my half-month's pay, a nice pile it was, I hid some for the bottle and that I drank at lunchtime today. It wasn't much, just to cheer me up, a man can go crazy, it's terribly sad. Am I not allowed to have a drink? Don't I make enough money? Ain't there enough to eat at home, father?" He felt his tongue getting entangled, and the spot where his left eye once was started burning even more.

"And she used to be like an angel, my daughter was."

"Who can deny it, Father? I don't remember if we ever had a single real fight. And I'd just opened the door when she jumped me, and look at what she's done with me!"

It seemed that only after the mournful words of his son-in-law did the old man see and realize what had actually happened. He scratched his cheek again, emptied the tumbler, and did not even feel it when several large tears rolled down on the table. Through tear-stained eyes, he looked at his son-in-law and the thought came to him that some alien force, distant and terrible, was walking their woods and fields. Nobody had seen it yet or encountered it anywhere, but it was right there. It drops in on every farmstead, stops by at every home, it sits on a tractor or on the ploughs in place of the coupler, and people do not see it, nobody recognizes it yet.

"It's spooky, somehow, Son-in-law."

"We've drunk quite a lot, Father."

"I can't understand very much anymore, Son."

"It seems to me, it was not my being drunk, Father ... And in such a way—to jump me like a stranger, like some murderer, She poked out my eyes, and all I can do now is moan or drink, like some good-for-nothing, nothing more. No way to get revenge, nobody to hit, you get blind as a mole smack in the middle of your own cottage, and that's it."

Gvildys became more and more drunk, he was gradually losing that guarded masculinity which can bear even the greatest calamity, the deepest sorrow, through one's entire life without uttering a word until the very fateful end. He felt a tremor start in his fingers and spread through his whole body while his right eye, not yet completely extinguished but suspiciously feeble, was twitching and closing spasmodically. In his mind he now likened himself to a nice kitten whom a child, on the verge of tears, is carrying to a river and, once there, is taking his sweet time to search for a stone while the kitten sadly comprehends what will come next although it cannot bring itself to sink its nails into the weeping child.

"What's happening, Dad, can you tell me what? You old man! You can't do anything at all, and that's it. And what'll I do? And where will I go now? Did you hear what they were saying at the dispensary? They are saying that the second one may also go dead. Have you any idea what that means?" Gvildys smashed his fist against the table, and his father-in-law, at a loss for what to do, seized his hand and started kissing it like crazy, tearful and impotent, as if kissing could erase the inexplicable crime.

"She'd never raise her hand against the tiniest animal, against a bird, and now . . ." the father-in-law made a try.

"It's easier against a human being, Father . . ."

"The rye's in bloom all around," the father-in-law said to himself as if he had not heard his son-in-law. "A fine dust's rising, and a man begins to feel warmer, good and true. The cuckoo will cry out, too, forgetting herself in midsummer, and all men see you and you can see through the others. How can you raise your hand against somebody if everybody and everything looks at you like you were the wisest and the best?"

"Ah! But the rye and the cuckoos haven't disappeared anywhere. All you want, and nobody's shooting the cuckoos yet, Father. But that's no help to me, Jesusandmary, no damn help at all; not even money's any help, or bread . . . I can hardly hear the cuckoo any more, its voice seems to slip away, like into some tar barrel . . . This evening when I climbed the hill, the tractors just kept crawling over the hills like wild boars, just kept crawling over piles of potatoes . . ."

"For me, it was a help . . ." the father-in-law sighed. "What can I tell you, now? Me, an old stump, how can I help you? I'm slobbering like a calf and yet I can't find a single word that's true. Whole ages are sticking to my throat already . . . My daughter Onute poked out your eyes and now her old father slobbers away drunk at your table . . ."

"What the devil can you tell . . ."

"You think I didn't understand that the first thing to do was to get you out of here and take you into the city without any delay. That's what I thought as soon as I found out. I ran to search for you, but then the closer I got to you, the sillier my haste seemed because I couldn't help you anyway, even if I took you to the hospital. I may be ranting from all that booze but if your wife poked out one of your eyes and the doctors can mend the other, it's not finished yet, is it?"

"So you want both of my eyes bandaged?"

"D'you understand that there's nothing you can do to make it like nothing had happened?"

"Ah, Father, why get mixed up! I already feel like I'm

chained—my legs and my tongue . . . Maybe, only time can make everything disappear. I remember, when I was a kid, I could never imagine how I'd be able to live after my mother and father died. And here it is—fifteen years have gone by and I don't give my parents a thought for months . . ."

"That's how it is. Only death—that's something else. You know that you're going to die, as soon as you learn to think. And that someone else will die, you know that, too, that it must be so . . ."

"And my wife's poking out my eyes, maybe that also had to be, only neither I nor anybody else knew that it would be like death—that it had to happen . . ."

They gulped down one more shot each, the bottle was empty now and only very few people were left although outside the windows some were pacing around, waiting. Then both got up—the old man and his son-in-law. The old man was solicitously leading his son-in-law by the elbow to make sure that he did not stumble against the chairs. Outside, Gvildys found his bicycle by the wall, leaned against it, felt it around, as if checking whether it was still firm enough, lowered his head:

"So I'll be going now, Father."

"Where can you go, it's night. Let's go to my place, there'll be time enough tomorrow, or you'll be able to go straight to the city from here."

"What's this about staying for the night, Father, as if I had no home." Gvildys staggered as he pushed the bicycle and mounted it."

The men dispersed, all had drunk quite a lot, but they still had some sense left in their heads to realize that it was not an ordinary man who mounted the bicycle, but someone unlike others, someone strangely different. And the old man who tried to run, stumbling after the bicycle, was not like the others, either.

Gvildys had already left the town behind him, he was already pedalling through the meadow, his head was shimmering like a white flag in the darkness and the swollen eye followed the road perfectly. As he pedalled farther away from the town, and aside from his home, he thought more than once about what his wife was doing now, and the children. He wondered why she had not run after him to the town, why she did not fall at his feet, like Christ's, and did not break out in tears. Didn't the old man slobber all over the place? Gvildys felt pity for his wife, his home and his children. The pity was almost sacred, and the painful longing was driving him ever farther away, as if it had occured to him to journey away to his childhood where we were all gods once.

Early the next morning, the old man hurried on horseback to his son-in-law's place. He found his daughter, Gvildy's wife, sitting on a potato furrow in the field, her eyes drained and herself a picture of woe. The old man became terribly frightened and spurred his horse onto the town. He then continued along the path his son-in-law had taken the day before. The people also anticipated something and rushed after the old man, some on bicycles or horses, others on foot. The tractors ground to a halt on the hills, like wild boars, and the tractor drivers scampered across the fields. The old man meanwhile, jumped off his horse and hurried on, stumbling, sniffing at footprints, like a dog.

They found the bicycle seven kilometers away from the town. Tears were already rolling down the old man's cheeks as he traced his son-in-law's footprints in the marshes. Suddenly, they all stopped as if thunderstruck. In the middle of the marsh on a lovely island, sat Petras Gvildys, his legs crossed, like a saint with a halo of white gauze, eating the lunch that his wife Onute had packed for him and that he completely forgot by the tractor.

Petras Gvildys sat there serene, it seemed that he saw neither the men who gathered around him, nor the old man who had turned white with astonishment. With his single eye, Petras Gvildys gazed through white gauze at a frightened cuckoo perched on a birch tree that grew at the edge of the little island.

Translated by Jeronimas Zemkalnis